Praise for *New York Times* bestselling author Lori Foster

"Lori Foster should be on everyone's auto-buy list."

—#1 *New York Times* bestselling author Sherrilyn Kenyon

"Foster's writing satisfies all appetites with plenty of searing sexual tension and page-turning action."

—*Publishers Weekly*

"Bestseller Foster…has an amazing ability to capture a man's emotions and lust with sizzling sex scenes and meld it with a strong woman's point of view."

—*Publishers Weekly* on *A Perfect Storm*

Praise for *New York Times* bestselling author Tawny Weber

"Ms. Weber's writing is better than ever, and the dialogue and banter between the characters are even stronger than before, which is saying a lot because it has always been Tawny Weber's forte."

—*Fresh Fiction* on *A SEAL's Temptation*

"Fiery hot sex scenes, strong characters and exciting action make this one of the best stories in the Uniformly Hot! series."

—*RT Book Reviews* on *A SEAL's Seduction*

Lori Foster is a *New York Times* and *USA TODAY* bestselling author with books from a variety of publishers, including Harlequin, Berkley/Jove, Kensington and St. Martin's. Lori has been a recipient of the prestigious *RT Book Reviews* Career Achievement Award for Series Romantic Fantasy and for Contemporary Romance. For more about Lori, visit her website at www.lorifoster.com, like her on Facebook or find her on Twitter, @lorilfoster.

A *New York Times* and *USA TODAY* bestselling author of more than thirty books, **Tawny Weber** writes sassy, emotional romances with a dash of humor featuring hot alpha heroes. It's all about the sexy attitude! A fan of Johnny Depp, cupcakes and her very own hero husband, Tawny enjoys scrapbooking, gardening, spending time with her family and dogs, and hanging out with readers on Facebook.

Fans are invited to check out Tawny's books at her website, tawnyweber.com. For extra fun, join her Red Hot Readers Club for goodies like free reads, complete first chapters, recipes, insider story info and much more.

LORI FOSTER

TAKEN!

ISBN-13: 978-0-373-28484-9

Recycling programs for this product may not exist in your area.

This edition published by arrangement with Harlequin Books S.A.

For questions and comments about the quality of this book, please contact us at CustomerService@Harlequin.com.

HARLEQUIN®
www.Harlequin.com

Printed in U.S.A.

CONTENTS

Also available from Lori Foster and HQN Books

The Ultimate series

Hard Knocks
(prequel ebook novella)
No Limits
Holding Strong
Tough Love
Fighting Dirty

Love Undercover

Run the Risk
Bare It All
Getting Rowdy
Dash of Peril

Men Who Walk the Edge of Honor

"Ready, Set, Jett" in
The Guy Next Door
anthology
When You Dare
Trace of Fever
Savor the Danger
A Perfect Storm
What Chris Wants
(ebook novella)

Other must-reads

A Buckhorn Bachelor
(ebook novella)
A Buckhorn Summer
(ebook novella)
All For You
Back to Buckhorn
(ebook novella)
Heartbreakers
Charade
Up in Flames
Turn Up the Heat
Hot in Here
Animal Attraction
(ebook anthology)
Love Bites
All Riled Up
The Buckhorn Legacy
Forever Buckhorn
Buckhorn Beginnings
Bewitched
Unbelievable
Tempted
Bodyguard
Caught!
Fallen Angels
Enticing

And don't miss the first book in the sizzling new Body Armor series
Under Pressure

TAKEN!

Lori Foster

CHAPTER ONE

THE HEAT SWELLED within him until he thought he'd explode with lust. This wasn't what he'd expected, wasn't what he'd planned on. Her nipple stiffened under the gentle abrasion of his rough fingertips and Virginia groaned, thrilling him, turning him inside out with need. She twined her fingers in his hair and said with a touch of desperation, "Please."

Dillon felt the silky smooth, pliant flesh of her breast, heard her choppy breathing and soft plea, and he forgot his purpose. He forgot that he had ulterior motives, that he wasn't actually attracted to this woman.

"Dillon..."

"Shh. It's all right, honey." And it was, better than all right. It was incredible.

He pushed her coat farther out of his way and shoved her blouse higher. Her breast, full and firm and heavy, nestled against his palm, and more than anything, he wanted her naked. He wanted to see the color of her nipples by the scant moonlight coming through the windshield, to see the pleasure in her exotic hazel eyes, eyes that were usually hard with determination and arrogance but now were soft with pleasure and desire. For him.

He pressed open-mouth kisses to the smooth skin of her throat and breathed in her unique scent. He'd never noticed before that she had a unique scent. He'd never noticed how sexy she was, or imagined how hotly she would respond to his touch. She gasped and he whispered to her, soothing her as his fingers plucked at her nipple, rolling and teasing. As her entire body trembled with need, she moaned and he wanted to moan, too. This wasn't right, but it felt too damned right.

What had started out as necessary seduction now seemed amazingly like blind sexual need. There was no way he could deny his enjoyment of this little rendezvous, or the way his blood surged through his body to settle into an insistent throb in his groin. He was as hard as a stone, hurting with it, and Virginia was far too astute not to notice.

The car was cramped, but it didn't matter, and even though it was a miserably cold night, they were cozy, sharing the warmth of the heater and their combined sexual heat as the wind whistled around them. He knew that inside the mansion, the party was still going full blast. Lights shone from every window, sparkling across the snow-covered lawn, and the rumble of music drifted on the air. What he was doing, and where he was doing it, was dangerous, but he finally had her alone and he wasn't about to lose ground. He needed to push forward; too much time had been lost already.

For thirty-six years he'd been a mean, determined bastard—traits his father had instilled in him, insisted upon. He never forgot his purpose, never wavered from his course. Tonight, though, right this minute, he couldn't seem to force the plan to remain uppermost in his mind.

He wanted Virginia lying naked on the narrow seat, wanted to fit himself between her soft plump thighs and slide deep, deep inside her. He wanted to ride her hard until she made those sweet little sounds again, until she begged him to give her what she needed.

"Dillon, wait."

Her tone wasn't authoritative now. It didn't carry the sharp cut of command it normally did. Instead, her voice was low, overcome with need, and purely feminine. As a man, he relished the thought of proper balance with this particular woman who didn't act the way he expected a woman to act, the way he needed her to act.

She whispered his name again, and when he ignored her, she tightened her strong fingers in his hair. Taking her reaction as one of encouragement, he worked her bra aside, nuzzling with his lips. Her breasts were extremely sensitive, and he liked that. He imagined how it would be to make love to her, to find all her sensitive places with his hands, his mouth, his tongue and teeth. He wanted to taste her, to draw her deep into the heat of his mouth, to suck her gently and then, not so gently, devour her.

He smoothed a hand over her soft, slightly rounded belly and heard her sharp groan. He needed to touch her, all of her. His fingers pressed lower, slipping between her thighs, seeking, probing, feeling the throbbing heat.

Suddenly, she jerked away. "Dillon, no."

He heard her gasping, heard the trembling in her tone. She pressed her head back against the seat and closed her eyes.

"I'm sorry. I can't do this."

Reality started to nudge his lust-fogged brain. *She* couldn't do this? He was the one who'd been forcing himself for the sake of his plan—at first. His sole purpose in coming to Delaport City, Ohio, had been to seduce her, and in the process gain answers. Reluctance was in no way the proper response from her to his lovemaking. In fact, it was so far out of line with his original intention that he scowled. "Virginia..."

"No," she said, shaking her head. "No, this isn't right. Hiding out here with you as if I'm ashamed. I shouldn't treat you so shabbily. Just because you work for the company and I have the authority to fire you doesn't give me the right to treat you with less than full respect."

As she spoke, her voice gathered strength and she straightened her silk blouse, pulling it down over her breasts. He tried his damnedest to catch a glimpse of that taunting nipple he'd wanted so badly to taste.

Then it sank in. She thought she was treating him badly because they were sneaking? They *had* to sneak, or his plan would never work.

He cupped her cheek. Long curls of titian hair had escaped their pins and now hung over her rounded shoulders. Those curls surprised him. Usually her hair was pulled up and tidy and he'd had no idea how long it was. Loose, it made her look almost vulnerable—not that anyone would ever think of Virginia Johnson in such human terms. It also made her seem very feminine. He toyed with a loose strand and it was incredibly soft against his fingertips. He wondered what she'd look like with it completely undone. That red hair of hers would frame her white body perfectly, maybe curl around her lush breasts, giving her an earthy, pagan appearance.

He shook his head at his meandering thoughts. He

must have been too long without a woman, but then, he'd had other priorities lately. Namely, saving his brother's ass. He had to get a grip, had to remember the purpose of this little seduction.

He summoned up his most bland tone, the one he knew she wanted and expected from subordinates. "It's all right, Virginia. You can't be seen with me and we both know it. Cliff would be outraged and your reputation might be ruined."

She shook that stubborn head of hers. In the two weeks he'd spent cautiously wooing her, he'd learned Virginia Johnson had stubbornness down to a fine, irritating art, along with arrogance and a complete lack of business modesty. She knew she was good at making corporate decisions and she wanted everyone else to know it, too, even if she had to shove the fact down people's throats.

"I don't care what my brother thinks. He's a snob and we seldom get along anyway. He doesn't own me and he has no say over how I live my life."

"That's not the impression he gives." Dillon knew he had to speak carefully so he didn't give himself away. Deferring to anyone wasn't customary for him. He led his life in a unique fashion, following rules of his own making. He lived by a code of honor that was independent of the strictures of society. Except for his father and his brother, Dillon owed nothing to anyone. But Virginia was a bossy, powerful woman, damn her, and as used to calling the shots as he. He cleared his throat. "Your brother is very protective."

"Ha! He's a bully and I'm the only one with the guts to stand up to him, because I control the majority of the money. Cliff knows that without me, he'd destroy the company in a matter of weeks."

Even in the darkness he could see the ire on her face. She wasn't exactly pretty—at least, he'd never thought so before—and she was entirely too headstrong and self-contained. She enjoyed giving orders to everyone in her realm. She was also a bit too plump. Only, she hadn't felt too plump against him a minute ago. She'd felt soft and warm and comfortably rounded. He frowned at himself. "Virginia, I can't let you—"

"Can't let me?" she interrupted, one thin auburn brow climbing high as she met his gaze. "You can't stop me, Dillon. I always do as I please—you know that." With efficient movements, she rebuttoned her coat and started to open the door.

He caught her arm. From the minute he'd first forced an introduction, he'd damn near bitten holes in his tongue to keep from revealing his true nature. Sometimes the urge to put her in her place, wherever that might be, almost overwhelmed him.

She glared down at where his hand circled her arm, then slowly raised those incredible eyes to his in a look that plainly said, *You dare?*

The little witch might have the hots for him, but she didn't want anyone telling her what to do, which probably accounted as much for her matronly status as did her excess weight and unremarkable features. Most of the men who worked for her steered clear because she frightened them half to death and they weren't willing to put their careers on the line. The rest simply weren't interested.

Dillon wasn't worried about his career. Working for the company was only a temporary sham, his way of getting close to her so that he could ultimately ruin her brother's destructive plans. But even if that hadn't been true, he would never have let a woman, any woman, dictate to him. There were easier ways to make a living than bowing under to the tyrannical rule of an iron maiden.

"Sweetheart, listen to me." He turned his secure hold into a caress to pacify her, and to some degree it worked. The only way he'd been able to get close to her had been to seduce her into wanting him. And seducing an iron maiden was no easy feat. He'd nearly depleted his store of ploys with her and he wasn't used to that. Women usually came to him easily enough, but Virginia had been so damn elusive his ego had taken a beating. Now the plan was more than a necessity; it was a personal challenge.

He'd finally been making headway, and then this. "Virginia, if you won't think of your own reputation, think of mine. If Cliff finds out about us, he'll fire me in a heartbeat. Is that what you want?" He had to keep their relationship secret so that later no one would suspect him.

She patted his hand in her condescending fashion. "Don't worry. I won't let him fire you. I hold controlling interest in the company. I have ultimate say over who goes and who stays."

He sighed, deliberately appearing put-upon. "I'm sorry, honey, but I won't have it. I'd look like a fool if I let a woman, any woman, defend me. People would start saying I was only after your money and—"

She waved a hand. "Nonsense. Everyone knows I'm never marrying, and that's the only way you could possibly get your hands on my money. We'd just be having an affair."

"Which is nobody's business but our own."

She frowned and he quickly retrenched, pulling together his frayed temper and gathering the remnants of his control. Why did she have to be so damn argumentative?

"I'm sorry," he said through gritted teeth, then managed to summon a calmer tone. "I didn't mean to yell at you. But what's between us is private. I want to keep it that way."

She still looked skeptical and he silently cursed her, while on the outside he did his best to appear hopeful. The damn shrew. What was it with this woman that she thought she had to control everyone and everything? Of course, he felt the same way, but it was different for him. He'd been raised to be cautious, to take control and guide the events in his life. His father's renegade lifestyle had carried over into parenting, and every survival value had been passed on. Dillon accepted his right to control as a means to protect those around him. It was what he was used to, the way he understood life.

Virginia had led a pampered existence, so she had no excuse.

Finally, she nodded. "Oh, all right, if you're going to be that sensitive about it, I'll keep our…association private. But I'm not going to make love in a car. It's ridiculous."

"Of course not." This was the opening he'd been waiting for, a culmination of two weeks' work and endless, nerve-stretching patience. "But we could take a day off, go somewhere private and indulge ourselves."

He swallowed, then forced himself to say, "I want you so bad, honey."

Now that he wasn't kissing and touching her, only listening to the grating, overbearing tone of her voice, all lust had died and he was once again filled with cold deliberation. She would be a pawn in the scheme of things, used and deceived so he could accomplish his goals, but he had no intention of making Virginia a victim. Though she might end up slightly humiliated, he wouldn't hurt her. He would go only as far as necessary to stop her brother and save his own.

True to her nature, she was already shaking her head no. "I can't take any time off right now. Too much to do. Just come to my home tonight. We'll leave separately so no one will know, seeing as how your reputation is so important to you."

He wanted to smack her for using that sneering tone. Obviously, she wanted just an hour or two with him, a quick toss in the hay, not the commitment of an entire evening. Although it was foolish, he felt very insulted; she might as well have labeled him a stud for hire. His male dignity was sorely tried.

He needed enough time to gain her trust and find the clues to the deception that threatened to destroy his brother. But he couldn't do that if Virginia's brother found out they were seeing each other. He answered her honestly. "No. It's too risky. Someone might see me at your place."

She heaved a dramatic sigh and glared at him, her hazel eyes appearing gold in the dark night. "Are you sure you really want to do this? I mean, for a man who only a few moments ago was in the throes of lust, you're setting up an awful lot of obstacles. I've never known anyone so ridiculously sensitive or so overly cautious."

Through narrowed eyes he searched her face, not quite sure how to answer her and keep the peace at the same time. Though her brother stood as a figurehead, it was Virginia who actually ran things. She was the only hope his brother had out of this damn mess.

She sighed again and said, "I'm sorry. That was uncalled for. To be honest, I'm not quite used to this."

He could believe that. What man would pursue a dragon lady? When he'd been kissing her and she'd been soft and pliant and feminine, he'd forgotten how cold and domineering she really was. But what he'd learned of her other side had been accidental. Not many men had ever tried to get past the brambles to see what lay beneath. If it hadn't been for Wade, he certainly wouldn't have tried. That thought bothered him and he shied away from it.

"Virginia, I know this is complicated, but I don't see any other way...."

"Maybe we should just forget the whole thing. I'm not exactly cut out for affairs and it's getting entirely too awkward."

"No!" Damn it, he couldn't waste time backtracking now. Getting her this far had taken longer than he'd expected. But here she was, lifting that damn supercilious eyebrow at his tone. He cleared his throat and had to clench his hands to keep from shaking her.

"What I meant," he said, painfully cajoling, "is that you can't change your mind on me. I need you too much." For good measure he kissed her again—then immediately forgot it was just for good measure and started enjoying himself. Her lips parted. Her tongue touched his.

Damn, but for a dragon lady she tasted fine—hot and sweet and sexy. Without making a conscious decision, he lifted his hand to that heavy breast again. Even through her sweater and coat, he could feel the softness of her as he kneaded her flesh. She moaned, and when he lifted his mouth from hers she whispered shakily, "Let me see what I can work out. I'll get in touch with you later in the week."

She had the door open before he could stop her, but it was just as well. The driveway was packed with cars and they could have been caught by anyone coming or going. He'd gotten so wrapped up in the job at hand he'd been careless.

No one knew who he really was and he had to keep it that way, because once he gained Virginia's confidence and ruined her brother's plans, Dillon would disappear. If anyone suspected him of having a relationship with Virginia, he'd fail. And his brother, Wade, would be the one to suffer.

CHAPTER TWO

WHEN VIRGINIA STEPPED back into the mansion, entering through the kitchen door, she ran smack into her brother, Cliff. He looked at her suspiciously.

"What were you doing outside?"

She pushed him out of her way and pulled off her coat. All that kissing and touching had her overheated. She'd rebuttoned the coat only as a sort of barrier, a way to shield herself from the overwhelming attraction and confusing emotions Dillon made her feel. Being so strongly drawn to a man wasn't something she was used to. And especially not a man like Dillon. She shivered in memory. "I was indulging in a secret liaison, of course."

"Ha, ha. Very funny." With his tone as bland as an angry brother could manage, Cliff glared at her. "Like any man would be foolish enough to tangle with you."

Virginia just shook her head. In one respect, Cliff was right. Men rarely pursued her—at least, not men who only wanted to have a heated affair. The term *sex symbol* had never been used to describe her, not with her excess weight and incisive personality. Men who wanted to try to marry her for her company connections showed up by the dozen each year, but their intentions were far from honorable or complimentary, which partially accounted for her ruthlessness. She'd decided to stay single because she couldn't find a man who suited her—they were all either immoral money grubbers or complete wimps.

She'd had high hopes for Dillon when she first met him. Unlike the other fools Cliff invariably hired, Dillon stood apart. His body was long and hard and honed, not the type of physique achieved in a gym, but rather the kind that came from hard work day in and day out, over a lifetime. With broad shoulders and thick thighs, he looked more than capable of taking on any physical task. And he wore a certain confidence, as if he possessed an alertness unknown to most men.

He had the kind of intensity that made a woman feel surrounded and closed in. It didn't threaten her—nothing did. She'd grown up a chubby, unattractive middle child who'd had to learn to fight for everything she wanted, including affection. She'd forced her way into the business and into her father's trust. After living through her parents' deaths and the battles for power that followed, she knew that very little in life had the ability to alarm her, including Dillon's pursuit.

Unhappily, Dillon was proving to be something of a pushover, just like the others. One little word from her, and he tripped all over himself trying not to anger her. Why couldn't she find a man who could deal with her head-on?

She was disappointed by his lack of backbone, but not enough to call a halt to the affair. With any luck, Dillon might surprise her once he learned her bark was worse than her bite.

"Yoo-hoo, Virigina. Anyone home?" Cliff peered at her critically. "What are you up to that has you so distracted?"

Virginia sighed. "I'm not exactly in the mood right now for your prying or your sarcasm, Cliff. Shouldn't you be entertaining guests or something?"

"That's my line to you. We have important associates here tonight."

"Is that right? Such as your personal assistant? I saw Laura dutifully following you around earlier. In fact, she's probably looking for you right now."

Cliff stiffened. "Ms. Neil is no concern of yours."

In all honesty, Virginia really didn't care what Cliff did with his free time or his secretary, although she suspected he'd promoted Laura to personal assistant only as a way to get her in bed. In spite of her disapproval, it wasn't her business, so she just shrugged. "True enough. Now, what do you want, Cliff?"

"I want to know what you were doing outside that was so important you neglected your duties."

"We've been through this before, Brother." She kept her tone level, hoping to avoid a prolonged fight. She wanted to be alone so she could contemplate how to proceed with Dillon. "What I do with my life is none of your business. Stop pushing me or you won't like the consequences."

Just as she expected, Cliff fumed in impotent silence and then stalked away. It was a shame he'd been born first. It was a bigger shame her father had believed the company needed to be represented by a man, regardless of the fact that Cliff was spineless and shallow and lacked the necessary business sense. Just because they dealt in sporting equipment, her father felt a man would be a more traditional head for the company.

Virginia would have done a much better job of it. She'd learned the business from the sales floor up, working part-time at their three mall locations while taking business courses and acting as an apprentice at the main offices. She'd absorbed every nuance of the business, and she thrived there, but regardless of all she was capable of, she wasn't male and that mattered most to her father. At least he'd had the foresight to leave her a controlling interest. No, she wasn't the president, and she didn't interfere overly in the daily running of the business, but no major decisions could be made without her. And that one small stipulation in her father's will had garnered her near hate from Cliff.

Her brother had always been a petty child, and he'd grown into a petty man. Still, they used to be able to get along, to find a middle ground. Now she hardly knew him—or her younger sister, Kelsey.

Kelsey also held a share of the company, but she hated to get caught in the cross fire between Virginia and Cliff, and usually gave her proxy to one of the other voting board members. She threw herself, instead, into her college studies and her computers, taking great pains to separate herself from the family business.

There were times, like tonight, when Virginia wished she had the same options. It would have been nice to be just an ordinary woman for once. Any woman. Then she wouldn't have to question Dillon's motives in pursuing her.

He wanted her; she knew that. He couldn't have faked his reactions in the car. She'd been more than a little aware of his erection, heavy and full, pressing into her hip. But there was more to it than that, she was certain. And if it wasn't a part of the company he wanted, then what?

She'd read his file when Cliff had first hired him to

oversee their security department, mostly because he didn't seem to be the typical Johnson's Sporting Goods employee. He didn't look as if he'd ever played a recreational sport in his life and every time he donned a tie, it seemed to choke him. No, with eyes so dark they almost appeared black, he looked more like a mercenary. Or a renegade. And his file had revealed that he'd never held a steady job for long. The man skipped around the country, and sometimes out of the country. It was for certain he'd been somewhere warm recently, because his skin was darkly tanned, contrasting sharply with the sandy-brown hair that hung beyond his collar.

His qualifications and references had been excellent, plus he'd had some military training, so Cliff had hired him regardless of the way he looked.

Dillon knew his business. In the first few days he'd instigated additional safeguards on several levels, approved by Virginia, that would save the company substantial funds in the long run. Ruthless in many ways, he'd already fired two night guards, claiming that the men had been leaving their posts, playing poker and not paying attention to their jobs. Dillon wouldn't allow any dereliction of duty. He now did a personal background check on everyone hired under his jurisdiction, which encompassed all the company offices and the store locations, as well. He took his responsibilities seriously and expected the same of everyone else.

The intelligence in his dark eyes was easy to read, as visible as his strength and every bit as appealing. Even his disdain of her family's business seemed sexy to Virginia. But still, he was an enigma.

She'd give him one night, she decided. Even if he did prove later to be a swindler with ulterior motives, it wouldn't matter. She'd never get drawn in by a wimp, so there was no risk of a bruised heart. She wanted a man who could stand toe-to-toe with her, a man to be her partner in life, who was her equal in every way.

But Dillon, with his incredible body and incredible kisses, would work nicely for now to fill a terrible void. Her aching loneliness had lingered too long, and she needed a little attention, the kind only a man could give a woman.

No, she could never get serious about a man like him. But every woman had the right to a fantasy on occasion. And Dillon Oaks was six feet two inches of hard, throbbing fantasy material. He'd do just fine.

THE MINUTE DILLON opened his door, Wade pounced.

"What happened? How did it go?"

Damn, this was just what he needed. The entire night had been irritating enough; he didn't need to be accosted by his brother right now.

He shrugged out of his battered leather coat and kicked off his low boots. "What the hell are you doing here? Are you trying to screw things up?" If anyone found out they were related…

"I was careful," Wade protested, looking wounded. "I took a bus to the corner and then walked the rest of the way. Besides, it's dark. No one could have seen me. Now, tell me what happened!"

His little brother, the personification of espionage excellence. What a joke. They'd been raised by different parents, and their upbringing and their outlooks on life couldn't have been more different. "Calm down, Wade," he said. "Nothing's happening yet. Hopefully, this coming week sometime."

"Damn it!" Wade began to pace, his turmoil the complete opposite of his usual, carefree lightheartedness. "What is the matter with that woman! No woman has ever treated you like this. Usually you're the one forced to turn them away."

Even though Wade's words echoed his own earlier sentiments, Dillon shook his head. "Don't be ridiculous. I'm no Romeo." Then he added with a frown, "And Virginia is no fool." A virago, but not stupid.

"Ha! She's a stuck-up bit—"

"Shut up, Wade." His defense of Virginia took him by surprise. He was automatically protective of women, the trait inborn, but of all the women he'd ever known, Virginia was least in need of his chivalry. Still, he didn't like the idea of using her this way, even if there wasn't any choice. Virginia had the answers he needed, and there was only one way to get them.

Fuming, Wade finally dropped into an overstuffed chair. "It has to be soon, Dillon. We're running out of time and I can't take much more of this. I keep having visions of being locked away in prison."

"I told you it won't come to that. I won't let it. If nothing else, I'll get you out of the country before that happens. You could come home with me to Mexico until I get things straightened out." Then he added, just to distract Wade, "How's Kelsey holding up?"

"She's got morning sickness." Wade looked ready to sink into the depths of depression. "She's sick and that damn brother of hers isn't helping matters by doing his best to separate us. He thinks that since I'm without a job and accused of a crime Kelsey won't want me. She's afraid to see me, in case he has me locked up right now. I have to settle for the occasional phone call and it's intolerable. At this rate, she'll be giving birth before we have a chance to get married!"

Dillon went into the kitchen and opened a can of cola, then began stripping off his shirt. For the sake of the party at the mansion and his scheme, he'd donned a dress shirt and tie. He hated ties. Wearing them to the office during the week was torture.

The lengths he went to for his brother.

Half brother, he corrected himself. They hadn't shared the same father, but Wade was still his brother in every sense of the word. Blood was blood, as his father had been fond of preaching. You didn't turn your back on a blood relative.

When their mother had died, leaving Wade alone, he'd made the effort to find Dillon, wanting him at the funeral, wanting to become a part of his life.

At the time, Dillon had just finished a stint in the military. He'd been living the life of a loner, independent of everyone, even his father, with no clue as to where his mother had gone or what she'd been doing, and not particularly interested in knowing. He certainly hadn't heard that she'd remarried and birthed another son. All his father had ever told him was that she hadn't wanted either of them, and that as soon as she could, she'd abandoned Dillon. She'd turned her back on both of them, and that said it all. They'd never talked about her; given the circumstances, it hadn't seemed necessary.

Women had come and gone in their lives while Dillon was growing up, but none of them had been all that important. His father's relationships never lasted; women were just a necessary convenience for him.

Though he and his father were close, Dillon had never really understood his attitudes on some things.

Discovering he had a brother had taken him by surprise, but he liked the feeling of having someone around who would depend on him, who wanted to be close to him. He'd never felt the need to bother his mother with his presence, but she'd given him a brother and for that he was grateful.

Dillon took over the chore of helping Wade financially through college. He'd given him advice and concern in addition to loans. After eight years of keeping in touch and visiting whenever possible, they'd developed the kind of blood bond his father had always lectured about. They were brothers, and that counted for a lot.

Dillon stripped off his shirt, then dropped onto the couch, propped his feet on the edge of the battered coffee table and downed his cola in one long gulp.

Wade shook his head. "Look at you! What the hell is wrong with that woman? Why doesn't she want you? I'd give my right ear to have a body like yours."

Dillon choked. "For Christ's sake, Wade, get a grip, will you?" He was well used to Wade's misplaced worship. He'd been putting up with it since the day they'd met, but he still wasn't comfortable with such open adoration.

"It's true," Wade persisted. "All the women at the company want you. The secretaries, the managers, every one of them! As long as I worked there, I never saw anything like it. The female corporate employees are usually so reserved, all buttoned-up businesswomen. Kelsey was the only one who ever paid me any mind. The rest pretty much ignored me. But they *all* gawk at you, and whisper behind their hands. Even Laura Neil, which is nothing short of a miracle."

"Why do you say that?" Dillon was aware of Laura's attention, but it had never felt particularly complimentary. More like wary curiosity.

"Since Cliff took notice of her, she hasn't left his side. She acts like a lapdog."

Dillon scowled at his brother's insulting reference to a lady. "Maybe she's just dedicated."

Wade snorted. "We used to have a thing going, you know. Before I met Kelsey. After we broke up, Cliff promoted Laura to personal assistant. I know he's not really interested. For him, her new position is just a convenience, keeping her close at hand." Wade said it with a sneer, emphasizing his dislike of Cliff Johnson. "Laura hopes he'll marry her, but it'll never happen. Maybe she's realized it, and that's why she's looking at you now. But then, as I said, all the women look at you that way. Kelsey told me some of the women even made bets about who would get you first."

Dillon could only stare. "I don't know about any bets."

"Trust me, the women know." Wade frowned in thought. "It's strange that Virginia is totally immune."

"She's not immune."

"Maybe Virginia's just not...you know." He bobbed his eyebrows suggestively. "Maybe she doesn't prefer men."

Anger surged through him, but he managed to restrain it. The explosive reaction didn't make sense, and he buried it deep, along with all the other confusing emotions he'd experienced tonight, thanks to one Virginia Johnson. "She likes men. There's nothing wrong with Virginia except that she's been given free rein too long. That and too many men wanting her money and not her."

"Not exactly a tough one to figure out." Wade's tone dripped with sarcasm. "Her money is the only appealing thing about her. My position in accounting only put me in direct contact with her a few times, thank God. She scared the hell out of me. With that razor-sharp tongue of hers, she could shred a man to pieces. Besides, she behaves like a dictator."

Actually, Dillon thought, fighting the urge to strangle his brother, Virginia's tongue was soft and tentative and inquisitive. At least when a man took the time to kiss her properly. He had the impression not many men had, and that caused him to feel a certain degree of possessiveness toward her, when he had no right to feel anything at all.

"So what are you going to do now, Dillon?"

"I'm going to wait. She said she'd make a decision this week sometime."

"Kelsey is going to be so disappointed if I don't get this settled soon. She's anxious to move out of the house, to get away from Cliff. She's been biding her time with school and volunteer organizations, but she's miserable."

Dillon shook his head. He'd met Kelsey several times at the company and because of Wade's infatuation he'd paid attention. In Dillon's opinion the woman was a spoiled brat. From what he'd learned of her through subtle queries, both Virginia and Cliff doted on her and tried to protect her from the world. Being the youngest, she'd taken the deaths of her parents the hardest. She was the type of woman Dillon avoided, the type who expected to be coddled and catered to. She knew nothing about coping with real life.

But then, Wade wasn't exactly a model of maturity himself. "You sure this is what you want, Wade? We could still try to fight this in court."

Wade shook his head, frustration apparent in his every feature. "There's no way to get Cliff to drop the embezzlement charges. He's set me up for a reason, and he'll have no qualms about putting me away for good. I don't know what evidence he'll come up with, so there's no way I can fight it, but Kelsey said he's really confident, bragging about nailing me red-handed. So whatever it is, it'll be solid. He'll be sure of that."

Many times, Dillon had considered just beating the hell out of Cliff. It would give him no end of pleasure, yet it wouldn't solve the problem in the long run. Dillon needed to find out what trumped-up evidence Cliff planned to use against Wade. Short of that, he had to find a way to force Cliff to drop the supposed "investigation." If it hadn't been for Kelsey, Wade wouldn't have known of the setup until it was too late. Thankfully, Kelsey had learned of her brother's plan and told Wade.

As yet, no legal charges had been filed, but Wade had been discharged from his position without pay or benefits while Cliff gathered together his evidence. Once the officials got involved, it would be too late. Time was running out.

Cliff was a powerful man and diffusing this situation wouldn't be easy. Dillon had to pull off a tricky unauthorized private investigation. He had to go through files he had no right to see, search records that weren't his to search and still find a way to keep his own butt out of jail. To do it, he needed Virginia. He didn't want her hurt, but she'd have to be the sacrificial lamb; it couldn't be helped. There was no way to switch course now.

He'd ridden some tricky fences in his day, but this was turning out to be the worst.

Though he already knew the answer, Dillon couldn't stop himself from asking. "Are you sure Cliff wouldn't change his mind if he knew Kelsey was pregnant?"

"Ha! Are you kidding? He'd probably forget handling things 'legally' and just take out a contract on me. He thinks she's way too young to get married."

Dillon hesitated, then leaned forward, propping his elbows on his knees. "You know, Wade, he wouldn't be entirely wrong. Kelsey is only twenty-two, and you're not much older. Marriage isn't something to be rushed into."

Wade stiffened and his hands fisted. "She's pregnant, Dillon. Am I supposed to abandon her now? I know from experience that a woman raising a child alone doesn't have an easy time of it. The baby deserves a father, and Kelsey deserves a husband."

"There is that, I suppose." Actually, Dillon wished they'd both shown a little more responsibility and not gotten into the situation in the first place, but rehashing that issue wouldn't help now.

Wade began to pace. "It's not like Kelsey is a child. It's just that she's the only family Cliff has. He's very protective of her, and you know my background isn't something to excite a prospective brother-in-law. No man is good enough for Kelsey, but I want a chance to try."

Dillon made a sound of disgust. He hated hearing

Wade harp on his unfortunate childhood. So he and their mother hadn't been rich. Dillon and his dad hadn't exactly lived a life of luxury, either. If anything, they'd lived a life of stealth.

None of that came out of his mouth, though. Instead, he heard himself say, "Cliff has Virginia, too."

Wade shook his head in dismissal. "They're not at all close. Virginia is too damn difficult. You know how she always bosses Cliff around. After their parents died, Virginia just took over. He despises her for it."

Dillon suspected that Virginia had taken charge because no one else could. Cliff certainly wouldn't have had the smarts to keep things together. And Kelsey had been a mere teenager. Gritting his teeth, Dillon snarled, "If Virginia means so little to him, then why does he worry so much about who she sees?"

Wade shrugged. "I should think he'd be glad to be rid of her. Most men would be. I suppose Cliff worries about someone marrying Virginia for her money—and her shares in the company. From what I've heard, a few men have tried that tactic, but Cliff doesn't want to take any chances on losing the little control he has."

Dillon surged to his feet. This night wasn't improving with conversation and he needed time alone to put things in perspective. He couldn't allow himself to feel protective of Virginia; he needed the ruthlessness his father had taught him. He needed to be able to do the job, without emotional involvement. "Go home, Wade. I want to get some sleep, and it isn't safe for you to hang around here for long. If anyone finds out we're related, the whole plan is ruined."

"I know. And I'm sorry. But I just couldn't wait."

"You're going to have to wait from now on." He spoke sternly in the way he knew commanded attention. "Don't come here again. Do you understand?" He waited until Wade nodded, then he added, "I'll get in touch with you when I find out something."

Reluctantly, Wade turned away. "All right." He walked to the door and then paused. "You know how much I appreciate all this, don't you, Dillon? I didn't have anyone else to turn to. The one lawyer I spoke with was useless. He said the company probably wouldn't press charges because they'd most likely want to avoid the scandal and the possibility of being discredited in front of their shareholders. If it was anyone but Cliff, I'd agree. But he won't be happy just firing me. He wants to ruin me completely. Kelsey and I didn't know what to do. Against Cliff's money, I didn't stand a chance. He'll be sure to have the best lawyers around and they'll make mincemeat out of me. I'd already be in jail and Kelsey would have to raise our baby alone. Cliff would have given her a hard time over the scandal—"

"Enough already, Wade." Damn, but the rambling melodramatics were enough to make him sick. Wade had missed his calling. Instead of becoming an accountant, he should have joined the theater. Still, Wade was his brother, so Dillon forgave him his shortcomings, just as he hoped to be forgiven for his own. "I told you I'd take care of things and I will."

Wade nodded once more, sent his brother a shaky, endearingly familial smile, then left.

Dillon locked up the apartment and turned out the lights.

When he was finally alone with his thoughts, he

wondered if he was doing the right thing. Maybe he should have tried to raise enough money to get good legal representation for Wade. Not the low-rate lawyer Wade had spoken with, but a sharpshooter who could match Cliff's. Dillon had property in Mexico he could have sold. That would have meant starting over, but then, he'd started over many times. He liked his home, but there were higher priorities to consider; he had to think about his father, too.

His dad lived with him now, and Dillon didn't want to uproot him. His father wasn't a young man anymore, and he had a few health problems thanks to the hard life he'd led.

Besides, if Virginia had been a typical female, this whole thing would have been simple. But no, she had to be difficult and unique and a pain in the backside. He'd never known a woman like her.

Naked, he slid between the sheets and stacked his hands behind his head. It was dark and cold and snowflakes patterned his window, making the moonlight look like lace against the far wall. He wondered how Virginia would react when she realized his sole interest in her was her personal files. He wondered how she'd react to the news that her twenty-two-year-old pampered baby sister was pregnant and wanted to marry Wade, a man accused of embezzlement, a man with a less than sterling background. *A man related to him.*

Most of all, he wondered how Virginia would react when she found out he wasn't the wimp she assumed him to be. Would she cry with hurt? He closed his eyes at the vision and shuddered with reaction.

Whatever she did, it wouldn't be the expected. There

wasn't another woman like her anywhere, and she had the knack of keeping him on his toes. She wouldn't make his job easy.

But he'd bet his last breath she'd make it interesting.

CHAPTER THREE

DILLON WAS IN Cliff's office when Virginia rushed in two days later. Lounged back on his spine in a casual sprawl, his legs wide, he made her forget why she'd wanted to see Cliff in the first place. Virginia noticed how the soft, worn material of his dark jeans cupped his heavy sex. His hands rested over a taut flat belly and his shoulders stretched the pressed material of his dress shirt. His hair hung to his shoulders, his collar was unbuttoned and his sleeves were rolled up. Her gaze traveled over him until she met his eyes. She shivered.

He looked totally relaxed, but his brown eyes were alert. She loved it when he acted so defiantly arrogant for her brother's sake. It made him look sexy and sinful and her heart immediately picked up rhythm.

She forced her gaze to where her brother sat behind a massive desk. One concern was replaced with another.

"What's he doing here, Cliff? Has there been some kind of trouble?" In the normal course of his job, Dillon didn't have much call to hang around Cliff's office.

Cliff glared at her—a look to which she was well accustomed to. "He's my head of security. Why shouldn't he be here?"

She strolled across the floor, trying not to react to

the almost tactile sensation of Dillon's eyes on her as he tracked her every step. Propping her hip on the edge of Cliff's desk, she asked, "Are we considering making some kind of adjustment or improvement? Is that why he's here?"

Cliff slammed down the pen he'd been doodling with. "Damn it, Virginia, don't you have a diet class or something to go to?"

That hurt. Her weight had always been a problem, but it wasn't something she wanted to discuss in front of Dillon. Usually the clothes she wore were loose enough so as not to accent the more obvious trouble spots. Today, her simple wool tunic over matching slacks worked wonders—or so she'd thought. Now she was uncomfortably aware of the width of her hips, the weight of her breasts, the roundness of her belly and thighs. She wanted to escape both men's scrutiny.

She lifted her chin. Low blows were a specialty of Cliff's. She should have become immune to them by now.

She didn't dare glance at Dillon. She didn't want to know what he thought of her brother's comment or, at the moment, what he thought of her. "I'm a busy woman, Brother, but I think I can spare some time to see what you're screwing up now."

Cliff snarled, almost ready to explode. At the last second he pulled himself together and sent Dillon an exasperated look of shared male insight, as if to say, *Women.* Virginia stiffened. Fighting Cliff had become a way of life, both in business and in her personal pride. "You do remember, don't you, Cliff, that any decisions have to go through me first?"

"How could I forget with you forever shoving it in my face?"

"So?" She waited, and finally he turned a sheath of papers toward her.

She studied the new property sheets for a moment before commenting. "The Eastland project." She ignored Cliff's surprise. He should know by now that there was no facet of the business she wasn't fully aware of. The company was her life, the only thing she was truly good at. She wouldn't let anything slip by her.

She approved the idea of expansion by purchasing the retail property in Eastland. Once the new expressway was built, the mall would flourish. Time and invested money were all they needed, and Johnson's Sporting Goods had both. Their expansion would add new life to the floundering area, drawing in other retailers.

"Actually, it looks good. Send some copies to my office today and I'll let you know later exactly what I think."

Through gritted teeth, Cliff told her, "Everything has been worked out. The security upgrades have even been tested and approved. I planned to work out a deal today."

"No. Not until I've had more time to study the cost sheets. There's no rush. It takes time to—"

Cliff shoved back his chair and stood. Startled, Virginia glanced up. He was practically seething, his hands curled into fists at his sides.

"There'll come a point, Virginia, when you push me too far!" He turned to Dillon and barked, "Be upstairs in the conference room in ten minutes."

He stormed out and Virginia was left there with

her mouth hanging open and an uncomfortable silence disturbing the air. It wasn't like Cliff to put on such a display in front of employees.

Without really wanting to, she looked over at Dillon. He hadn't moved. He seemed unperturbed by Cliff's overreaction, but his dark eyes were cryptic. She tried a shaky smile. For some stupid reason she felt defensive. Having the world know her own brother reviled her had the same effect as being nicknamed "Chubby" in grade school.

"Well, I certainly pushed the wrong buttons this morning, didn't I?" she said, relying on flippancy to save her pride.

Dillon narrowed his eyes. "Or the right ones."

"What does that mean?"

"Why do you deliberately provoke him, Virginia?"

She pushed away from the desk and started for the door. Discussing family business with employees—regardless of how gorgeous they might be—wasn't done. Still, she couldn't resist one righteous parting shot. "I have as much right to know what's going on in this company as he does. Or more so!" When she turned, Dillon was right behind her. She gasped, took a step back and hit the door. She hadn't even heard him move.

He took another step closer, looming over her. His fingers touched her chin; his dark gaze touched everywhere else. In a rumble, he whispered, "There are gentler ways for a woman to get what she wants. Especially from her own brother."

For one instant she felt frozen by his touch. Her stomach curled and her nipples tightened into sensitive peaks. Then she shook her head. "So I should play meek and mild just to placate Cliff? I don't have a meek or mild bone in my body. I thought you understood that, Dillon."

He didn't smile. "Are you going to make time for me this weekend, Virginia?"

"Are you being pushy?" she asked automatically, still stinging from her brother's remarks.

To her disappointment, he backed down, both physically and mentally. For a single heartbeat, he looked frustrated, almost angry, but he took a safe step away from her and shook his head. "No, of course not. I'm just...anxious."

If he was really anxious, he'd insist she make a decision, she thought. But then, it wasn't fair of her to try to force her own dominant spirit on him. She went on tiptoe to kiss his chin. "I need to be here Friday for a meeting, but I can take off Thursday."

His gaze heated. "What time?"

"Whenever you like. You tell me."

Without hesitation, he said, "Early. We could spend the entire day together. The waiting is just about killing me."

After her brother's crack about her weight, Dillon's obvious desire was a welcome balm. She pressed closer to him for a kiss and felt his large hand cup her backside, gently squeezing. With her brother's comment still lingering fresh in her mind, she was uncomfortable with the touch and stepped away. His gaze searched her face, questioning, and she tried not to blush.

Other men who had come on to her had been discreet with their touches, never venturing so boldly in broad daylight as Dillon seemed prepared to do. In thirty years, she'd had two lovers, and they'd both made it a practice to have sex in the dark and under the covers, which suited her just fine. The entire experience had always been rather nice. Safe and predictable and uncomplicated. The sex itself hadn't been spectacular, but the sharing, the holding and touching had comforted her in a way nothing else could.

She hoped Dillon wouldn't prove too difficult about the arrangement. Surely he'd be satisfied with proper bedroom convention.

"This isn't exactly the best place, is it, Dillon?"

At first he didn't answer and her heart raced in both dread and anticipation. He shook his head. "No, it isn't. I'm sorry."

Virginia sighed. "Since I know you're worried about appearances, we'll meet in the mall parking lot by my home. That way no one will see us leaving."

"Can you be ready at six?"

"*That* early?"

His tone dropped to a husky rumble. "It'll give us more time together."

"All right, then." She smiled. "Where did you want to go?"

Dillon hesitated, then touched her cheek again. "Why don't you let me take care of that. It'll be a surprise."

"Hmm. A secret?"

He nodded. "What did you need to see Cliff about?"

She stared into his eyes, amazed by the mixed messages there. Hunger, but also…regret?

"Virginia?"

"What?"

He laughed, a low, rough sound that made her belly tingle. "You rushed in here to see Cliff, but got sidetracked. Was it important?"

"Oh." She paused. "Oh! Damn it, I needed to talk to him. Something's wrong with my car. I wanted to use his."

"That's not a problem." He dug in his pocket and pulled out a large key ring, then unhooked one gold key. "Here. You can use the company car. I left it in the garage, lower level, personnel entrance. But what's wrong with yours? Maybe I can help you with it."

"I'm not sure." Virginia accepted the key, feeling awkward with Dillon's concern. She wasn't used to anyone asking after her in such a solicitous way. For as long as she could remember, she'd taken care of herself. "Something's wrong with the brakes. I started out of the parking lot, then remembered some papers I needed on my desk. When I went to put on the brakes, they felt sluggish at first, not really catching, and when I pumped them, the pedal went all the way to the floor. I ran into a guardrail." She scowled, thinking of the damage that had been done to her bumper. "It's lucky I found out they weren't working before I tried to leave the garage. You know how the exit ramp slopes down right into the main road."

"And into heavy traffic," he added in an ominous whisper. Dillon's brows were lowered and a muscle ticked in his jaw. Suddenly, his arms surrounded her and he gave her a tight squeeze. With his mouth against her neck, he murmured, "You could have been killed."

Pushing herself away from his hard chest, Virginia laughed, trying to make light of his reaction. "Nonsense! It wasn't all that dramatic or life threatening, I promise. I'd barely gone three feet before I found out they weren't working. But I do intend to give my serviceman a piece of my mind. I had my oil changed not two weeks ago and he told me he'd topped off all the fluids."

Dillon bent to press his forehead to hers. "I'll take a look at it. You…might have had some damage to the brake lines."

Virginia shook her head. "Dillon, looking after my car isn't part of your job and not at all a necessary part of our relationship. Besides, I already called the tow truck. I can take care of myself, you know."

He looked as if he wanted to argue, but held his tongue. In this instance, Virginia appreciated his restraint. She liked her independence and wanted no infringements on it. She smiled her approval. "You know, it's too bad I have to check in here Friday morning." She smoothed her open palm over his wide chest and sighed. "I think I'd like a lot more time with you, truth be told."

His slight frown and the darkening of his eyes were confusing. He reached around her and opened the door, suddenly in a hurry to leave. On his way out, he muttered gruffly, "Save your wishes for something important, honey. You never know when you might need them."

She wondered what he meant, or if he'd meant anything at all. Dillon was an elusive man and most times she wasn't at all sure how to take him. But she did feel certain about one thing. She would definitely enjoy her fling with him.

"DON'T EVER SPEAK to me like a lackey again."

Cliff whirled around and stared. Dillon closed the door quietly behind him and stalked forward. He knew he wasn't precisely angry at Cliff, at least not over anything new. But he made a fine target. And right now, Dillon needed an outlet.

He hadn't reached Virginia's car before it was taken away, but he'd still had his suspicions confirmed. Someone had cut her brake lines. Reddish brake fluid made a large puddle where her car had been parked. This was no mere leak.

Cliff backed up two steps before he caught himself. "What are you talking about?"

Dillon flattened his palms on the highly polished table and leaned toward Cliff. "Don't give me orders. If you want to meet with me, say so, but don't get pissed off at your sister and then bark at me."

Cliff tried a show of umbrage. "Now, see here…"

"I'm a damn good employee, Cliff. I've upgraded your entire security system and saved you a bundle in the process. I've found glitches most men would never have noticed. That's my job and I do it well. But I don't need this job and I don't need to be talked down to. Understand?"

Dillon was pushing it, but Cliff seemed to gain more respect for him every time he asserted himself. Unlike Virginia. It made sense to Dillon. He'd be damned if he'd want some marshmallow in charge of protecting the interests of his company. Not only was Dillon in charge of securing the actual property against theft, both at the offices where Cliff and Virginia worked and at the retail outlets, but he evaluated the security potential and estimated costs of future retail sites. He also oversaw the personal security for employees, including the boss. Johnson's Sporting Goods wasn't a nickle-and-dime operation.

Dillon recognized his value to the Johnsons. He'd

learned his trade from the best. His father had taught him how to secure, and how to breach, the legal and the illegal, which made him unique, and one of the best in the business.

Cliff needed him, especially with Virginia constantly breathing down his neck.

Besides, now that he believed Virginia was being threatened, he wasn't quite up to maintaining his pretense with Cliff. Virginia had finally agreed to some intimate time alone with him, and it was entirely possible he'd be able to settle things just by getting a few good leads from her. Surely Virginia would know what trumped up evidence Cliff had manufactured. If she would talk.

God, he hoped it would work out that simply. He hated playing the dutiful employee. He preferred working for himself, hiring himself out on short-term jobs, spending his free time in Mexico with his father and his horses and his land.

Dillon figured that once he established a relationship with Virginia, he could quit the company. Virginia would undoubtedly find him more appealing as a free agent; there would be no reason for her to think she was being used.

Dillon shook his head. He didn't like the warmth that swelled over him when he considered pleasing her. It didn't matter what Virginia thought or would think. If her bright golden eyes were angry or aroused. None of it mattered. None of it *could* matter.

A heartfelt sigh from Cliff broke into Dillon's thoughts.

"You're right," Cliff said. "I do value you as an employee. It's just that Virginia can be so damn arrogant, and I've got enough on my mind right now without her harassment."

Very slowly, Dillon straightened. "Oh? Anything I can help with?" Little by little, Cliff opened up to him, making him a confidant, wanting him for a cohort in his grievances against his sister.

Cliff waved dismissively. "It's a matter that came up before you were hired. I have people already on the problem."

"What exactly is the problem?"

"A little matter of internal embezzlement. A former employee used his position to siphon funds from the company. The theft occurred mostly in insubstantial amounts, so it was hard to notice. I knew it was him, and I fired him on the spot, but of course I can't accuse him officially without solid evidence. Finding proof is taking some doing. You know how difficult it can be to trace numbers. However, I believe we finally have him nailed. We should be able to wrap things up any day now."

"What kind of evidence do you have?" Keeping his tone so mild, so bland, was more than difficult when he wanted to grab Cliff and slam his fist in his mouth. He wanted to force him to admit it was all a scam. Wade couldn't be guilty.

Except… Cliff didn't look as though he was scamming. He looked smugly confident. It shook Dillon.

"My lawyers have advised me not to discuss the case. Suffice it to say, when we go to court, we won't lose." He pushed a button on the intercom, then requested that Laura bring in coffee. Cliff stacked some files and turned to face Dillon. "The others will be joining me soon, but I wanted to talk with you for a minute or two first. Virginia interrupted us downstairs. But now is as good a time as any."

This was curious. Dillon considered telling Cliff why Virginia had interrupted, about the cut brake lines, but decided against it. Cliff could be the very one who had tampered with Virginia's car. At the moment, he wasn't willing to put family loyalty to the test, especially not in Cliff's case.

Dillon hid his thoughts well as he gave Cliff his attention. "I didn't realize we were having a meeting. Is your sister invited to this one?"

"Hell no." Cliff chuckled. "I try to keep her as much out of the way as possible. You've seen firsthand how offensive she can be. No, the meeting is about expanding the downtown operation."

Not again, Dillon thought, tired of that tune and trying to explain to an idiot that opening an outlet downtown was a waste of funds. Unless the entire area was revamped, Cliff would be better off withdrawing and investing his money on renovations elsewhere. Though Virginia had told Cliff that countless times, it didn't take someone with her business sense to see it. Dillon had backed up her reasoning, on a security level. Cliff wasn't listening.

"You know how I feel about that, Cliff. I can upgrade all the systems there, hire good people to work in shifts, but it won't do you any good. Even without the petty theft, which is rampant and you know it, that store is a money hog. There's not enough business to warrant the effort."

Cliff gestured with his hand, looking distracted and annoyed. "That's not what I want to speak to you about. No, I want to talk to you about my sister."

Dillon turned his back to look out the third-story windows. Below him was human congestion, smog and noise. The sides of the street were piled high with blackened snow and sludge. Traffic flowed, the same traffic Virginia had almost encountered, without brakes. He shuddered.

He hated being here in Delaport City on this ridiculous ruse. He wanted to be home again, listening to his father grumbling and recounting all his old adventures. This didn't feel like an adventure. This felt like one huge mistake. "You want to talk about your sister? What about her?"

"I, ah, know from your file that your expertise includes surveillance."

"My *expertise* covers a lot of activities that aren't exactly part of a legitimate job résumé, especially not for the position you hired me for. I only gave you a few facts because I figured you'd need something to recommend me." The information was accurate, just in case Cliff had the sense to look, which Dillon wasn't certain of. But Virginia would have checked, of that he had no doubt. So he'd supplied the names of the few companies he'd ever worked for. Like his father, he could ferret out trouble—or cause it. With equal success, according to who was paying the most. It wasn't a trait he felt any particular pride over. Just a way of survival.

"Virginia insisted on checking into your employment background. She was impressed, which says a lot, even though your lack of consistency with any one job concerned her. Has she ever spoken to you about it?"

Dillon still faced the window. He was afraid if he looked at Cliff, all his anger would show. "No. Other than a few casual exchanges, we've never spoken."

"Excellent! Then she'll never suspect you."

"Suspect me of what?" He did turn to Cliff now. "What is it you want me to do?"

"I want you to spy on her, of course. She's up to something, seeing someone. God only knows what that woman's capable of."

Dillon grunted. He knew she was capable of making grown men cower, of scaring off any advances, of isolating herself completely with her sharp tongue and smothering arrogance. She was also capable of making him burn red-hot.

Was she capable of making an enemy who would wish her harm?

Dillon shook his head, feeling his tension simmer once again. "What do you mean, she's seeing someone?"

"The other night at the party, I caught her sneaking back into the kitchen."

With a dry look, Dillon said, "I can't imagine Virginia *sneaking* anywhere. It's not in her nature."

"No, you're right. She strutted back into the house, bold as you please, when she'd been out there conspiring with someone against me."

Dillon pulled out a chair and straddled it. Cliff's stupidity never ceased to amaze him. "Conspiring? How do you know she wasn't with a lover?"

He grinned. "That's exactly what she said! How about that—you two share a similar sense of humor."

Dillon heard a noise and looked up. Laura Neil stood in the doorway, holding a tray with fresh coffee and two mugs. Dillon wondered how long she'd been standing there, but then decided it didn't matter. He was more interested in the way the woman watched Cliff, sheer adoration clouding her eyes.

Cliff nodded to her and she entered. She leaned close to him while she poured the coffee, and asked if they needed anything else. Every so often, her gaze darted to Dillon. He almost felt sorry for her. It was obvious she was infatuated with Cliff, and just as obvious that Cliff had used his position to take advantage of her. To Dillon's mind, it was one more reason to despise Virginia's brother.

Cliff dismissed Laura. Dillon sipped from his cup, waiting. He knew his silence would annoy Cliff, so therefore his patience was its own reward.

After only a few seconds, Cliff exploded. "Well? What do you say?"

Dillon glanced at him over his mug. "To what? You haven't asked me anything yet."

"Oh, for… Will you check into it? Find out what Virginia is up to and who she's involved with?"

"What's in it for me?"

"A five-hundred-dollar bonus. Twice that if you come up with something concrete."

The irony of it amused Dillon—that Cliff would be paying Dillon to spy on himself. But the little bastard was also spying on his sister, and Dillon's suspicions were growing. He didn't trust Cliff, not at all.

Dillon let Cliff wait while he pretended to think things over. Of course he'd agree to do it. It made perfect sense. If *he* was checking into things, Cliff wouldn't be hiring someone else who would get in his way.

Dragging out the inevitable, and hoping for any tidbit of information that might help him, Dillon asked, "Any clues at all who it might be? Any leads?"

"Just the obvious. The guy must be someone who could benefit Virginia in some way, someone in the company who might be able to sway votes."

From what he'd heard, Virginia always won every vote, so that theory didn't make sense. He refrained from pointing that out to Cliff. "Anything else?"

Cliff shrugged. "The guy's most likely passive, ineffectual, a spineless sort. You know how Virginia is. She'd never be able to get a man like you to put up with her carping and demands for some scheme of hers. And Virginia insists on complete obedience. She wouldn't accept any defiance."

Dillon couldn't help himself; he grinned. "So I'm looking for a wimp?" The description was apt.

"Yes, but a wimp with connections. Someone who could do her some good."

"But you're a hundred percent positive she's not involved in a personal relationship she just doesn't want you to know about?"

Cliff was already shaking his head. "Not Virginia. Men are interested in her for one reason—to use her. And I'd want to know about that, too. Even though she's sworn she'll never marry, I have to protect her from those sorts. She's too abrasive and too overweight to attract anyone with genuine feelings. She'd only end up hurt, or hurting the company."

Abruptly, Dillon came to his feet. One more second with the loving brother and he'd throw him out the damn window. "I'll check into things." He crossed to the door, then turned back. "By the way, Virginia had some brake trouble today." He watched Cliff closely, waiting.

"Oh?"

"She's all right, but her car's out of commission for a while. I gave her the company car to use."

Cliff waved a hand, already distracted, as he gathered together the notes for his meeting. "That's fine."

Dillon clenched his jaw. He hadn't been asking for permission, but rather watching for a reaction. He didn't get one.

He jerked the door open and started out, saying over his shoulder, "I'm taking the rest of the day off. I'll be in touch later."

Cliff didn't argue. He couldn't have anyway. Dillon had already slammed the door.

CHAPTER FOUR

VIRGINIA HAD JUST hung up the phone when the rap sounded on her office door. She glanced up, frustrated by the way her day had gone. First the problems with her car, then her run-in with Cliff. And her meeting hadn't gone at all well. Today was not her day, and she was tired. A hot bath and a long night's sleep seemed just the cure.

"Come in."

Dillon stuck his head in the door. "You about ready to head home?"

As always, one glance into those sinfully dark eyes turned her insides warm and jittery. With every minute that passed, she anticipated her day alone with him more. "Mmm. I was just about to call a cab. What's up?"

She didn't particularly relish the idea of doing any more business tonight, but for Dillon, she'd make an exception. Spending time with him was seldom a hardship.

He stepped into her office and closed the door behind him. His features were etched in a frown. Virginia sighed, knowing why he'd come by. "If you're here to tell me about Cliff's plans to rework the downtown office, I've heard all about it."

Dillon stiffened. "It's not my job to tattle on your damn brother."

She lifted a brow at his tone as well as his words.

"No? Your loyalty to a prospective lover doesn't go quite that far?" Virginia knew she was taunting him, but damn it, her day had been rotten, and just once, she wanted to see Dillon lose his temper, cut loose and prove to her what a powerful man he could be. But instead, he merely narrowed his eyes and waited.

Virginia took pity on him. "I'm sorry. I was just about to head home and I'm a little out of sorts. It hasn't been the best of days."

"That's why I'm here," he said. "To offer you a ride."

"Chauffeuring is part of your job description?"

"Why not?" He stepped closer, his expression inscrutable. "I'm in charge of security. It's my responsibility to see that you make it home safely."

She couldn't help but smile. "That's stretching it, Dillon."

"Not so." He looked at her intently, his gaze unwavering. "I think your brake lines might have been tampered with."

She waited for the punch line, and when it didn't come she got to her feet and crossed to the closet to retrieve her coat. Before she could slip it on, Dillon was behind her, holding her shoulders. "I'm serious, Virginia."

"That's ridiculous." She turned to face him. "So some vandal picked our parking lot to play around in. We'll just increase security."

"That's just it." He raised his hand to her cheek and stroked it. "Maybe it wasn't a vandal. Maybe whoever did it targeted your car."

"So now I have an enemy?" She could see he was serious, but she couldn't feel the same way. It was entirely too far-fetched. "You've been working too hard, Dillon. I think you need a day off more than I do."

His jaw tightened and his hands slipped to her shoulders again. After a deep calming breath, he said, "All right, then just humor me, okay? Let me drive you home tonight."

"I'm a big girl, Dillon, all grown-up. I don't need a caretaker."

He smiled, a beautiful smile that made her toes curl. He kissed her and she forgot they were standing in the middle of her office and someone could walk in at any moment.

He pulled back only far enough to speak, but his breath was warm on her lips, his tone husky. "You don't have to convince me of that, honey. I know it all too well." He kissed her again, a quick, hard kiss, then stepped back. "What did your mechanic say?"

Virginia had trouble bringing herself back under control. Lord love him, the man was a temptation, and she was quickly growing tired of resisting him. She stared up at him and tried to find her aplomb.

"I haven't talked with my mechanic yet. He won't have a chance to look at the car until tomorrow."

"Then will you please—for my sake—be extra cautious until then?"

She thought about denying him, if for no other reason than reasserting her independence. She'd always had to fight so hard to prove herself, she sometimes didn't know when to quit fighting. But truth be told, she loved the idea of him taking her home. Maybe he'd come inside, maybe he'd stop being so skittish about appearances and make love to her this very night. The mere thought caused her body to heat. "All right."

Dillon stared down at her a moment longer before he nodded. He held her coat while she slipped into it, then led her out the door.

DILLON DIDN'T WANT to explore his satisfaction too deeply. Having Virginia accede to his wishes made him feel like a conqueror. It hadn't happened often, and he had a feeling it wouldn't happen again anytime soon. Virginia wasn't a woman to let a man call the shots. Right now, she was quiet. Too quiet. And he wondered if maybe she was regretting her small show of weakness. He didn't consider caution a weakness, but he knew she would.

"Turn left up here."

Startled out of his thoughts, Dillon reminded himself that he wasn't supposed to know where she lived. He had to keep his mind on what he was doing, rather than trying to dissect Virginia's psyche. He'd already discovered many times over what a futile and frustrating effort that could be. He just couldn't seem to help himself; she fascinated him.

For the rest of the ride, he waited for her directions, even though he knew the way. Before getting hired on at Johnson's Sporting Goods, he'd done a complete check on her.

When they pulled into her driveway, Virginia started to open her door. Dillon ignored that and walked around to her side of the car. She stood there, embraced by selective moonlight, on this dark, cloudy night. Her head was tilted back as she stared up at him, her eyes wide, and he wanted her.

He hated himself for it, but he wanted her. The iron control he'd always depended on seemed to evaporate where this woman was concerned, and it didn't make sense. He didn't even like her.

"Do you want to come in for a while?"

He hesitated. It didn't take a genius to see the direction of her thoughts and, seeing that, he become instantly, painfully, hard. But making love to Virginia, especially now, wasn't a wise thing to contemplate. He racked his brain for any excuse that would be believable, but before he could speak, a shadow caught his eye and he jerked toward the house. He could have sworn he saw a curtain move.

He shoved Virginia behind him as he stepped deeper into the shadows. "Do you have any pets, honey?"

"No. Dillon what are you—"

"Shh. Someone's in your house." His senses rioted, telling him all he needed to know.

"What?"

"Give me your key."

Thankfully, Virginia complied, but when he told her to get into his car and lock the doors, she refused. As he inched closer to the house, she followed, leaving him no choice but to stop. "Damn it, Virginia." His whispered voice was guttural, his temper on the edge. He grasped her shoulders. "You can't—"

"It's my house. I know my way around a lot better than you do."

He shook her. He hadn't meant to, but she was so obstinate, so annoying, he couldn't help himself. "This isn't a game, damn it! For once, will you—"

They both heard the back door slam, the sound carried easily on the cold, quiet night. Dillon squeezed her shoulders hard. "Stay put!"

He took off at a run. Even before he reached the

backyard, he knew the chase was useless. Woods bordered her property on two sides, and he had no doubt the intruder would have long vanished into the black shadows. He cursed, then cursed again when Virginia touched his arm and he almost threw her to the ground in reaction. In the split second before he touched her, he realized who she was.

Without a word, knowing she wouldn't follow an order even if her life depended on it, he dragged her up the back steps and into the house, keeping to the side so he wouldn't destroy any footprints that might have been left behind. His temper was on the ragged edge, the ruthless aspects of his personality ruling him.

He found two light switches just inside the door. One illuminated the kitchen with blinding fluorescent light and the other flooded the backyard. Dillon scanned the yard, but there wasn't a single movement caught in the glare.

"Call the police," he whispered.

She answered in kind. "Why? Whoever it was is long gone now."

"Unless there was more than one guy. Just do it."

She bristled, but he didn't have time to cajole her. He waited only until he saw her lift the receiver, then cautiously made his way down the hall, turning on lights as he went. Quickly, methodically, he went through the downstairs rooms, then trotted silently up the carpeted stairway to the upper level. He had explored all the rooms before Virginia finished making the call.

"Dillon?"

"It's okay." He answered from her bedroom, the last room he'd found. Virginia joined him there.

She glanced around, looking uncomfortable. "The

police are on their way. They said to stay in the kitchen, not to try to be a hero."

He grunted. "This is what I'm trained to do, Virginia."

"To be a hero?"

He knew she was teasing. He could see it her golden eyes, shining now from the excitement. He shook his head. "Your bedroom is a surprise."

That small observation removed the smile from her lips. She stiffened and drew her auburn brows together. "What's that supposed to mean?"

He left the room, Virginia hot on his heels. With a deliberate shrug, he said, "It's a little more feminine than I had expected, that's all. I mean, I hadn't pictured you having ruffled pillow shams or lace curtains."

She apparently didn't know what to say to that, so Dillon changed the subject. "How about some coffee?" He approached the back door, examining it closely. "I'm sure the cops would appreciate it on a cold night like this."

He'd no sooner said the words than the sirens could be heard. Sure enough, the police were more than willing to swill coffee as they gave the house another examination. To everyone's surprise except maybe Dillon's, nothing seemed to be missing.

Still, the police wrote up the incident as a simple break and enter.

One young officer held his hat in one hand while cradling his coffee in the other. "With a house like yours, in this neighborhood, a burglar would be in heaven."

Another policeman confirmed what Dillon already knew. "They came in through the kitchen door."

"But how?" Virginia didn't seem unsettled by the

whole affair—she seemed furious. "My doors are always locked."

"They picked the lock somehow." The cop shrugged. "Leave your floodlights on tonight. In fact, you should get a timer to turn them on as soon as it gets dark. And put in an alarm system, as well. A woman living here alone—"

Disgusted, Dillon interrupted. "I'll see to it tomorrow."

Virginia frowned at him, but kept her peace. Dillon's position, his reason for being with her, had already been explained. Since then the cops had been giving him a wide berth.

The policeman nodded. "Yeah, well, we'll patrol through the neighborhood the rest of the night, ma'am. You should be safe enough. Very seldom does a perpetrator return once he knows he's been discovered."

Dillon didn't agree, and he told Virginia so as soon as the officers had left. "You shouldn't stay here."

"Now, don't start, Dillon. I'm tired and I want to go to bed. I'm not about to start uprooting myself tonight."

He paced, trying to think while she glared at him, looking her most imperious. "What is the matter with you? You've been entirely too high-handed this evening and I've about had enough!"

He should have known she'd get her back up and make this more difficult than it had to be. "Virginia, has it escaped your notice that you've been threatened twice in the same day?"

She rolled her eyes. "I've had car trouble and a simple break-in. That's doesn't exactly add up to a life-or-death situation."

He clenched his fists tight, fighting for control. It

seemed he fought that particular battle more since meeting Virginia than he ever had in his entire life. "How do you think the guy got inside?"

She shrugged. "He picked the lock."

"There's no evidence of a forced entry. What if he had a key?"

Her eyes widened and she took a step back. "What exactly are you saying, Dillon? You think someone I know is trying to hurt me? Who?"

He should probably have admitted his suspicions that he thought Cliff might very well be the one harassing her. But something held him back. Despite all her bravado, all her indignation and affronted pride, she was still a woman, soft and vulnerable. From what he knew of her, Virginia had never had an easy life, and she'd never had anyone to love her. To find out now just how big a scoundrel her brother could be might well devastate her. He couldn't bear that.

To his shame, though, he had another reason for hesitating. The possibility that if he forced the issue, she might blame Wade for threatening her. To Virginia, Wade would be a much more likely suspect. Her brother had accused him of embezzlement, and he'd been fired. Didn't that give Wade motive enough, in her mind, to want revenge? If he convinced her the threats were real, would it backfire on Wade?

Wade could end up being accused not only as an embezzler, but an assailant as well. And then, if Virginia thought Wade was guilty, she would let her guard down. The real assailant would have a clear field. It was too risky. And if Virginia got hurt because he was preoccupied with his brother…

Impulsively, he put his arms around her and pulled

her close in a careful hug. She resisted, holding herself stiff in his arms until he said, "I'm sorry. I know I've been on edge tonight. But Virginia, at least give me the right to worry about you a little, okay?"

She smiled up at him. "If you insist. But it isn't necessary. I'll be careful. I'm not an idiot."

"I know." He kissed her and didn't want to stop kissing her. Her lips were warm and soft and she tempted him. He opened his mouth over hers, gently moving, savoring her taste. She made a small sound deep in her throat when his tongue licked over her bottom lip.

Cursing inwardly, Dillon set her away from him and reached for his coat. "Will you be all right tonight?"

He could tell by her expression that she wanted to ask him to stay; pride would keep her from it, though. And this time, he was glad. In less than twenty-four hours, everything had changed. His plans thrown into turmoil, he had to adapt. False accusations of embezzlement were no longer the only issue, and took a back seat to Virginia's safety. This new threat was much more tangible, much more immediate.

He felt responsible for Virginia, whether she liked it or not, and he'd do his best to protect her, even while helping his brother. If he had to be ruthless to accomplish both goals, so be it. In all fairness, he gave her one last chance to do things the easy way. "Why don't you take a vacation? Disappear for a while until things calm down?"

"What things? You really are overreacting."

His hands fisted at his sides. "This wasn't a simple break-in, Virginia."

"Of course it was—"

"Nothing was taken, damn it! How do you explain that?"

She shrugged. "It's like the police said. We probably interrupted the burglar."

He grabbed her arms, his patience at an end. "What if you'd walked in here alone? What if I hadn't been with you? Do you think whoever it was would have run?"

She stared at him blankly, her lips parted in surprise at his vehemence. With an effort, he eased his tone.

"This is what I do, honey. I know what I'm talking about. To be safe, you should get out of here for a while. Go to a motel. I'll join you Thursday, just as we planned."

She rubbed his shoulder as if to soothe him. "I have responsibilities here, Dillon. And the police really don't seem to think there's anything to be alarmed about."

Dillon drew a deep breath and released her. "Surely the company can survive without you for a few days." Without having to worry about her being threatened and with free run of her office, he could not only get the information he needed to absolve Wade, but most likely nail the bastard who was harassing her as well. All he needed was a little time.

She began loading empty coffee cups into the dishwasher, and when she glanced at him, a gentleness had entered her eyes. "I like you, Dillon, and I want to spend time with you. But one long afternoon will have to be enough for now. Don't ask for more. My first priority will always be running the company—you know that."

Only, it wasn't her company, it was Cliff's. And

Dillon had a feeling Cliff had gotten tired of sharing it with her.

Her stubbornness knew no bounds; she wouldn't relent. He closed his eyes a moment, accepting the inevitable, knowing what had to be done, knowing his options had just become severely limited. From the moment he'd involved himself in this mess, he'd felt equal parts protective and possessive of her. He wouldn't let anyone hurt her. He'd protect her despite herself. Never mind that she'd probably despise him for it. Her hate had been guaranteed from the first.

He had one more day, Wednesday, to watch over her, while at the same time rearranging his plans and making new ones. He had a lot to accomplish in the time left to him, including the installation of an alarm system at her house that would put a stop to intruders.

He sighed as the ramifications of his new plan sank in. Virginia would miss her meeting on Friday after all. But at least she'd be safe.

CHAPTER FIVE

DILLON HEARD THE ringing as if from far away. It pierced his subconsciousness, but wasn't enough to get him out of the dream. And he knew he was dreaming, knew it wasn't real, but he couldn't force himself awake.

The cell was dark and cold, and in his dream he accepted that he would spend many years there, yet strangely enough, that wasn't what bothered him most. No, it was Virginia, standing outside his cell, round with a late pregnancy. His child. He broke out in a sweat. Cliff was pointing and laughing from the background, and Virginia's eyes looked wounded—and accusing.

The ringing became more insistent, sounding like a small scream, and he jerked awake. His heart thundered and all his muscles felt too tight, straining. He had an erection.

Unbelievable. He ran a hand over his face, drew several deep breaths. His stomach slowly began to unknot.

The covers were tangled about his legs and he felt like he'd been in a furnace he was so hot. The dream, and his reaction to it, made no sense, and even if in some twisted way it did, he shied away from probing the reasons. He didn't want to know what it meant, didn't want to dwell on the strange things Virginia made him feel. Kelsey was the one who was pregnant, and Dillon planned to do only what he had to do. He would save his brother, protect Virginia, but he wouldn't touch her. So there was no chance of the dream coming true.

Still, he felt a drip of sweat slide down his brow.

The bedside alarm continued its shrill call, and feeling drugged, Dillon reached for it. He glanced at the face of the clock. It wasn't quite five a.m. and he had to meet Virginia at six. Today was the day.

His heart still thundered from the dream—which hadn't been a dream at all but rather a damned nightmare. Dillon ran a hand through his hair, shoving it away from his face.

Peddling his legs, he kicked the blankets to the end of the bed and let the cold winter morning air wash over his naked body. The sweat dried quickly and he chilled as he considered what was on his agenda.

He was going to kidnap Virginia Johnson.

Ever since the break-in he'd tried to think of another way to do things, another way to protect her *and* his brother. But he'd come up blank, without a single alternative. She refused to take the time away from the office, refused to listen to reason or take extra precautions. He'd come up with only one solution.

And his stomach had been in knots ever since.

Anyone who'd met Virginia for more than two minutes would know how she'd react to being held prisoner.

Everything in her would rebel. Hell, he'd had to fight her tooth and nail just to get the alarm installed at her home yesterday. He'd hired the very best agency, interviewed them himself, selected the alarm. Virginia had been outraged, only grudgingly giving over to his greater experience. Dillon had made sure the system was installed that very day, in case she changed her mind.

Virginia, on the best of days, was hard-nosed and contrary and independent to a fault. She wouldn't be an easy victim, and in the normal scheme of things, with a real kidnapping, her sarcasm and sharp tongue could get her hurt. Not that he would ever hurt her. He didn't hurt women, and the very idea of harming Virginia made him ache. She'd been hurt more than enough over her lifetime.

Poor Virginia. A brother who ridiculed her to employees and a spoiled little sister who thought only of herself. No wonder she'd become such a tough woman. She'd had to to survive the jackals, the people who would use her without regret.

And now he would be no better.

All his life he'd thought there were only two kinds of families. The type he and his father had, that existed on guts and strength and commitment. Their lives centered on survival, and they watched each other's backs, because they only had each other. Their bonds ran deep with the bare bones of necessity.

Then there was the other kind, the one filled with love and tenderness. Children playing, dogs barking, barbecues in the backyard and family outings to the amusement park.

Now he realized there were many kinds, because Virginia didn't fit into either group. She was as strong as an iron spike, but she didn't have the respect and dedication from her family that same trait would have earned for a man.

Neither did she have the love or tenderness. Maybe none of that even existed. Maybe it was just something he'd conjured in his brain when things had been hard and he'd foolishly tried to imagine the life he would have had with a mother. He was damn lucky his father had stuck by him, lucky the man had seen fit to teach him how to get by in the world.

Dillon glanced at the clock again. In one hour he'd be picking up Virginia. She would be expecting a day full of intimacy. He was going to give her the fright of her life. More than anything, he'd like to simply walk away, to forget Virginia and her damn dysfunctional family. The ridiculous dream that couldn't mean anything, no matter how it made his guts churn, was just that, a dream. He didn't, *wouldn't,* care for her, but for some damn reason, he wanted her. And he wanted to protect her. Chemistry, unaccountable and indisputable.

It wouldn't be easy, not with the complications growing every day, but he'd manage. Once Virginia was safely stowed away, he could concentrate on Wade.

He wondered if Cliff was using Virginia's distraction with the embezzlement to try to hurt her, to drive her away from the company. He hadn't heard Virginia mention the embezzlement, so she might not even be aware of Cliff's treachery. Or maybe she had gotten too close to discovering her brother's underhanded tactics. Virginia took her obligations to the company very seriously; she wouldn't put up with falsifying evidence. Was Cliff afraid of her finding out?

Either way, Dillon knew in his guts that Virginia was threatened. And he knew Cliff would be closing in on Wade very soon now. They couldn't have much time left. He had to get into the files and find the real embezzler before it was too late. Taking Virginia was the only option open to him, the only way to settle both problems at one time.

Virginia wouldn't like it, wouldn't understand his motives. But Wade would. He knew it had to be now or never. He had no choice. Just as his father had watched out for him, he now watched out for Wade, regardless of personal feelings or conflicts. That much, at least, he understood about family.

With cold resolution he climbed from the bed and headed for the shower.

VIRGINIA COULDN'T HELP but be excited. She'd arrived at the parking lot fifteen minutes early. It was dark and cold and everything was covered in ice. The world sparkled beneath streetlamps and moonlight, looking new and clean and magical.

Headlights curved into the lot and then blinded her as they slowly crept her way. Her heartbeat picked up rhythm, and she closed her eyes, trying to calm herself. Somehow, she knew Dillon wouldn't be like the other men. He wouldn't be satisfied with half measures and fumbling in the dark. The thought shook her, but in a small part of herself that she'd kept hidden for so very long, she was excited by the notion. She felt sexy.

Absurd, a woman her age, with her weight problems and practical outlook on life, but she couldn't help it. She'd even worn sexy underclothes. A silk teddy, garters and silk hose. Instead of twisting her hair into a tight knot, she'd left it looser, more like the romantic Gibson-girl style. Little curls fell around her ears. She'd felt silly when she looked in the mirror, but she didn't redo it.

She wore a long winter-white cashmere tunic and

skirt, with ankle boots of the same creamy color. Even her thick cape was a matching off-white. Her red hair was the only color. And the blush on her cheeks.

The vehicle that pulled alongside her, facing the opposite direction, wasn't the same car Dillon had kissed her in the other night. No, this was a big, mean, ugly truck. She squinted through the driver's side window and saw Dillon step out, holding on to the truck door because of the ice. He'd parked so close only a few feet separated them. He reached out and opened her door.

"Be careful. It's like a frozen pond out here. Nothing but ice."

She put her gloved hand in his and carefully stepped out. He held her securely, protectively. For a moment she allowed it, and then she realized what she was doing, how she was being treated, and she pulled back.

All day yesterday Dillon had hovered over her. He'd fretted, much like a mother hen, and she knew it was because he was worried. The break-in, though no big deal to Virginia, had upset him. Despite his capabilities, he was a mild-mannered man in most instances, and she supposed the circumstances might be unsettling to someone without her constitution.

In a way she thought it was sweet that he'd been so concerned for her welfare. But being independent had become second nature to her. It was her greatest protective instinct. "I'm fine. Just let me open my trunk and get my bag."

"Your bag?"

Flustered, she fiddled with her car door. "You can't expect me to spend the entire day with you and not have...other stuff with me. I didn't know if we'd go out for dinner, or if you'd just want to...stay in the room."

Her voice trailed off. She'd packed things to refix her hair, anticipating that it might get rather mussed, and she'd brought something sexy to wear for him when they went to bed, as well as a cocktail dress. She'd never before planned a rendezvous and wasn't certain of the protocol. But she had no intention of explaining all that to him.

"It's not important, Dillon. Just let me—"

"No. I've got it." He took her arm and, still holding on to his own door, pulled her toward his truck. "Just slide in on this side. I wouldn't want you to fall and bruise anything."

"I might fall, but you wouldn't? Does being male give you better coordination?"

In the dim light, she saw him close his eyes, saw his breath puff out in a sigh. "Virginia, if I fall, I don't care. And I can guarantee I'd be landing on a lot more solid muscle that you would."

She didn't know if that was a slur or not, but she didn't ask him to clarify because she didn't really want to know. Handing him the keys, she looked away and mumbled, "Fine. Suit yourself."

He tugged her close as she tried to slide past him. His forehead dropped to hers. "Virginia."

This close, she could see the dark sweep of his lashes, feel the warmth of his breath. He smiled. "You have an incredibly sexy ass. You know that, don't you?"

Her heart tripped with the rough compliment. He sounded sincere, and she peeked up at him. He looked sincere—and as if he was waiting for her acknowledgment of the fact. "You have a wonderful way with words."

His beautiful mouth tipped in a crooked grin, and

once again his lashes swept his cheeks. "Sorry. Was my language too…colorful? I hope you won't mind. I don't know a lot of pretty words. But I do know a pretty bottom when I see one." His firm palm went to that area and gently squeezed.

She was eternally grateful for the darkness hiding her blush. As it was, he probably felt the heat from her that seemed to pulse beneath her skin. Sex talk was new to her. And the raw, spontaneous way in which Dillon spoke was far from the practiced lines she usually heard.

She tightened her lips and tried not to laugh. "Thank you."

His gaze lingered over a curl trailing past her cheek. "I like your new hairdo, too. Did you wear it this way for me?" His hand moved back to her waist.

Ironically, he didn't look at all pleased by the notion. A more sophisticated man wouldn't have asked. He would have assumed, and maybe been flattered, but he wouldn't have embarrassed the woman by mentioning it. Virginia started to reply, but Dillon interrupted her.

His eyes were narrowed, and he looked reluctant to speak, but the words emerged anyway, low and raw. "Do you let it loose when you make love?" His gloved fingertips slid over her cheek, then over the upsweep of her hair. His gaze followed the path of his hand. "How long is it?"

Oh my. How could she possibly regain control if his every word made her mute with anticipation? Dillon lowered his head and kissed her. His fingers tightened on her skull and the kiss gradually grew more intimate until his mouth ate at hers, voracious and invading. Her fingers wrapped over his wrists, not to pull him away, but to hang on. His passion made her almost dizzy. It wasn't what she was used to. He was too unrestrained, too natural, too much man. The thought made her heart jump.

He drew back slowly, in small degrees, his tongue licking her lips, his teeth nipping. Finally, his forehead rested against hers and she felt the cool, soft sweep of his long hair over her cheek. His sigh fogged the air between them. "Get in the car. I'll throw your bag in the back and we can get out of here."

Virginia glanced into the back of the battered truck and saw that the bed was covered by a tarp. "Whose truck is this?"

"Mine. It gets better traction in the snow." He opened the trunk of her car, pulled out a small overnight case and cautiously picked his way back across the ice. He stowed the bag beneath the tarp while Virginia watched, then he carefully checked to see that her car was locked up tight. She held out her hand for her keys, but he'd already shoved them deep into his jeans pocket.

"Dillon…"

"In you go, honey." Not giving her a chance to comment on his high-handedness, he lifted her off her feet, then unceremoniously dropped her into the truck.

He slid in beside her and locked the door.

Virginia fumed. "Don't you *ever* do anything like that again!"

He didn't answer, disconcerting her with his silence. In fact, he seemed different; the very air seemed different. Somehow charged. He put the truck in gear and began pulling away. She heard ice and snow crunching beneath the tires, even over the sound of the blowing heater.

She shifted in her seat, nervousness creeping in on her by slow degrees. Speaking her mind always helped her overcome her fears, helped her to reassert herself, to regain control of any situation. She'd learned that trick while still in high school, throwing student bullies who would pick on her about her weight into a stupor with her blunt honesty and virulent daring. She'd employed her skill throughout college and in the family business after her parents' deaths. So hitting people broadside with arrogant bravado earned their dislike? It also earned their grudging obedience. And that had been good enough for her, because through most of her life, she'd needed every advantage she could gain. Cliff was the oldest and the heir; Kelsey was the baby—the sweet, *pretty one.*

Virginia filled the distressing spot of chubby middle child.

She huffed to herself and tightened her cape around her, regretting the brief stroll down memory's bumpy lane. Such thoughts always brought up her defensive feelings and the feeling of loneliness. Only, she wasn't alone now, and what always worked for her would work at this moment.

She turned in her seat to face Dillon and prepared to blast him with a few facts of life, namely that she was still the boss and as such, due all courtesies.

"Put on your seat belt."

Of all the nerve! Her spine went rigid and her nostrils flared. "If you don't stop ordering me around, we can just forget this little escapade altogether!"

Jaw clenched, he reached for the center floorboards

of the truck, where a small thermos sat in a molded plastic car caddy so it wouldn't tip and spill. Two lidded cups, already filled, were beside it.

"Here." He handed her a cup. "I thought you might like something hot to keep you comfortable on the trip. I got you out of bed so early I wasn't sure if you'd have time for coffee at home."

He glanced at her, and she knew he was judging her mood, trying to decide if he'd managed to placate her. She still felt affronted, but accepted that he was trying. And in a small way, his take-charge attitude stimulated her. In a *very* small way.

"Thank you."

He smiled, looking dramatically relieved, then he made a teasing face. "If I ask nice, will you also put on your seat belt? These roads are like a skating rink, and I don't want to take any chances with you."

She rather liked his teasing, and his concern. She smiled as she buckled her belt. "There. Happy?"

"Yes." He reached over and, fingers spread wide, put his large hand on her thigh, gripping her in a familiar way. She held her breath and her stomach flipped sweetly. She waited to see what he would do next, but he seemed preoccupied by the deserted road, almost distracted. An occasional streetlamp or passing car lit the interior of the truck cab and she saw his gloved hand looking wickedly dark and sinful against the pale material of her skirt. He didn't move, didn't speak. But that heavy hand remained on her leg, and she was incredibly aware of it, of him. She wondered if that hadn't been his intention all along.

She sipped her coffee, then cleared her throat. "Would you like your cup?"

"In a little while."

"Where exactly are we going?"

He flashed her a look she couldn't read, then his gaze dropped to the cup she held. "It's a surprise." He returned his attention to the road.

She didn't want to spoil the adventure, but his strange mood put her on edge. She'd survived a long time by trusting her hunches, and right now, it felt as if things weren't aligned quite properly. She never felt like this about men, and they never acted like this around her. Always, Dillon had gone out of his way to speak with her, to turn on the charm. But now he seemed so distant, sitting there in a manner that felt very *expectant*.

Did he want something of her? Was she supposed to be doing something? If so, she didn't know what. Dillon didn't behave like other men, which was both exciting and a bit unsettling.

She continued to sip her coffee, trying to push the mingled uneasiness and anticipation away.

After a moment, they turned onto a deserted southbound expressway, heading for Kentucky. Virginia hadn't gotten enough sleep, so the silence, combined with the easy driving and the early-morning darkness made her eyelids heavy. She closed her eyes and rested her head against the seat. "Where are we going, Dillon?"

His hand left her thigh to rub softly over her cheek, then around her ear. "You look like a snow bunny, you know that?"

His words were so soft. They drifted over her like his lazily moving fingers. With considerable effort, she forced her eyes open and turned her head in his direction. "I wanted to look nice for you," she whispered, then closed her eyes again, wondering where in hell that bit of confession had come from. She held tightly to her coffee and sipped. The mug was almost empty, but that was okay; she didn't want any more. She wanted to sleep.

She heard Dillon sigh. "I'm so sorry, Virginia. Remember that, okay?"

Something wasn't making sense. He sounded pained, but somehow determined. She frowned and forced her eyes open again. Everything was blurred and it took her precious seconds to focus again. Dillon kept glancing at her curiously, his brow furrowed, his gaze intent and diamond hard.

Suddenly, she knew. Her chest tightened in panic and she stared at him. Her breath came fast. "You bastard. *You poisoned me.*"

"Not poison," he said, but his voice was strained and there was a ringing in her ears. None of it made sense, at least, in no way she wanted to contemplate. She wouldn't let the fear take her, wouldn't let him take her. Hadn't he warned her himself that someone was threatening her? But he'd been with her when the intruder had been in her house. Unless they were working together…

She narrowed her eyes on him and saw his worried frown. They were moving quickly down the expressway, too quickly. Farther and farther from home. The roads were empty, the day still dark and cold. She felt weaker by the second, and she fought it. She'd have to use her wits before they deserted her. Later, when she was safe, she'd let the hurt consume her. But not until she was safe—and alone once again.

DILLON WISHED SHE'D say something, anything, rather than stare at him in that accusing way. It reminded him of the dream and his stomach cramped. She had to be frightened, and he hated doing this to her. Nevertheless, his body was tense, prepared for whatever she might try.

"What have you done to me?"

He felt cold inside. "I drugged you, just as you assumed. It's a sleeping drug. It won't hurt you. Even now, you're getting drowsy. You might as well stop fighting it, Virginia." More than anything, he wanted her to sleep so he wouldn't have to see the disgust and mistrust in her eyes.

She shook her head as if to clear it. "Where are we?"

"Nowhere yet." He pulled off the main highway and onto a less-traveled rural route, slowing the truck accordingly. It would take longer this way, but there wasn't likely to be any traffic at all. "We've got a while to go."

Her head lolled on the back of the seat, and she looked out the windows at the scrubby trees, the endless snow. Dillon knew what she saw; no one had cleared this area, and the road was almost invisible between the trees lining it.

It had turned bitterly cold, and the wind whistled around the truck. He saw Virginia shiver and rub her eyes and a strange tenderness welled up in his chest. "Honey, don't be afraid, okay?"

"Ha! I'm fine," she managed to snap in slurred tones. She held her shoulders stiff and her hands clenched in her lap. He knew she was fighting the drug and her fear with everything she had. But it was useless.

"As soon as we get to the cabin and you're awake, I'll explain what's going on. I don't want you to worry."

"I'm thirsty," she whispered, ignoring his speech. He supposed, given the circumstances, his assurances *were* bizarre.

"Sure. Here, there's a little coffee left." She glared at him and he added, "Mine. This isn't drugged. See?" He lifted the mug to this mouth to demonstrate, and that's when she hit him.

He should have seen it coming, but he hadn't realized she still had that much strength. Her doubled fists smacked into the cup, jamming it into his mouth, cutting his lip and clipping his nose. He cursed, dropping the cup and doing his best to steer the truck safely to the side of the road. He hit the brakes and shifted gears. They spun to a rocky stop after sliding several feet.

Already, Virginia was working on her door. He'd locked it, of course, and she fumbled, crying in frustration as she tried to find the way to unlock it. He'd put a large piece of electrical tape over the lock switch, just in case.

His hands closed on her shoulders and she turned on him, twisting in the seat and kicking wildly with her small boots. She hit him in the thigh and he grunted.

Subduing her without hurting her proved damn difficult. He finally just gave up and threw his entire weight on top of her. She gasped and cried and cursed as he captured both her hands and held them over her head. His chest pressed against her breasts, his thighs pinned hers.

"Virginia, shh. Baby, it's all right."

She looked up, and stark fear darkened her blurry eyes, cutting him deeply.

"Aw, damn." He closed his eyes, trying to gather his wits. "Honey, I swear, I'm not going to hurt you. Please believe me."

"Then why?" She began to struggle again, but she was weaker now, her eyelids only half-open. He lowered his chest, forcing her to gasp for air, to go completely still.

"I promise I'll explain everything at the cabin."

"What cabin?" she cried, the words slurred and raw.

"The cabin where I'm going to keep you for just a few days, until I'm sure it's safe. Now, can I let you go?"

She stared up at him, blinking slowly, still fighting. "Your lip is bleeding. And your nose is turning blue."

"I think you might have broken it." He tried a small grin, but with his lip numb, it might not have been too effective. "You pack a hell of a punch, especially for a drugged lady."

"I don't understand you. You're not the man I thought I knew."

"No, I don't suppose I am. But I won't hurt you. And in a few days, I'll take you home. Okay?"

Slowly, she nodded, and when he cautiously released her, she dropped her head back on the seat and took several deep breaths. After a moment, she pulled herself upright. It seemed to take a great deal of effort, but he didn't touch her. He didn't want her to slug him again, or possibly hurt herself jerking away.

Her gaze went to the door and the electrical tape. "I should have noticed."

"It was dark." He dabbed at his split lip with a hankie. Thankfully, his nose felt more bruised than broken, but it still hurt like hell.

"I have to use the bathroom."

That stymied him for just a moment. He lifted his hands. "There's nothing for miles, no gas station, no restaurants..."

"I need to go now. I can't wait."

He measured the wisdom of letting her out, but then he looked at her face. He wanted more than anything for her to trust him just a bit. He frowned at his own weakness. "All right. But stay right beside the truck. I'll turn my back."

She swallowed and her face flamed. To Dillon, she look remarkably appealing and feminine. Her hair was half-undone, long strands tumbling around her shoulders, waving around her face. Her strange topaz eyes were slumberous, filled with a mixture of muted anger and anxiety. She breathed heavily, slowly, her lush breasts rising and falling. He hated her fear, hated being the cause of it. But he hadn't had a choice.

Icy wind and wet snow assaulted him as he opened the door and stepped out. He turned and reached in for Virginia. She swayed, then offered him her hand to allow him to help her out on the driver's side. That was his first clue. Virginia never admitted to needing help with anything or from anyone. She especially wouldn't do so now, while she felt so angry and betrayed.

The realization hit just before she did. This time her aim was for his groin, and her aim was true, though thankfully not as solid as it might have been, given her lethargic state.

Air left his lungs in a whoosh and he bent double, then dropped to his knees in the icy snow. He ground his teeth against the pain and cursed her—the stubborn, deceiving little cat. This time when he got his hands on her…

Virginia tried to run, but her legs weren't working right. She was clumsy, stumbling and falling again and again. She headed for the scraggly trees, even though they wouldn't offer a speck of concealment. Dillon forced himself to his feet, leaning on the truck as he watched her. She moved awkwardly, hampered by her fear, the drug and the thick snow. He took one more deep breath, which didn't do a damn thing for the lingering pain and nausea, and started off in a lope after her.

She must have heard his pursuit because she turned to stare wildly at him—and tripped. Dillon saw her go down, saw her land heavily on the ground and not get back up. His heart stopped, then began to thud against his ribs. Oh God.

"Virginia!" He forgot his own pain and charged to her. She lay limp, her face in the snow, and he fell to his knees beside her. She didn't move. He gently lifted her head and felt for a lump of any kind. There was nothing; the snow had cushioned her fall.

She opened her eyes the tiniest bit and glared at him. In a mere whisper, she said, "You're a miserable jerk, Dillon."

"I know, baby. I know." He smoothed the silky red hair away from her face while cradling her in his arms. "Easy, now. It's all right. How do you feel?"

"You've drugged me." Her head lolled, her words almost incoherent.

"It'll be all right, Virginia. I promise. I would never hurt you."

He heard a low, weak cry, and knew the sound came

from Virginia. "Shh. It's all right. I swear it's all right." He listened to his ridiculous litany and wanted to curse himself. Nothing was all right, and he had the feeling it might never be again.

He cuddled her close to his chest, rocked her. "Just relax and go to sleep, sweetheart. I'll take care of everything. I'll take care of you. That's all I'm trying to do, you know."

Her eyes shut and her body went limp. But just before she gave in, before she let him have his way, she whispered, "You never really wanted me at all." She sighed. "You never wanted me. Damn you, Dillon… damn you, you never wanted…"

He listened to her breathing. She was asleep. Deeply asleep. Quickly, the cold slicing through him, he hefted her into his arms and started back for the truck. His groin ached and his nose throbbed, but that was nothing compared with how his heart hurt.

For Virginia's own safety, he wouldn't take any more chances. She had proved to be a creative captive, and he knew she'd fight him tooth and nail if he gave her the opportunity. That meant taking certain precautions that she wasn't going to like.

For the second time that day, he lifted her into his truck. But as he strapped her in, as he looked around to make certain there were no witnesses, his brain played her words over and over again. *You never wanted me.*

SHE WAS SO WRONG, so damn wrong. He wanted her more than he'd ever wanted any woman. And it made no sense. He didn't like her family or her problems or the confusion she made him feel.

She'd passed out cursing him. Typical of Virginia to fade out while raising hell.

He smoothed his hand over her head, which lay in his lap, her cheek against his expanding fly. He knew it was only his imagination, but he thought he could feel the soft warmth of her breath there.

He was a sick bastard, kidnapping a woman and then getting aroused over her sleeping body. But he couldn't help himself. Everything about her excited him, and he was helpless against her. He wouldn't violate her, never that. But he had taken advantage. He was the one who'd pulled her so close. And even as he drove, trying his damnedest to distance himself from what he'd done, he was pulling the pins from her hair and smoothing it with his fingers. He'd told himself he only meant to make her more comfortable, but he knew it was a lie.

Her flaming hair now lay thick and full and shiny over his lap and his belly and his thighs. He shuddered, feeling in his mind and body how it would be if he and Virginia were naked. He tangled a fist in the sinfully sexy mass and pulled it carefully away from her face.

Thick brown lashes lay over her pale cheeks, her lips slightly parted, all arrogance and dominance washed away. She didn't look like a virago or a witch. She was simply an incredibly enticing woman. But he knew better, and he could only imagine how she'd react when she awoke. It would be a while yet. She'd been sleeping for only an hour. Still, he hadn't given her that much of the drug, just enough to make certain she couldn't figure out where they'd gone. He hadn't wanted her to know where they'd be staying.

The sun was trying to show itself on this hazy winter morning and they'd almost reached their destination when he felt her fingers move, clasping weakly at his thigh. She made a small moaning sound and he stilled. He wanted her to sleep just a little longer. There was one more thing he had to do—one more precaution to take—once they reached the cabin, and it would be easier for both of them if Virginia slept through it.

Because he knew without a single doubt, Virginia would never willingly give up her clothes.

He didn't plan to give her a choice.

CHAPTER SIX

VIRGINIA OPENED HER eyes and accepted the feeling of dread that swirled around her. Cautiously, not sure what was wrong or why she felt so disoriented, she lay perfectly still and peered at her surroundings. Her head pounded as she took in the rough plank walls and bare floor. She was in a narrow bed piled high with quilts, cozy and warm, but the air on her face was cool. The cabin, or more like a shack, didn't appear to have modern conveniences, but the fireplace across the room blazed brightly, the flames licking high and casting an orange glow over the otherwise dark room.

Memories returned in bits and pieces, and with them came a deep ache in her heart. She closed her eyes and bit her lips as the emotional pain swelled.

That rotten, deceiving conniver. That miserable creep. He'd kidnapped her! He'd played her for a fool, pretending to want her, when in truth it had all been a game. She opened her eyes and willed away the tears that threatened. Virginia Johnson did not cry.

After taking several uncertain breaths, she worked up the nerve to turn her head and look for Dillon. She didn't see him anywhere. The minuscule cabin had only one separate room, not much bigger than a closet. Through its open door she could see it was a bathroom, butting up next to the kitchen area. There was one narrow counter, a stove, small freezer and refrigerator situated around a metal sink. The cabin's one and only window, mostly blocked by snow on the outside, was situated over the sink.

There were two chairs, one a wooden rocker, the other a threadbare armchair, facing the fireplace. The bed she was lying in—a cot, really—hugged the back wall. Beside the cot was a small dresser that served as a nightstand, holding a clock and a tiny lamp with no shade. In the middle of the room was a badly scarred pine table and two matching chairs.

There was no sound other than the snapping and hissing of the fire. She swallowed, wondering if she might have a chance to escape.

Damn the cold and the snow and whatever distance they'd covered. She would not accept being a victim without choices. It didn't matter to her if she had to run all the way home.

But as she cautiously sat up in the bed and the quilts fell to her lap, she realized something that had escaped her notice thus far.

Dillon had taken all her clothes.

She stared, appalled, at her barely covered breasts. She had on her teddy, thank God, but other than that, she was as bare as the day she'd been born. Her nipples, stiff now with the washing of cold air, could be plainly seen through the material. Her nylons were even gone, but it didn't matter.

Mortification hit her first. He'd removed her clothes! He'd viewed her imperfect body, no doubt in minute detail. He'd looked at her at his leisure and found the evidence of her extra pounds—her rounded hips and thighs, the softness of her belly, the fullness of her breasts. She wondered if he'd chuckled as he stripped off her clothes; had he been amused by her attempt at seductiveness?

She felt queasy, sick with embarrassment. Her face flamed and her vision blurred. It was more than a woman could accept, more than she could bear.

Thankfully, outrage hit next, bringing with it a bloodcurdling scream of rage that erupted from her throat and resounded through the tiny cabin again and again.

The door crashed open and Dillon came charging in, his body strangely balanced as if for battle, his gaze alert as he made a quick, thorough survey of the room. He held himself in a fighter's stance, his black gaze steely and bright. Virginia could only stare.

Oh my. Closing her mouth slowly, she looked him over. He'd shed his civilized demeanor and hadn't left behind a single trace. His long hair, held off his face by a red bandanna rolled and tied around his forehead, gave him a pagan appearance. The bruise shadowing his nose and the corner of his mouth, discolored even through his sun-browned skin, added to the impression of savagery. His jeans were faded and torn, displaying a part of one muscular thigh and two bare knees. The material over his fly was soft and white with age and cupped him lovingly. His heavy coat was gone, and his flannel shirt lay open at the throat, the sleeves rolled high over a gray thermal shirt. Incredibly, he seemed to be sweating.

His black eyes lit on her, then perused her body, lingering on her throbbing breasts and the shadowed juncture of her legs. Belatedly, Virginia grabbed the quilt and snatched it to her throat. Her insides seemed to curl up tight.

"What's wrong?" he demanded.

Virginia stared at him. His chest heaved from whatever activity had made him sweat, and possibly the fright she'd given him. She realized that he must have come charging in prepared to rescue her from some unknown threat. She wanted to laugh—after all, he was her only threat—but she couldn't manage it.

When she remained mute, he firmed his mouth into a grim line and headed back to close the door he'd left hanging open. "Stupid question, right? Do you always screech like a wet cat when you wake up?"

She was taken aback by his uncharacteristic sarcasm, and it took her a moment to gather the wit to speak. "Where the hell are my clothes?"

"Gone."

That flat answer caused her heart to skip in dread. "What do you mean, gone? Damn it, Dillon, what's going on here?"

He walked over and sat on the edge of the cot, prompting her to scurry back as far as she could. The wall felt cold against her shoulder blades, but the alternative would have been to touch him, and that was out of the question. She could already smell him—a cold, fresh-air scent mixed with raw masculinity and clean sweat. His dark eyes had never looked more intense as he took his time gazing at her features.

In a low, awe-filled voice, he asked, "How the hell did you manage to hide so much hair in that tight little knot you usually wear?" His gaze followed the length of one long curl as it rippled over her shoulder, almost to her lap. Words beyond her, Virginia squirmed under his scrutiny.

He reached out and twined a thick strand around his finger. "I've never seen hair like yours."

Virginia jerked, then winced at the tug on her hair. Dillon released her.

He chewed the side of his mouth, all the while studying her. "I was outside chopping wood. I meant to be in here when you woke up so you wouldn't be frightened. But as you can see, the only heat we're going to have here is from the fireplace and stove."

"Let me go."

"No." He pulled the bandanna off and used it to wipe his face. His long hair fell free and she caught another whiff of that enticing scent unique to him. "After I finish splitting the wood, I'll put on some soup or something and you can eat. I'll have you comfortable soon enough."

No longer was he the man she knew. He didn't act or move or speak like the old Dillon. There was no feigned deference, no show of politeness. He told her what he would do, and seemed to think she'd simply accept it.

But her mind shied away from that, from the ramifications of being stolen away by a man she didn't know—*this* man. So she skipped the questions clamoring uppermost in her mind and concentrated on another, more immediate one. "Where are my clothes, you bastard."

He made a tsking sound, amusement bright in his eyes. "Such language, and from a lady of your standing."

Without thought, she swung at him, her burst of anger overshadowing her better judgment. When he caught her fist, he was grinning with genuine humor. "I can't tell you how relieved I am you're not wailing and crying and shivering in fear." He moved, flipping her down on the bed and catching her other fist, too, as she swung it. He leaned over her, his big body hot and hard, covering her own. In a whisper, he said, "Don't fight me, Virginia. You can't win."

His gaze bore into hers, and he was so close she felt his every breath. Then, suddenly, he sat up and moved away. The racing of her heart and the jumping of her stomach refused to subside. She didn't move, too intent on trying to calm herself from what felt like a tussle with a large male animal. Which wasn't far from the truth.

He caught a chair from the table and swung it around, straddling it so he could face her. "I took your clothes so you won't try running off again. I can't let you hurt yourself, and that's exactly what would happen if you tried to escape me."

Slowly, keeping a watchful eye on him, she sat back up and rearranged the quilt to cover her body. "What would you do to me if I tried?"

Deep dimples creased his sun-bronzed cheeks as he laughed. "I don't intend to do anything to you."

The words, combined with his misplaced humor, hurt more than she wanted to admit. Virginia lifted her chin. "Of course I realize now that you never wanted me, that pretending to want me was only a nasty little scam to fool me. That's not what I meant."

The humor left as quickly as it had appeared. "We're a long way from anything," he said, biting off the words. "There's nothing but ice and snow and freezing cold out there. If you tried to find your way home or find help, you'd never make it. The snow has gotten worse, burying all the roads. Taking your clothes was just a way to discourage you from even trying."

"I won't run, I promise. Just give me my clothes."

He eyed her, his gaze drifting lazily over her face. "I know you, Virginia. I know how your mind works. You'll try to run because sitting here doing nothing is the one thing you won't be able to abide."

"Yes, you know me so well," she sneered, wanting to hurt him the way he'd hurt her. But she couldn't because he didn't actually care about her. He never had. "You've been working on this plan for a long time, haven't you? When exactly did you come up with the idea?"

"To kidnap you? After the break-in at your house."

"Ha! Can't you be honest even now? Do you expect me to think you were *ever* sincere, that anything between us has *ever* been real?"

His gaze never faltered, but she saw his hands tighten into fists, saw the muscles of his shoulders bunch. "I got myself hired on at the company and talked you into coming away with me, all for a single purpose."

Knowing it and actually hearing it were too different things. She fought back the lump that formed in her throat and tried not to sound as wounded as she felt. "That's what I figured. What an idiot I've been."

He cursed and she jumped at the sound. "You're not an idiot, Virginia. I'm just very good at what I do."

"Lying, you mean?"

His look was quelling. "You know that's not what I meant."

"Then what?"

He shook his head and she knew the subject was closed. "Are you hungry? Or do you want something to drink?"

"And have you poison me again? No, thanks. Maybe next time you'll kill me."

He growled and came off his chair with a burst of energy. Pushing long fingers through his hair, he paced away from her, then jerked back around to face her, his expression fierce. "I'm not going to hurt you. Just the opposite, damn it. I'm trying to keep you safe."

"Oh?" She raised one eyebrow, deliberately egging him on. Somewhere, deep inside, she refused to be truly afraid of him. She'd spent better than two weeks getting to know him, and she couldn't believe her intuition had been so flawed. She refused to accept that she could have made such an enormous error. But she was hurt. Very hurt. And that made her almost blind with anger. "I suppose I should accept the word of a kidnapper? A pervert?"

He propped his hands on lean hips and his jaw worked. "I am not a pervert."

"You stole my clothes while I was unconscious!" She still couldn't bear the thought of it. "You…you looked at me! That's the lowest, most despicable…"

He stalked closer and bent low until he was nose to nose with her. "I'll take the rest of your damn clothes with you wide-awake if you don't stop trying to provoke me!"

Again, she cowered, wondering why she'd ever wanted a man who would stand up to her. Right now, she'd gladly trade Dillon for a man who would do her bidding.

The look on his face and the set of his body told

her there'd be no swaying him. She swallowed and wisely decided against saying anything that might agitate him further.

Dillon shook his head in disgust. He straightened and took a small step away from the cot. "Damn it, I don't want to yell at you. I don't want to frighten you."

"Could've fooled me," she muttered, forgetting herself again while still keeping watch on him.

His head dropped forward and he laughed. "Ah, Virginia, you just don't know when to quit, do you?" He scrubbed both hands over his face, then raised his gaze to her again. He no longer laughed, but his smile lingered. He shook his head when he saw how he'd confused her. "You're a unique woman, you know that?"

The softly spoken words wiggled down deep into her heart, and she almost choked on her bitterness. She would *not* play the fool again. "Are you forgetting, Dillon, that the game is over? There's no reason for you to continue to flatter me with your nonsense. I've already been duped. Your plan succeeded."

He sat back in his chair with a deep sigh. "Would you like to know what the plan actually is, or are you happier to sit there and bitch?"

Virginia felt the words like a slap and she scowled. "How dare you?"

"What? Are you going to fire me?" He laughed again. "Grow up, Virginia. We're on new ground now. You'll find I can dare to do whatever I choose."

Her pulse fluttered in dread, but Dillon just made a sound of disgust. "Now don't go rounding those big gold eyes at me. I'm not going to hurt you. I've already told you that."

"You're threatening me," she said indignantly.

"Not at all. Just trying to explain to you what I have in mind."

Virginia tightened her hold on the quilt and glared at him. "Well, you can save your breath, because I already figured it out."

"Is that so?" He waved an encouraging hand at her. "So tell me, Virginia. What have you deduced in that quick little mind of yours?"

"You want money. But that's plain stupid, and I hadn't figured you for stupid." She looked him over with as much contempt as she could muster, then added, "A criminal, maybe, but not a stupid one. Surely you realize there's no love lost between me and Cliff. In fact, he detests me. I won't be surprised if he refuses to pay you a single penny. He'll probably be glad to be rid of me."

"That's part of what had me so worried, truth to tell," he admitted, his words sharp and filled with anger.

"Ah, that bothers you, doesn't it? You're stuck with me and there's no way to collect. Now what'll you do?"

Very deliberately, he stood and put his chair back at the table. As he retied the bandanna around his forehead, she watched the flexing of his biceps and the bunching muscles of his forearms and thick wrists.

"Virginia?"

Her gaze shot back to his glaring face and she reddened, knowing he'd caught her staring.

"I think I'll save the conversation for later. If I stay in here and listen to you go on, I might be tempted to violence."

"Ha! You said you wouldn't hurt me. Are you a liar as well as a kidnapper and a pervert?" She silently cursed the words once they'd left her mouth, but right now, words were all she had. She felt defenseless and vulnerable and emotionally wounded. She hated it. She almost hated him.

Dillon headed for the door. "No, I'm not a liar. And I won't hurt you. At least, not the way you're implying. But if I hear you putting yourself down like that again, I will turn you over my knee. And trust me, you won't enjoy the experience." As he opened the door he looked at her over his shoulder, and his black gaze lingered on her hips. "Although, considering what you've put me through these past weeks, I think *I'd* probably enjoy every second of it."

The door slammed closed behind him and Virginia let out her breath. Good grief, she felt scorched by that look and the words that had accompanied it. Put herself down? Was that what she'd been doing? And why should he care anyway?

Dillon wasn't the man she'd believed him to be. He definitely wasn't the meek, considerate lover she expected. No, Dillon would never accept half measures in the dark; she had a feeling that when he made love, he did so with the same intensity he'd just shown her. He wouldn't be *nice* about it; he'd be demanding, taking everything a woman had and giving her back just as much of himself.

Virginia shivered at the thought of making love to this new Dillon. He was hard and commanding—but for some reason, she still, ultimately, felt safe with him. At times his expression seemed foreboding, but she never feared any real harm or she wouldn't have given her mouth so much freedom. Dillon would not hurt her.

His contradictions—the way he used his strength

and power with such devastating gentleness—thrilled her to the center of her feminine core. Every time he looked at her, her heart knocked against her ribs and her stomach tightened with desire.

She still wanted him, probably more than ever. But to him she was only a means to an end. For that, she would never forgive him.

She closed her eyes on a silent groan. She had to be the biggest fool alive because she wanted him anyway. Until now, she hadn't known such a need could exist. If she didn't get away from Dillon soon, she'd probably end up begging him to take her.

She couldn't let that happen.

CHAPTER SEVEN

CHOPPING WOOD PROVED to be cathartic. Dillon could release his tension, both sexual and emotional.

Seeing her sitting there, her thick mass of hair loose and silky, her heavy breasts with the large dark nipples barely restrained by her sheer lingerie, had cost him. When he'd undressed her, he'd tried to be detached. He hadn't looked any more than he had to, and he'd detested himself because he got aroused anyway.

With Virginia wide-awake and spitting venom at him, he hadn't *not* been able to look. He wanted her. He wanted her so bad he couldn't stop thinking about it. He lingered on the memory of those rounded breasts in his palms, and he wanted, at this moment, to know the taste of her nipples, to suck her and lick her and hear her moan for him.

He should have explained it all to her. That would have put her at ease, at least on one level. But she'd have been devastated to know the lengths Cliff had gone to to get rid of her. He wanted to demolish Cliff, and before this was over, he probably would.

Virginia might not believe him if he told her all his suspicions right now. She'd admitted to knowing how little Cliff cared for her, but Dillon knew she didn't think he was really capable of hurting her. She disdained Cliff, she didn't fear him.

Still, Dillon should have explained about Wade. Then maybe she wouldn't consider him a mercenary bastard driven by monetary rewards. She would have known, too, the absurdity of her charge that he didn't want her. He wanted her too damn much.

But putting some distance between them had been the most immediate necessity. He'd kidnapped her, and once this was over, he'd leave. That was an irrefutable fact. He wouldn't complicate things by giving in to his need. Throwing in the threat of a paddling had been sheer self-defense. He had to find a way to get her to stop baiting him, so he could find a way to keep his distance and do what he knew to be right. But with every word out of her mouth, she tempted him in a way no other woman had. He wanted to kiss her quiet, to prove his dominance over her, to be male to her female.

Not that he would ever raise a hand to her. His father had taught him that hurting anyone smaller or weaker than himself was a sign of true cowardice. Even worse was to hurt a woman. Females were to be protected, looked after. Just as you protected your family. Only, Virginia didn't want or need anyone to protect her. Disregarding physical strength, she was the most capable woman he'd ever met. Which meant he had no place in her life at all. What he had to give, she didn't need. And when all was said and done, she wouldn't want him around anyway.

But he wasn't going to explain his feelings to Virginia. If she feared him just a little, maybe she'd keep her insults behind her teeth and give him some peace. He enjoyed her show of defiance, but right now he needed to enjoy her a little less so he could maintain some control.

His arms loaded with firewood, he kicked the front door open. He automatically looked toward the bed, and Virginia, but she wasn't there. Only sheer instinct caused him to drop the wood and roll away a split second before a heavy frying pan came swishing past his head.

He cursed, then grabbed her bare ankles and jerked. She went down hard on her bottom, screeching curses so hot it was a wonder they didn't melt the snow. He snatched the frying pan out of her hand when she tried again to heft the damn thing toward his skull.

"Goddammit!" It was like wrestling with a wild woman. He did his best not to hurt her when he slammed down on top of her, using his knee to spread her bare thighs so she couldn't kick him and holding both her wrists in one tight fist. "Keep still, Virginia, before you hurt yourself!"

"You're the one hurting me, you cretin! Let me go." She thrashed and her hair whipped around her face, slapping against him.

"No." Dillon dropped his forehead to her shoulder, then quickly flinched away when she tried to sink her teeth into his neck. Clasping her chin with his free hand, he growled, "Maybe I should give you that paddling now."

"Try it and I'll emasculate you!"

So much for empty threats, he thought.

She wiggled and he felt the softness of her, the giving of her feminine body cradling his own. He clenched his jaw even as his muscles hardened and his penis followed suit. From one breath to the next he was as hard as a stone, pressing into her soft belly. "You already tried emasculating me, remember? I may never father children."

The low, husky sound of his voice gave away his dilemma, and Virginia stilled, her eyes wide on his face. In a whisper, she asked, "Criminals don't want to father children, do they?"

The absurdity of it hit him. How could this woman, whom—he kept reminding himself—he did *not* like, keep making him lose his head? It defied reason.

"Forget I said that." He pushed up, coming to his knees between her spread thighs. She gasped and struggled, but he held her wrists.

Staring hard into her eyes, he asked, "Why did you attack me?"

"Because I can't let you use me."

Despite his best intentions, Dillon gazed over her body. Her legs were sprawled around him, the teddy pulled tight to her frame, showing every curve and hollow. Damn but she was lush and rounded and generously built, the way a woman was supposed to be built. She would cushion a man with her feminine curves. He felt all that giving softness beneath him, and the feeling tempted him. Damn but it tempted him.

Forcing himself to look away from the outline of her feminine cleft, the hint of soft curls, he raised his gaze to her face. He saw her flushed cheeks and the wariness in her eyes. He understood. He himself could barely breathe. "Virginia, I have no intention of forcing myself on you. You don't have to be worried about rape."

Her mouth fell open before she narrowed her eyes and hissed, "I wasn't talking about that, you ass! I was talking about your using me in some moneymaking scheme."

She strained against his grip, and he struggled to subdue her. "In that, you have no choice." He touched her shoulder where an angry red welt had risen against her white skin. "Did I hurt you when I yanked you down?"

"This is insane!" Her voice now sounded shaky and he continued to soothe the small injury with strokes of his fingertips. "First you kidnap me and now you're concerned about giving me a bruise or two?"

"You have other bruises?"

The flush spread to her breasts and she looked away. "No, I just…"

"Show me, Virginia."

Her chest heaved and she briefly closed her eyes. "Get off me, you oaf."

When she looked at him again, he could see her embarrassment in the way she squirmed. He tilted his head, then surveyed her lush hips, remembering how hard she'd hit the floor. "Your bottom? Did I hurt you when I pulled you down?"

He could feel her trembling. "Dillon, *please,* this is ridiculous."

He released her and stood, then caught her upper arms and pulled her to her feet. He didn't like hearing her beg, didn't like seeing her fear of him. Holding her a moment longer than was necessary, he studied her downcast face, the way her hair fell like a curtain, hiding her expression and a good portion of her body. He dropped his hands and took a step away. "Get in the bed before you catch pneumonia. This floor is like ice."

Her back stiffened. "Why don't you just give me back my boots then?"

No matter how he tried, he couldn't put the thought

of other bruises from his mind. He studied her, his gaze lingering again on her hips.

"Dillon?"

He shook his head. "No. I like you better just the way you are, honey."

Her beautiful eyes narrowed and she hissed a vicious curse at him.

He couldn't help but laugh, then he chucked her chin. "Face it, Virginia. Like this, you're more manageable. Now get in the bed before I put you there."

He picked up the frying pan and stepped over scattered logs as he went into the kitchen, not bothering to see if she obeyed. A moment later, he heard the cot squeak, and when he looked, Virginia was again buried beneath the quilts. She stared toward him, her expression stony.

After washing his hands, he opened the refrigerator and found a small roast. He put it on a battered old cutting board. "Cliff is charging my younger brother, Wade, with embezzlement."

Using a sharp knife—one he vowed to remember to hide after he finished his chore—Dillon cut the meat into small chunks and put them in a stew pot. "I know you had no idea Wade Sanders is my brother. Actually, we're half brothers, so our last names are different and we don't look a hell of a lot alike. We share the same mother, though I never knew the woman." He glanced at Virginia to see how she took his explanation. She watched him, blessedly silent for a change.

"Wade is innocent, of course, but since I don't know what trumped-up evidence your brother has on him, I couldn't defend him. We obviously don't have the money your family has. Taking this to court would be ludicrous. Your brother's high-priced lawyers would crucify Wade. I had to think of another plan."

He added water to the pot and lit the stove. After throwing in a chopped onion and putting on the lid, he went to the fireplace and piled on more logs. Sparks leaped out at him, then landed harmlessly on the dusty wooden floor, where they faded away.

Personally, he thought the room was already too warm, but then, he was fully clothed. And damn near fully aroused.

He glanced at Virginia. Her entire body was rigid. "This may come as a surprise, but Wade and your sister, Kelsey, are in love."

He heard her gasp and their eyes connected. He felt touched by her anxiety, but forced himself to ignore it. It was past time she got things straight.

Small logs were scattered all over the floor from where he'd dropped them when she'd attacked. He began gathering them up, more to give himself something to do than for the sake of neatness. "On top of all that, and regardless of what you think, someone is trying to hurt you. I don't know for sure who it is yet, but I have my suspicions." He wouldn't come right out and name her brother. That would serve no purpose, at least not yet.

"You're the one trying to hurt me, Dillon."

He stilled in the process of stacking the wood by the fireplace, unable to ignore her sneering tone. Without looking at her, he said, "Never. I didn't lie about that, Virginia. When this is all over, I'll take you back and then disappear. You don't have to be afraid about that."

"After you've collected your money?"

"I'm not asking for any money. I need to clear Wade.

But I couldn't do that, not while I was distracted worrying about you."

She appeared to chew that over. "You said you'd leave when this is done. Where will you go?"

He shook his head. He couldn't tell her he'd be flying to Mexico, back to his home. The less she knew about him, the better. "With you out of your office, I should be able to go through some files, do some checking."

"You kidnapped me to get me out of my office? You drugged me and dragged me to this dirty little cabin in the middle of nowhere, stripped me and scared me half to death, just so you could access my files?"

She sounded appalled by such logic. She also seemed to have forgotten the fact of her own threatened circumstances. But he wouldn't remind her of that again. "Cliff hates Wade, and he's trying to railroad him. All I need is a little time to prove it."

"You could be wrong."

"No. I'm good at reading people."

"I used to think the same thing," she said with a great deal of disgust.

He went on as if she hadn't interrupted. "I've gotten to know your brother pretty well. He's a petty bastard who wants things his own way whether that's the right way or not. He objects to your involvement because it injures his pride, not because he thinks it isn't necessary. And he's accusing Wade of embezzlement because he doesn't want him involved with Kelsey, not because Wade is guilty. Cliff is insecure, and he deals with his problems in an underhanded way."

She didn't respond and Dillon cleared his throat. He didn't have it in him to force the issue of Cliff's violent tendencies right now. "Anyway, Wade and Kelsey will be married."

"No!" Virginia shot forward on the bed, her expression and tone frantic. "Kelsey is too young and—"

"And Wade isn't good enough?"

"That's not what I was going to say!" she nervously smoothed her hands over the quilt and licked her lips. "Kelsey doesn't know what she's doing. She's only twenty-two."

"Almost twenty-three, and she'd disagree with you. She thinks she knows exactly what she's doing. She claims she loves Wade. And I know he worships her. He'll take good care of her, Virginia."

"No, Dillon, please. You have to let me talk to her, reason with her. Please."

Dillon walked to her, holding her gaze as he approached. There was no fear, only anxiety. He caught her chin between his fingers. "Don't ever beg for anything, Virginia. It doesn't sit well on your shoulders."

"Damn you!" She reached out one small fist and thumped his thigh. "This isn't a joke."

Her eyes plainly showed every emotion she felt. He shut his heart against her turmoil. "I'm sorry. But Kelsey is pregnant, with Wade's baby. Do you know, he wasn't as worried about going to jail as he was concerned with leaving Kelsey alone as a single mother. Wade is determined to take his responsibilities seriously."

Tension vibrated through her body. She bunched the quilt in her lap and held it tight. "If that was so, he wouldn't have gotten her pregnant in the first place."

Dillon lifted his brows. "I suppose that's true enough. But it's spilled milk now. Or rather, spilled—"

"Don't say it!"

He couldn't help it. He chuckled. "You know, Wade didn't exactly act alone. They both played and they both got caught."

"There are alternatives to marriage."

He didn't want to hear her make any suggestions, didn't want her to consider giving the baby away or disposing of it. Narrowing his eyes, he tried to deny the tightening of his gut. "Such as?"

"I could help Kelsey raise it. Women these days don't need a man around to take care of things. Single mothers survive every day. And I could more than provide for them both. She's my sister. The baby would be my niece or nephew."

He relaxed, enough to be distracted by her incredible hair again. He ran his fingertips down a long red curl that reflected the firelight with hints of gold. His fascination with her hair didn't seem to be dwindling as he got used to looking at it. Just the opposite.

And this time Virginia didn't move away. "You're saying Wade would be denied his child? Is that your ingenious plan, Virginia?"

"No… I don't know. I need time to think about it."

"There is no time. Decisions have to be made now. Wade and Kelsey *will* marry. Wade being a member of the family ought to protect him from Cliff in the future. It wouldn't do to have one's brother-in-law in prison, now would it?"

"How do you know Wade didn't do it?" Virginia licked her lips and refused to meet his gaze. "From what I remember, there was pretty strong evidence against him."

His fingers trailed over the curl, then tucked it behind her ear before tilting up her chin. "Do you know what the evidence is?"

A mulish expression came over her face. "You think I'd tell you? In case you're missing something, you're the bad guy in this scenario. I'm the victim. I certainly can't make it easy for you."

He grinned, thinking just how *hard* she made things. "No, I don't suppose you can. Fair enough. You don't give me any details, and I won't give you any more."

Slowly, her brows drew down in a suspicious frown. "Now, wait a minute. That's not fair. I need to know what's going on."

"You need to know only what I tell you."

"That is *not* acceptable!"

"We're not at the office, Virginia. You can't give me orders, because I won't obey them. I don't work for you," he enunciated clearly. "From here on, I'm the one in charge. I know it'll be a new experience for you, but you might as well get used to it."

She practically hummed with anger. "If that's the way you want it, *fine*. But don't expect me to miss the next time I come at you with a frying pan!"

He sat on the edge of the cot. Virginia held the quilt up to cover her breasts, and her rich titian hair hung almost to her elbows. She shook it back. This time, she didn't cower from him when he leaned close, caging her in. Instead, she squared her shoulders and thrust her chin toward him in a silent challenge.

She looked so enticing, which shouldn't have mattered. And it didn't, not in the big picture. But here, closed into the cabin with her, he could feel her presence, could smell the light womanly fragrance of her. He loved how women smelled, and Virginia seemed especially inviting. He braced one hand on the bed beside her hip and used the other to cup her chin, making certain he had her mutinous attention.

"So you deliberately missed the first time, but you won't be so considerate again? I appreciate the warning, sweetheart. Now I can take necessary precautions."

"What…what do you mean?" Some of her defiance faltered.

"Did you notice that this is the only bed in the room, Virginia?"

Her lips parted and she surveyed the bed as if seeing it for the first time. "It isn't exactly a bed," she sputtered. "It's a narrow little cot that's barely big enough for a single body."

"Then I suppose we'll have to scrunch up real close, won't we? Maybe lay spoon fashion."

She shook her head while color rushed into her cheeks. "You are not getting into this bed with me, Dillon, so forget it."

He grinned, but decided to let her statement pass. "Since you were generous enough to warn me of your intent to lay me low, I guess I should warn you, too. Tonight, I'm going to have to tie you up."

"No!"

"I'd like to wake in the morning with my brains intact. That means," he said, flicking the end of her nose, "I have to restrain you and your more violent tendencies."

"Dillon…"

"Why don't you rest for now, honey? We'll have lunch in a couple of hours."

He walked back into the kitchen, grinning, knowing he'd just set himself up. Virginia would go out of her way to keep from being tied up. But he could handle her. And he'd rather deal with her anger any day than her hurt or fear. Even now, she was probably planning his demise.

He only wished he weren't looking forward to her efforts.

CHAPTER EIGHT

He was a good cook—she'd give him that. But with him watching every bite she took, she felt obliged to skimp. She knew she was overweight, and she didn't want him thinking of her as a glutton. Vanity had no place on a victim's shoulders, but then, she refused to think of herself as a victim. Somehow she'd find a way out of this mess. This wasn't the time to deal with her insecurity about her figure. Besides, she'd already spent years trying.

"Is that all you're going to eat?"

He'd been quiet for so long and her thoughts had been so personal Virginia gave a guilty start. She had to make a grab for the quilt as it started to slide down her body. Dillon watched the path it took and the way she then clutched at it. His gaze locked with hers and remained there.

Awkwardly, she tucked and tugged until the quilt shielded as much of her body as possible. She knew she looked ridiculous with the thing wrapped around her like a sarong, but Dillon flatly refused to return her clothes to her, and she refused to continue cowering in the bed. It was a clash of wills that she fully expected to win. "I, ah, I'm not that hungry."

He made a small sound—a male snort of acknowledgment, then looked away. "You need to eat to keep up your strength. You can't very well give me hell if you're lying in bed too weak to argue, now can you? And I know you haven't eaten all day, so you have to be starved. Come on, finish up."

"No, thank you."

Her stomach muscles tightened, then fluttered, at the searing look he sent her way. "I never thought of you as the fainthearted type, willing to wilt away like a martyr. I thought you were made of sterner stuff." Soft sandy-brown hair fell over his brow as he shook his head in mock regret. "You've disappointed me, Virginia."

She thinned her mouth and glared at him. "I have to watch my weight."

Speaking around a large spoonful of meat-filled soup, Dillon asked, "Why?"

He looked genuinely puzzled and she wanted to hit him right between his gorgeous eyes. But he wasn't obtuse, and she assumed he was toying with her. Automatically, her chin lifted. "Because I'm ten pounds overweight, that's why."

"More like twenty." Again, his gaze slid over her, and she felt the touch of it everywhere. "But it looks good on you. Damn good. Makes you nice and round. Skinny women are too pointy. Pointy bones, pointy breasts, pointy hips. Most men prefer a woman with a little meat on her." His gaze lingered on her breasts and her nipples pulled tight in reaction. "Provides a nice cushion."

In her entire life, Virginia had never heard anything so crudely put, or so ridiculous. How dare he speak to her that way, correcting, insulting and complimenting all in the same breath! Flustered and confused, she went for a show of umbrage. "Well, thank you, Mr. Dillon Oaks, for your masculine insight, but..."

He laughed. "Dillon Oaks *Jr.* to be exact. I carry my father's name."

Halted in midtirade, she stared at him. "You're a junior?"

Dillon finished his soup and then carried his bowl to the sink. "That's right, though I don't share that fact with just anyone. My father is rather...infamous in this country. If the connection was ever made, it could lead to a lot of questions I don't usually want to answer."

Virginia couldn't begin to fathom a Dillon Oaks Sr. One man of Dillon's caliber, of his appeal and arrogance, was more than the female populace should have to contend with. "Don't tell me your father is a kidnapper, also?"

Dillon glanced at her over his hard shoulder, then began running water in the sink to clean the dishes. Virginia thought he seemed to be much more domestically inclined than she was.

"Eat the rest of your soup and I'll tell you."

Obligingly, she ate. What the hell—she was hungry, and as Dillon had pointed out, he already knew she was overweight, although he didn't seem to mind. Starving herself for spite didn't make a bit of sense. Plus he was a wonderful cook. All he'd done was add canned vegetables and a few spices to meat, but it tasted better than good. Virginia always ate more when she was excited or upset; right now, she felt equal parts of both.

Nodding in satisfaction as Virginia dipped her spoon into the bowl, Dillon launched into his first story.

"My father was close to forty and set in his ways when I was born. The military had become his life, and my mother pretty much took him by surprise when she caught him in the States on leave and dumped his newborn infant in his lap. He says it was the biggest shock of his life." Dillon grinned, twin dimples flashing in his darkly tanned cheeks.

"My mother made it clear she didn't want any part of me, and Dad said he could tell by looking at me that I was his kid. Even as a newborn, I had the same dark eyes and light brown hair, and our features are the same, even to this day. Looking at Dad is like looking forty years into the future."

Virginia tried to imagine Dillon as an older, less powerful man, but she couldn't manage it. Somehow she thought Dillon would have a raw strength about him regardless of what exalted age he reached.

He chuckled now, a low rich sound that danced down her spine and sank into her bones. "When my mother started to hand me to Dad, I spit up on her. That was exactly what he wanted to do, but rudeness to a lady went against his grain. Since I'd done it for him, he gladly accepted me. Gradually, he left the military to take on the dubious role of parent."

The image of a man just like Dillon caring for an infant squeezed something in Virginia's heart, leaving her breathless and captivated.

Dillon tidied the kitchen efficiently, cleaning off the stove and scrubbing the pans. He didn't look as if he needed, wanted or expected her help, which was just as well, because she would have refused. The kidnappee did not help the kidnapper tidy his prison.

Dillon glanced at her, a half smile still hovering around his mouth. "Now, leaving the military might not sound like much to you, but you have to realize my father was an old war dog. He was in active duty in World War II, the Korean War, even the early stages of Vietnam. He had the military haircut, the tattoos and the salty language testifying to his past. He had no idea how to be a civilian, but he did know that without a wife, he couldn't very well raise a child and stay in the army."

Pulling her legs up onto the chair and bracing her heels on the edge, Virginia settled herself more comfortably. She made sure the quilt covered all her vital parts, then wrapped her arms around her knees. The cabin was now cozy and warm, except for the cold air drifting over the hard floor. She leaned her chin on her knees and regarded him. "Did your father ever consider putting you up for adoption?"

He made a rude grunting sound of disbelief. "Not my dad. He admits he didn't know much about parenting, and there were some real rough times, but he'd always believed in taking care of his own. Blood is blood. And you never, for any reason, turn your back on family."

Virginia supposed that accounted for Dillon going to such lengths to rescue Wade. Not that she forgave him just because he had a reason. "So what did your father do then?"

Dillon shrugged. "He tried off and on through the years to get a regular job. But Dad is the original renegade. Ordinary life doesn't suit him. He's not...domestic enough. He doesn't fit in with society, and society is scared to death of him. There's a rough, almost dangerous edge to him that people pick up on within seconds of meeting him." He sent her a mischievous grin.

"It scares the hell out of most men, and excites most women."

It sounded as if there was a lot of his father in Dillon, she thought, letting her gaze stray over his hard body, taking in the broad muscled back, the tattered jeans over solid thighs and tight, narrow hips. He had a natural arrogance that set him apart from other men, a self-confidence that went beyond being big and handsome and capable.

There was an aura of danger about him—something about the intensity of his eyes—that was very appealing. She could easily believe he shared that trait with his father. Curiosity got the better of her and she asked quietly, "Were you ever afraid of him?"

Dillon turned to face her, leaning back on the counter and crossing his arms over his broad chest. "No. I was afraid for him a lot, though. There were times when he'd be out of the country for long stretches—a month or more. I'd get antsy and nervous, but he always came back."

"Who watched you then? Who raised you?"

Dillon chewed the side of his mouth, his gaze on a far wall. "Dad always had one woman or another hanging around. They swarmed to him. When he had to leave, he'd give one of them money to make certain I made it to school and ate regular."

Virginia couldn't imagine such an existence. Knowing her words to be cruel, but unable to help herself, she said, "Maybe you would have been better off adopted. At least you would have had a parent who spent time with you!"

He gave her a pitying look and shook his head. "Dad spent more time with me than most kids ever hope to get. He taught me everything he knew—how to protect myself, how to get what I need, how to stay ahead and take care of those people who depend on me. He taught me morals and values and personal ethics and self-worth." His gaze was hard, almost accusing. "He taught me about the world."

She shouldn't ask. Knowing about Dillon's life and his family would only get her more involved. But the words couldn't be held back. She *wanted* to know everything about him, even more than she wanted to be free. "If he was such a great father, why did he leave you?"

When Dillon turned back to the dishes, Virginia wondered if she'd pushed too far, if maybe he wouldn't answer her at all. Then his voice, soft and low, came to her. "Dad became a mercenary. He continued to do the things he knew how to do best, but he did them on his own time...and for a lot more money."

For some reason, she wanted to go to him, to hold him. She shook her head. Touching him would be a very dangerous thing. To her heart.

"Your father was a hired killer?"

"You make him sound like an assassin." He cast her a glance. "He didn't exactly run around slitting innocent throats. His job was generally to apprehend and hold. And more often than not, it was the government who hired him for assignments they couldn't get sanctioned through the regular channels. Not always, though. He worked for other agencies, too. And he came through for them every time."

"You sound proud." If her parents had taken part in illegal activities, she would have died from shame. But

Dillon actually seemed pleased by his father's sordid accomplishments.

He flattened his palms on the edge of the sink and looked out the window. "I don't know that 'proud' is the right word. But I know my dad did whatever had to be done so he could keep me. He made certain I understood how much he cared about me, that I was the first priority in his life. I've always known that no matter what, he's there for me. It doesn't matter if I'm right or wrong, if I'm in danger, he'll back me up." Dillon was silent a moment, then added, "That's what family's about. Unqualified support."

She'd never thought about her family in those particular terms. Sure her parents had loved her, even though she hadn't been their favorite. But Dillon spoke as if life was a war, filled with risks and hazards and deviousness. She supposed, given his upbringing, that might have been the only world he'd known.

She felt that tightening in her chest again and had to take several breaths. She would *not* feel sorry for him. What he'd done was unforgivable. She didn't for a minute believe that nonsense about taking her to protect her. He planned to ransack her office and defend his brother. If Cliff caught him at it, Dillon would go to jail. She had to find a way to reason with him. He had to let her go.

Dillon carried a dishrag to the table and began to wipe the surface. "I'm proficient with every weapon there is, but I'm especially good with my hands. Dad started teaching me self-defense when I was about six, after he got home from a mission to find out his girlfriend had taken off and left me alone. He wanted to be sure that if it ever happened again, I'd know how to take care of myself. He taught me all about security, how to create it, how to break it." He grinned. "That information is what got me hired by your company."

Hesitating for only a second, she asked, "Have you followed in your father's footsteps? Do you hire yourself out as a mercenary?"

"No." His black eyes flashed, and he smiled. "Kidnapping you is the only time I've walked on the wrong side of the law. I own a horse ranch, and Dad lives with me now. For the most part, that keeps me plenty busy enough. Over the years, before Dad mellowed and settled down, I bailed him out of a few situations that hadn't gone quite as planned. And I went with him on a few jobs. But they were legit, and I learned a lot. And I have to admit, my skills have come in handy recently."

Virginia sighed theatrically. "Wonderful. I get to be your guinea pig?"

He leaned his hip against the table and considered her. "Yeah. But I swear I think storming an enemy platoon would have been easier than taking you." He touched the swollen bruise on the bridge of his nose. "Do you plan to keep abusing me?"

"Not if you plan to turn me loose anytime soon," she replied sweetly.

Dillon chuckled again. His mood seemed to have improved quite a bit. In fact, she couldn't remember him ever being so relaxed. She wasn't sure she liked it; it made him appear less dangerous—and more appealing than ever.

As if he'd read her thoughts, he laughed and then tapped her chin. "Want to play cards?"

The quick switch threw her and she stared at him. "You're kidding, right?"

"We're stuck here for a while, Virginia. There's no television, certainly no outdoor activities. I can see that active mind of yours churning, but I won't be letting you go, so relax. Why make us both miserable?"

"Because you deserve to be miserable?"

"But you don't. So why not loosen up. We still have a few hours before bedtime."

Thinking of bedtime made her shiver and she looked away; beneath the quilt, her body turned warm, too warm. Nothing in her life had prepared her for this man. She had no idea how to deal with him. At the moment, sarcasm seemed her only option, the only way to keep the distance between them. "Do you plan to leave me here alone while you ransack my office?"

"Yes, tomorrow morning. But you don't need to worry. You'll be safe enough."

"Safe? What if something happens? I mean, there's no phone anywhere around here for me to call for help. And I assume we have no close neighbors."

He went to a cabinet and pulled out a battered deck of cards. "No. There's no phone nearby, no one to hear you scream. When I leave to check things out, you'll be on your own. But as you keep telling me, you can take care of yourself. It'll only be a few hours."

She struggled not to reveal her reaction to his words. If he left her alone, she'd finally have a chance to escape. Surely the truck would leave tracks, and she could follow them to the main road. There would have to be traffic of some kind, and she'd hitch a ride—

Damn, she needed her clothes! She couldn't very well go outside in what she wore now. Not only would she freeze, but no one would pick her up. They'd all think she was a lunatic.

Realizing that, she glared at Dillon. "I'm cold. Why don't you at least give me back my sweater." She'd work on the other clothes as she went along, slowly earning his trust and gaining back her whole outfit, especially her boots. They weren't exactly designed for treks in this kind of weather, but they'd have to suffice.

Dillon laid out a game of solitaire. Without looking at her, he said, "You're not an idiot, Virginia. You should know better than to underestimate me." He glanced up, and there was regret in his eyes, but determination, as well. "There is absolutely no way for you to leave this cabin. We're miles from everything, and the snow is piling up. By morning, it'll be a couple of feet deep."

She lifted her chin. "You plan to leave."

"The truck is four-wheel drive. You're not. If you tried to leave here by foot, you'd freeze to death—even with your clothes. If you're not worried about your own hide, think of the company. Under Cliff's sole guidance, it wouldn't last long. We both know it."

Frustration nearly smothered her. "Bastard."

He seemed unruffled by her insult. "I can make you a deal, you know."

Oh, the way he said that, with his voice husky and low and suggestive. Her thighs tightened reflexively, and she searched his face for a clue to his mood, but his expression was inscrutable. Cautiously, she asked, "What kind of deal?" Her voice broke, and she had to clear her throat. Even with his head down, she saw Dillon smile.

"Virginia, Virginia," he chided. "What are you thinking? Here I am, offering you a legitimate exchange, but you insist on laying evil deeds at my door."

Her feet hit the floor hard and she put both palms on the table. His teasing made her feel like a fool. "Let's see. Beyond kidnapping, drugging and stealing a woman's clothes, what else might you be capable of? I'd say the possibilities are endless!"

His humor vanished, and his tone turned gentle. "I told you I wouldn't hurt you."

"You also told me you—" Appalled, she stopped herself. Had she really been about to berate him for not wanting her sexually? The truth of that hurt, but damned if she wanted to let him know it. She crossed her arms tightly over her chest and slouched back in her chair.

A strained silence fell between them. She could feel his gaze, but she refused to meet it. Instead, she stared at the fireplace until her vision blurred and she could breathe normally again.

Somehow Dillon seemed to know the moment she regained control. He returned his attention to his cards as if nothing had happened. "You give me the evidence Cliff has on Wade, give me a chance to prove it's false, and I'll take you back that much sooner. Maybe you could even help me figure out who the embezzler is. I know you're a woman who likes control, who needs to be kept informed. You might enjoy the challenge."

He never looked at her, just continued to play the game, moving and adjusting the cards at his leisure. His attitude infuriated her, but she didn't think she could stand not knowing. Her pride had forbade her to ask again, but now he had offered.

And what would it matter if he knew the evidence? If anything, it might convince him to get his brother out of the country, instead of involving Kelsey in his ridiculous scheme. One thing was certain, though. Never would she tell him it was she who had found the evidence of missing funds, not Cliff. Dillon's reaction to that news wasn't something she wanted to experience while she remained his captive.

She drew a deep breath, considering. Dillon laid the ace of spades at the top of his line of cards.

"Will it make things easier on you if I tell you what evidence Cliff has?"

"It might hurry things along a little. But the outcome will be the same either way." Now he did look up, and the hardness in his expression chilled her. She shivered and wrapped her arms around her knees.

"Regardless of what you do or don't tell me, I'm not letting my brother go to jail to satisfy Cliff's warped sense of obligation to his sister."

Virginia couldn't look away. "That's what you think all this is about? You think Cliff got upset because Kelsey was seeing your brother, so he concocted this whole scheme just to get Wade out of the picture?"

"That's how a coward fights. Backhanded, through lies and deception."

"Coming from you, that doesn't say much!"

"I give as good as I get." He flipped another card. "Kelsey knew how Cliff would react. It's my opinion that's why she started chasing Wade in the first place. At the time, he was involved with Laura Neil and wouldn't even have noticed Kelsey. But she knew you two would have a conniption if she got involved with the hired help."

"But we didn't know!"

"Cliff found out. And not long after that, he decided Wade had been embezzling."

God, had she inadvertently handed Cliff the perfect tool for revenge? When she'd given him the faulty accounts, she'd known immediately that his satisfaction, in balance with his rage, had been too keen. At the time, she hadn't suspected anyone, she'd only wanted the matter looked into. She was even running her own private investigation. But Cliff had jumped on it, and it hadn't taken him long at all to blame Wade Sanders.

She leaned forward and rested her elbows on the table, but that drew Dillon's gaze to her breasts, and she quickly sat back again. Frowning, she tried to understand his reasoning, to sort it all out in her mind. Blaming Wade may have been convenient, knowing how Cliff felt about Kelsey. He considered her his only ally, his family, in a way Virginia had ceased to be soon after their parents' deaths. Cliff wasn't beyond doing something so reprehensible if it suited his purposes. She just didn't think he was quick-witted enough to concoct such a scheme.

There were also a lot of facts to deal with, beyond the emotional issues. Virginia felt as if too much was hitting her a one time. She couldn't quite sort it all out. "You're telling me Cliff's known for some time that Kelsey and your brother were seeing each other, but he never mentioned it to me?"

"I think he expected to take care of it on his own, without your interference." He flipped over another card, only briefly scanning the deck before returning his gaze to her face. "You treat Cliff like a little boy. It's no wonder he sneaks around trying to do something, anything, on his own."

"You're defending him!"

"Don't get me wrong. I think he's a fool—" his gaze

narrowed on her face "—for letting you dictate to him. A real man would have taken charge long ago."

Virginia forgot her precarious position as victim; she forgot that she needed to trade information and sort out facts. She forgot everything except her pride. Running the company was all she had, the only truly wonderful thing she'd ever accomplished. It defined her life, her integrity, her strength, her independence. And now Dillon would strip that from her with a few callous words. She'd worked hard to get that modicum of business respect; she wouldn't let him or anyone else take it from her.

She came to her feet so fast her chair tipped over, landing with a crash in the silent cabin. She whirled to storm away, only to come up short when Dillon grabbed the back of the quilt. Like a dog running out of leash, she jerked to a stop. Staring straight ahead, she saw nothing but the walls, a tiny enclosure with no place to go, no place to run. She nearly choked on her bitterness, and then Dillon began tugging on the quilt, reeling her in.

She would have released it, but then he had her arm in an unbreakable grip, and it took only one small yank for her to fall solidly into his lap. Without any real effort on his part, he subdued her struggles. To her mortification, tears threatened. She'd never felt so vulnerable or helpless. Or hurt. She didn't like it. Lifting one fist, she thudded it against his shoulder, which felt like hitting a boulder.

Dillon didn't so much as flinch. "Don't you want to know how I would have taken control, Virginia?"

She shook her head, or at least she tried. Dillon had curled her so close her cheek pressed into the solid wall of his chest. Beyond all her anger and frustration, she felt an awareness of him, of the hardness of his body, his incredible scent, the gentleness of his hands as one coasted over her back and the other tangled in her hair. Effortlessly, he had surrounded and invaded her.

"I'm going to tell you anyway."

She felt the light touch of his mouth against her hair, and everything inside her seemed to shift and swell. Her body pulsed with awareness. She didn't know what that small kiss meant, or what she should do about it.

"Virginia, I would have made you a visible partner. I would have used your obvious strengths for the benefit of the company. Anyone who meets you knows you have an air of command, that you can aptly take charge of any situation. Cliff's biggest mistake is in trying to steal from you what you do best, instead of using it to his and the company's advantage. By giving you the credit you deserve, he would have gained a portion of that control."

The praise stunned her. Carefully, she tipped her head back to see his face. His mouth was only a few inches from her own, his expression implacable and hard. At the moment, there seemed to be no tenderness about him, but she knew better. "You're only trying to soften me up."

"No, baby. You're soft enough as it is."

Her eyes narrowed, but before she could speak, his fingers tightened in her hair like a rough caress and he kissed her temple. "You know what I say is true, Virginia. Cliff could only make himself look better with you at his side. He's a fool for keeping you in the shadows."

"So I've told him."

Dillon grinned and those dimples, so seldom seen, charmed her, adding to the heat that kept gathering beneath her skin, weakening her muscles. "I know you have. Repeatedly and with a great deal of vehemence. It's the way you tell him that makes him dig in his heels. You need to learn a little about compromise."

Virginia couldn't help but grin, too. "Lectured by a kidnapper. What's the world coming to?"

Dillon cupped her head, his fingers thrusting deep into her hair. "Tell me what evidence he has, Virginia."

She sighed. There was really no harm in telling him, even if his motives hadn't been firmly established. And for some reason, she felt more generous now than she had a few minutes ago. "All right."

She straightened, prepared to leave the warmth and comfort of Dillon's lap, but his hands tightened and she knew she couldn't move unless he let her. It didn't seem worth the struggle, so she relented. She really didn't want to move anyway.

She had to pick her words carefully, to give him only the bare bones of it, leaving out her own involvement. "As you probably already know, Wade Sanders was fired. I wanted to give him an indefinite leave of absence, but Cliff wouldn't hear of it. I believe he gave Sanders some vague excuse about too many errors at first, not wanting to tip anyone off." That had actually been her suggestion, the only one Cliff had listened to. Though Cliff had been adamant about firing Wade, Virginia hadn't wanted to take the chance that they might fire the wrong man. Wade had been with them for several years and never caused any problems.

Why wouldn't Cliff listen to her? Now look at the trouble they were in.

Of course, she hadn't known Kelsey was seeing Wade. Which wasn't surprising. Other than organizing the donations made by the company to various charities, Kelsey never involved herself in business. She and Kelsey and Cliff all led separate lives, with different priorities. Virginia made the business her life, while Kelsey chose to keep herself apart, both emotionally and physically. Lately, the two sisters seldom talked.

The gentle movement of Dillon's fingers on her scalp lulled her, and she went on with a sigh. "It was all done quietly, with no suspicions being announced. That way, if Wade wasn't the one embezzling the funds, the embezzlement would have continued and they could have trapped the person responsible. But since Wade was fired, no more money has been taken."

She looked at Dillon, at the concentrated frown on his brow, the dark eyes intense with thought. She wanted to soothe him, to comfort him, because in her heart she believed his brother to be guilty. And she knew it was going to come as a terrible blow to him.

He had some antiquated notion of family honor that wouldn't allow him to believe his brother capable of embezzlement. The contradictions in him amazed and intrigued her. He was by far the most dangerous man she'd ever met, but at the moment, bizarre as it seemed, she trusted him implicitly. The same code that would force him to risk his own life for his brother would keep him from ever deliberately hurting her. When he said he only wanted to save his brother, she believed him.

"Dillon, since the day Wade was relieved of his position, no more money has been taken," she repeated. "The investigation has been very quiet. Other than the two professionals Cliff hired to find proof that it was embezzlement and not accounting errors, no one knew except Cliff, Wade and me."

Idly, Dillon traced his fingers up and down her bare arm while he stared toward the fire. His light brown hair shone with highlights from the flames and his dark, dark eyes seemed almost fathomless. More contrasts, Virginia thought, and not only his coloring. He seemed contemplative and regretful, but beneath it all, the internal conviction of his brother's innocence was still there.

"Dillon? Don't you see? No one else knew except Wade. Not knowing the theft had been discovered, the embezzler probably would have continued to steal. But it didn't happen. The fact that the embezzlement ended the day Wade left the company almost proves his guilt." Almost, though Virginia wanted solid proof, and that's why she'd set up her own investigation.

Dillon finally looked at her. His large rough hand rose to cup her cheek, his thumb stroking over her temple. Slowly, inexhoribly, he urged her closer, and his mouth began to lower.

Virginia didn't know what to think, what to do. A whispering roared in her ears, and she accepted the fact that she wanted his kiss more than was wise. Pride, determination, common sense, seemed to evaporate. All she could concentrate on was the scent of Dillon, the hard comfort of his body, the way her own body reacted to him.

When his mouth touched hers, without passion but with tenderness and concern, she wanted to snuggle closer and stay safe, with him, in this cabin.

The thought appalled her, but before she could pull away, he lifted his head and then set her on her feet.

"It's almost bedtime, honey. Why don't you go take a shower or do whatever it is women do to get ready for bed."

Stupified, Virginia stared down at him. She swayed before catching herself and locking her knees against the weakness he caused. "Didn't you hear what I said? Didn't you understand? Wade is guilty."

Dillon gathered up the cards and stacked them neatly in his palm. "Go on, Virginia. There are clean towels in the bathroom, and I unpacked your shampoo and cleanser and all that other feminine stuff you had in that tiny bag."

He stood and Virginia reached out to clutch at his shirt. Dillon stared down at her, his expression veiled. She wanted to shake him, to make him understand that this would never work, that he was trying to save his brother against all odds.

"Dillon, you can't go through with this! You'll only implicate yourself in Wade's actions."

He pried her fingers loose from his shirt and then held her hand close to his chest. "You're wrong, honey. You say Wade is the only one who knew, but don't you wonder how I knew it was embezzlement he was suspected of, before any charges could be made? Don't you wonder how Wade contacted me so quickly that I was able to set this whole damn thing up *before* Cliff even began his investigation?"

"I… I hadn't really thought about it." She felt a stirring of dread, of sick premonition.

Dillon turned her toward the bathroom and gave her a light push. "It's easy, Virginia. Someone else knew. If Cliff didn't make it up or take the money himself, and if there really is money missing and Wade doesn't have it, someone else is guilty. Maybe the same person who's trying to hurt you. Maybe even the person who warned Wade in the first place."

"Why would anyone do that?"

"For the same reason you tried to keep it quiet. If the embezzlement stopped, Wade would look guilty. And who could look more innocent than the person trying to save him?"

She held on to the bathroom doorknob and looked back at Dillon. She felt both hope and dread that it might be all over. "If Wade didn't do it and you think you know who did, then the problem is solved. We can forget this little charade and go home. I promise you I'll do all I can to settle this."

But Dillon shook his head. "Are you forgetting the threats against you? And don't shake your pretty head at me, damn it. Someone cut your brake lines. And someone came into your house, using a key. If I hadn't been with you, I don't know what might have happened. But I do know I don't like the idea of anyone hurting you. I won't let it happen."

He took a step toward her, before stopping himself. "I'm sorry, Virginia. But the *problem* is far from solved. In fact, things just got a whole hell of a lot more complicated. Because I happen to think the two problems are related. And that narrows our suspect list down considerably."

CHAPTER NINE

SHE WANTED HIM to explain, but Dillon couldn't find the heart to tell her the truth. Not yet. Not until he had more information. Explaining to Wade was going to be tough enough, something he already dreaded.

He'd gotten used to the idea of blaming Cliff, and it felt good to blame him. But Cliff couldn't have been working alone because he wasn't savvy enough to pull off such a stunt. He should have realized that sooner.

Dillon believed the embezzlement charge and the threat to Virginia were related. That meant Cliff was the one tampering with her car and hiding out in her house or he'd hired someone else to do it. Either way, Dillon intended to destroy them all. He only hoped Virginia wouldn't be destroyed in the process.

Facing the fireplace, he listened to the sound of the shower and knew Virginia was only yards away, naked and wet and worried. Lord, he wanted her, wanted to hold her and comfort her and protect her from her damn deranged family and their deadly manipulations. Kissing her earlier had been so sweet, an odd feeling he'd never experienced before. There had been no passion, at least not on the surface where she would detect it. He'd simply been holding her on his lap, aware of her turmoil, sensing her insecurity. And he'd kissed her as a sign of comfort and understanding.

It was the first time he could recall sharing such a thing with a woman. Usually, if he kissed a woman, it was a foregone conclusion that they'd end up in bed. He didn't have the time or the interest for romantic relationships, so he settled for sexual ones. He'd always been discreet, and very careful with his health and the issue of responsibility, but he'd never claimed to be a monk. He enjoyed women, and in return he made sure they enjoyed him.

Yet he'd kissed Virginia, knowing he couldn't make love to her, knowing she was the one woman off-limits to him. And it had been so incredibly tender he'd wanted to go on holding and kissing her all night.

Of course, that hadn't been the only feeling storming him at that moment. Having her on his lap caused his body to surge in awareness. The firm pressure of her behind had been incredibly arousing and had stirred up visions of how they could mate, leaving his brain muddled with erotic images of her naked and warm and wet.

Not only did he want to comfort and gentle her, he wanted to claim her, to make love to her while she sat on his lap in just that way, her breasts vulnerable to his hands and mouth, her legs draped over his flanks. He wanted to break down her rigid defenses and force her to be a woman, his woman. He wanted to hear her whisper his name while he manipulated her to a blinding climax again and again. He would bury himself so deep inside her lush body she'd forget everything and everyone else. But that was impossible, as well as unconscionable. He wouldn't take advantage of her, no matter how severe his own need became.

So he'd settled for that one chaste kiss of comfort, and strangely, he'd reveled in it.

The shower finally shut off and Dillon closed his eyes, imagining her drying her body, the soft towel moving over her generous curves, around her full breasts, between her plump thighs.... His erection was almost painful, but he couldn't control the reaction of his body. He stood, then paced to the window over the sink. The snow fell continuously, burying everything, serving his purpose nicely. The deeper it got, the less he had to worry about Virginia trying to run off when he left her in the morning. Travel would be difficult enough for him, even with the truck. He'd have to adjust his time frame to accommodate the extra hours it would take to maneuver the icy roads.

The bathroom door opened and he turned to see Virginia peeking out.

"I need something clean to put on."

He sighed, ruthlessly bringing himself back under control. "We've been over this already, Virginia. I'm not taking any chances, which means the less you wear, the safer you'll be."

Her lips firmed and her slim auburn brows drew down in a frown. The severe look was a familiar one to him, but mixed with the incongruity of her cowering body behind the door, it almost made him smile.

"Fine. I understand that. But don't expect me to put on the same thing I've been wearing all day. Give me something else."

He considered that for a moment, then nodded. "I'll be right back."

As he headed for the door, she said, "Dillon!" and he heard the alarm. It made his insides twist with regret, because he was solely responsible for making her so uncertain, for stealing away her cockiness and arrogance. "I'm not leaving, honey. I'm just going out to the truck to fetch one of my shirts."

He saw every thought that flashed through her quick mind, and he laughed. "Don't get any ideas about bashing me over the head and stealing my clothes or my truck. I've disconnected a few things on the engine, and it won't run again until I reconnect them—easy enough for me, but unless you know a lot about mechanics, you won't get the thing started. And my suitcase only has a few shirts and clean skivvies anyway. Except for trying to strip my jeans off me, you'd have to leave here bare assed."

Her response was to slam the bathroom door in his face.

As Dillon dashed through the snow to the truck, he realized he wore a sappy grin on his face. Damn, but the woman amused him with her flash temper and biting wit. Now that he was no longer constrained to keep his natural responses to himself, he actually enjoyed her sharp tongue. They played a game of dominance, and even though he knew he'd come out ahead, that in the end he could conquer her if that was his wish, the game still thrilled him. Virginia proved a worthy adversary and she kept him on his toes.

When he returned to the cabin with a spare white T-shirt for her and a few things for himself, he did so cautiously. He didn't doubt her ability to take him by surprise; she'd already done so numerous times. But Virginia was still in the bathroom, and when he knocked, she merely stuck her hand out through the narrowly opened door.

After she'd snatched the shirt from him, he heard a muttered, "Thank you." He went back to sitting by the fire.

He didn't know quite how to handle her now, but he had decided to give her options. He'd found in the past that it was easier for people to accept the idea of having choices than being totally dominated. Not that he was looking forward to his next move. Hell, it would likely be much harder on him than it would be on her. At the moment, she pretty much detested him—rightfully so—while his feelings came nowhere close to such a negative emotion. But he didn't want her fighting him, either, and possibly hurting herself. He had to find a way to gain her compliance so she could get some badly needed sleep and he could relax his guard.

Turning as the bathroom door opened again, he watched Virginia creep across the floor with the quilt thrown over her shoulders and held close to her breasts by a tight fist. It dragged behind her like a queen's robe and suited her haughty stature better than she could know.

She wore his shirt. He could see the hem of the white T-shirt brushing her dimpled knees as she walked, and the sight filled him with a primitive satisfaction. The shirt signified a claim, a stake he couldn't make but wanted all the same.

Ignoring her wary gaze, Dillon came to his feet and braced himself for the newest confrontation. "Into the bed, Virginia."

She faltered and her beautiful eyes widened, looking more amber than gold in the dim room. They seemed to dominate her face, a face scrubbed clean of makeup, pink and fresh and young. He knew she was thirty years old, but at the moment, she barely looked nineteen. As usual, her chin went into the air and her shoulders squared.

"What are you going to do?"

He picked up the rope he'd laid on the mantel. Gently, he said, "I told you I'd have to tie you, remember?"

"No!"

"I can't take a chance on you doing anything foolish."

"You're not going to tie me, Dillon."

The warning was there, but the trembling in her tone belied the vehemence of her words. He felt like an animal, and he hated himself, hated what he had to do. He clenched his hands into fists, tightened his abdomen and said, "There's only one other choice."

Hope shone in her eyes, mixed with the caution she tried so hard to hide. "What choice?"

"I'll have to sleep with you." She took a quick step back, and he said, "It's one way or the other, Virginia. I'm a light sleeper, and if I'm right beside you, I'll know if you try anything. But if you hate the thought of having me so close, I can sleep in a chair. It wouldn't be the first time." He stared at her, refusing to back down from the accusation on her face, refusing to acknowledge the stirring of lust that twisted his gut and tightened his groin. "But then I'll have to tie you. Those are your choices."

"Which leaves me no choice at all."

The rope slid through his fingers as he wound and rewound it. "Don't be bitter, honey. Accept what has to be. We both need some sleep."

With her gaze on the rope, she chewed her lip and

squirmed, and it was so unlike her, this indecisiveness, that he almost relented. Hell, he could go another night without sleep. He could easily sit by the fire and watch her all night as she rested; it would be an apt punishment for involving her in all this, for using her.

"All right."

Taken by surprise, Dillon stared at her, wanting no mistakes, no illusions. "All right what?"

"You can sleep with me."

She tried to scoff, shrugging her rounded shoulders and shifting her feet nervously. She wouldn't meet his gaze, no matter how he willed her to.

"I mean, what's the big deal? You've already made it clear you don't want me. Right?"

He didn't—couldn't—answer. Surely the woman wasn't blind to his lust; at thirty years of age she'd had lovers, or so he'd understood. Virginia was in no way a naive spinster who wouldn't recognize the signs.

The material of his worn jeans was straining he was so hard. He felt huge, hot and throbbing, and it wouldn't take much more than a single touch from her to make him come. The thought caused a shudder to skip down his rigid spine. He held his breath in reaction.

Even an inexperienced woman would notice such an obvious arousal. He wasn't a small man, not in any way. But then, Virginia tried not to look at him, and he'd never seen her this distracted, this...*shy.* His heart twisted.

When he remained silent, she went on, determined to brazen it out. "We'll be separated by a quilt and we could use the shared warmth tonight when the fire dies down."

"Fine." Dillon put the rope back up on the mantel and snatched up his own change of clothes as he headed for the bathroom. Right now, he needed a cold shower, and given the size of the hot water tank, that was likely all that was left. "Get into bed. I'll be there in just a few minutes."

He didn't wait to see Virginia's reaction to his curt order. He didn't want to be tempted further by the sight of her, by the length of her gorgeous, sexy hair, her bare feet or wide-eyed gaze.

He didn't want to think about lying close to her warm soft body but not touching her in all the ways that tempted him most.

In the bathroom, he leaned back against the door, then opened his eyes and met the sight of her pale silk teddy draped over the towel bar. She'd rinsed the thing out, but the material was so sheer it already looked dry in places.

Like a sleepwalker, he stepped over and raised it in his hand. Cool, smooth. Damp. He lifted the material to his nose and drank in her woman-soft, musky scent, knowing the delicious smell would be so much stronger on her body, her heated skin. His pulse throbbed and he rubbed the slippery material over his cheek. Finally, disgusted with his self-torture and the expected results, he draped the teddy back on the towel bar and turned on the water.

It took him only minutes to realize the cold shower wasn't cold enough. His skin prickled with the chill, but still he felt hot and aroused, his loins full and heavy, his muscles drawn too tight. He couldn't go to her this way, on the very edge of exploding. Not only would he frighten her, he'd be testing his control beyond dangerous limits. Since no woman had ever had this effect on him, he felt angry and helpless at his inability to deal with it. With a curse, he made up his mind.

The shower was barely wide enough for his shoulders, but he braced his back against the icy tile wall and closed his eyes. The freezing water sprayed his face and chest and groin like sharp needles and he allowed that feeling, allowed it to grow and torment him until he couldn't breathe. Then he relieved the pressure.

It didn't take much, not with the way he'd been aroused all day. When his climax hit, he clenched his teeth and growled, pressing his shoulders hard against the cold wall. The feelings went on and on and finally he slumped on a ragged groan, his body slowly relaxing.

With his lust diminished but far from gone, he left the shower. His thighs still trembled, his breathing still uneven. Shivering, he briskly dried himself, then pulled on his underwear and shoved his legs back into his jeans. Normally, he slept in the nude, but lying beside Virginia without the protection of sturdy denim would be disastrous, even after his release. He wasn't a fool, and he knew his own limitations. After finger-combing his hair and brushing his teeth, he quietly left the bathroom.

The cabin seemed too silent, and he wondered for a brief instant if Virginia would launch another attack; he wasn't at all up to fending her off. But then he saw her in the bed, curled on her side, the quilt tucked tightly around her, her hands beneath her cheek. The fireplace cast a dancing golden glow over everything, but especially on her hair, which fanned out behind her and covered a good portion of the bed, including the part where he would lay.

She kept her eyes tightly closed, even though he knew she wasn't asleep.

Shadows in the darkest parts of the cabin seemed to insulate them from any intrusion. The fire hissed and the air smelled pleasantly of winter and wood smoke and Virginia.

The bed dipped as he put one knee beside her hip. She clutched at the edge of the mattress to keep from rolling toward him. He watched her eyes squeeze a little tighter, her shoulders hunch, and he wanted to yell, to shout out his frustration like a madman. Ill equipped to handle sleeping chastely with a woman who turned him on, he felt angry, at himself and her. He remained poised beside her for several heartbeats while he took deep breaths and resigned himself to the inevitable.

"I'll have to curl around you to fit on the bed."

She didn't respond. Cautiously, he stretched out full length beside her, pulling the spare quilt over his body, then flipping the extra over her so that she was covered by both quilts. The room would get chillier as the night wore on and the fire burned down. Virginia never moved a muscle.

Reaching over, he caught her waist and pulled her snugly against his body. She made a small sound, then went perfectly still again. His body hummed with tension. "Try to relax, honey. I never bite a woman unless she asks me to."

Her elbow came back with surprising force. He grunted even as he grinned, then tightened his arm in a quick hug. "That's better. I thought maybe you were concentrating on playing possum."

"Actually, I was concentrating on pretending you don't exist."

He chuckled at her continued sarcasm, able to see the irony now that she wasn't so frozen beside him. "You know that's not going to work. Not with us both so cozy in this bed." Feeling her bottom tucked snug against his groin worked wonders to revive his libido; his earlier release might never have happened.

"It could work if you'd shut up and let me get to sleep."

He hugged her again, pressing his nose to the back of her neck and breathing in the sweet fragrance of her hair. It felt soft on his face, and he wondered how soft it would feel on the rest of his body. Just as quickly, he chased the stirring thought away, sensing disaster. "Good night, Virginia."

Several minutes passed, and she remained motionless. Dillon thought she had dozed off until she whispered, "Dillon?"

"Hmm?"

Again she was silent, before finally asking, "What would you do if Wade was guilty?"

He nuzzled her ear, unable to help himself, and was rewarded with her slight shiver. He decided masochistic tendencies must be part of his genetic makeup. "First, I suppose I'd beat the hell out of him."

Virginia half turned to see him and they nearly bumped noses. Her face showed astonishment as she searched his gaze for sincerity. "Your own brother?"

Firelight licked over her cheekbones, turning her eyelashes to gold and making her skin glisten. Dillon tucked a loose curl behind her ear, that damn tenderness tightening his chest again, mixing with the lust to confuse and agitate him. "Especially my brother. I couldn't let him go to jail, but I'd definitely want him to understand that what he'd done was wrong, and there's always a price to be paid. We'd eventually talk about it, I suppose, and hopefully I could make him understand so the situation never occurred again."

Virginia considered his words, then turned back to her pillow. "I think it's really nice that you care so much. Not many families are that way."

"What about you, Virginia?" he asked tentatively, trying to find the right words. "What would you do if you found out Cliff or Kelsey had broken the law? What if Cliff resorted to blackmail...or Kelsey put herself at risk for money? What would you do?"

She shook her head. "I don't know. Things aren't as clear-cut for me as they are for you."

"You love your brother and sister."

"Yes. But we don't usually see eye to eye. We don't have the rapport that you evidently have with Wade and your father."

He smoothed his hand up and over her shoulder, then back to her elbow. "You could have, if you'd be willing to work for it." He wanted to stop touching her, but he couldn't seem to help himself and his fingers lingered on her soft white skin.

"It might be too late now. If you get your way, and Kelsey marries Wade, nothing will ever be the same again. Our family will be more divided than ever."

"You can't know that. Problems have a way of either destroying a family or bringing it together. If you'd give Wade half a chance, and trust my judgment just a bit, you might find things are in better shape than ever."

"Ha!" Again she twisted to see him and her cheeks were flushed with righteous indignation. "Not only do you kidnap me, but now you refuse to tell me who you suspect of setting this whole thing up. How can I possibly trust you?"

"Give me a little time." He splayed his fingers over her belly and heard her audible gasp. Her soft stomach quivered before he felt her muscles tighten. "Give me a chance to check things out, to get my facts straight, and then I'll tell you what I know."

"When?"

"Tomorrow when I get back."

"I could leave while you're gone, you know."

"But you won't." Dillon was painfully aware of their present situation, their lying together in intimate surroundings, the night dark and the fire warm, talking in bed like an old married couple. Virginia seemed to have put her uneasiness aside for the moment. That alone proved some measure of trust. "You're not afraid of me, for yourself or your family. There's no reason for you to run."

"You can't know what I'm feeling!"

"But I do. You trust me not to hurt you. Trust me enough to find out what I can tomorrow, then we'll decide together what to do."

She chewed her lip in indecision. "You'll tell me everything? All your suspicions? Anything you find out?"

"I promise."

Her sigh was long and dramatic. "It's a sorry day when I take the word of a kidnapper, but I suppose I have no choice." She dropped her head back to her pillow and wiggled to get more comfortable. It was Dillon's turn to suck in his breath. Virginia seemed to have difficulty getting settled, and finally she punched her pillow. "Cliff is going to give me hell for this whole mess."

Dillon grabbed her hips to still her movements before he forgot his good intentions and shoved her T-shirt high and threw the quilts off the bed. He wanted to feel her bare buttocks moving against him. "I have no doubt you'll give as good as you get. Cliff doesn't stand a chance."

"Good night, Dillon."

He let his body ease against hers, moving his arm around her waist, the other under her pillow, supporting her head. *He* wasn't comfortable; he was too alert for comfort. But he thought he might eventually sleep. Tomorrow would be horrendous, filled with confrontations, and he'd need a little sleep if he was to deal with the difficulties in the best way.

About a half hour later, he heard Virginia's breathing taper into sleep and her body sighed into his, warm and feminine and soft, fitting against him perfectly. He stared into the fire and thought about all the problems and all the players involved, while his fingertips continued to smooth over her skin. With only a few words, everything had gotten more complicated. And there was no way he could protect Virginia from what would come. He realized he didn't want her hurt, not in any way. Somehow, someway, he'd begun to really care about her. He could no longer attempt to convince himself that he didn't like her, because he liked her far too much.

Admitting what was in his heart, even to himself, scared the hell out of him, but it was too big to deny.

The odds of getting away from this damn scheme unscathed had drastically diminished.

THE HEAT DISTURBED HER, covering her in thick, pulsing waves, mixing vividly with the dream. She moaned, trying to force herself awake and away from the tormenting heat. As she stirred, she curled her fingers, and felt them dig into solid muscle. She panted for breath, for recognition.

The scent of hot, excited male filled her nostrils as she sucked in a long breath. Stunned and disoriented, unable to move with any speed, she lifted her eyelids.

Her nose twitched, tickled by the dark hair of Dillon's chest, close to one flat brown nipple. Her heart skipped a beat, and she couldn't seem to get her thoughts organized other than to realize her face was pressed to Dillon's bare chest and her pelvis was perfectly aligned with his. The solid length of his erection burned against her bare belly, even through his jeans. A sweet, insistent pressure between her thighs made her shudder. Confused, she raised her head just a bit. Dillon's diamond-hard gaze immediately snared her.

Lazily, he murmured, "You're awake."

The husky rumble of his voice rubbed over her and she moaned. That was when she realized his thigh pressed against her in the most sensitive of places. Her legs straddled him and one large calloused hand anchored her naked bottom in place, his fingers pressing into her flesh, roughly caressing. Somehow the quilts were pushed low on the cot and her T-shirt had gotten shoved to her waist. His fingers dipped, sliding between her buttocks, moving down toward her mound, and she jerked in startled, excited embarrassment. *"Dillon?"*

His smile was gentle, even as those fingers slid lower, coasting over her, probing, seeking. "I like waking up with you hot and wet for me, Virginia. I like it a lot." He closed his eyes as one finger circled her, briefly pressing into her body. "Do you feel how wet you are, babe? How hot?"

A slight trembling started deep inside her. "I don't understand."

"You crawled right on top of me." As he spoke, his gaze moved over her face, lingering on her lips, then her throat, where she knew her pulse raced. He lowered his thick lashes, hiding his eyes.

She swallowed, wanting to deny his statement, but how could she when she made no effort to move away from him? She didn't want to move. She'd gone to sleep excited, wanting him so much, more than she'd ever thought it was possible to want anyone or anything. The things he did to her now, the bold way he touched her had to be forbidden. But he continued, and she didn't try to stop him.

Dillon had a strength she'd never imagined, but there was also a gentleness about him, the careful way he wielded his strength. His power was a sexy, vital part of him and she wanted him.

Unable to help herself, she squirmed. Dillon pulled his hand away, then raised his thigh a bit more, pressing hard against her while her body moved of its own volition to a rhythm she hadn't known until he showed her with a guiding hand. She gasped at the acuteness of the sensation, closing her eyes and pressing her head back.

She felt his fingers tangle in the length of her hair, moving it over his chest and shoulders. "You are so sexy."

She couldn't stand it. She shook her head, knowing it wasn't true, knowing she behaved shamefully, practically attacking Dillon in his sleep. He palmed her breast, weighing it, his fingertips rubbing roughly over her aching nipple. It pebbled hard and he lightly pinched the very tip, tormenting her. Her body become more sensitive, more alive with each small movement. She cried out.

"Do you have any idea what you do to me, Virginia?" His whispered words added to the quickening building beneath her skin. "I couldn't sleep, not with you so near at hand. And then you crawled over me, cuddling close, and you touched me, just my chest, but I felt it to my very bones."

His leg thrust higher, forcing her forward and she cried out again, arching her back to add to the delicious pressure. "Dillon..." The embarrassment was there; she'd never done anything like this before, certainly not with a man watching her so closely. And she'd never felt this way, scattered and fractured and ready to explode, *wanting* to explode. She could feel her own wetness, her heat, and she kept moving against him, seeking the sharp pleasure that kept expanding but seemed just out of reach.

Dillon lifted her breast higher and bit her nipple lightly through the cotton shirt. "I want to taste your nipples, Virginia. Hell, I want to taste all of you."

She opened her eyes, staring at him, uncomprehending. He smiled and touched her face with a trembling hand. "Let me help you, honey. You need me right now, don't you?"

"I don't know." But she did know. She wanted Dillon inside her, she wanted to know what it was to be loved by this man, even if the lovemaking was a sham. He'd lied about wanting her, lied about being attracted to her, but he wanted her now. She could feel his body moving in subtle shifts, his huge erection grinding against her belly.

"Trust me, Virginia?"

He made it a question, not an order, and she groaned, hardly able to think with his hands teasing her and showing her how to move, urging her harder against him, faster. "I do."

In the next second, Dillon flipped her onto her back, shoving her T-shirt up and over her breasts. His slim hips planted firmly between her widely spread thighs. Virginia clutched at him, stunned and excited and a little scared by the way he made her feel so out of control, so uncaring about everything in the world but the pleasure of him and the ache inside her.

Then his mouth was on her nipple while his hand held her breast high, like a sacrifice. He sucked and licked and Virginia didn't know if she could stand it, it was so exciting. She bit her lips to keep from begging, to stop herself from crying out like a wild thing. But she couldn't hold still and she writhed under him, holding his head, feeling the hollows of his cheeks as he sucked her hard, mercilessly.

The torture went on and on. He switched from one breast to the other, never quite satisfied, and she did cry, only it didn't deter him from his course. He seemed intent on driving her out of her mind, his mouth and hot tongue first light and teasing, then frightening her with sharp little nips of his teeth and rough kisses. She thrust her mound against him, rubbing and seeking, anxious to gain her own pleasure. But whenever she got close to that mystical realm of satisfaction, he would hold her hips and force her to be still, even while he continued to taste her and whisper hot, forbidden words to her.

"Damn you, Dillon." Her gasping breaths made it difficult to speak. Her words sounded high and weak.

"I want you to remember this, honey, to remember me." Now he used both hands to lightly pinch her nipples, tugging and rolling, keeping her poised, her back arched while he watched her respond with satisfaction. "I want to give you something you've never had before."

"I can't stand it…."

"Shh." He bent to lave her nipple with the very tip of his raspy tongue. "I'm not giving you a choice. Not this time."

The words sent an erotic thrill of warning down her spine. "Make love to me, damn you!"

One hand left her breast to trail down her side, then over her belly. "Not a good idea, Virginia. You want me now, but when this is all over, you're liable to hate me."

"No." She moaned as his hand slid over her, separating her slick folds, teasing her further. When she cried out, he pushed two fingers deep inside her, high and hard. Instinctively, she tried to twist away. Dillon wouldn't let her.

"Don't hide from me, Virginia. Give over to me. *Trust me.*"

How could she trust him when it seemed he only wanted to make her crazy? If he wouldn't make love to her, then why torture her so thoroughly? But she couldn't think, couldn't find a rational thought, not with his fingers stroking her, stretching her.

"Open your legs wide for me, baby. Wider…." He groaned. "That's it."

He kissed the sensitive underside of her breasts, then her ribs, counting each one. When she felt his mouth low on her belly, she held her breath, wanting to protest, but unable to speak or even think past the heightened sensation and acute painful need.

He sat back on his heels and looked at her. Using his thumbs, he spread her open, slicked up and down, sometimes dipping, then rubbing over her.

"No," she moaned, pushing his hands away and trying to cover herself. But he caught her hands and pinned them to her sides. Their gazes met and she shuddered at the hot, determined look in his eyes. "I like to see a woman touch herself, Virginia, to watch her play with her own body. But not now, not yet. Right now, I'm playing."

"Bastard." But the word was only a whisper and she didn't fight him anymore.

He released her hand and said, "Do you want me to stop?"

She trembled, then shook her head. "No."

"Then don't move. Do you understand me, Virginia?"

She didn't think she could move even if she'd wanted to. Meek compliance went against every fiber of who she was. But she knew she'd die if he stopped now, so he left her no choice. She swallowed, then turned her face away and whispered, "Yes."

"Look at me."

Again she seemed to have no choice but to obey. Her heart pounded so hard it hurt.

He trailed his fingers down her ribs, watching as she trembled from the tickling sensation that only added to her raw nerves, making her body more frenzied. Both hands stopped at the top of her thighs and he pushed, spreading her even wider.

"You look beautiful like this."

She knotted her hands in the sheets and tried to concentrate on the sight of him, his hard body, the way every muscle seemed drawn tight right now. His jaw was rigid, his eyes were burning. He traced her femininity with one rough finger, then tweaked her curls, smiling and saying, "So pretty." As he toyed with her, he asked, "Hasn't any man ever really looked at you, honey?"

She shook her head, unwilling to voice the words. Caught in a maelstrom of embarrassment and overwhelming need, she didn't dare speak for fear of what she might admit.

"Fools. I could look at you forever."

Just as he had done with her nipples, he caught her swollen bud between the very tips of his fingers and thumb. Her body bowed, lifted high, and he held her like that, lightly abrading her, stroking, pulling. If she started to close her thighs, he'd stop and rearrange her again before returning to his torment. She bit her lips and sobbed and then he bent low and she felt his breath.

Carefully now, he slid his fingers back inside her, adding a rough friction while his hot mouth closed over her, drawing gently. Everything in her tightened, the sensations all rushing to that one spot, then radiating out again in rolling waves. His lips nibbled over delicate, throbbing flesh and suckled gently while his fingers continued to fill her, and she exploded, her climax taking her by surprise as her legs tightened and her vision went blank and her body screamed in a rush of unbelievable pleasure. The power of it was so devastating, like an attack to her every nerve ending, that she honestly wondered if she'd survive—and didn't really care.

The sensation went on and on, stealing all thoughts. She wasn't even sure what it was now that Dillon did with her body and it didn't matter, as long as he continued to do it. He murmured to her, encouraged her and praised her, until she trembled and her body went utterly limp. She tugged weakly at his hair, unable to bear it a second more, hardly able to breathe.

Dillon released her with one last, leisurely lick, and she collapsed back against the bed, her skin damp with sweat, her heart pounding against her ribs, her body tingling yet almost numb. She waited for him to enter her, to gain his own pleasure. But instead she felt a gentle kiss, as soft as a breeze, over her belly, then on each breast. She was so sensitized to his touch she groaned.

Forcing her eyelids open, she saw Dillon looking down at her, his cheekbones flushed darkly, his eyes bright and burning, his lips parted and wet. He leaned over and kissed her nose, her mouth. She could taste herself and she could feel the heat of him, the repressed energy as it seemed to sizzle between their bodies. "Go to sleep, Virginia."

She blinked, barely able to keep him in focus. The firelight worked like a hypnotic drug, lulling her. "Don't you want to…?"

One side of his mouth quirked. "Oh yeah, I want to. Now, go to sleep."

When she started to speak again, he covered her mouth with his fingertips. They were still damp and scented by her body. She shuddered. "Sleep."

Though she fought it, her eyes did shut, and the last

thing she remembered was Dillon gathering her close again, half pulling her over his body and covering them both with a single quilt.

Cozy and comfortable and for the first time in her life totally, completely sexually satisfied, she must have slept like the dead. She couldn't recall stirring a single time the rest of the night, even though she'd never actually slept with a man before.

When she awoke late in the morning, her head felt muzzy and full of cotton, as if she'd drunk too much. She shifted and her body complained, sensitive in places she'd never thought about before. She winced, remembering what she'd done, what she'd let Dillon do.

How could she face him now? What would he say?

Cautiously, her eyes darting around the room, she sat up in the bed. The quiet penetrated and she gasped. No, surely he hadn't left without waking her! Not after last night. She crawled out of the bed, untangling herself from the quilts, and rushed to the door. Before she opened it she saw the note on the center of the table.

Dillon was gone.

CHAPTER TEN

THE COLD, HAZY blue-gray day could have accounted for Dillon's mood, except he knew the real reason, and it didn't sit right with him. He wasn't the sort of man who normally suffered extremes of temperament. And he wasn't the sort of man who normally felt the need to dominate a woman so completely.

Much as he missed Virginia already, he didn't look forward to facing her again. He'd slunk out of the cabin like a coward, and felt perverse satisfaction at the way she slept on undisturbed, too replete, too sated, to wake.

Last night had been the most incredible sexual experience of his life, and he hadn't even taken her.

He scratched at his rough-whiskered jaw as he pulled the truck into the parking lot of his apartment building. When he opened the door, wind whooshed past him, flapping his coat and sapping his heat. Even though the truck's heater was adequate, he felt frozen through and he worried about Virginia, wondered if he had brought in enough wood to keep her comfortable until his return. He wanted to get his business over with quickly.

He glanced at his watch as he bounded up the apartment stairs, and saw that he had less than an hour to get to Cliff's office. He wanted to be there, to go through

Virginia's files before anyone else arrived. Once it became known she wasn't going to show up, the uproar would begin, and stealing information would be even more difficult. Already his head ached, both from wanting Virginia and because he needed to leave before he got any more wrapped up in this emotional mess.

He rushed into his apartment, prodded by more than time limits. He needed to get back to Virginia, to make sure she was okay after last night. He'd pushed her, and the reward had been sweet. But would she understand?

This time, Dillon needed a hot shower to relax his stiff muscles and clear his head. With any luck at all, it would also wash away the insistent ache of unrequited lust, and the more disturbing element of overwhelming tenderness.

CLIFF WAS SITTING BEHIND his desk, poring over a stack of mail. Dillon walked in unannounced and sprawled in a plush padded chair. He waited impatiently for Cliff to finish reading. He was anxious to get this over with.

Owing to his position within the company, he had keys to every office, and as early as he'd arrived, Virginia's secretary hadn't yet been at her desk. He'd entered the inner office with no problem. He'd expected to have to weed through endless files to find any information, but he'd been surprised by a thick envelope lying in Virginia's inbox. The package was without an address, blank on the outside, but tightly sealed. Without remorse, he'd opened it, and found two computer discs, along with a brief note. He'd taken the discs, together with Virginia's laptop computer, out to his car. He'd drive home, grab his truck and head back to the cabin to confront her. Anger still simmered just below the surface, where he hid it from Cliff.

He shouldn't have been surprised to discover Virginia was running her own investigation. In fact, he should have anticipated it. She took charge of everything, so why would this situation be any different? But he felt oddly nettled. She hadn't trusted him enough to confide in him. She obviously had her own suspicions about the embezzlement, but she'd kept quiet. Was it because she, too, wanted to pin the charge on Wade?

His hand fisted. He now had more than one reason to see the conniving little witch again. And he wasn't feeling overly patient.

All he needed was for Cliff to become aware of Virginia's absence, which should be any minute now. The calendar on her desk had her marked for an early meeting. But Miss Virginia Johnson was at present mostly naked and stranded in a deserted cabin. When he'd left, she was sleeping, exhausted from the pleasure he'd given her. Just the way he wanted her.

His muscles twitched in impatience. Dillon knew Cliff, knew his habits, and going through mail like a little boy hoping for a Christmas card was one of them. Sometimes it seemed as if Cliff could only believe he was really the head of the company by opening mail addressed to him as "President."

"So." Cliff looked up after laying aside the paperwork. "Have you found out anything?"

"I assume you're inquiring about your sister?"

"You're damn right. I have to know what she's up to. Do you realize she wasn't here at all yesterday? Didn't show up for work. She told her secretary she was taking the day off, but didn't say where she was going."

"Yes, I know. I went through her date book, but she didn't have anything personal written down for yesterday."

Cliff looked stunned, then very pleased by the idea. "Her date book. I never would have considered that. But maybe I should look at it, too. I mean, it's possible something that looked harmless to you could have been a meeting with a conspirator."

Dillon shook his head. He felt he had to protect Virginia's right to privacy from Cliff, even though he himself had invaded it only minutes earlier. "No. I recognized all the appointments. They were legitimate."

"Damn."

"I'm not surprised I didn't find any suspicious names there. Virginia isn't stupid or careless. If she's doing something behind your back, she certainly wouldn't make a note of it."

"Oh. I suppose that's true."

Cliff appeared to make the admission grudgingly. It probably felt too similar to a compliment for his tastes. He seemed struck by another thought. "If you knew you wouldn't find anything, why the hell look there in the first place?"

"I didn't say I wouldn't find anything. I said I wouldn't find anything concrete. What I was checking for was unaccountable time. Virginia is very organized and she strikes me as a woman who marks down all her appointments religiously. If there had been an hour or two left free, with nothing penned in—"

A knock on the door interrupted Dillon's well-rehearsed speech. Laura Neil breezed in with fresh coffee and an expression of concern. Predictably, Laura hovered near Cliff, who ignored her. He took the coffee without even a polite platitude. Dillon waited, his body in its usual negligent sprawl, but his muscles tightened in expectation. Finally, when Laura didn't leave, he saw the frown gather on Cliff's forehead.

"What is it, Ms. Neil?"

She stiffened at his tone, but otherwise showed no emotion. "Ms. Johnson's secretary says she hasn't arrived yet."

Cliff's brows rose. "Virginia's late?"

"Yes, sir. She had an appointment thirty minutes ago. Mr. Wilson from financing is downstairs waiting. He said the meeting was very important."

Without a word to Dillon, Cliff picked up his phone and punched in a number. "Damn irritant. Not like her to oversleep. What is she thinking," he muttered. Dillon, very aware of Laura listening, wanted to drive his fist into Cliff's face. He forced himself to sit still, to wait. After a moment, Cliff slammed down the phone. "She didn't answer at home, either. She's probably on her way in."

To Laura he said, "Call downstairs. Have Mr. Wilson escorted up here. And have Virginia's secretary bring me his file, right now."

Laura hesitated. "Ms. Johnson could get here any minute…."

"And I don't want to wait! Do what you're told."

Dillon heard Laura's gasp, but his biggest concern was conserving Virginia's business relations. The office door closed with a quiet click and Dillon stood. "Maybe you should think about this for a minute."

Cliff's face darkened and seconds later he flew out of his seat, cursing and pacing around the desk. He looked to be at loose ends, not quite sure what he should or shouldn't do. Dillon decided to give him a nudge in the right direction.

"For the sake of the company's reputation, why not just tell Mr. Wilson that Virginia is ill. There's a nasty flu going around. I'm sure Mr. Wilson would be willing to reschedule. No matter how important the meeting is, it can surely wait a day or two."

"You don't think I can handle things?"

The tone of Cliff's voice showed mingled concern and anger. "I think it will look bad for the company if anyone gets wind of the fact Virginia didn't show."

"Where the hell could she be?"

Surprised, Dillon narrowed his eyes and studied Cliff. "You sound almost worried."

The phone rang and Cliff, still pacing, pushed a button so that the call came over a speaker. Virginia's secretary responded to Cliff's curt hello, saying she didn't have the keys to Virginia's desk or file cabinet and that she couldn't access the files without them. Cliff swallowed. "What's on her agenda today?"

"Three meetings here at the office and a business lunch."

"Keep trying her home number. Let me know if you reach her, or when she shows up."

"Yes, sir."

Cliff disconnected the call. After a long hesitation, he started to reach for the phone again, then cursed instead and pressed his fist against his forehead. "Yesterday and today. Something isn't right."

This wasn't quite the reaction Dillon had expected. He leaned forward on his seat. "What is it?"

Cliff drew several breaths, then dropped his hands to his sides. "Something must have happened. In all the years she's been part of this company, Virginia has never, *not once,* missed an appointment."

Dillon slowly got to his feet. This show of brotherly concern, of near panic, was rewarding in its own way, reassuring him that Virginia wasn't totally despised by her family. But it also made him wonder about his own conclusions on things. If Cliff was guilty of sabotaging Virginia's car, why would he now look so worried about her welfare?

Every time Dillon turned around, things got more complicated. "What do you think could have happened?"

"How the hell should I know? Maybe Virginia screwed up. Maybe whoever she was working with turned on her. She was involved with someone, and I knew—*I knew*—it wouldn't turn out good. She ought to understand by now that no man pretending to be interested in her would be sincere. She should know better than to trust anyone like that."

Dillon's shoulders ached from strain. He wanted, needed, violence. The urge to hit someone or something almost overwhelmed him. "You have to give her credit for having some common sense. She wouldn't put herself at risk."

"Ha!" Cliff stabbed Dillon with an incredulous look. "She's too damn pigheaded to be cautious. She storms through life as if she alone owns it, and everyone will bow to her wishes."

Dillon thought of the way she'd writhed beneath him, pleading, crying in need, then screaming with an explosive orgasm. She hadn't been bossy then; she'd been more than eager to follow his commands.

"Damn her! What has she gotten herself into?"

Cliff's outburst cut through Dillon's heated memories. He was through playing. He needed to get back to Virginia, the sooner the better. Once they had this all wrapped up, she could deal with her brother however she wished. It wouldn't be his problem.

Summoning his most authoritative tone, the one he knew Cliff would automatically listen to, he said, "Tell Mr. Wilson that Virginia took ill. Tell him she'll have to reschedule when she's feeling up to it. The last thing you want right now is panic running through the building. I'll go check out her house, make certain everything is secure there. I'll talk to a few people, find out who saw her last."

Cliff stepped back to lean against his desk as if he needed the support. "You think something's wrong, too, don't you?"

His face was white, and for the first time, Dillon wavered in his hatred of the man. "I have no idea. But to be on the safe side, I'll look into it." He started toward the door. "I'll get in touch with you later. Don't worry. And don't spread the news around, whatever you do."

Just as his hand closed on the doorknob, a knock sounded. He opened the door and there stood Laura with Mr. Wilson. Dillon stepped back. Cliff reached out his hand to shake Mr. Wilson's. After rapid introductions, where Dillon greeted the older man, Cliff said, "I'm sorry for the inconvenience, but Virginia is home sick today. She got taken by surprise with a case of the flu. I was hoping I could reschedule for her."

Dillon relaxed, seeing that Cliff could handle things. But as he pulled the door shut behind him, he caught the surprise on Laura's face. She stood near her desk, watching him with a worried frown. So she, too, had wondered about Virginia's well-being? Dillon nodded to her, but she caught his arm as he passed by. "She's truly okay?"

Laura was a nice woman, if a bit standoffish; it was a damn shame she wasted herself on Cliff. Dillon patted her hand. "She's fine. Just under the weather."

"You're certain?"

His own gaze sharpened. "I'm certain. Don't give it another thought."

She didn't look convinced, but she forced a smile. "Good. I was...concerned."

Dillon stood watching her a moment longer as she seated herself behind her desk. "Ms. Johnson will appreciate your concern."

"Will you give her my regards, tell her I hope she'll be feeling better soon?"

One brow lifted. "You'll likely be seeing her before I will, Ms. Neil." Crossing his arms over his chest, he waited. He didn't like it that the secretarial pool was speculating on his relationship with Virginia. And that's what it was. Laura's concern now seemed more like curiosity.

"Oh. Of course. What was I thinking?"

"I'm sure I have no idea." With that, he left, feeling ridiculous for getting huffy with a secretary. Before much longer, everything would be settled, and when he left, all gossip would be put to rest.

His chest tightened at the thought. He knew Virginia was the type of woman he could have easily had a relationship with. She was headstrong, capable of standing up to him and anyone else. Her intelligence was appealing and her wit sharp. She was also the most sensually responsive woman he'd ever made love to, even though the lovemaking hadn't included total consummation. He knew having Virginia Johnson beneath him, open to his gaze, her soft flesh touching his, her taste on his tongue, was an experience he'd never forget. When he left her, he'd leave a part of his heart behind.

He figured he'd owe her at least that much.

HE HEARD THE SCREECH when he pulled up in front of the cabin. Given the howling of the wind and the fact that the cabin's only window and door were closed, it must have been a mighty loud screech. His blood seemed to freeze in his veins, and then his instincts kicked in.

Dillon had the door open and his body braced for any number of threats in less than a heartbeat. What he saw was Virginia, wearing nothing but his white T-shirt, frantically wielding a ratty broom and racing around the floor. "Virginia?"

Her wide, panicked eyes swung around to him, then she threw the broom and flew into his arms. An unexpected rush of emotion gripped him and he held her to him, cradling her close. But Virginia had other plans. She practically climbed his body, still yelping and babbling. He had little choice but to lift her as her frantic urgency sank in, and in the process, the T-shirt ripped. Her gaze searched the room, and Dillon, holding her secure, did the same. Then she pointed and began struggling against him again.

A big black spider, looking totally harassed by all the commotion, scuttled around the dusty floor, going first one way, then the other.

"Kill it!"

He couldn't help laughing. In the next instant, his head was ringing from the blow to his ear.

"Damn you, it's not funny. *Kill it!*"

She screamed suddenly as the spider made a haphazard, indirect line toward them. The sound caused his ears to ring yet again. He nearly dropped her when she launched into a renewed frenzy. Tightening his arms, he stepped toward the spider and, with the side of his boot, swept it out the open door. Virginia hid her face against his neck, her arms so tight around him she nearly choked him. Which was good, because it helped to keep his chuckles muffled.

Once the spider was dispatched, Dillon kicked the door closed. His earlier anger with her seemed to have evaporated as he relished the feel of her warm weight against his chest. "It's all right now, Virginia. The bug is gone."

She kept her face hidden and her grip didn't loosen at all. "It wasn't just a bug. It was a huge hairy spider and it…it *chased* me."

His lips twitched, but he sounded calm when he said, "Spiders don't have hair and they're more afraid of you than you are of them."

"Not that one. I was going through the wood, to add to the fire, and it jumped out of the pile and looked right at me. Before I could even run, it came after me. I kept pushing it away with the broom…." She shuddered and pressed her face closer, her warm breath feeling like a caress. "It wouldn't go away."

"How do you know it was looking at you?" he murmured, rubbing his cheek against the softness of her hair. "Could you see the evil glint in its eyes?"

"Yes, damn you, I could!"

He laughed, and this time she didn't hit him. He

kissed her cheek, her temple. “It’s all right now. I’m sorry you were afraid. I got back as quick as I could.”

She sighed, pressing even closer, not lifting her face a single inch. “I feel like an idiot, you know.”

“Is that why you’re still hiding?”

She nodded. “I really truly have no liking for insects.”

“Really truly, huh?” Dillon glanced toward the door, smiling slightly. “I’m sure that one isn’t particularly fond of you, either. It’s damn cold outside.”

She leaned her upper body away from him, and her cheeks were bright red. Dillon was more than a little aware of her soft thighs resting on his forearm. Beneath the T-shirt, she was naked, and his body was slowly coming alive to her scent, the feel of her in his arms.

She drew a trembling breath and his gaze dropped to her breasts, then stayed there. The neckline of the T-shirt had ripped and one soft nipple was partially visible, taunting him, making his body shudder with a violent rush of hot lust. He closed his eyes, and then Virginia’s voice, strained and quavery, sounded in his ear.

“Put me down. Right now.”

CHAPTER ELEVEN

VIRGINIA FELT LIKE CRYING, and that infuriated her. This morning she'd been first so angry she could barely see, then so filled with remorse that she felt hollow inside. The realization that she loved Dillon had come slowly, but the thrill of it had invaded her body and soul. She knew when he left her, she'd be empty. She also knew he wouldn't, *couldn't* stay. He hadn't lied to her, hadn't led her on. He'd only made her love him, only showed her what she could have if things were just a bit different, if she were a different woman, and the knowing almost killed her.

All she could hope for now was to seduce him, to make him give her physical love, since there was no hope for emotional love. She wanted that desperately, wanted to make him feel the same things she'd felt last night. She wanted memories and awareness so that when he was gone, she'd still have a part of him. She knew her life, knew what goals she could reach and those that would never be. There would never be another man for her. Never.

So she'd intended to greet Dillon while lying on the bed, to play up to him, to be soft and feminine until he gave up and gave in. Instead, she'd raced into his arms like a lunatic, hysterical over a damn spider. Shame bit into her pride. She'd more or less forced him to hold her, when she knew she was no lightweight; she could feel his arms tremble with the strain. Never had she felt so unappealing.

"Put me down, Dillon."

He didn't answer, except that his arms tightened. Virginia peered at him and saw where he was looking. She looked down, too, and heat washed over her. Her breast was bared to his view, pushed up by the position of his arm, one nipple exposed. "Oh."

She started to reach for the shirt, to readjust it, but Dillon said, "Don't," and she went still. His eyes had turned black, filled with heat. It seemed an effortless endeavor for him to lift her even higher, enough so that his mouth could close over her nipple, and Virginia gasped. Her fingers tangled in his silky soft hair, cool from being outside, and she moaned.

He took his time, licking, sucking, rocking her slightly in his arms. He seemed in no hurry to relinquish her weight. She drew an unsteady breath. "Dillon… Put me down. I'm too heavy for you."

In answer, he raised his face and his mouth came down on hers, voracious, hungry. He bent her head back over his arm while he ate at her, thrusting his tongue possessively into her mouth, sucking her tongue into his. She felt him moving, but didn't know what was happening until her back came into contact with the cool quilts on the cot. Dillon followed her down, still kissing her, his hands busy shoving the T-shirt up. "You're not heavy, Virginia. You're perfect."

He placed biting, open-mouth kisses on her throat, her shoulder. He shoved the T-shirt out of his way and again drew on her sensitive nipples, a little roughly, shocking her, thrilling her. He moved down her ribs and belly.

"No!" Virginia caught at his hair, certain where this would lead, when what she wanted was so much more.

He lifted his face to look at her. He was so sexy, so gorgeous, she caught her breath. "No, Dillon."

His chest heaved and he leaned back to look at her, first her face, but his gaze quickly moved over her naked body. His nostrils flared, his jaw locked tight. "I want to give you pleasure, sweetheart."

The endearment touched her soul, made her feel vulnerable. She lifted her chin. "Make love to me, then."

He was shaking his head before she'd finished her request. "I can't, Virginia. You know that."

Brazenly, she cupped his heavy erection in her hand, then shuddered at the size of him. In a husky whisper not at all feigned, she taunted him, wanting to break his control. "Surely you're up to the task, Dillon."

His eyes closed and he groaned. "That's not what I mean and you know it."

"I don't care what you mean. I want you to make love to me, damn it."

"Contrary to what you believe, Virginia, you can't always have what you want."

He was set on refusing her, and she almost hated him—wished she *could* hate him. "Then leave me alone. I want everything or nothing."

"You want too much."

Disappointment choked her and she shoved him away, scrambling to her feet. She flipped her long hair over her shoulders and stalked to the kitchen, where she leaned against the counter and tried to collect herself. She would not let him know how he'd hurt her. She couldn't.

She heard the bed squeak and turned to find Dillon sprawled on his back, one forearm over his eyes. Never had she seen such an appealing sight. He'd thrown off his coat and his shirt was pulled tight over bulky, solid chest muscles and broad shoulders. His throat was tanned and she wanted to lick him there, to taste his skin. His worn jeans hugged lean hips and a tight abdomen, and his thighs, half-off the bed so that his feet rested flat on the floor, were thick and hard. In his reclining position, the tight jeans clearly defined his erection, and his size and thickness took her breath away. He was an impressive male, in every way possible.

She swallowed audibly, a little afraid of so much masculinity, but drawn to him just the same. On silent feet, she approached him, and without warning, her palm smoothed over him. He jerked, dropping his arm and eyeing her cautiously.

She straddled his lap and heard him growl. "All right, Dillon," she lied. "If you won't give me everything, then at least be fair and let me take from you what you took from me."

She felt him jerk, felt his erection move against her buttocks. His mouth opened and he sucked in air. "Virginia…"

"Shh." She caught his hands as he reached for her, and mimicking him from the previous night, she pressed them down at his sides. "Don't move."

His eyes narrowed at her familiar arrogant tone, and his smile twisted. "You haven't got the nerve."

She caught his flannel shirt in two fists and, staring him in the eye, gave a vicious jerk. Buttons flew across the room, pinging off the wall, rolling across the hardwood floor. Dillon watched her, not saying a word, but as her palms smoothed over his bare flesh, her fingers tangling in his chest hair, his eyes closed and he groaned. She shoved the shirt off his shoulders and down his arms until it caught at his elbows, where he'd tightly rolled the sleeves. She left it like that, trapping his arms, tangled above his head. His biceps bulged; his shoulders strained. She shifted, scooting on his lap, and he growled, lifting his hips.

Virginia leaned forward and lightly bit his nipple. He cursed and went still again. She licked the small wound, touching him everywhere on his upper body. His chest hair was dark, like his eyebrows and eyelashes, contrasting sharply with the sandy-colored hair on his head. She traced the bulges of muscles on his chest and shoulders, felt the silky softness of the hair in the hollows of his arms, then counted down the rippling muscles in his abdomen. She dipped her tongue into his navel and heard his harsh breathing.

"Virginia..."

"Don't you like this, Dillon?"

His words were low and guttural. "I don't think I've ever been so turned on."

She smiled and said, "Good," then nipped his erection through his jeans.

His hips lifted sharply, almost unseating her.

She nibbled on him, thrilled by his response. One hand crept lower, cradling him where he was softer, and his moans grew harsh.

In a rush, Virginia sat up and unsnapped his jeans. When she started on the zipper, he jerked his hips to the side. "Easy, baby. Slow."

Feeling how tight the material was around him, she understood the need for caution. Carefully, she eased the zipper downward, and his erection pushed free of the restriction. Heat enveloped her. His dark briefs weren't sufficient to contain him, and Virginia stood, turning her back to him and straddling one leg to tug off his boot and sock. She knew Dillon had propped himself on his elbows, that he watched her with hot eyes and a small smile. She didn't care.

Stumbling forward as the first boot came free, she steadied herself, then dropped the boot and straddled his other leg.

Dillon made a sound of approval. "I do love the view, honey."

She jerked hard and his boot slipped off. She dropped it, too, and turned to him, dusting off her hands. "Good. I love your whole body."

Fisting her hands in his jeans, she pulled them down. Dillon lifted his hips to help her. "I've never had a woman molest me before."

"I've never been kidnapped before."

His underwear came off next, and once she tossed the briefs with his jeans, he pulled his arms free of the shirt. Virginia would have reprimanded him for that, except she was too busy ogling his body. He was all hard bone and muscle and overwhelming masculinity. He lay there on the bed, propped on his elbows, watching her at his leisure.

"You going to chicken out?"

She shook her head, but couldn't find adequate words.

"It's all right, Virginia. I won't hurt you."

She didn't quite believe him. She'd had only two

lovers in her life, and neither of them had been built like him. How could he not hurt her?

"It doesn't matter." She sat on the side of the bed and wrapped one small hand around him. She couldn't circle him completely, and that fact made her heart race with mingled fear and excitement. He felt heavy and hot and incredibly hard.

He breathed heavily. "Take off your shirt, honey. If we're going to do this, let's do it right."

Virginia shook her head, then leaned forward. Her hair fanned out over his belly and thighs. Dillon groaned, his hands tangling tight in the quilt, his body rigid. When her lips slid over him, he shuddered and curled forward, one hand sliding down to her bottom, the other cupping the back of her head, guiding her. He pulled her shirt up so his hand could touch naked flesh, and when she sucked him, opening her mouth wide to fit him in, his fingers bit into her flesh.

"That's it." Dillon caught her up and tossed her backward on the bed. "I can't take it, Virginia. I've wanted you too long."

"You did it to me."

Despite his arousal, he grinned. "It's just a little different."

Tears welled in her eyes, no matter how she tried to hold them back. "Don't leave me, Dillon. Make love to me. Please."

Their eyes locked for a long instant in time. Dillon cursed low. "I have your laptop in my truck. I have discs from your personal investigator, along with a note that claims unwavering evidence. It'll end today, Virginia, one way or another. And then I'll have to go. Do you understand? I can't stay here. I…"

She opened her arms to him. "Then make love to me now, before it's too late. Let me have what time I can. Everything else will wait."

He hesitated only a moment more, then jerked her legs open and positioned himself between them. His mouth was everywhere at once, urgent and hot. He helped her get out of the shirt, then whispered, "Promise me you won't hate me."

"Never."

"Don't be afraid of me, either."

"I'm not." Virginia found it difficult to talk with his naked body covering hers, moving over her. She clutched at his hard shoulders, relishing the feel of him, his heat and his enticing scent that made her heady with need.

Dillon's mouth touched her cheek, and he spoke against her skin. "You'll take me, Virginia. It'll be a snug fit, so snug I'm liable to lose my mind, but I'll make sure you enjoy it."

She shuddered, lifting her hips into the rhythmic pressure of his; neither of them seemed capable of holding still. She didn't see how it would be possible, but she wanted to feel him inside her, all of him. "Do it now."

"Oh no. You're not ready. And no way in hell am I going to rush this." His hands were at her breasts, his thumbs teasing her nipples. "I have only one condom with me."

"I have a whole box." She spoke before she thought about it, and heard Dillon's laugh.

"A whole box, huh? You really did have some high expectations for me, didn't you?"

Her body ached. Her stomach quivered, and he

found the wit to joke? She pounded on his shoulders. "Dillon…"

"All right, baby." He snagged his jeans off the floor and retrieved the condom from his pocket. It was only late morning, but the cabin was still dim due to the cloudy day and the lack of windows. The firelight was mellow and golden, not bright. As Dillon opened the foil packet with his teeth, Virginia took the opportunity to touch him, to familiarize herself with his body. When she again leaned down to kiss him, mesmerized by his response to her mouth, he groaned and pushed her back on the bed.

"You're going to be the death of me, woman."

He slipped the condom on and came down over her. "Wrap your legs around me."

Nervously, anxiously, Virginia did as directed. Dillon kept his gaze glued to hers and hooked his arms beneath her legs, lifting them even higher. She felt open and vulnerable, and in a small part of her mind, she admitted she liked it. As he started to push into her, she winced, automatically tightening her body.

He crooned to her, keeping up the subtle pressure, the slow steady rocking of his hips. "Relax, sweetheart. Don't fight me."

She tipped her face back, not wanting him to see her discomfort. Her teeth sank into her bottom lip.

Dillon released one of her legs and reached down between their bodies. With the rough pad of his thumb, he stroked her. She jumped, startled. The feeling was too acute and she tried to shy away from it.

"Shh. I'll help you, honey. Just relax." He continued plying her most sensitive flesh, determined. "Lift your breast for me."

Virginia whimpered, already in an agony of sensation.

"Do it."

With shaking hands, she cupped one breast and offered it high. His mouth clamped onto her nipple and he drew gently. "Umm."

"I can't stand it," she said, her voice high and tight.

He licked, circled her nipple. "Yes, you can."

She felt him sink a little deeper into her body. The intrusion burned, but at the same time soothed. Her body seemed to be demanding conflicting things. There was an emptiness that she wanted him to fill, and the aching pressure of him doing just that. She wanted to pull back, but she also wanted to draw him nearer.

"Dillon…"

"Just a little more. Come on, Virginia. Open up for me. You can take all of me." His thumb pressed and manipulated and she cried out. "That's it. A little more."

Her heart raced, urged on by the gentle friction of his thumb, and she gave a broken moan, lifting herself to him, hearing him groan in return, and then he thrust hard and filled her.

She recoiled, shocked, but he held her hips, keeping her still, keeping himself buried deep inside her. His chest heaved against her.

It was too much; she felt stretched too tightly, felt him much too deeply. She hadn't imagined anything like this, lovemaking out of her control, both physically and mentally. She couldn't seem to draw a breath, couldn't move because he held her so close, pinned by his body.

Slowly, she became aware of other things, of the furious gallop of Dillon's heartbeat, the strain of his muscled body over her as he struggled to remain still, his harsh, deep breathing. God she loved him, and he was hurting as much as she.

Virginia smoothed her hands down his back and kissed his shoulder. After a shaky breath, she said, "I'm okay."

He laughed, a strained sound. "I know it. But I'll admit I'm glad you realize it. I don't know how much longer I could've waited."

When he began to thrust, slow and smooth, it both hurt and tantalized. He filled her, and each deep push dragged against her sensitive flesh as surely as his thumb had. She kept her arms around his neck, her legs tight around his hips, and held on, half-afraid to let go. Dillon tangled a hand in her hair and turned her face up to his, kissing her deeply, fusing their mouths as well as their bodies. Virginia felt the first stirrings of a climax gaining quickly on her, the sizzling heat began to swirl low in her belly. *"Dillon."*

He lifted her hips in his large hands and pulled her more snugly to his body, touching her so deeply she screamed. "Yes," he groaned. "Now, baby, please, now."

He shouted, his head thrown back, every muscle in his body taut and delineated, showing his incredible strength and the wonderful way he tempered it.

Virginia watched him through a haze of pleasure and tears, loving him, missing him already. As Dillon slowly lowered himself over her, she held him close, and their heartbeats mingled. Whatever else happened, she would never regret meeting this man. And she'd never love this way again.

HE WISHED SHE'D put on some clothes. Making love to Virginia three times in as many hours hadn't satisfied his need. He felt desperate to tie her to him, to take all of her that he could while he could. Fighting his growing need for her, biting back the words he wanted so badly to say, was keeping him on edge.

But Virginia, now that she'd decided they should be lovers, held nothing back. She kept touching him, tenderly, *lovingly,* in ways he'd never been touched before, and that would set him off. Even a simple touch to his back or shoulders held special meaning when her golden eyes were smiling at him. Especially since she still wore only his shirt, even forsaking the damn quilt. She'd look at him and her lips would tremble and he'd get a hard-on every time. He wanted to drown in her scent, and had tried to do just that until she'd cried and begged and threatened to kill him if he didn't take her. He'd placed one last kiss on the warm, sweet heat of her body and then thrust into her, giving her the release she needed.

Even in bed, she was a demanding, bossy woman. She pleased him more than any woman he'd ever known or could have imagined. Leaving her would be the hardest thing he'd ever done, but he had no choice.

After a hasty lunch of sandwiches, he'd set up all her computer equipment on the rickety table and she was in the process of reading the discs. Dillon couldn't have read them at work because he didn't have the necessary password to find the files, but he was looming over her shoulder, not willing to trust her a single inch. She typed in the words *You got it.*

"That's the password?"

She laughed. "Yeah. Every time I ask Troy to do something almost impossible with computers, he says—"

"You got it."

"Right." As she spoke, she sorted through files. "Troy is my inside guy. He helped me set up some stuff on the company's computer system."

"Stuff your brother knows nothing about."

Virginia grinned at him. "Yep. You see, each computer terminal is coded. So not only does the person using the computer have a user ID, but we can track who used which computer. According to Troy's note, it got complicated tracking the embezzler because—Ah, here we go."

She read a moment, Dillon peering over her shoulder, then suddenly she stiffened. Dillon read on a moment more before he began to snicker. "Ms. Johnson," he said with mock severity. "So you were the culprit all along."

Virginia didn't think it was funny. She turned to glare at Dillon. "That bastard used my ID!"

He kissed her mouth, then didn't want to stop kissing her. She clutched at his shirt. When he pulled back, she asked, "You don't really think—"

He kissed her again, quick and hard. "Of course not." He took her hand. "Honey, did you see which terminal was used?"

Virginia glanced back at the screen. "No, I…"

Dillon waited. "It's your brother, Virginia."

"Ridiculous. Cliff would have no inkling how to do anything this elaborate." She scanned the typed words, then frowned.

"But he would surely know your user ID and all the passwords. And it was the computer in his office."

Without responding, Virginia hit a button on the keyboard and backed up several pages. "Ha! That transaction took place during a week when Cliff was out of town."

Dillon stared thoughtfully at the screen. "You're certain?"

"I think I know what's going on in the company, thank you."

"Okay, so that only means he's working with someone, which is what I suspected all along. I had hoped, for your sake, that he wasn't involved, but it's the only thing that makes sense."

"And who would he work with?" As she spoke, she turned to face him, swiveling sideways in her chair. Seeing her naked legs and the shadow of her nipples through the T-shirt made reasoning very difficult.

Dillon knelt in front of her. "Honey, you have to realize you've collected a few enemies along the way."

"The employees respect me."

"I know that. But a lot of the management, especially the men, resent you. Don't you think it would be easy for Cliff to find a cohort if he chose to?"

"I suppose." Then she narrowed her eyes and crossed her arms under her breasts. "You told me yesterday you suspected someone. Cliff was it?"

Dillon chewed on the side of his mouth, debating what he should say to her, how he should say it. Virginia slapped a hand on the table. "Stop it! You promised to tell me everything, but now I can see you calculating! Just for once, be truthful with me."

He didn't like her tone or her attitude. Slowly, he straightened, glaring down at her. She glared right back. He didn't want to hurt her, but she did deserve the truth. Virginia, more than any woman he knew, could handle the truth. "I think it's possible Kelsey could be involved."

She sat frozen a moment, then chuckled. "Oh, Dillon, really. Kelsey is a child."

"A child having a child? She's pregnant, she's a little desperate and from what Wade tells me she resents the constant animosity in the family."

"And you're telling me she blames me alone? Cliff's as much at fault as I am."

"Unless Cliff has convinced her otherwise. Kelsey isn't like you, babe. She's wants to be a wife and mother, not a corporate leader."

Virginia turned her face away. "I want those things, too." She shrugged, looking suddenly small and defensive, and Dillon wanted to hold her, to carry her back to bed and try to keep the world at bay. But he knew he couldn't.

"I haven't been given a lot of choices in what I want to do with my life, Dillon. The company is all I've had."

He shoved his hands deep into his jeans pockets. "Are you saying you'd give it up? That you'd walk away from it to be a wife, to have babies?"

He watched her hands curl into fists on the table, watched her shoulders stiffen. "Why couldn't a woman have both? This is a new era. A huge percentage of women work and have families."

Dillon felt the last of a small dream die away. Virginia would never leave her family's company, and he had to take care of his father in Mexico. There was no future for them, and never had been. He'd known that from the first. He'd warned himself time and again that touching her would be a mistake. It had been nothing but foolish romanticism making him wonder if whatever she felt for him could ever be more.

Dillon pulled out the chair opposite her and straddled it. Virginia wouldn't quite meet his gaze. "I see no reason you couldn't have both, honey. If any woman could pull it off, you could. I wish you all the best, you know."

Virginia sighed. Her eyes were shiny with tears, but he pretended not to see, knowing how badly she'd hate the sign of vulnerability. She propped her head on her hand and sent him a small, shaky smile.

"I wish you the same."

They stared at each other until Dillon cleared his throat. "Well, unfortunately, the embezzlement is only part of our problem. There really was a physical threat to you. Someone got into your house using a key, and since I was with you, we'll never know what might have happened. But someone also tampered with your brake lines, and that intent can't be misconstrued. They knew what you'd be driving into, that you could have been killed. Think about it. Who would gain if you got hurt or lost your standing in the company, other than Cliff. And Lord knows that man resents your intrusion."

"I'm not intruding! I have every bit as much right to be involved as he does."

"I believe you, but does Kelsey? Does she think you might be stepping on some toes, angering her brother and in effect causing family problems?"

"You're suggesting that my family—*my brother and sister*—would deliberately do me harm."

He hated the way she looked, that obstinate set of her shoulders that told him how much he'd wounded her. He took her hand and held tight when she would have pulled away. "I just don't know, Virginia. Before today, I would have said yes, that Cliff was more than capable of such a thing."

"What happened today? Did Cliff suddenly grow a halo?"

"No. When Laura told Cliff you hadn't shown up for work, he all but panicked. He looked more concerned than I've ever seen him. In fact, I'm supposed to be looking for you right now."

"Is that right? Working a side job for Cliff?"

He started to tell her about his side job, that Cliff had hired him to keep tabs on her, but saw no point in it. She was hurting enough. "As soon as we finish reading through the results of your investigation, I can take you back, and Cliff will no doubt welcome you with open arms."

She made a face. "Don't push the bounds of reality, Dillon. If Cliff wants me kept safe, it's because he knows he can't run the company without me, regardless of the fuss he makes sometimes. That in itself proves he couldn't be the embezzler. But I suddenly have an idea who it might be."

Dillon waited, but Virginia only shook her head. "Let's finish seeing what Troy turned up, and then we'll know."

They pulled their chairs together and continued reading the data entered in an organized way. Each case of missing money was noted, and which terminal had been used, plus the user's ID. Several of the initial thefts had been done using Wade's password. After that, things got sketchy. Small amounts were removed using Cliff's ID, Virginia's and several others. They were all taken from the same terminal. Dillon narrowed his eyes as he came to the same conclusion as Virginia.

"The necessary info could have been stolen from Cliff. Only the people with highest security clearance would have had access to all those codes."

Virginia nodded. "I keep my important files locked up, but Cliff isn't nearly as responsible. It's possible that someone with access to his office could have found the codes, without knowing that the terminals were also monitored."

"Laura Neil." Dillon stared at Virginia as so many things started to take shape in his mind. "It makes sense. The original thefts were blamed on Wade, and he used to be involved with her before he met Kelsey."

"And Cliff got her on the rebound. I hate to say it, but he hasn't treated her well. She knows that we argued about her, that I tried to convince Cliff to have her transferred if he was going to become involved with her. But he refused and I let it go. Now it appears their affair is over, but she's in the awkward position of still being his secretary."

Dillon leaned back in the chair and rubbed his eyes. "I felt sorry for her today, Cliff was so indifferent to her. She acts like she's still very hung up on him."

"'Acts' being the operative word. It wouldn't do for her to show she despised him. If that happened, she might get fired, and that would put an end to her skimming money."

"Damn, I can't believe I overlooked her. She just seemed so…pathetic."

Virginia made a rude sound. "Face it. You overlooked her because she's female and you wanted to blame Cliff."

With a raised brow, Dillon admitted, "That, too."

"We have to get out of here. I need a phone so I can

call Troy. He can put a personal audit on Laura. We should be able to figure out if the money has shown up in her accounts. Plus he knows her. Any fancy new cars or expensive vacations might prove interesting."

"Troy can access her accounts?"

"He's a top-notch hacker, which is the main reason I keep him around and pay him a damn good wage. I want him working for me, not against me."

Virginia stood, then looked at Dillon expectantly. "I'll need my clothes."

Once again, his gaze skimmed her body; he relished the sight of her, the lush curves and feminine roundness. "Not yet. I have a cellular in the truck. Let me get it and you can call Troy from here."

"Why not just go back to my place and call?"

With his hands on her shoulders, Dillon bent low to give her a direct look. "Because someone wanted to hurt you, which you seem to keep forgetting. I'm not taking any chances with your safety. Once I find out if it really was Laura, then we can contact the police and go from there."

He could tell Virginia wanted to argue, but he ignored her protests and went out to the truck. She could make her calls, but there was no way he would let her put herself at risk. He might not always be around to protect her, to cushion her from the world and her own prickly pride, but he was here now, and he wanted her to know how important she was to him. He couldn't tell her, but he could try to show her.

VIRGINIA HUNG UP the phone. It was nearing six o'clock and Troy had been diligently applying his computer expertise for the past several hours. She turned to Dillon, feeling equally relieved and sad. They had the information they needed, and that was a relief, but it also meant their time alone was over. Dillon would take her from the cabin and the real world would intrude. She felt the loss like a physical blow.

"What did he find out?"

Virginia had been jotting down all Troy said, and now she flipped the piece of paper toward Dillon. "Laura had enough of the deposits in her accounts, in the same amounts as the missing funds, to prove her guilt. Stupid, really, but I suppose she thought the amounts were small enough not to matter. I mean, a couple of hundred here and there is really not all that noticeable when taken from so many different sources. Troy said she also has her house for sale."

"The amounts might have been small, but they really added up." Dillon stood and stretched his shoulders. "I guess that cinches it."

"If it's okay with you, I'd like to go by the office and get all the files on this together. We can notify the police in the morning from my house."

She watched him, hoping he wouldn't argue. They should probably move tonight, but she was so tired, and she hoped to have one more night alone with Dillon. His sad smile showed he had the same thought. Though they'd made love for hours while waiting for news, it hadn't been enough. Virginia didn't think a lifetime would be enough, but every day was precious.

"Tomorrow is fine," he told her softly.

He stepped close and kissed her, holding her face between his large warm hands and lingering until she thought she might beg him to stay at the cabin with her. But she knew that couldn't be. According to Dillon, Cliff was worried, and she could only imagine how relieved Wade would be to know he was in the clear. Those people deserved to be told as soon as possible.

Dillon brought Virginia's clothes in from the truck and laid them by the fire to warm while she showered. A half hour later, they were on the way home.

CHAPTER TWELVE

DILLON KNEW SOMETHING was wrong the second the elevator opened onto the floor. He couldn't exactly explain his unease to Virginia, because it wasn't anything concrete, just a gut reaction that told him she was in danger.

She'd been holding his hand since they left the truck. No woman had ever held his hand, not even when he was a kid. He never had a mother, and the endless string of women his father had brought around weren't interested in a little boy. The gesture now seemed sweet and almost protective. He didn't want her to let go. But he had to keep her safe.

"I want you to wait downstairs with the night-shift guard."

Virginia raised her brows. "Why? Cliff is surely gone for the night, so you won't get a chance to confront him, if that was your thought."

She was too astute for own damn good. "I would have done that. In fact, I'd like to break his damn nose. But right now I have other concerns." He hesitated a moment, then admitted, "Something doesn't feel right."

Smiling, Virginia tugged on his hand and started him down the hallway to Cliff's office. "Let me guess. You expect to find Laura Neil brandishing a bazooka and threatening the masses?"

Dillon pulled her up short and shoved her behind him, staring down the dim hallway. "Now who's underestimating a woman?" He nodded toward Cliff's office and they both saw that a light was on, shining dully through the etched window in the door. The entire floor should have been shut down and locked for the night.

Virginia stared. "Well, hell. What is that brother of mine up to now?"

"Shh. Not another word out of you or I'll lock you in a closet." When she started to protest, he said, "I mean it, Virginia. I have the keys in my pocket, so don't test me."

Luckily for his peace of mind, she didn't argue. Dillon pressed her down on the floor, in the shadows of a large decorative plant. "Stay here. I'm going to see what's going on." He narrowed his gaze on her. "Don't move."

Glaring, Virginia gave him a mock salute. He answered by kissing her. "I couldn't stand it if anything happened to you, honey." As he crept away, he could feel Virginia's eyes on his back.

The door to Cliff's outer office opened silently. Dillon peered in, saw the inner office was the one brightly lit and slid through the doorway. As he moved along the wall, nearing the inside door, he could hear the muffled tones of people speaking. Rather than burst in, he took his time, listening and assessing the situation.

It didn't take long to figure out that Laura had already guessed her game was over. Cliff feebly tried to claim he loved her, gaining even more of Dillon's disdain, but Laura only laughed. Her voice overrode Cliff's panicked one.

"You always were a sniveling bastard, Cliff. You deserve anything I do to you."

"I thought you cared about me."

Her words took on a hard edge. "Yes, maybe at first. When Wade dropped me, I was content to set him up, to make him pay. You'd fired him, and that was enough punishment. But your sister insisted on investigating everything. She wanted to ruin all my plans, including my plans for you."

"Virginia had nothing to do with me and you."

"You're so naive, Cliff. You pretended to care about me, and I stupidly thought you'd marry me. I knew the only hindrance would be Virginia. She'd go to any lengths to protect this damn company, and that means she'd keep digging about the missing money until she finally caught up to me."

"You did something to her?"

There was indifference in Laura's tone. "I didn't really intend to hurt her, just distract her from the investigation. I figured if she had to worry about her own life, she wouldn't have time to stick her nose into the business."

Dillon heard Cliff clear his throat. He could almost taste the man's fear and assumed Laura had a gun trained on him. Cliff's voice shook when he spoke.

"But then I lost interest in you, so that changed everything?"

"Not really. I'd already realized that even if you married me, it wouldn't have mattered. Eventually Virginia would have succeeded in totally discrediting you. She's the ruling factor in this company, not you. So I decided to take one more hefty sum and get out. It was stupid of you to show up here tonight, Cliff."

“I was worried about my sister, damn you.”

“Hmm. And that surprises me. I thought the two of you hated each other. Or were you worried because you know without Virginia, you’d fail completely?”

For the first time, Cliff sounded angry. “*Bitch.* She’s my sister, and regardless of our differences, I love her. This damn company has nothing to do with it.”

Dillon sensed Virginia’s presence even before she touched his arm. He turned. She stood in the darkness right behind him, tears glimmering in her eyes. He wanted to curse, wanted to throttle her and lock her away someplace safe, but he couldn’t do a damn thing. Any noise at all would distract Laura, and after Cliff’s melodramatic confession, he really didn’t want to see the man shot.

Dillon raised a finger to his lips as Laura again spoke.

“I do wonder where your errant sister is.”

“If you’ve hurt her, Laura, I’ll kill you.”

That caused a burst of hilarity. “I’m the one with the gun, Cliff. And believe me, I wouldn’t mind putting a bullet through your cold heart. But first, finish transferring the funds as I told you. We’ve done enough talking.”

There was the almost silent pecking of the keyboard, and then Cliff said wearily, “It’s done.”

“Excellent. Now, stand up and come over here.”

“You can’t shoot me in the office, Laura. The night guards would hear. And you know, since hiring the new security manager, the men working are more than capable.”

“Shut up while I think.”

"You know why I grew tired of you so quickly, Laura?"

"Shut up."

"Probably the same reason Sanders did. You play the role of lapdog to perfection. You can complain about my sister all you like, but at least she's an intelligent woman. She provides conversation and wit, not just babbling."

"Shut up, damn you!"

"All I got from you was blind adoration, and at times it almost made me sick."

Laura lost her temper, screeching in rage, and that's when Dillon threw open the door. Laura whirled, getting off a wild shot that missed Dillon as he rolled across the floor. Cliff ran to the outer office, almost knocking Virginia down as she stuck her head in the doorway. Dillon effectively tackled Laura, gripping her wrist and squeezing until she dropped the gun. Virginia, much to his dismay, ran in and picked up the weapon. Laura still fought him, scratching his neck and the side of his face, kicking her long legs wildly.

When Virginia realized Dillon planned to do no more than hold her, regardless of how she injured him, she knelt by Laura's head and whispered, "Put one more mark on him, and you'll have me to deal with."

There was enough venom in her tone to make Laura go completely still. Dillon grinned at Virginia, then came to his feet, holding Laura's wrists in one hand.

Security guards rushed in, guns drawn, and they took control of Laura. Dillon removed the automatic weapon from Virginia's hand, giving her a chiding glance. "You were supposed to stay in the hall, safe."

Before she could answer, Cliff began a hysterical

recitation of the events. Dillon listened with half an ear, most of his attention on Virginia, who looked pale. The guards handcuffed Laura and led her to the outer office. The police had been called and would arrive shortly.

"It's really over, isn't it?"

Huge tears welled in her eyes and Dillon had difficulty swallowing. "Don't do this, baby. You're killing me."

"I love you, you know."

He closed his eyes, drawing a shuddering breath. "I have to leave now. My father's waiting for me in Mexico. Nothing will change that."

Cliff sidled up to them and clamped a hand on Virginia's arm. "Oh, this is rich. I'm here, almost getting shot, and you've obviously been off whooping it up with an employee!"

Dillon gave Virginia an apologetic look, his eyes never leaving her face, and with his left hand, socked Cliff right in the nose. The smaller man went down like a stone.

His hand, no longer fisted, cupped her face. "If you ever need me, honey, just let me know."

Her expression changed, became almost desperate. "No, you can't leave now. I won't allow it."

Her panic twisted his insides. "It's better if I don't get tangled up with the police. You can handle things."

Cliff writhed on the floor next to them, holding his bloody nose and cursing.

"Dillon—"

He leaned forward and kissed her, a kiss of tenderness and regret. "I love you, Virginia." The tears spilled over and he groaned in genuine agony. "Shh.

God, don't cry, Virginia. If I could change things, I swear I would."

Her chin lifted. "I'm glad you kidnapped me."

He managed a smile at her false bravado. "I have a feeling it'll always be my fondest memory." He touched her cheek one more time, then turned to go. As he passed through the outer doorway, he heard Virginia bark, "Oh, come on, Cliff, get up. We have to take care of this mess."

Dillon smiled. She would be okay. She didn't need him. The truth was, he needed her. She'd filled him up, made him whole and gave credence to his beliefs about life and love and reality. His gut cramped painfully, more so with every step he took, and he decided he might as well get used to the feeling. Because he knew that for the rest of his life, he would feel empty.

He figured it was no more than he deserved.

A month later—

"WADE SAYS HE GOT a hefty promotion, along with a bonus."

Dill Sr. laughed. "A little retribution to ease the guilt?"

"I suppose. Virginia was responsible for the promotion. Cliff, believe it or not, provided the bonus as a wedding present, and from what Wade said, it was a large one."

"Good for him. Doesn't hurt to start off a marriage financially sound. True love will take you only so far."

Dillon stared at his coffee for long moments, lost in thought, then finally tipped the cup to his mouth and took a large gulp. The bitter taste suited him just fine on this hot, dusty morning. He put Wade's letter aside.

Staring at his father, seeing a glimmer of amusement in the dark eyes so like his own, he said, "Virginia is handing over a lot of the control to Cliff. According to Wade, Cliff's learned his lesson."

"So why the long face, then? You know, I'm getting damn tired of watching you brood."

His father grinned when he said it, had been grinning since the moment Dillon walked back in from his week-long buying trip a few hours earlier. "I'm not brooding. There's just something I don't understand." He ignored the toast his father pushed toward him and concentrated on his coffee, instead. "According to Wade, resolving the problems in the company has brought Virginia and her family closer together. Virginia even offered to sell out to Cliff, but he wouldn't take her offer. He says he needs her guidance and input until he learns how to run things on his own. Kelsey has gotten involved, too, along with Wade, so they're lending a helping hand."

"Sounds like a real family-run organization."

"I suppose. But I can't see Virginia offering to sell out. That company means too much to her. It's her whole life. I'm afraid something's not right."

"You're just afraid you made a damn fool mistake, that's all. I keep telling you, you should go back for her. You find a woman like that, you don't just let her go."

Dillon had heard it endless times. For weeks, his father had picked his brain for every detail. Dillon hadn't admitted to loving Virginia, fearing his father would suffer guilt, rightfully assuming that Dillon stayed only because his father needed him.

"Tell me again what she looks like."

"Dad..." Talking about Virginia, remembering, hurt like hell.

"Long red hair, right? Round in all the right places."

"Yeah." Dillon grinned despite himself. "And soft and sexy, but so mule-headed she scares most men away."

"Humph. Not my son."

Dillon grunted at his father's misplaced pride. "She's strong. And a fighter."

"A woman like that'd make a damn good wife and mother."

Thinking of Virginia that way tormented Dillon. He could so easily see her with a baby in her arms and a corporate report on her desk. She'd make beautiful babies, with tempers as fiery as her own. And between the two of them, their children would never feel alone or afraid.

But it wouldn't happen. Dillon had told her that if she ever needed him to let him know. She could easily have gotten his address from Wade, but he hadn't heard from her. She'd gotten on with her life, just as he'd told her to do, but the reminder of what he'd lost ate at him day in and day out.

He finished off his coffee and shoved back his chair. "I have a fence to repair today and the vet's coming to check over the new mares I bought. I gotta get out of here."

As Dillon started to stand, his head swam. He sank back into his seat, cursing. His father grinned.

Dillon couldn't get sick now, because that would give him too much free time to think about Virginia. Since returning to the ranch, he'd filled his days with the hardest physical labor, working from sunrise to sundown. His nights were the worst; he filled them with endless paperwork and expansion plans. None of it helped. Virginia was never far from his thoughts.

He looked at his father, but his face wouldn't come into focus. "What the hell is going on?"

He heard a door open and Virginia stepped into the kitchen. Dillon blinked, not sure he was seeing right, wondering if he'd only imagined her because he missed her so damn bad. He lifted a heavy hand toward her and she dropped to her knees by his chair. "I love you, Dillon."

"God." He must be dreaming. "You can't be here."

"Oh, I'm here all right. It's payback time. You told me to let you know if I needed you. Well, I do. But I need you forever, not just for a little while. You didn't come to me, so I'm taking you."

He could feel himself fading. "What did you do?"

"I drugged your coffee."

And his father, through his chuckles said, "Damn, but she learned from a master, didn't she?"

As Dillon started to slump, Dill Sr. called out, "Come and give the lady a hand, boys. My son is no lightweight."

Virginia, a touch of worry in her tone, said, "Thank you, sir, I wouldn't want him to get hurt."

"Call me Dad. We're going to be related, after all."

And Dillon smiled groggily.

DILLON AWOKE NAKED. He opened his eyes slowly, looking around. He felt silk sheets beneath him, nothing over him. At least he'd had the decency to leave Virginia in her lingerie, providing her a bit of modesty.

He'd even covered her with a quilt. Of course, Virginia wouldn't show such consideration, the witch. He chuckled.

This...*palace* was nothing compared with the cabin he'd taken her to. There was champagne chilling in a bucket of ice beside the bed and a gas fireplace blazed brightly. He started to sit up, and that's when he realized his hands were tied. He looked over his shoulder. A soft, woven velvet rope was knotted around his wrists and then looped through a scrolled newel post on the back of the bed. His body stirred, his loins tightened.

Virginia opened a door and walked in, her bare feet sinking into the thick carpet. "You're awake!"

He tugged on the ropes, working up a believable frown. He didn't want to spoil her fun. "Was this necessary?"

Perching on the side of the bed by his hip, she surveyed his naked body. Her gaze lingering on his erection. "What have you been thinking about, Dillon?"

"About making love to you right now."

Her eyes brightened and her cheeks flushed. "Yes, well... I do believe we have a few things to get straight first."

"Take off your robe."

She made an exasperated face at him. "Really, Dillon. I'm the one in charge right now. That's why you're tied down. You have a tendency to run roughshod over me."

"You like it. Now, take off the robe."

She hesitated a moment, then shrugged. "Suit yourself." The gold satin robe slid down her shoulders to pool at her hips. She stood, then pushed it aside. Dillon stared at her lush body. "I missed you something terrible, baby."

She lay down beside him, one hand resting on his taut stomach, her head on his chest. "Not as bad as I missed you. Every day, I wanted to call you, to insist you come back to me. But you were so final when you left, and it...it hurt too much to think you might turn me away again."

"I never did that, honey."

"I know. Wade told me that you'd never leave your father. He said he thought you wanted to be with me, but that your loyalty would keep you in Mexico."

Dillon kissed the top of her head, carefully testing the strength of his restraints. He didn't know how much longer he'd be able to wait and let her lead the way. "I knew you wouldn't leave the company, and I couldn't leave Dad. I'm all he has, Virginia."

"I understand. But the company doesn't mean that much to me. I thought it did, because it was all I had. But then I had you, and I knew nothing else mattered as much."

"You offered to sell your share of the company to Cliff so you could come back to Mexico with me."

She surprised him by leaning up and shaking her head. "No. I can't see me living in Mexico *and,*" she said when he started to object, her expression stern, "you will let me finish. I'm not good at roughing it, Dillon."

He glanced around at his surroundings. "So I can see."

"Well, I'm sorry, but being chased by huge nasty spiders and having my feet freeze aren't memorable moments."

He narrowed his eyes. "And what about the rest of it?"

"The stuff women dream of."

He grinned.

"Kelsey will give birth in a few months, and Cliff still needs me to guide him, at least until he catches on a little better. I'm going to be a consultant for him."

"I see."

"Living in Mexico would really complicate things, put me too far out of reach."

Dillon fought back his rising anger. "You're not leaving me again, Virginia, so you can forget it."

She kissed him, long and deep, her body moving over his, her hands exploring. Finally she lifted her head, and Dillon felt sharp frustration.

"Your father and I have it all worked out."

He groaned. "You've been plotting with my father?"

"We talked quite a bit while you were out of town. He wants to live with his housekeeper."

"With Maria?" Dillon couldn't quite take it in. Maria was a wonderful person, ten years younger than his father, and not at all his type.

Virginia laughed. "They're in love. They want to get a small house and take care of each other. I thought we'd hire someone to check up on them twice weekly, just to make certain they're doing okay." Her brows drew together in a frown. "As big and powerful as your father seems, he's still old enough to need a little help, I think."

Dillon chuckled. His father was six feet two inches tall, weighed almost as much as Dillon and still had a commanding air about him. "Lately he's had a few health problems, but he doesn't like to admit it. Come to think of it, Maria is the only one he lets pamper him. Now I know why."

Virginia toyed with the hair on Dillon's chest, not quite meeting his eyes. "Don't get mad, okay?"

He stilled. "What did you do?"

"I bought a ranch." She spoke quickly, giving away her uncharacteristic nervousness. "It's a little bigger than the one you have in Mexico— Damn it, Dillon, stop shaking your head at me! It's not like it's a bribe or anything. Once you sell your ranch, you can pay me half on it, okay?"

"No, it's not okay." He tugged at his restraints, but stilled when she huffed out a curse.

She sat up, her legs astride his hips, her arms crossed under her bare breasts. "This is why I tied you down! You're so damn stubborn!"

He choked on that, distracted from the enticing view of her body. "Me? You think *I'm* stubborn?"

"Yes! I love you. I want us to be together. I'm willing to let Cliff run the company now, but I can't let him ruin it, and I can't just sit idle. So I'm starting my own business. The ranch and the business property I just bought are in the States, not that far from your father, but closer to my family so I can check up on Cliff and we can visit with Wade and Kelsey and the baby when it gets here."

"Virginia—"

"You'll love the area, Dillon, I promise. It's in New Mexico, due north of Albuquerque, and the ranch house is huge and the land is beautiful and the people who owned it raised horses but then they had to sell and… well, it's perfect…for us."

Dillon dropped his head back and laughed. She could make him nuts with her take-charge attitude, but he'd missed her so much. "All right. I'll look at the ranch. But I'm paying you back for all of it. I'm not going to live off your money, Virginia." He didn't want her ever to wonder at his motives, not when so many men had tried to use her.

She snorted. "Then I won't live off yours, so if you won't let me pay half for the ranch, I can't live there. I guess that leaves us at an impasse."

Quietly, he studied her rigid posture and mutinous expression. He knew she felt free to be so bossy, given that he was tied down. He decided to put an end to that before things got out of hand. They might as well start things off right. "Honey, move for a minute."

She looked hurt first, then angry, as she scuttled off his abdomen to stand beside the bed. Dillon laced his fingers together tightly, flexed his arms and broke the small spindle off the back of the bed. Virginia stood there, her eyes wide, and gaped at him as he loosened the rope and tossed it aside. He turned to her with a narrowed gaze. "Now."

She launched herself at him, knocking him back on the bed and sprawling over him. Her hands tangled in his hair and she held his face still while she kissed him all over, his nose, his chin, his eyes. "I love you, Dillon. Please, say you'll marry me. Let's have babies and a home and grow old together."

He locked his arms around her and rolled her beneath him. She was so beautiful to him, so determined and gutsy and proud. Her hair fanned out over the pillows, wild and tangled and as fiery as the hot temper he adored. Her cheeks were flushed, but her golden eyes seemed filled with doubt, and he wouldn't allow it. He didn't like her being humble, not when she had arrogance and bravado down to a fine art. "I love you," he growled, tightening his hold. "One way or another, I'm never letting you go, so you might as well get used to it."

She grinned as he kissed her, tears seeping from her eyes. When Dillon lifted his head, he said, "Everything will work out, Virginia. I really do love you."

"I love you, too." She spoke softly, almost shyly, peeking up at him. "And I adore your father. He made me promise we'd have some babies right off." Her gaze flicked up to his face, then away again.

Dillon kissed her nose. "I'm willing."

"I told him if he got rid of that horrid tattoo of a naked lady on his arm, he could be a surrogate grandfather to Kelsey's baby, too."

Astonished and momentarily distracted from his need, Dillon croaked, "You're kidding, right?" When she just blinked up at him, he said, "You tried telling my father what to do?"

She snorted. "I didn't try. I told him. He can't possibly be around children with that...*thing* on his arm. It's obscene." She shuddered. "Do you know where he got that? He told me the most outrageous story—"

Dillon kissed her quiet, the love inside him almost more than he could bear. She was incredible. No wonder his father was so anxious to see him married to Virginia. He couldn't think of another woman who'd ever dared to try to boss his father. More than anything, Dill Sr. respected courage, and Virginia had that in spades.

He'd also loved being a father, despite his claims of incompetence. Dillon had no doubt his father would make an excellent grandpa, but he was pleased to let his dad begin with Wade's baby. He could start all over again with the lectures on family bonds and loyalty, and this time, he'd have Dillon and Virginia to help him.

Dillon decided he'd make a show of sizing up the ranch, just to keep Virginia from getting the upper hand. But in truth, he didn't care two cents for where he lived, as long as she lived there with him. Having her for a wife, having children with her, sounded as close to perfection as he was ever likely to get.

Then Virginia moaned softly for him, accepting him as he slowly joined his body to hers, and he knew he'd already reached perfection. She was a bossy little woman, but she was his, and it couldn't get any better than that.

* * * * *

Books by Tawny Weber

Harlequin Blaze

Nice & Naughty
Midnight Special
Naughty Christmas Nights

Uniformly Hot!

A SEAL's Seduction
A SEAL's Surrender
A SEAL's Salvation
A SEAL's Kiss
A SEAL's Fantasy
Christmas with a SEAL
A SEAL's Secret
A SEAL's Pleasure
A SEAL's Temptation
A SEAL's Touch
A SEAL's Desire

Cosmopolitan Red-Hot Reads from Harlequin

Fearless

And don't miss
Call to Honor
coming soon from HQN Books

A SEAL'S SEDUCTION

Tawny Weber

Thank you to all of the men and women
who serve their country.
You are amazing heroes.

CHAPTER ONE

And they who for their country die shall fill an honored grave, for glory lights the soldier's tomb, and beauty weeps the brave...

—Joseph Drake

A LOUD BLAST FILLED the air as seven guns exploded in succession. Once, twice, thrice. Twenty-one shots. Faces implacable, the honor guard shouldered their guns and stood as tall and rigid as the oaks lining the cemetery.

The echoing silence broke when the bugler sounded taps. Lieutenant Blake Landon stood at attention, his eyes narrowed against the bright morning sun. The chaplain's words of honor, bravery and sacrifice rolled over him like the gentle breeze, teasing, hinting but not really making an impact.

There was no mention of Phil's sense of humor, of how he always carried a rubber snake on missions to break the tension. That he'd hit a McDonald's the minute they were stateside for a bagful of French fries. The chaplain didn't know that before jumping from a plane, Phil always kissed his mother's picture, then rubbed a rabbit foot. He wouldn't mention Phil's love for the beach. It didn't matter how godforsaken hot their assignment might have been, the minute he was off duty, he'd hit the beach—sun, surf and girls in bikinis. He'd often said those were his reward for getting shot at on a regular basis.

But that wasn't the Phil they were honoring right now.

Here, at Arlington National Cemetery, Lieutenant Phil Hawkins was a soldier. Here, the sacred tradition of honoring the noble warrior focused on service, dedication and sacrifice to country.

The entire SEAL platoon in attendance, Blake stood shoulder to shoulder with his team. His squadmates. The men he served with, fought with, trained with. Prepared to offer up the ultimate sacrifice for their country.

Later tonight, they'd all celebrate Phil, the man. Their squadmate, buddy, friend. The Joker.

He clenched his jaw, his eyes glancing off the flag-draped casket, then shifting to the distant trees again when the captain began the ritual of folding the red, white and blue material. As the chaplain offered his final words of comfort, the captain gently placed the folded flag into Mrs. Hawkins's hands.

Blake's focus locked on that triangle of fabric and didn't waver as the funeral finished. The people around him moved, shifted, left. He didn't. He couldn't.

They'd gone through BUDS training together. He, Phil and Cade. All cocky as hell, all determined to push their limits, to be superheroes. The Three Amigos, the rest of the team had called them. Inseparable.

Now permanently separated.

A large, beefy man joined him, scattering his thoughts. Grateful for the distraction, Blake directed his attention to the admiral. His hair as white and gleaming as his uniform, the older man topped Blake's own six feet by at least two inches.

"Lieutenant," Admiral Pierce greeted quietly. "I know this is a hard loss for you and your team. You have my sympathies."

"Thank you, sir," Blake said, his words stiff as he watched Phil's mom softly smooth her fingers over the folded flag, as if running her fingers over her son's cheek. Blake cringed when she lost it, her slender shoulders shaking as she sobbed into the triangle.

Desperate for distance, he ripped his gaze away. He looked at the trees. Oaks, mighty and strong, stood tall. Symbolic, probably. But he was having trouble finding solace.

"It never gets easier," the admiral said.

"Should it?" Blake asked, looking at the older man. His superior. His trainer. His mentor.

"No." The admiral glanced over at the trees. He sighed, then looked at Blake again. "No. But it's something you'll revisit. One way or another. Make sure you don't let it get in your way."

Just like that? Blake wanted to protest. To call bullshit on it being that easy to simply push the loss of his comrade, his friend, aside. But years of training, the respect he had for the man who'd recruited him to the SEALs, eliminated that thought almost before it formed. Instead, he inclined his head to indicate he'd handle it.

Clearly expecting exactly that, the admiral nodded. Then he cast an assessing glance around the graveside.

"Lieutenant Commander," the admiral called, his words carrying over the gentle grasses and soft murmur of the milling crowd.

Cade Sullivan, Blake's team commander and the third amigo, subtly came to attention. With a quiet word and a brush of his hand over Mrs. Hawkins's shoulder, he turned and strode across the lawn.

"Sir?"

"I'm assigning your men leave."

Blake and Cade exchanged looks. All it took was two seconds, a slight furrow of the brow and a shift of their shoulders to know both men were in perfect accord. They didn't want to go on leave.

"Sir?"

"Two weeks R&R, effective immediately."

For the second time since joining the navy—and both in the space of the last few minutes—Blake wanted to protest an order. He didn't want time off. He needed distraction. Work. A mission. Preferably one that included blowing up large buildings and letting loose vast amounts of ammo.

Fury was like a storm, brewing and stewing inside him.

It needed an outlet. The shooting range would work. Or the base gym.

As if reading his thoughts, the admiral inclined his head, offered a stern look and added, "You've just finished a tense mission, and lost one of your own. I hope you have places off base to stay, as I'll be leaving word at the gate that you're on inactive duty until September seventeenth."

For a second, Cade's usual charming facade cracked, the same anger Blake was dealing with showing in the other man's vivid green eyes. In an instant, it disappeared, and his smile—the one that lulled friend and foe alike into thinking he was a nice guy—flashed.

"Looks like it's time for a trip home. My father will be thrilled. Thank you, sir. I'm sure the team will be excited about the R&R."

You had to admire Cade's talent for lying. The man had a way with sincerity that, when added to that smile, was pure gold. At least it was if you weren't the one he was conning. The truth was, the team was going to be pissed, Cade hated visiting home and his father hated having him there. Yet the guy still smiled as if he'd just been pinned with the Congressional Medal of Honor.

That's why Phil had always called Cade Slick. Blake was Boy Scout. By the book, a goody-goody, his whole life was focused on being prepared. On being the best SEAL he could be. And Phil? He'd been the Joker. The last thing he'd said before that bomb had blown him in two? Knock knock.

Knock knock.

Jaw clenched, Blake glared at the sleek black lines of the casket.

Cade excused himself to inform the other men of their spiffy little vacation, leaving Blake and the admiral standing alone. The rest of the mourners were dispersing, civilians leaning against each other, shoulders low as they made their way across the lawn.

"Landon?" the admiral prodded. As if there was any option. Cade, like the admiral, was Blake's superior. He'd accepted the order, so it was a done deal.

"I'm sure I can find something to do," he said quietly. Not go home. He was less welcome in the trailer park he'd been raised in than Cade was at his big fancy mansion.

The guys were meeting later at JR's, the local bar and dance club Phil had favored. After that, Blake would go back to California. Drive up the coast, check out Alcatraz, the Golden Gate. Anything.

"I'll see you on the fifteenth."

Blake frowned. "I thought we were ordered off base until the seventeenth."

Had he misunderstood? Hell, it was only two days, but he'd take them.

"My retirement party. I expect you there. You can meet my daughter." With that, a stern smile and a clap to the shoulder that would have put a lesser man a foot into the ground, the admiral strode off.

Leaving Blake to contemplate those last words.

Meet the admiral's daughter?

Shit.

HOT. HOT. *HOT.*

There were a lot of things to be grateful for in life. Good friends. A healthy body. Chocolate-covered caramel.

All good.

But not nearly as good as the sight of a gorgeous, mostly undressed man. The kind of man who made a woman very aware of all her girlie parts.

The one striding along the water's edge was that kind of guy, Alexia Pierce's girlie parts assured her. Gorgeous, built and, since he seemed oblivious to the women he left panting in his wake, as humble as he was hot.

Tall, she'd bet his body lined up perfectly with her five-ten frame. Long legs ate up the sand as he strode toward the ocean, his deliciously broad shoulders straight, his flat belly framed by a tapered waist. He had that sleek, muscled look that said he could kick some ass, but didn't have the bodybuilder bulk that screamed mirror-whore.

Dark hair, a little too short for her taste, had just a hint of curl. She wrapped her finger around one of her own ringlets, figuring a guy who fought the wave would have a little sympathy when humid days made her look like a demented poodle. She couldn't see his eyes from this distance, but he had those dark, intense brows that made guys look ferociously sexy. Either blessed genetics or the summer sun had washed his body with a pale golden hue.

She wondered if he was just as golden beneath those summer-blue swim trunks. Was it too much to hope a big wave would help out in giving her a peek?

C'mon, waves.

The guy was a potent combination, guaranteed to make a strong, independent woman whimper with desire.

At least, in her own mind.

As she mentally whimpered, Alexia shaded her eyes against the bright arcs of sunlight reflecting off the Pacific and interfering with her view of the gorgeous specimen of manhood as he dived into the ocean.

She actually envied the water as it slid over that rock-hard body.

"Want a towel?"

"Hmm?" she murmured, absently taking the soft fabric that was handed to her. Frowning, she glanced at the red beach towel, then at her brother. "What's this for?"

"To wipe your chin."

"Goof." She laughed, tossing the towel back at him before sitting back on her beach chair, her toes digging into the warm sand. "That's sweat from the sun. I'm not used to it being this warm the second week of September."

Or, admittedly, to seeing a man sexy enough to make her sit up and drool.

"Right. It's the heat." Michael was a master at sarcasm, his words as dry as the sand beneath their feet. "Aren't you in a relationship?"

Even as Alexia waved that question away with a flick of her wrist, she yanked her gaze from the water. She didn't know why. Even if she were in a relationship, looking wasn't cheating. And at this point, she and Edward were just colleagues who'd dated a few times. Friends—without benefits. Buddies, even.

"Not so much in a relationship as considering one. Dancing around it, maybe," she admitted. More like trying to justify pushing herself into taking a handful of dates and a solid friendship and making them something more. Something bigger. Of course, she'd been trying to talk herself into it for three months now. If there was one thing Alexia was good at, it was talking. "I don't know what we are, to be honest."

Michael tilted his red sunglasses down to peer at her. His eyes were the same dark, depthless brown as her own, but he was blessed with thick lashes while she was stuck relying on volumizing mascara. It'd be so easy to hate him for that. "You moved across the country for a guy. That says relationship to me."

Alexia lifted her bottle of water and sipped, her eyes sliding back to the ocean. All she could see of the swimmer was the occasional elbow. Why did that turn her on so much more than the idea of seeing all of Edward, naked?

Which was the problem in a nutshell. She liked everything about Edward. The man was brilliant, one of the foremost scientists specializing in psychoacoustics. She'd studied under him for two years when he was in New York, before he'd moved to California to take over the Science Institute. They had a lot in common, enjoyed each other's company and always had a ton to talk about.

The only problem was, she wasn't sexually attracted to him. And she couldn't imagine a relationship without sex. Without heat. Excitement and orgasms and spontaneous wall-banging releases. Those were as high on her relationship list as honesty and communication.

"I moved across the country for a once-in-a-lifetime job. That says career to me," she said as she dug her bottle back into the sand. "This position is off-the-charts exciting. I'll be doing in-depth research into correcting and enhancing sexual recovery for abuse victims by means of subliminal messaging, neurolinguistic programming and brain-wave technology. And get to be the face of the Reclaiming Yourself project. I'll meet with investors, promote the project and make a difference in how it's perceived by the press."

"You're an acoustical physicist with a minor in psychology. How does that translate into PR shill?"

Alexia grimaced at her brother's irritated tone.

"Show a little more enthusiasm, why don't you," she said, swiping her towel at him. "It got me back to California, so you should be grateful. Investors want to talk to someone directly involved who is working on the project. I'm better at the social stuff than Edward is, and since the project focuses more on female sexuality, it's better to have a woman front and center."

"In other words, Dr. Darling isn't as good at talking sex as you are?"

Alexia grinned, but as the words sank in, her smile dimmed. Yeah. Edward was great at the science of sex. But talking about it? Doing it? She wasn't so sure.

"I'm just giving you a bad time. I really am excited that you're back home," Michael said, patting her shoulder. He gave her a cheeky look. "With you here, publicly talking sex all the time, the heat's going to be off me with the parents. So thank Dr. Darling for me, 'kay?"

Alexia's smile disappeared completely.

"They're going to have a fit, aren't they?" she murmured.

"Yep."

By the time she'd started third grade, Alexia had known three things. One, that she was much, much smarter than the average bear. Two, that she didn't quite fit in anywhere—not with kids her age, not with the agenda her parents lined up for her and not with what her child psychologist had deemed *society's norms.* And three, that her father would never love her. After a few years of exploiting the first while trying to hide the second, she'd finally realized that there was nothing she could do about the third. At thirteen, with a slew of academic awards, a couple of skipped grades and a social calendar filled with normal, acceptable, shoot-me-now-I'm-going-crazy boring activities, she'd done a tight one-eighty.

She'd stopped socializing and started failing classes. She'd turned to fatty food and sugar for comfort. She'd explored more ways to numb herself than she liked to remember. And to this day, she wasn't sure if her father had noticed any of that.

But he had noticed when, at sixteen, she'd been picked up by the base MPs, drunk and half-naked with an ensign thirteen years her senior. That'd been the second turning point in her short life. Her father's fury hadn't mattered. His blustering and disgust had barely dented her hangover. Seeing that, the admiral had proceeded to show her once and for all where she got her brains. In an ice-cold voice, he'd promised that the next time she stepped out of line, she'd be out of his house and no longer a part of the family. She'd shrugged, saying that she didn't care. He'd nodded, as if he'd expected exactly that response, before adding he'd then send Michael to boarding school overseas.

Michael. The one person who loved Alexia. Who accepted and celebrated her. Who she'd be cut off from until he was eighteen, if their father had any say in it.

Yep. The admiral was a scary man.

"Don't stress about it," Michael said quietly, clearly tracking her trip down memory lane. "Mom's thrilled you're back and Dad will come around eventually. They might not like what you're talking about, but the prestige of seeing you on TV, hearing you're at the big fancy billionaire parties like any good socialite will bring them around."

"Sure, as long as they ignore the part about me publicly talking sex." Alexia sighed. As much as she wanted to be tough and emotionless when it came to their parents, a part of her still craved—with the desperation of a small child—that approval. But she couldn't—wouldn't—change who she was to get it.

"You could almost feel sorry for them." Michael

laughed. "We're not exactly their idea of poster children, huh? To make it easier on them, when I go to Sunday brunch, I pretend to be straight. Not an easy thing for the headliner of Sassy's Fancy, an all-male revue. Last month I mentioned my photo shoot for Calvin Klein and you'd have thought I tried to jump the waiter, the way Dad choked and Mom sputtered."

"Maybe they'll focus more on the fact that this research project will potentially help abuse victims overcome their fears than the sex part of things," Alexia mused. When her brother looked at her as if she'd jumped right over naive into delusional, she wrinkled her nose.

"So enough about how proud we make the parents," Michael said with a dismissive wave to both the topic and the low-level guilt Alexia was starting to feel. "What's the real deal with you and Dr. Darling?"

"Edward's last name is Darshwin," she corrected for the zillionth time, following his lead and sitting up to reach for the sunscreen. Unlike many redheads, Alexia didn't have a problem tanning. She did, however, turn into one giant freckle after too much sunshine. "And I don't know what the deal is, really. He's a sweetie. Smart, cute and really big on communication. A guy who likes to talk feelings. What's better than that?"

"A guy who makes you feel things worth talking about," Michael ventured quietly.

Yeah. She sighed. That.

"When did you get so smart?" Alexia slanted him a look. Spread out on a bright turquoise beach towel, he looked too pretty, and honestly too vain, to offer up such deep thoughts. Sleek and toned, he was a man who made his living by looking good.

"Babe, just because I'm not a superbrainiac like you doesn't mean I'm not a pretty sharp cookie."

Wasn't that the truth.

Joy, as warm as a big squishy hug, filled her. Alexia could have turned down the job offer that'd brought her back to San Diego. But between her dream job and a chance to live close to her brother again, she hadn't been able to resist. They'd grown up as military brats, and the only steady thing in their lives had been each other. And while she didn't look for a lot of steadiness these days, she needed love. Needed to feel important. Special. If only to one person—and even if that person was her brother.

As if taunting her with Michael's words, her gaze sought out the gorgeous specimen of manhood again. Now, *that* was a guy who'd make a girl feel things worth talking about. She let the sight of his body, cutting strong and sure through the ocean waves, soothe her. Relax away the tension and worries.

Then he stepped out of the water.

And a whole new kind of tension seeped into her body.

At the same time, all thoughts, and most of her brain function, vanished. Every cell of her being was focused, like a laser, on his body.

His gorgeous body.

Sleek muscles, from the top of his sexy head to his well-shaped feet. The man was a work of art. Not in the bodybuilder-obsessed way, but pure streamlined power.

Him, she was sexually attracted to. Him, she could easily see herself begging for.

"You know, I might have questioned your judgment and hairstyle over the years," Michael said quietly. "But I've never faulted your eyesight. That is one fine-looking man."

"He's okay," she downplayed as if her body wasn't melting just looking at him.

"Okay? Just okay?" Michael's voice rose in indignation, as if she'd just insulted gorgeous men everywhere. "What'd New York do to you? You say you're not in a relationship, but your butt's still planted on this towel. Why aren't you going for it?"

"Because, as you pointed out, I'm in a relationship."

"*Considering* a relationship."

"Which means I should *finish* considering before I do anything crazy," she retorted. "Like hit on some stranger just because he's gorgeous."

"Gorgeous is the best reason to hit," Michael mused. Then he gave her an arch look. "Of course, he might not be your type."

"I don't think he's yours," she said with a laugh, eyeing the sexy swimmer. A man who exuded that much sexual energy, who made her wonder how many hours it'd take to try her top ten favorite *Kama Sutra* positions, gay? That'd be a crime against women everywhere.

"Let's find out, shall we?" Michael suggested as the man walked toward them, either because his stuff was up the beach past where they sat or maybe in response to intense do-me signals Alexia was mentally sending.

"Michael," she hissed, suddenly wishing she were on a plane back to New York. Or buried in the sand. Either would be better than what she knew was coming. "Don't you dare."

"Did you say dare?" Michael's grin shifted to one hundred degrees of wicked.

"Michael." Jackknifing upright, Alexia made a grab for her brother's arm. And growled when she missed.

"Oh, hey, excuse me," he called as he slid gracefully to his feet. "Do you have a second?"

Gorgeous slowed, walking toward them. His eyes—yes, just as fabulous as the rest of him—bypassed Michael to lock on to Alexia.

His gaze was like being bathed in a deliciously sensual bath. The dark blue depths were warm, luxurious and bone-meltingly wonderful.

Alexia swore she felt the world shift. Or maybe it was just the sand beneath her butt as her brother hurried forward to offer his hand.

"I'm Michael," he said, his smile big and bright as he gestured her way. "That's my sister, Alexia."

"Blake," the man introduced quietly, his voice carrying just a hint of the South.

"I was wondering if you wanted to join me, us, for a drink?" Michael reached into the cooler and pulled out a bottle of water, offering it. "It'd be a great favor. You can help settle an argument between my sister and I."

BLAKE GLANCED AT PRETTY BOY, and the proffered water, then at the sexy beach siren lounging at his feet. She looked like a parting gift from summer, as hot as the season itself. All red hair and gold skin, she made his mouth water.

Any other time, he'd have made a move to join her. But instead of offering healing, solace, the last two weeks had simply hammered home his grief. Made it worse. He'd hung out at Cade's apartment for a while. Only back a couple of days from a visit home, Cade had been lousy company. Silent, morose and distant, wallowing in the bitch of a mood that always went with dealing with his family. So Blake had escaped to the beach.

The sun hadn't helped. Neither had the surf. And he was sure talking to strangers was just as pointless. *Just make an excuse and go,* he told himself.

"What argument?" he heard himself asking instead.

"Alexia thinks a hot date is dinner and a movie," the guy told him, tilting his bright red sunglasses down his nose to offer a comical eye roll. "Boring, right? Me, I think a club and dancing is the way to go. What's your take?"

The bottle of water halfway to his mouth, Blake paused to stare.

Was the guy hitting on him?

Tempted to laugh, Blake offered the redhead a baffled look. Her answering smile was like a ray of sunshine, reaching out to pull him out of a dark hole he hadn't even realized he'd been hiding in.

"Both," Blake said. "Dinner and dancing. I'm traditional that way."

"Ah." The guy's smile didn't shift, his attitude didn't change. But his nod made it clear he'd got the message that he wasn't Blake's type. "Then I guess it's a draw."

"You'll have to excuse Michael," the redhead said. "He's a nothing-ventured, nothing-gained kind of guy."

"Can't fault him for that."

"You're sweet," she decided softly, her smile flashing bright. At first glance, her features weren't traditionally beautiful. They were too striking, too bold. Eyes almost too large for her face were direct under a slash of dark brows. Her jaw was strong, her lips full

with an obvious overbite that spelled all kinds of sexy to Blake's suddenly wide-awake libido.

A red-rose tattoo on her shoulder twined down her biceps, twisting and circling. Her body, hot enough to make a man grateful for summer, was stunning. Packaged in a tiny purple swimsuit that hugged and highlighted curves, he suddenly wished like hell he'd met her another time. One when he could lavish on her every bit of attention she deserved.

Blake was the kind of guy who'd built his career on doing the right thing. Who lived his life by the rules. He not only followed the book, but double-checked it to ensure the rules he was following were exactly as written.

Anal?

It worked for him.

At least, it had.

The image of Phil flashed through Blake's mind, the last thing he'd seen from his buddy was his big, cheesy grin just before the shrapnel had pierced his helmet.

Phil had followed the rules.

The entire team had, to the letter.

And they'd still lost their teammate.

Overwhelmed by the memory, Blake turned to stare toward the ocean, trying to find peace again. The water wasn't giving any up, though. Of its own volition, his gaze returned to the stunning redhead.

She didn't look like the kind who followed rules.

Maybe that's what he needed right now.

His eyes traveled over the smooth golden skin of her bare belly, noting the tiny strings tying her bikini bottoms to her slender hips. His body stirred. Blood pumped. For the first time in two weeks, he felt alive.

He'd come here to heal, though.

And as much as losing himself in a body as lush and welcoming as Alexia's appealed, he knew better. A smart man fighting demons avoided addictive substances. Alcohol, drugs, gambling. Gorgeous, sexy women. Anything that let a man numb himself to the memories.

Blake's body screamed a number of ugly epithets at him. Ten years in the navy meant it had a ton to choose from. Still, he'd put his body through worse than denying it a gorgeous woman. He'd get over it.

"Thanks," he finally said, splitting his smile between the brother and sister. "But I've got to go."

Before he could change his mind, he lifted the water bottle in acknowledgment, and strode away. And regretted every step.

CHAPTER TWO

"EDWARD, I'VE THOUGHT about it a lot," Alexia said, her tone low in an attempt to keep their conversation private from the rest of the diners. After her talk with Michael on the beach that afternoon, she'd realized she had to deal with the issue before she started work the following week. "I value our friendship, it's really important to me. But I don't think we should risk it by trying to turn it into more."

After uttering those totally uncomfortable words, Alexia held her breath and waited for Edward's response. Sounds suddenly amplified, forks against plates, the rushing servers' feet against the tile floor, even the sound of the still-warm tortilla chips sliding into salsa.

The smile not shifting on his handsome face, Edward blotted his lips with his napkin, then took a sip of his water. Buying time to sort his reaction, Alexia realized with a wince.

"I'm sure we'll be fine. Nerves are natural before taking a big step in a relationship. Don't let it worry you."

No. Anticipation was natural. Excitement was. And sure, nerves if they were along the lines of *will he like seeing me naked* and *is he open to kinky positions*. But this stomach-churning, feet-twitching-to-run, little-voice-screaming-nooooo feeling? This wasn't normal.

What did she have to say to get through? She really didn't want to hurt him.

But after her reaction earlier that morning to hot, sexy and gorgeous on the beach, as she still thought of the hottie named Blake, there was no way she could settle for a sexless relationship. Spark, desire, passion, they were too important. It'd been all she could do not to chase the guy down the beach, throw herself at his feet and beg him to let her make up for her brother's odd behavior by licking her way up his body.

Heck, she'd stayed so turned on and sexually charged thinking about him, she'd come twice in the shower preparing for this dinner. Clearly her subconscious was sending her a strong message that she and Edward weren't meant to be a couple.

But he wasn't listening to her subconscious. Or her words, for that matter. What did that say about their wavelength? Edward had a habit of believing that if he ignored something he didn't like, it'd eventually go away. Having tried that often enough, and still having the parents to prove it didn't work, Alexia could empathize.

"Sweetie, we have a great time together," Edward said brightly, dismissing her concerns with a wave of his fork. His blond hair glinted in the colorful piñata-shaped lights and his perfect teeth flashed. "We're great together. We're on the same wavelength, totally in tune. Our interests, our goals, our values, they all click. That's what counts, right?"

Alexia forced her lips to curve in agreement. Because he was right. They were in tune and did have a great time. But that wasn't enough.

"That's all important," she said, pushing her barely tasted enchiladas aside to reach across the table and take his hand. "But those are things that make for a strong friendship. Not a…"

She couldn't do it. Alexia wanted to pound her head on the table a few times to try to shake the words loose, but didn't figure it'd do much good. So she took a deep sip of her pomegranate margarita—her third—instead. How was she supposed to say that she had absolutely zip sexual interest in him? She specialized in the art of subliminally messaging the center of the brain that controlled sexual response. She was about to start a job that required her to be front and center, publicly talking about how to heal and stimulate sexual responses. How could she work with test subjects and expect people who'd had sexual trauma to trust her to help them if she couldn't even talk about her own sexual needs?

"Look," Edward said, twining his fingers with hers. "I know what you're worried about. That mythical spark isn't blazing between us. You think there should be some energy, some physical manifestation of attraction."

It was all she could do not to throw her hands in the air and say *duh.*

"And you don't?" She'd worked enough in the field of sexual health to know there were men who couldn't perform. Others whose libidos were so low, they had no interest in sex. But she wouldn't have thought that Edward fit that category. He was a geek, sure. And a little socially awkward sometimes. But if he had issues, he wouldn't hide them. He'd self-diagnose and dive into treatment, using himself as a test subject.

"Our species was made to experience sexual connections," she said, shifting the discussion into scientific mode instead of personal, and instantly relaxing. "You know the statistics as well as I do. The odds of a romantic relationship lasting without sex are slim."

"Alexia, relationships based on sexual heat don't last. They flare hot and intense, then burn out just as fast." Edward leaned forward, his words as sincere as the fervent look on his face. "Better to base a relationship on more solid, long-lasting emotions. Like friendship and similar interests. We share the same values, the same goals in life. That matters more than a few paltry orgasms."

Well, sure. If they were paltry, she could see his point. Who needed that? Alexia thought, dumbfounded.

"We're scientists who specialize in sexual health," he continued. "Layering the physical elements into our relationship won't be an issue. And when we do, it'll be done in a well-thought-out, practical and measured way. Just as it should be between two intelligent scientists focused on the long term."

Well… Wasn't *that* sexy.

Alexia drained her margarita, the bitter tang of the pomegranate matching the taste on her tongue. Was that how she came across? As the kind of woman who would settle for measured practicality? In bed? There was only one thing she wanted to be measuring in bed.

Edward must have sensed her disquiet, because he shook his head, as if to stop her from saying anything.

"Think about it," he said, giving her fingers one last squeeze before trading them for his fork again.

"In the meantime, don't worry about us. Get settled in your apartment, enjoy the weekend. Maybe reacquaint yourself with some of your old haunts. That'd be fun, right? Don't you have a family event this weekend?"

"My father's retirement party," she acknowledged with an inward cringe. How fun was that going to be? The only thing that might appeal more was finding a gynecologist with a hook for a hand. Alexia signaled the waiter for another margarita.

"Just let it go for now. Let your subconscious work it through. I'll wait awhile before I bring it up again." He looked so sincere, so sweet, that it actively hurt to have to set him straight. But she wasn't going to change her mind, and the sooner he accepted that, the sooner they could reestablish their friendship on its original terms. Alexia sighed, then, not seeing any choice, opened her mouth to tell him that she'd made up her mind already.

As if reading her intention, he hurried to say, "In the meantime, did I tell you about the latest round of crackpot threats the institute is getting?"

"The bitter women's brigade is protesting sex again?" she asked, giving in and graciously letting him change the subject. That was part of the art of communication. Read the signals in order to know when to talk and when to let things go until a better time. Between his sidestepping the issue, refusing to listen and stiff-shouldered body language, she might as well give up. For now.

He nodded. "Oh, we hear from the women's brigade about once a week. But this was a new one. A European gentleman wanted to offer us a grant to study anger and aggression."

"There have been a number of studies in that area,"

Alexia said, smiling her thanks to the waiter as he swapped her empty glass for a full one.

"Not with the focus of using subliminal messaging and brain-wave manipulation to incite anger."

"Incite? Isn't five o'clock on the 405 freeway enough to do that?"

After a brow-furrowed second, Edward quirked a smile, then shook his head. "Apparently not. This gentleman offered a huge sum of money. Enough that I was actually tempted, if not for the fact that we're already so committed to the current project that it'd hurt our reputation to pull out at this point."

Well, *goody* for future funding and the need to keep up one's reputation. She hadn't signed on for anger management, and didn't like the idea that Edward and the institute's focus could be bought. Alexia gripped her fork so tight it left a dent in her fingers, but managed to smother the anger before she made a nasty remark. Dating, friendship and the rest aside, Edward was still her boss. Calling him a greedy weasel was probably a bad idea.

But she'd taken the position at the institute because she wanted to help people. Because she knew the power sexual satisfaction could offer and truly believed that everyone deserved a chance at that kind of pleasure. Not to make money for whoever had the deepest pockets.

Her mind flashed back to hot, sexy and gorgeous on the beach that afternoon. As she let herself focus on the image of his butt, so tight and solid beneath those wet swim trunks, the red edges of anger faded from her vision. Now, *that* was the kind of guy who inspired fantasies and made a woman very, very aware that she was female. But for women with issues, whether from conditioning or abuse, that delight was out of reach.

Too bad she hadn't gotten a chance to see if the reality of hot, sexy and gorgeous was as delicious as the fantasy. She could have called it work incentive.

Or just mind-blowingly awesome sex.

AN HOUR AND A HALF LATER, Alexia paid the cab and stepped onto the shell-encrusted sidewalk in front of JR's. The club-slash-bar fronted a long stretch of beach, both lit up like carnival attractions.

She wasn't sure why she was here. She definitely didn't need another drink. But she didn't want to go home, either. And the idea of spending any more time with Edward, pretending that everything was peachy keen, was enough to make her scream. She wanted to dance. To relax in a crowd of strangers. And JR's was the only bar she knew well enough to feel safe. A regular hangout of the navy locals, it wasn't that it didn't get rowdy or wild. But it had three major advantages. One, it was a familiar place so she knew what she'd get when she walked through the door. Two, she was there to dance, and if anyone tried to push for more, her get-out-of-trouble-free card, aka the mention of her father's name, would cut them off at the knee. And three, she'd never get involved with a military man. Ever. She'd had enough of the military growing up to know that a sailor's first priority was to his very dangerous, often secretive career. And while she respected that, she had no interest in being background noise in someone's life.

Still, walking into the club was like stepping face-first into chaos. Noise, so loud the music had to be felt instead of heard, pounded through her. Heat from the crowd of bodies swirled with an ambitious air conditioner. Lights flashed, strobed and glowed, depending on which way she turned her head.

Maybe she should have just gone home.

But she'd have gone crazy there, with only her thoughts and guilt for company. Michael was on a date, and three days back wasn't enough time for her to have made any new friendships. So she was on her own.

And she needed action. Movement. Something to shake off the sexual tension that'd been driving at her all afternoon. Since hunting down the sexy guy from the beach wasn't an option, she'd figured she'd do the next best thing to release body tension. *Dance.*

About to head for the flashing lights of the dance floor and kick up the heels of her favorite Manolos, a man at the bar caught her attention.

Blake?

The hot, sexy and gorgeous from the beach?

A slow, wicked smile curved her lips at the sight.

He was just as appealing dry and clothed as he'd been wet and half-naked. In jeans and a simple T-shirt that did wonders for his broad shoulders, he looked like a guy who just wanted a drink and some alone-time. Too bad for him, though, since a blonde barracuda was tiptoeing her red talons up his chest. Was that his type? Blatant, busty and ballsy? He grabbed the blonde's hand on its downward sweep, shaking his head. She didn't back off. Alexia bit her lip to keep from laughing at the range of emotions chasing across his face. Irritation, confusion and just a hint of amusement. Poor guy, he probably hadn't realized this was a navy bar. Which meant pushy, desperate women all focused on one thing. Catching themselves a sailor boy.

He looked as if he needed saving.

Sliding and pressing her way through the crowd of bodies, she made a path to the bar. The music was quieter here, but the cacophony of voices made up for it. She was about five feet away when Blake's gaze found her. Delight flared in those blue depths, making her girl parts feel oh-so-happy. Happy enough that she hesitated. Getting all hot and wet over a stranger wasn't a bad thing. But it wasn't where she was at in her life right now, either. Despite what she'd told Michael, she had feelings for Edward. Ones that deserved to be explored. She couldn't explore feelings for one guy while another was tickling her girlie parts. It just wasn't right.

But could she leave Blake there at the mercy of the red-taloned barracuda?

As if sensing her struggle, Blake gave her a wide-eyed look of desperation. *Hurry up,* he mouthed. Alexia's lips twitched, but her feet started moving again.

She bypassed the blonde and positioned herself behind Blake. Heavily made-up eyes glanced her way, dismissing her with a flick of false lashes.

It was going to take stronger measures, Alexia realized. Warning her girlie parts not to get too excited, she moved in close, draping her arm over the broad muscles of Blake's shoulders. He was like steel. Solid, strong, sleek. Her mouth watered. To give it something to do before she actually drooled, she leaned forward to brush a friendly kiss over his cheek. He smelled like the ocean. Clean, salty, intoxicating.

"He's with me," she said, giving the blonde a go-away tilt of her head.

"He's not wearing a ring."

Alexia's expression didn't change. All she did was

curve her hand over Blake's shoulder. Possession. Then she leaned her body closer to his. Whether he knew what she was doing or he was preparing to use her for a shield, he wrapped his own arm around her waist, pulling her tight to his side.

Desire sent her body into a tailspin at his touch. Warm tingles swirled, heating her nipples to pebbled warmth before trickling down to her belly. Because he was sitting on the bar stool and she was standing, his head was level with her shoulder. All it would take was for him to turn his head and his lips could brush her nipples.

Alexia had to force her breath to steady, her vision to clear. She couldn't do anything about the damp heat between her thighs as her girlie parts did a happy dance, though.

"Like I said," Alexia repeated as soon as she knew her voice was steady, "he's with me."

Proving that brains and bleach weren't mutually exclusive, the barracuda hissed through a smile clenched so tight her jaw had to ache, then shrugged.

"Fine. You two have fun," she said. Flicking a challenging look at Alexia, she leaned against Blake, pressing so tight her silicone squished out the sides of her tank top. She sank both hands into the sides of his neck, pulled his head down and slapped a slurpy wet kiss on his shocked mouth.

"Just in case you change your mind," the blonde said when she released him.

Grinding her teeth, Alexia almost reached over Blake's shoulder and smacked the smile off the blonde's face. Whether it was just her nature, or a by-product of the red hair, anger was an emotion she visited daily. But jealousy was brand-new to her. Trying to tamp down the green-eyed gnawing fury in her belly, she decided it wasn't one she liked.

Still, her fingers curled into a fist and her eyes narrowed as she sized up the other woman. At five-ten and dedicated to her gym membership, Alexia was pretty sure she could take her.

"I guess I'll join my friends now," the blonde said, looking a little afraid.

Subliminal messaging at its best.

Realizing that she still had her hand fisted, Alexia took a deep, calming breath and relaxed her fingers. Then, because she really needed the rest of her body to relax, too, she shifted away from Blake. Touching him was anything but calming. It took another deep breath before she had enough control to put on a friendly expression and walk around to face him.

"Thanks," he muttered, shaking his head as he watched Blondie sashay away. Like if he took his eyes off her before she'd reached a safe distance, she might ricochet back and plaster herself all over his body. "She wasn't interested in hearing no."

"It's a hard word for some people to accept," Alexia agreed with a grimace, thinking of her dinner date. "I spent most of my upbringing trying to get people to listen when I said no. Or yes. Or anything, actually."

She tried to laugh away her discomfort at oversharing. Communication was important. But it was a two-way street, not a one-way emotional dump. Blake didn't look uncomfortable, though. More…curious.

"You don't seem like a wimp to me," he said after a long contemplation.

"Well, aren't you the sweet talker," she said, both

amused and relieved. Not that she figured on tossing him over her shoulder and carrying him off to have her wicked way with his body or anything—mostly because he was too heavy to carry. But she'd hate to think that she was on par with the barracuda when it came to scaring guys off.

"Sweet talk is a game, isn't it?" he said. Then he shrugged. "I don't play games."

Ooh. Intriguing. If his sexy body hadn't already caught her interest, the idea of finding out if he was for real—or if that statement was simply a game in itself—would have hooked her for sure.

"That must be tough, being a nongame kind of guy in an arena like this." She twirled her fingers, indicating the lights, the bar, the bodies. "In here, like in life, almost everyone is playing a game of some kind."

He looked around the bar, his expression blank. Just a little lost. As if he wasn't sure how he'd got there. Alexia's heart clenched. He was so wounded. She wanted to wrap her arms around him and pull him close. Let him rest his head on her breasts while she combed her fingers through his dark hair.

Her nipples tightened as if preparing for just that.

What'd happened that he felt so much pain? Maybe if she got him talking, he'd open up. Let it out so he could start healing.

Radiating damp heat and fresh off the dance floor, a guy tried to get past her to order a drink. Alexia wedged herself between Blake's body and the bar stool. Now it wasn't the music throbbing through her body. It was desire, hot, intense and needy. Nothing wrong with that. She was a red-blooded woman with a healthy appreciation for her sexuality. Didn't mean she was going to act on it.

Maybe.

BLAKE WATCHED THE SEXY redhead closely, mulling over her comment. He didn't like to think of himself as a game player. But she was right. Everyone probably did play games in one way or another. Hell, the military called them war games. A test, pitting man against man. Even man against himself. The endurance and strength training, weren't those games of sorts?

And the mental gyrations he'd been playing before the blonde had tried to dig her lethal claws into him. It'd be a game, pure and simple, trying to convince himself that he'd exaggerated Alexia's impact in his mind. That she wasn't as sexy, as gorgeous, as appealing as he remembered.

But now that she was standing in front of him again? She had the same impact as an unexpected fist to the gut. Shocking, intense and demanding an instant response.

Her personality was as bubbly as her looks. Fiery curls, golden skin and molten dark eyes topped a body that made a man want to get on his knees to offer thanks…among other things.

The memory of her body, each and every delicious curve of it highlighted by tiny scraps of purple fabric, was etched in his mind. So he didn't begrudge the loose fit of her dress, high at the neck but leaving her shoulders bare, the turquoise pleats barely skimming the tips of her breasts before draping to midthigh. Her legs were bare. Yards of silky golden leg stretched between the bottom of her dress and skyscraper heels.

"So," she said after a long pause, her voice a little breathless. He wondered where her mental trip had taken her. And what kind of games it'd included. And if he'd been there. Maybe naked.

"So," she said again, clearing her throat then giving him a bright, friendly but not flirty smile. "What brings you to a club like this? It doesn't seem like your kind of place."

"Why not?"

"This is navyland," she said, waving her hand around the room. "Soldiers and sailors, this is their hangout. Most guys avoid it unless they're stationed at Coronado."

Blake frowned into his beer before taking a drink. "You don't think I belong here?"

He didn't know how to take that. He'd joined the navy the day after he'd graduated high school, and had found his home. His place in the world. With the SEALs, he'd found family. He'd never wanted to be anything else.

"Oh, I don't know. You've got the body and the, well, energy, to be a sailor boy," she said, her tone still teasing as she gave him a slow once-over. Her big brown eyes slid from his face and down his body. Proving he was alive and doing damn well, his body stirred in reaction. Hardened.

"But?" he prodded when her eyes stayed a little too long on his jeans. A few more seconds and she was going to be seeing a whole different terrain down there.

"But you don't have that bravado I usually associate with soldiers," she said a little breathlessly, looking into his eyes again.

"Bravado, hmm? Is that a requirement, something

they issue along with the uniform?" He grinned. Maybe Cade was right. Maybe he was burned out. He liked the sound of that better than wallowing in grief. Whatever it was, he kinda liked that Alexia didn't know he was a sailor. With her, he wasn't Lieutenant Landon, decorated Navy SEAL, radioman, linguist and teammate. He wasn't a finely honed weapon, a highly trained warrior. He wasn't a military paycheck, or a score to be notched.

He was just a man.

That was so damn appealing.

"I think bravado is intrinsic," she decided. "It either fits, or it doesn't. But a uniform probably helps."

"And you like the uniform?" Figured. Most women did. Most women didn't even look past it. Plenty of guys didn't care. Whatever bait worked, they reeled 'em in. Blake was pickier than that, though. And oddly deflated to think that Alexia wasn't.

The bartender delivered a fresh drink and took the empty. Blake nodded his thanks and lifted the bottle, ready to wash some of the bitterness off his tongue.

"I'm not a fan, actually."

Thirst forgotten, Blake slowly lowered his beer. *Not a fan? Seriously?*

Seeing his shock, she grinned. "Don't get me wrong. I appreciate our servicemen and women. They are amazing. But when it comes to relationships, I'd rather steer clear."

"Relationships?" He pulled a face. Women always used that word. What it meant was sex with a soldier—and let's face it, SEALs did everything, including sex, better. Or a golden ticket to a soldier's paycheck and benefits without the day-to-day work of being a wife.

Blake realized that this was probably the first time since he'd enlisted that he'd had a flirt going on with a woman who was only focused on him. Not the SEAL thrill. Yeah, this just-being-a-man thing was wildly appealing. He didn't consider it a lie not to tell her he was navy. She'd made the assumption, after all. He was just letting her go with it.

"Yes, relationships." She laughed, bringing him back to the conversation. "I'm a fan of the concept."

How much of a fan? A groupie type? A desperately chase-after-it type? Blake frowned. Was she in one? Would she be here if she was? You never knew with women. He debated asking. The problem was, once that discussion door was open, it went both ways.

"But most women here," she continued, waving her hand again to encompass the loud club. "They're all about the goal, not the relationship."

"What's the goal?"

"Fishing. They're here to fish for sailors," she said, shifting closer so she didn't have to shout the words. Close enough that her body heat wrapped around him, her scent filled his head with the image of sun, surf and sex. "Some, like Blondie, are catch and release. Others are looking for a keeper."

"That's awfully cynical," he observed, laughing even though her words echoed his own thoughts. "Aren't you women supposed to stick together? You know, group bathroom trip, the girl code, the secret sisterhood?"

Dark eyes dancing, Alexia leaned closer. Blake almost held his breath so as not to be tempted by her scent. Coconut, spices, just a hint of something floral and purely female. Then he remembered he was a solider. A navy SEAL, for crying out loud. He was brave enough to deal with sexy.

"Oh, believe me, if she was a friend I'd be distracting you while she slid that hook into your mouth," she assured him with a laugh. "But tonight, you look like you could use someone on your side."

Nonplussed, Blake stared. And saw the sympathy in her eyes. As if she'd seen into his soul and wanted to soothe the pain there.

God, he was a mess. When had he lost it? Blake had been captured by the enemy once. They'd been furious with his implacable refusal to show emotion or reveal information. But tonight all it took was three beers, and a sexy redhead could read his secrets?

He figured he had three options. Say goodbye and walk away before she delved any deeper. Open up and share the confused emotions tangled in his gut. Or distract her.

But he never gave up, and he wasn't into sharing. So option three was it.

"Which category do you fall into?" he asked, giving in to the need that'd been gnawing at him since that afternoon and reaching out to touch her. Just the ends of her hair, like silken heat between the tips of his fingers.

"I don't think I can be categorized," she murmured. "It's too easy to be dismissed once a label's been posted, isn't it?"

Beautiful, sexy and smart? She might as well be wearing a sign proclaiming her dangerous territory.

A woman this perceptive was better to hustle along as quickly as possible. When a man's defenses were down, it was smart to keep the threats to a minimum. Out of the corner of his eye, he noticed Cade and a group of SEALs saunter into the club. Now that his teammates were here, she'd find out he was navy soon enough. Still, Blake figured it was better to hurry her along before he was tempted to do something stupid.

"Everyone can be categorized. The only question is, are you in the catch-and-release group?" he asked quietly. "Or are you looking for a keeper? And if it's not the uniform that gets your attention, what's a guy got to show? His bank statement?"

There. That should piss her off. Blake sipped his beer with only a little regret that he was driving away what could have been the most incredible encounter of his life.

CHAPTER THREE

HER TEMPER WAS A WORK OF ART. First Alexia's eyes flashed dark fire. Then they narrowed as if she was contemplating where she wanted to punch him. Blake didn't bother to steel his core. He deserved the hit, and he'd take it full-on. After all, that'd been a cheap shot.

"C'mon," she said, tilting her head toward the exit.

Not sure he'd heard her right, Blake frowned in confusion as she wriggled between him, the bar stool and the three guys blocking her way.

Blake's groan was lost in the noise of the club. With her in heels, her lips were within kissing distance of his. Her breasts, full and soft under that flowy dress, skimmed, just barely, his chest. He knew it wasn't deliberate. He'd been hit on enough to tell. But it was the sexiest move he'd ever felt.

"C'mon," she said again, this time waving her fingers in a *let's-go* gesture.

Still baffled, but with the rational side of his brain sputtering due to the feel of her breasts sliding like white heat against his chest, Blake followed. His eyes on the sway of her hips as he headed for the door, he didn't lose sight of her even as he took a short side trip to where his friends were waiting.

"I'm outta here," he said, tilting his head toward Alexia's back.

Cade followed his gesture, gave an impressed arch of his brows and a thumbs-up.

"Glad to see you're using your time wisely," he said with a grin before heading toward the heart of the club noise to party it up in his usual style.

Blake didn't worry about blowing off his buddy. And given that the lieutenant commander was wearing a T-shirt that claimed Navy SEALs Don't Make Deals, he didn't feel bad about not making introductions, either.

He did, briefly, think joining Cade and the rest of the guys might be smarter than following Alexia outside. Those guys were trained to have his back. But some missions just had to be done solo.

Stepping out the club doors into the warm night air, he gave himself a second to adjust to the lack of noise. Nothing better than silence, with a little ocean music, to set a chewing-out to.

Alexia stood toward the end of the building, where the wooden walkway curved toward the ocean. Hands fisted at her hips, she sucked in a breath through gritted teeth, her eyes flashing fire.

"You sure you want to tear me down for the insult privately?" he asked before she could say anything. He flashed his most charming smile to indicate that he knew he had it coming and wouldn't protest her angry retaliation. "Don't you want witnesses?"

"Actually, I figured you needed a little air. You know, to clear the testosterone idiocy out of your head before you said anything even stupider." Then, the fury clearing from her eyes, she laughed.

Laughed? Where had the anger gone? She was like mercury, changing so fast he could barely keep up.

Damned if that wasn't tempting. She was sexy and fun, with so much energy he felt alive again. He wasn't sure if he wanted to, though. Maybe it'd be smarter to turn heel and go back into the club. Or, he fingered the keys in his pocket, hop in his truck and drive away.

"Not that you don't deserve a little teardown," she continued with a shrug that highlighted well-toned shoulders and the golden glow she'd got at the beach that morning. "But I figure a guy smart enough to know he's made an asinine comment is smart enough to not make it without a reason."

Huh? Blake rocked back on his heels, trying to figure that one out.

"I got too close, right?" she guessed. "You're upset about something and here I come, a total stranger, poking and prodding like I have the right to peek into your privacy. So you slapped me back. That's natural."

"Are you for real?"

"Why? Because I didn't have a hissy fit?" She tilted her head to one side, her curls bouncing around her face. "Do you think women are that easily categorized?"

"I think this is where I got in trouble," Blake mused. He still wasn't buying the no-games line. But he was intrigued enough to want to see if she could change his mind. "Want to walk?"

She gave him a narrow look, then glanced at the tiny boardwalk leading to the beach. Smart women didn't wander off with strangers, so he didn't take offense. But since there was a party going on along the beach, it looked like a wedding or something, she must have decided there were enough numbers for safety.

She gave him a considering look. As if she was

debating something beyond safety. For a second she looked as though she might think he had the potential to haul an ax out of his back pocket. Then she lifted her chin and offered a bright smile.

"Sure."

As soon as they reached the point where the wooden slats gave way to silken sand, Alexia stood on one foot to remove her shoe, then switched to the other. Not sure when he'd become a gentleman, Blake held her hand to help her balance. Her fingers were dainty. Slender and fragile. Warm. Strong.

The kind of fingers that would feel incredible skimming over his naked flesh. Tugging his zipper down and gripping his hardening erection. Stroking, guiding.

Hell. As soon as she was barefoot, he not only grabbed his hand back, he put a safe couple feet between them. The woman was potent.

"You're not taking yours off?" she asked.

"Nope." To end the discussion, he strode onto the beach, his tennis shoes sinking, sand filtering into his socks. Didn't matter. He had the feeling he'd do better to keep every article of clothing intact.

Although he didn't have Cade's track record and fancy-faced looks, he'd had his fair share of women hitting on him. Hitting back always depended on three things.

Timing. Was he fresh off a mission and in need of shedding some pent-up energy, or about to embark on a mission, which would provide him with an inarguable exit strategy?

Spark. A lot of guys he'd served with banged anything that moved. For the notch, for the cheap thrill, to stroke their ego. Whatever. Blake didn't want notches, thrills or strokes when he got naked with a woman. What he did want was spark. Heat. Something wild and intense, like the rest of his life.

But the most important return-hit factor was the commitment perspective. Years of SEAL training had sharpened his instincts to a razor's edge, and years of avoiding commitment had honed his ability to discern a woman's intentions—even if she didn't realize them herself.

Timing and spark didn't mean jack if the woman's perspective was skewed toward long term.

The redhead smiled. A slow, wicked curve of her lips. It didn't matter that the look wasn't aimed at him. Blake's muscles still bunched, his senses sprang to full alert and his dick hardened. Yeah. There was plenty of spark. It was the timing, and the scary depths of her perception, that worried him.

"I've missed the beach," Alexia said after a few minutes of silent strolling along the water's edge.

"Where've you been?"

"New York." She gave him a saucy look, her eyes sparkling in the moonlight. "Can't you tell from my accent?"

Before training for the SEALs, Blake had served as a cryptologic technician. In civilian terms, a linguist. He spoke fluent Spanish, Russian, Arabic and Persian. And once in a while, pretty decent English.

"I meet a lot of people from a lot of places," he told her. "Most are easy to place by their accents. You don't have one, though."

"Seriously? I don't have any accent?"

He grinned at her affronted tone.

"I'm an expert," he assured her. "Take it from me, you're accent free."

Then, maybe because he was starting to relax for the first time since watching Phil's helmet blown to smithereens, he decided to show off a little.

"Bet you moved around a lot as a kid. Not just the U.S. Your tones are too rounded to be purely American. Europe. Maybe Asia?"

She stood rock still, music from the party ahead filling the air with a Motown beat, her hands fisted on her hips, and gave him a narrow-eyed look. "Did Michael track you down and say something this afternoon?"

Blake laughed. There wasn't a whole lot to do for entertainment on a ship in the middle of the ocean, so he'd built a rep guessing where the guys were from. *Name that accent in ten words or less,* Phil had called it.

His laughter faded. The memory didn't hurt as much, though. Maybe it was the dark. Or the company.

"Your brother didn't spill any secrets," he assured her. "I told you, I'm good at accents."

"You really are clever." She laughed, the sound as alluring and mysterious as the ocean itself. "I'll bet it's a handy skill. Does your job involve languages?"

"Yep." But he didn't want to talk about his job. He wanted to escape it right now. He watched her dip her feet in the surf, kicking up droplets and catching them in her fingers. What'd it feel like to be that free? That comfortable with yourself, with life. "What about you? You a psychologist or something?"

"Like I said. Clever," she complimented as they reached the edges of the party. People milled about, dancing in the light of tiki torches, diving fully clothed—and in a couple cases totally unclothed—

into the night surf. "I have a minor in psychology, actually. But I don't practice."

"What do you do?"

"Until recently, I worked at a private New York lab as an acoustical physicist."

"Seriously?" he asked, throwing her word back at her.

A science geek? With a minor in psychology? Blake fingered his keys again, figuring he could make it up the beach to his truck in about six seconds flat.

"Yes, seriously," she chided with a laugh. "I specialize in psychoacoustics."

What was that? Crazy talk?

He shifted on the balls of his feet, gauging the sand's inertia effect on his escape.

"And psychoacoustics is…?" he asked tentatively.

"The technical definition is the study of sound perception, measuring the psychological and physiological response to sounds."

"So you do research?"

"Research, development," she agreed with a shrug before giving him an arch look. "My current research is focused on correcting and enhancing sexual health through subliminal messaging, neurolinguistic programming and brain-wave technology."

Intrigued, a little confused and, since she'd mentioned sex, totally open to being turned on, Blake settled his weight again, raised one brow and invited, "Tell me more."

From the amused look she gave him, it was clear she knew which part he wanted to hear more about.

"If done right, subliminal messaging offers an opportunity to bypass the brain's critical factor and speak directly with the subconscious. This is where the changes happen. Not just changes like smoking cessation or breaking a sugar addiction. But true physical changes. When trauma or conditioning are too strong for someone to overcome, the best way to make changes is on a subconscious level. This could be a powerful tool in helping abuse victims overcome blocks, in making inroads to libido dysfunction, healing emotional confidence."

Between the animation in her voice and the way she was practically glowing with excitement, it was clear this was a woman who got passionate about her work. He gave her a questioning look. "So you're talking about using sound to do the work of a psychologist?"

"Sure. It's a little deeper than that, and should actually be done in concert with psychotherapy instead of replacing it, but you have the general idea of it right."

Blake was all for a little mood music while doing the deed, but this was wild. Then again, he was getting pretty turned on just listening to her talk, that husky voice so passionate and excited—even if it was about her job rather than something more personal, like his body.

"How'd you go from acoustical physics to sexual health?" he wondered.

"While getting my psych degree, I interned at a clinic that helped abuse victims. It was heartbreaking," she said quietly, staring out at the water. "Years, lifetimes were impacted by a single event, and no matter how much these people wanted to overcome that, or how much we tried to help them, there were things that the mind just wouldn't let them get past."

Blake didn't say anything. He couldn't. His own

mind was taking its oft-hourly trip back to the mission, to his last sight of Phil. She was right. Some things, they just didn't go away.

"I'm boring you, aren't I?" she asked, giving him a rueful look, the moonlight glistening off her down-turned lips.

"Hell, no. I'm fascinated. Besides, I like a woman who gets this excited about sex," Blake said with a wicked grin.

"Done right, sex is the ultimate excitement," she said, her voice as sultry as the night itself.

"And done wrong?"

She smiled, slow and wide. Her look was filled with empathy, a sort of deep sympathetic understanding that told him this was a woman who cared. Not just about her job. But about people, about helping. About making things better.

And he'd thought she was scary when she was just perceptive.

Trying to regain control over the needs raging through his libido, Blake focused on the scenery. A few yards from the water's edge, a crop of boulders marked the end of the beach. Up the dune, a large white tent sheltered the bulk of the wedding party, music pouring a soft wave of romance down toward the surf.

"Want to sit?" he asked, gesturing toward the bench-like rocks. "Or are you ready to head back?"

She nibbled her bottom lip, making him want to beg her to let him do it for her instead. The full flesh glistened, damp, in the tiny white lights twinkling around the tent. Since grabbing her would pretty much guarantee an end to the evening, he forced himself to be patient while she decided.

"We can sit for a few minutes," she finally said.

Waiting for her to settle herself on the rock, watching her carefully arrange her shoes next to her, he wondered what she'd been thinking. What had been the deciding factor between staying or going?

"So you love your job," he said, leaning his hip against the rock so he was half facing her, half facing the water. "What else are you passionate about?"

Her fingers toyed with the tall grasses growing between the stone, the blades black in the moonlight. It was hard to tell since he couldn't see her eyes, but she suddenly seemed sad. As if he'd rapped his knuckles on a healing bruise. Since he felt like one giant bruise himself, he could sympathize.

Before he could change the subject, she glanced up, her lashes a feathery frame to the intense look in her eyes.

"You know, I don't think I've been passionate about anything except work for a long time. I learned pretty young that my passionate exuberance for certain things in life was a problem. So I pulled it in. Focused it. First on school, then on my career."

Her words were matter-of-fact. But so sad, he felt like a self-pitying fool for settling into a pit of grief the way he had. For hiding instead of facing life the way Alexia did.

He should ask about her past. Find out what had hurt her, how she'd overcome it. Give her the comfort of getting it off her chest.

But the idea of that made his gut ache like no amount of enemy fire or threat of torture could. Feelings, emotions, opening up. They all seemed passive. He was a man of action. So he went with comfort-option number two. His body gave a silent woohoo.

He lifted her hand, amazed at its softness. Long, slender fingers trembled once. He watched as she took a quick breath, stilled her hand and lifted her chin. In a rare move, his body reacted without his say-so, hardening.

"All work can't be good, even when it's work you enjoy," he said. "You should share that passion. Spread it around to other things. You know, maybe a hobby."

"Hobbies are good," she agreed softly, the look on her face both amused and patient. As if he was a cute little kid who entertained her. Not quite the image he'd been going for.

"But I think there are other things I'd rather be passionate about," she said, her words almost lost in the pounding of the surf.

Or was that the pounding of his heart?

SHE WAS IN TROUBLE. Knee-deep, sinking-fast, scream-for-help-before-it's-too-late trouble.

Alexia knew all the signs.

Her heart was racing, even as her feet twitched, warning to run.

Anticipation curled, tight and low in her belly. Somewhere between desire and terror, it waited. Hope and fear entwined, making it impossible to know which to root for.

Her mind screamed warning, but her body wanted him, badly. Her nipples tightened and her thighs melted in anticipation. It was all she could do not to close the space between them, lean into that rock-hard body and trace her tongue over the hint of stubble along his jaw. She'd bet he tasted yummy.

Catching herself just before she fanned her hand in front of her face to try to chill, Alexia desperately grabbed control, reeling it tight.

It was time to make an excuse and leave. She had a very narrow window—maybe five minutes, tops—before she did something really, really stupid. And she'd spent a lot of years weaning stupid behavior from her repertoire.

She was proud of that. Even as a sneaky part of her brain whispered that she'd been good for so long, she deserved a little bad. Just a little, now and then.

Mostly now.

Then Blake stepped closer. Her eyes widened. Her pulse tripped over itself before racing off so fast it made her light-headed.

"I know it's too soon," he murmured, his words as dark and deep as the night sky, "but I have to taste you."

Alexia's mental gymnastics melted away, right along with her resistance. Desire swirled down into her belly in a slow, sinuous slide.

Then his lips brushed over hers and she didn't care about stupid, resistance or the fact that they were on a public beach.

His breath was warm. His lips soft. The fingertips he traced over her shoulder a gentle whisper. It was sweetness personified. She felt like a fairy-tale princess being kissed for the first time by her prince.

And he was delicious.

Mouthwatering, heart-stopping, panty-creaming delicious. And clearly, he had no problem going after what he wanted, she realized as he slid the tips of his fingers over the bare skin of her shoulder. Alexia shivered at the contrast of his hard fingertips against her skin. Her breath caught as his hand shifted, sliding lower, hinting at, but not actually caressing, the upper swell of her breast.

Her heart pounded so hard against her throat, she was surprised it didn't jump right out into his hand.

She wanted him. As she'd never wanted another man in her life. Years, she'd behaved. She'd carefully considered her actions, making sure she didn't hurt others. She'd poured herself into her career, into making sure her life was one she was proud of.

She had a man who wanted her in his life. A nice, sweet man who she could talk through the night with and never run out of things to say.

But she wanted more.

She wanted a man who'd keep her up all night screaming with pleasure. Who'd drive her wild, who'd send her body to sexual places she'd never even dreamed of. She wanted orgasms. Lots and lots of orgasms.

Even if it was only for one night.

And that, she realized, was the key. One night of crazy. One night of delicious, empowered, indulge-her-every-desire sex with a man who made her melt.

One night would be incredible.

One night would be enough.

"This is crazy," she murmured against his lips.

"Yeah," he agreed, his tongue sliding over her lower lip before he nipped the tender flesh. When she gasped, he soothed it with a soft kiss. "But crazy feels damn good."

It did.

She wrapped her arms around his neck, leaned into the hard, solid wall of his muscled body and gave a low moan of delight. He felt really, really good.

Blake pulled back then, giving her an intense look. As if he was trying to see past her heart, into her soul. As if he knew all her secrets, her every desire.

Then he smiled. A slow, wicked curve of his lips. As if he'd just figured out how to make every one of those desires a reality.

Now, *that* was a scary proposition. Scarier still, she was pretty sure he could.

She wanted him. Wanted nothing more than to strip him naked and run her hands over every inch of his hard body. To touch, to taste. To feel. Oh, God, she wanted to feel him. To give herself tonight to feel, to enjoy. To live.

"Did you ever want something you knew you shouldn't have?" she asked, her words so soft they almost disappeared in the sound of the surf. She traced her fingertip over his lower lip, then sighed and met his eyes. "Something you knew you'd be better off not even considering, but were so tempted by?"

"No."

Figured. Alexia laughed helplessly, dropping her forehead to his shoulder and closing her eyes.

"But I know what it's like to want *someone* that bad," he said quietly, his voice so intense she had to raise her head to look at him.

He shifted, sliding his hands in a whisper-soft caress up her cheeks, then tunneling his fingers into her hair. Cupping her head just above her ears, he tilted it back just a little and stared deep into her eyes.

Alexia shivered. Her heart skipped, then tumbled over itself trying to catch up.

His gaze was hypnotic. Penetrating. The moonlight glowed, glancing off his cheekbones and giving him an otherworldly air. As if he was straight out of one of her fantasies, sent by the universe as a reward for her being such a good girl for so long. A chance to be bad again for just a tiny little bit of time, and then she could go back to being on her best behavior.

She wanted Blake, and this feeling between them. His hands skimmed through her hair, fingers tangling softly in her curls. This delicious, overwhelmingly intense feeling of excitement. Her body hummed, her senses went on hyperalert. It was as if each touch of his fingers was amplified, exciting her more than she'd ever been before. More than she'd even imagined.

"Shouldn't we talk about this?" she asked, desperately trying for sane and practical. "Make sure we know what we're doing?"

"Babe, I promise you, I know what I'm doing."

Whether to prove it, or to shut her up, he shifted again, his fingers strong, firm against the back of her head as he held her face up for his lips.

His tongue tangled with hers, demanding a response, pulling passion out of its worried hiding places and daring it to dance. Alexia's fingers dug into his shoulders as her mind gave up the fight to be rational and dived into the delights he offered. To hell with discussing it. Who needed a clear understanding of what the parameters of this exchange were when the communication between their bodies was coming through loud and clear.

Sexual nirvana, his body promised.

Hers couldn't respond with anything but *Let's rock.*

CHAPTER FOUR

BLAKE SPENT A GREAT DEAL of his life under fire. He'd honed his body to be a strong, powerful weapon, ready to face down and beat any danger.

He was pretty sure he'd never felt so out of control as he did right now. It was as if Alexia was a sudden addiction he couldn't do without.

"You feel so good," she breathed, her hands gripping his shoulders, then sliding down the hard muscles to curve over the rock-hard roundness of his biceps. "So strong. Big."

"You ain't seen nothing yet," he said, his laughter a whisper of air over her throat.

"Then show me," she challenged. Using her nails, she scraped a soft line back up his arms and shoulders, then down his shoulder blades, pulling his body closer against hers.

He groaned in reaction, both to her move and her aggressive attitude. She was clearly a woman who knew what she wanted, and wasn't shy about getting it. Was there anything sexier? Still, they should probably go somewhere. Since he lived on base, and was currently banned, he'd been bunking at Cade's. So that was out. A hotel seemed tacky. Her place?

She leaned in, her breasts softly pressing into his chest as she placed tiny, nibbling kisses along his jaw.

When she reached his ear and blew a soft gust of warm air, he groaned again.

He wasn't going to last till they found somewhere else. He had to have her. Here. Now.

Eyes narrowed, he peered up the beach. Their chances of being caught were slim. To narrow the odds even more, he swept her into his arms.

"Whoa," she exclaimed breathlessly, automatically wrapping her hands behind his neck for balance. He shifted her tighter against his chest and strode around the copse of boulders, far away from curious eyes.

"Better," he decided as the dark blanketed them, the rocks blocking the party, the lights and the people. He gently set her on a stone ledge, the height of it putting her breasts at mouth's reach. He stepped between her legs, nestling there. Exactly where he wanted to be. "Perfect."

Before she could comment, or worse, protest, he took her mouth again. She tasted sweet. Like sunshine and smiles and a hint of strawberries. Delicious. He was starving for more.

He rested his palms on her knees for a second, warming her skin before he caressed his way up the smooth, silky warmth of her thighs. He felt her shiver. Her breath caught. So damn sexy. He traced the edge of her dress, the fabric soft and smooth, but nowhere near as soft as her skin.

She was his escape. When he touched her, everything in his mind shut down. All the dark thoughts, the emptiness, they went away. It was as though the hollow desolation of the last month just disappeared. Instead, he had a single focus. Pleasure. Feeling it, giving it.

And keeping her totally focused on this passion between them, so she wouldn't think to slow it down. Because he was pretty sure if she stopped him, he'd make an embarrassed fool of himself and do something really crazy.

Like beg.

His tongue danced soft and slow over hers as he skimmed his hands down to her knees, then back up her thighs. He cupped the back of her thigh in one hand, shifting her so that her legs rested against his hips. With the very tips of his fingers he traced a gentle path along the edge of her panties, right there in the crease of her thigh. Hip bone to the top of her thigh, then back. A little deeper, a little closer to her core. Then back to her hip bones. His fingers slid down again, slipping under the slender elastic as they went. Teasing, loving how tight she felt as he wound her up, he stopped just short of her tempting flesh.

Her fingers dug into his arms, her thighs trembling at his touch. Her breathing intensified, and he could feel her heartbeat beneath his fingers, fast and furious.

He shifted his mouth over hers, taking the kiss deeper. Their tongues dueled, each fighting for control. She challenged him, stirred up a desperation he'd never felt before. The taste of her was beyond words. So delicious. So incredible.

Then she shifted. Her body beckoned, her warmth luring him closer. He needed more. He had to feel her. His fingers slid along the elastic of her panties again, this time hooking into the tiny lace band holding the sides together. He pulled.

She gasped as the fabric slid down her legs, then caught. Moving fast, again, needing to touch, to taste, he shifted so he pulled her panties away, then tucked the fabric into his back pocket. In less time than it took her to inhale, he was back. Right there between her thighs. Her warmth.

Delicious.

The movements had pushed the wildly patterned fabric of her dress higher, to the crease of her thighs. The moonlight shone on the hint of curls peeking from beneath. Beckoning. Tempting.

Blake didn't have the power—didn't want to find the strength—to resist temptation when it came in the form of Alexia. Starting at her knee again, he slid his index finger up the inside of her thigh. Wanting to see her reaction, he locked his gaze on hers. His fingers combed softly through curls that were gratifyingly damp, then skimmed the swollen bud nestled there.

Her gasp filled him with as much pleasure as touching her did. She squirmed a little, as if trying to intensify the pressure. Always glad to make a lady happy, he did just that. She gave a breathy moan, her hands now roaming his chest, scraping a delicate path of fire down his pecs and making him want to strip naked and see what she'd do next.

Her touch was perfect. Just the right blend of rough and delicate as her fingers scraped lower, along the flat planes of his belly. He sucked in his gut, wanting her to delve lower, to touch him the way he was touching her. Wanting to see how fast, how hard, they could go at each other.

Pulling his mouth from hers, he buried his face in the delicate curve of her throat, breathing deep her scent. It turned him on even more.

"You're delicious," he told her as he pinched her swollen clitoris softly. It was like triggering a switch.

Her entire body stiffened, her breath coming in gasps now. She went up fast. He'd bet she was wild once she caught fire. Wild enough to take anything he had, to handle the intensity of his sexual appetite.

SHE WAS ON FIRE. Hot, intense and wet, Alexia gasped at the pleasure Blake's body offered. She let her suddenly too-heavy head rest against the rock as his fingers slid, first one, then two, deep into her core. Slid and swirled. Heightening and tightening.

It was as if he had her entire body, her entire being, in the palm of his hand. Literally. His to control. His to pleasure.

Oh, please, yes. More pleasure.

She pressed herself tighter against his hand, her hips undulating, circling, trying to take him in deeper. Her breath came in gasps, all of her being focused on his fingers. On the feelings he stirred. The scent of the ocean mixing with Blake's subtle cologne adding to the surreal, out-of-this-world feeling she had.

It turned her on even more.

The sound of people partying, just on the other side of the rocks, made her nerves sing, worry about one of them venturing this way adding a whole 'nother level of intensity to the feelings Blake's fingers were creating.

She'd never been an exhibitionist. She'd never been turned on by the idea of public kissing, let alone semipublic orgasms. But this was…

Oh, my God.

Her breath came faster as his fingers worked her.

Her heart raced, trying to keep up with the wild, intense feelings rioting through her body. She couldn't think, could barely breathe. Everything she had, everything she was, centered on Blake. His fingers, the pressure.

Oh, baby, the pressure.

Desperate for him to feel as good as he was making her feel, she skimmed her fingers, just the tips, along the hard, rounded muscles of his arms. His body was incredible. Masterful.

She wanted to touch him, to fan her hands all over the firm, sculpted planes of his body. But she couldn't find the energy to move. Not while he was doing such lovely things with his fingers. She was so focused on that, she barely noticed his other hand slide under her dress, up to her breasts, until he cupped one, squeezing tight.

"Oh, God," she moaned breathlessly, staring up at the stars overhead through blurry eyes.

His thumb brushed over her nipple. Sensation, sharp and enticing, shooting from her clitoris to her breast like lightning. With a quick flick, he unsnapped the front closure of her racer-back bra, the fabric breaking loose under her trapeze dress. The constrictive straps slid down her shoulders. Hating the trapped feeling, she quickly shrugged off the white satin, not caring where it fell.

She grasped his head with both hands, pulling his face to hers. She had only a brief glimpse of the flaring heat in his blue eyes before her mouth attacked his. Ate him up in big, gulping bites.

His fingers pinched, rubbed, swirled. Her nipples hardened, aching for more. As if hearing their pleas, he pressed harder, flicking his thumb back and forth, back and forth. Her body tightened. Her girlie parts wept with pleasure. His fingers moved faster between her thighs, plunging deeper into her core.

Then he pressed her aching bud tight with his thumb, his fingers—all of them—still tormenting.

The climax grabbed her so fast, she couldn't stop the cry of pleasure. Vividly aware that there were people nearby, she tried to stifle her screams, so instead they came out strangled gasps. Everything spun in circles. Her head, the stars, the hot delight low in her belly.

Before she could come back down, before her body was even through shuddering, he moved. She was vaguely aware of the sound of ripping foil as he readied himself. Her thighs fell wide, as if begging to feel his hard power there, thrusting deep.

Instead, though, he grabbed her, lifting and turning at the same time so it was him bare against the rock.

She cried out in surprise, then in pleasure, as he pulled her close. Her body, still quaking from that lovely climax, wrapped around his.

His hands were so big, each one covered a cheek. He pulled her forward, gripping her flesh with strong fingers, positioning her. The velvet knob of his penis pressed, just there against her still-quivering flesh, as if begging for entry.

"Ready for some passion?" he asked, his words husky and low.

"Sure," she breathed, linking her fingers behind his neck and preparing for what she hoped was going to be a wild ride. "Because so far it's been pretty bland."

His laughter rang out, the sound making her ego feel almost as good as her body did with his pressed against it.

Then he slid, hard and deep, inside her.

She'd been wrong.

Nothing, ever, had felt this good.

It was as if her nerve endings all picked up and moved between her legs, every single sensation in her body connected to the feel of his cock driving in and out.

He moved slowly, with just a hint of undulation as he plunged. His hands gripped her butt, his strong fingers adding a whole new level of pleasure to the experience.

"You're going to come for me," he muttered, his words tight, low. Intense.

As if under his command, she instantly went over.

Alexia's body shook with the power of her climax. Her breath came in gasps, pleasure so tight, so intense, it bordered on pain. Her ears rang out, the surf disappearing so all she could hear was her own pounding heart.

As her body slowly settled back down to earth, she tried to catch her breath. Tried to reconnect with reality. Given that tiny trembling orgasmic aftershocks were still rocking through her, it wasn't easy.

All she could hear was his breathing, and the sound of her own heartbeat, loud and throbbing in time with his thrusts. Despite their semipublic love nest, she had a surreal sense of being outside the real world. As if this side of the rocks sheltered them in their own little bubble, away from real life. Away from repercussions or choices. Her head fell back, making way for his lips along her throat. For his kisses. His tongue.

It was as if he was flipping the switch from hot to blazing, bring her back to life, back to total awareness. Of the warm night air. The sound of the surf. The feel of his shoulders, so strong beneath her fingers. And his erection, still so hard and huge inside her.

"More?" she murmured.

"At least two more," he promised.

She gave a breathless laugh. No way. She didn't think she had two more orgasms in her. She had him in her, though, so she was ready to be proved wrong.

"Big talk," she teased, her fingers twining through the short hair at the back of his neck.

"Hold tight," he said, shifting his grip so his fingers were tighter on her butt. "Proof is on its way."

Then he leaned down, unerringly finding her pebbled nipple through the fabric of her dress and sucking hard. She shuddered, moaning over and over in time with his thrusts.

The tension wound again, tight and low as she gave herself over to the power he had over her body. Clearly he was a man who liked a challenge, and if he said two more orgasms, then dammit, she'd be reveling in two more mind-blowing orgasms.

He nipped, his teeth working her nipples through the wet silk. Alexia popped like a champagne cork, pleasure spewing from her in an explosion. Her nipple beaded, hard and aching beneath his lips. Her stomach constricted as heat curled lower, spinning tighter.

"That's one," he counted breathlessly.

And zero for him. As her body drifted back to earth, Alexia realized that he was calling all the shots. Not a bad thing, since those shots felt so damn good. But she wasn't the passive type, and she had a few shots of her own. She wanted him to go over. Wanted to drive him so crazy, he couldn't control himself. Wanted to feel him explode, to know that he felt as wild for her as she did for him.

But she couldn't use her hands because letting go of his shoulders meant she'd probably land on her butt in the sand. If she leaned forward to use her mouth, he might lose his grip, or worse, the perfect position he'd found that had his dick sliding against her clitoris with every thrust.

All she had were her hips, and those were in his hands. Still…

Calling on her thrice-weekly pilates training, she constricted her core muscles, her glutes flexing so she could grip him tight, like a fist, as he slid inside her.

He gasped. Groaned. His next thrust was hard and deep. Then he sucked in a breath and yanked himself back under control.

Oh, so he thought he could resist, did he? She gave a wicked grin. And clenched him again, this time swirling her hips against his.

The move sent yet another orgasm spiraling through her, her clitoris quivering, her breath rasping in and out.

That's all it took to send him over.

He thrust, hard, out of control. Intense, pounding pleasure poured through her as he gave a low moan, his body shaking as he poured out his climax.

Alexia's head dropped against his shoulder, her thighs trembling too hard, muscles too liquefied to keep them wrapped around him any longer. So she let them drop, her toes sinking into the soft sand. She felt as if she'd run a marathon while having a deep-tissue full-body massage and eating herself into a chocolate coma, all at the same time.

Pretty damn incredible.

Blake shifted, just a little, making the sand beneath her feet cave in a few inches. The sounds of music, of the partyers' voices, carried on the night air, dancing just above the surf.

Suddenly, awareness poked its sharp fingers through the fog of sexual delight. Made Alexia aware that she was practically naked, although her dress kept her modesty intact. That she'd just had three screaming orgasms with a virtual stranger, on a public beach, with a bevy of other strangers just yards away.

Holy cow, what had she been thinking?

Where had her good sense gone?

And why did she know, without a doubt, that given the chance, she'd do it all over again? What did that say about her? And, suddenly going all girlie, she cringed and wondered what Blake thought about her actions. Other than gratitude for one hell of a fine ride.

Cold, even though the temperature hadn't changed, she stepped out of his embrace. Unable to look at him, she rubbed her hands up and down her arms and made a show of looking around for her underwear.

"Well, I guess you showed me," she said, her words as shaky as her laugh. She would have pushed her hands through her hair, but between his fingers earlier and the sea air, she knew she was probably already rivaling Bozo in volume. So she settled for twining her fingers together.

Alexia jumped when his hands closed on her upper arms. She automatically looked into his face, meeting his gaze. Warmed by the calm affection in his blue eyes, she felt a little of the tension drain away. Why was she ashamed? Healthy sex, between two consenting people? She gave a mental eye roll at the sudden, silly and totally not-her inhibitions that'd taken hold.

And wished like crazy that the eye roll was enough to make them go away.

Blake let go of one of her arms, reaching up and rubbing his thumb over her lips. A gentle caress quickly followed by an equally gentle kiss. When he pulled back, she sighed.

"I'd say we showed each other," he said quietly.

It wasn't a promise or declaration. It probably wasn't even meant to be a reassurance. But she felt as if it was both. A promise that he didn't think less of her and the reassurance that he'd stepped just as far outside his normal as she had.

"I guess we did." Her smile was about as big as her lips would stretch, but still not even close to how large and bright the bubble of joy inside her chest felt. "I suppose you should get back inside and meet that friend?"

She nibbled on her bottom lip, anxious to hear his response. He didn't make her wait long.

"Nah. We can go inside and have another drink if you'd like, though." He didn't sound excited. But he didn't let go of her, either, so she took his lack of enthusiasm to be for the drink, not the company.

Alexia took a deep breath. She'd told herself one night. And she'd already proven that she wasn't a chaste good girl who required a ring—or hell, even dinner—for a sex romp. So there was nothing to stop her from grabbing on to her *entire* night.

"Did you want to go back to my place?" she asked. "I just have to call a cab."

His lips shifted, a slow, sexy smile curving his

mouth. The kind that lit up his eyes and made her want to hug him close because he was so damn cute.

"I've got my truck." He let go of her and reached into his pocket, handing over her panties. "You might want these, though. I held on to them so they wouldn't get all sandy."

"Aren't you the gentleman," she teased, gratefully taking the tiny scrap of silk.

"You know it. And I'd like to think the only abrasions you're going to have on your thighs are coming from my whiskers."

Alexia's breath caught. Her heart danced. And her body—which should be sexually satisfied enough to last for weeks—did a giddy little cheer.

"Then let's see how soon we can make that happen," she said, wriggling into her panties, then holding out her hand.

When he wrapped his fingers in hers, she began the mental chant *one night, one night, one night.*

One helluva night.

CHAPTER FIVE

Everywhere Blake looked was desert. Weapons fired around him, shots flaring like fireworks, bright and loud. Their quick in-and-out rescue had taken a left turn. Not a problem. SEALs were always prepared. He radioed in to report the ambush while Phil and Cade pulled the rocket launcher out of the pack.

"Knock knock." Phil grinned.

Blake jackknifed into a sitting position. One fist rose in fury, the other slapped to his hip for his sidearm. But his hip was naked.

Just like the rest of him.

Shuddering, he swiped his forearm over the sweat trickling off his brow and took stock.

Naked. In bed. Sexy female body curled in the sheets next to him. Sunrise was peeking through uncurtained windows. Other than a long dresser and a stack of moving boxes, them and the bed, the room was empty.

Alexia's condo. Where he'd been for two incredible, sex-filled, erotically intense days. He turned his head. She was splayed across the satin sheet where she'd collapsed after their last round. Facedown, vivid red curls curtaining her face and shoulders, so only a hint of her rose tattoo peeked out, she was totally zoned. Given that they'd slept maybe a sum total of six of the last fifty-two hours, he wasn't surprised.

But he was grateful.

Wanting air, needing space, he carefully slid from the bed, grabbed his jeans and left the room. He skirted packing boxes, still lined and neatly labeled against the living-room wall. She hadn't been kidding when she said she'd just moved from New York. Most of her stuff, except a few large pieces of furniture, was still packed.

He was pretty sure she'd been here a week or two. Wouldn't most women have hit the boxes, hung the curtains, filled the space with doodads by now?

Not that they'd talked much, but he'd got the impression during one of their between-sex rest breaks that she wasn't in any hurry to settle in. Why? Missing New York? Not a fan of the California sun? He knew she'd lived here before, but not when. What'd made her leave? Was the job going to be enough to keep her here this time?

And why did he care so much?

Caring, wanting to know she'd be here long-term, curiosity about her past, her present, her future. Those were all off-limits. Bad ideas for a man who played Russian roulette for a living.

He crossed the cool living-room floor, his feet silent on the Mexican tiles, around the dining table and into the nook of a kitchen. A coffeepot, a single pan and a pair of wineglasses were all that were visible. He skipped the glass and stuck his head under the faucet, letting the cold water wash away the remnants of nausea his dream had caused.

He hadn't used sex to numb the memories, but if

he'd been the type to do that kind of thing, it sure as hell hadn't worked. He shook the water off his hair, grabbing a paper towel to dry his face, and stared out the small window at the smaller garden beyond. Bright tropical-looking flowers bloomed, innocent and welcoming.

He felt happy and alive and filled with the weirdest sort of contentment with Alexia. She made him laugh. Watching her the few times she'd slept had filled him with a scary sort of peace. Her body was a wonderland, one he wanted to explore and lose himself in over and over again.

He didn't belong here.

He didn't do relationships, for one. And even though she'd made sounds like she wasn't looking for one either, she was the relationship kind of woman. Or maybe just the kind of woman who meant relationships to him.

He was due back on base the day after tomorrow. Most likely out of the country before the end of the week. And she didn't do navy guys. At least, Blake winced, she didn't when the guy was honest and up front before she'd done him.

Time to cut it short. Say goodbye, get back to real life. His gaze dropped from the view to his hands. Hands that just hours ago had been all over Alexia. Had touched, explored every inch of her delectable body. Hands that were as competent with a weapon as they were at bringing her to a screaming orgasm. Hands that *were* weapons.

He remembered the devastation on Phil's mom's face at the service. Blake's only comfort had been that nobody would be that torn up if he ended up in a flag-covered box. His only relation was his mom, who probably wouldn't sober up enough to attend. It was better that way.

Better not to get involved with someone. Not to ask them to risk caring, to risk being hurt.

Easier.

ALEXIA WOKE WITH a slow, moaning sort of sigh. Every muscle, every inch of her body was soaked in satisfaction. She could barely move, and wasn't even sure she wanted to wake. Except in sleep, she'd miss out on the fun and games. And she really, *really* liked fun and games with Blake.

With a soft, purring sort of moan, she rolled onto her back, shoved her hair out of her face and scanned the bed. The wide, empty expanse of bed.

She frowned. Where *was* Blake? His belt was still draped over her dresser handle, and his shoes there by the door. She should go look for him, but she needed a break. Time to figure out why she felt so empty waking without him next to her.

That was stupid, she told herself. He was a one-night guy who'd simply extended the party a little. She wasn't going to be a cliché and start wishing he'd ask for more. They'd both made it clear that wasn't what they wanted. And she'd be damned if she'd be the one to renege on that. Of course, if he happened to have changed his mind, she wouldn't say no, either.

Shoving her hand through her hair again, she tugged the curls a few times, hoping it'd shake loose some of the confusion. That her thoughts would line neatly up into nice, manageable rows the way they were supposed to.

Maybe if they talked?

But she'd noticed that Blake wasn't much of a talking kind of guy. Maybe because his mouth had been so busy doing other things. Delightful things. Deliciously wonderfully sexual things.

Whew. Alexia waved her hand in front of her face. Shower time. Hopefully the cool water would chill down her thoughts, and her body, so she could focus.

Climbing from the bed with less grace than usual, she winced at the delicious soreness between her thighs. Clearly, her gym workouts didn't address toning hot, wild sex muscles. The few feet to the bathroom sent new tingles of pleasure through her. Her body a vivid reminder of why she was on them, she took her birth-control pill. As she reached for the spigot in the shower, she caught sight of her reflection.

Her hair was a red halo, framing a face that almost glowed with residual ecstasy. Her lips were swollen, eyes heavy. Whisker rash spread over her entire torso and lower, below the mirror's view, like a sunburn. Proof that there wasn't an inch of her body that Blake hadn't kissed. Worshipped. Pleasured in ways she'd only read about.

With a shuddering breath, she flipped on the spigot, not bothering with the hot water.

Thirty minutes, and not a few shivers, later, she made her way down the hallway with a frown. Why hadn't Blake come in? Not that she thought she was so irresistible that he couldn't keep his hands off her for the time it took to shower, but still...

She stepped into the still-unfamiliar living room. Tension she hadn't even realized was knotted in her shoulders unraveled. There he was at the table, reading the paper with his bare feet propped on a chair. Bare feet didn't scream *time to run away,* did they?

"Hey," he greeted. He folded the newspaper and smiled. Friendly enough, but Alexia suddenly felt as if she was under the icy-cold shower again. "I figured on letting you sleep awhile. You must be pretty worn-out."

"That's sweet," she decided, belting her robe tighter and moving into the center of the room. Did she give him a kiss? Just act casual? She wasn't sure. "But you haven't had much sleep, either. Aren't you tired?"

"I'm used to going without."

For his job? Because he didn't like to sleep?

"Why?"

He got to his feet, offered a half shrug and a smile, then reached out to pull her into his arms.

"Good morning," he murmured just before his lips covered hers.

Alexia forgot her question—hell, she forgot her name—as his mouth took hers in a slow, decadent morning dance of delight.

"You hungry?" he asked against her lips.

"Hungry?"

"Yeah. I'm starving. I figured I'd wait to make us both something. You ready to eat?"

"Um, sure." She stood there, a little confused, as he pressed a quick kiss to the tip of her nose, then released her to head into the kitchen.

Food was good. It was a nice, nonsexual way to spend time together, she told herself, wandering after him into the kitchen.

Her toes barely touched the linoleum when he turned and waved her back.

"Have a seat, relax. Read the paper. I've got this."

A guy who cooked and didn't expect—or want—help? Well, well. Too surprised to protest, Alexia turned right back around and made her way to the couch. Once there, she still didn't know what to say. He'd booted her out of her own kitchen. To cook for her. Should she be irritated or thrilled?

For a woman who prided herself on her communication skills, she was having some definite issues figuring out how to converse with Blake. Of course, the fact that she couldn't figure out how she felt about any single thing probably didn't help.

Might as well quit worrying and just enjoy the experience, she finally decided.

As delicious as two days of naked romping, rolling and rocking were, even rabbits had to take a break from time to time. Knees a little weak as she recalled their last naked, rolling romp, Alexia snuggled deeper into her silk robe and watched Blake scramble eggs.

What was sexier? A man in the kitchen whipping up something delicious and nutritious? Or the sight of him, jeans unsnapped and slung low on his slim, tanned hips. *Oh, baby.* Alexia sighed, propping her chin on her fist. The man's body was a thing of beauty. Pure muscle, with not an ounce of fat anywhere. His shoulders were wide, his skin golden in the morning sunlight that streamed through her kitchen window.

"I didn't even realize I had eggs in the refrigerator," she said, her brain starting to awaken from its sexual stupor. She tore her gaze off his body to look at the counter between the condo's living room and kitchen. Orange juice, toast, a bowl of grapes. "Did you go to the grocery store?"

"Just next door," he said. "I borrowed some food from your neighbor."

Then he turned, frying pan in hand, to face her. Alexia actually felt her brain sputter as it sank under the waves of sexual heat again.

"I'm sorry. I should have had something here to feed you. A guest having to forage for his own breakfast fixings? That's a loss of major hostess points." She felt guilty as she slid to her feet. His eyes narrowed, locked on her body, then heated. Suddenly aware that her robe was gaping open, Alexia adjusted it with trembling fingers. Her breath hitched. Her pulse raced.

She'd lost count of the number of orgasms they'd shared, the multitude of ways they'd pleasured each other's bodies. She shouldn't be reacting like this. So hot, so easy. Shouldn't she know more about him before feeling so much more than desire? Shouldn't they have spent a lot more time together, clothed, before she started wishing he'd be giving her Halloween orgasms and Christmas orgasms and oh, please, Valentine's orgasms?

"I like cooking. Besides, you fed me dinner last night," he said with a shrug, dismissing the guilty apology she'd almost forgot she'd issued before diving down the emotional rabbit hole of worry.

He divvied eggs onto two plates, added toast and pushed them across the counter. Alexia frowned at the unspoken command—the guy was good at that—but picked them up and placed them on the table anyway. She came around the counter to get silverware while he carried juice and fruit to the table and sat.

"I fed you leftover fettuccine and steamed vegetables out of a freezer bag," she said with a laugh as she added forks to their plates. She pulled out a chair, but before she could sit, he grabbed her by the waist and swung her onto his lap.

Giggling, delighted, Alexia wrapped her hands behind his neck and tilted her head to the side. Her still-damp hair was chilly against her bare skin where the robe gaped yet again.

His eyes darkened to a midnight hue, narrowed with desire. She knew that look now. Knew the promise of it. Blake was demanding in bed. And in the shower. And on the balcony at two in the morning. Wherever their lovemaking took place, it was as if he grabbed inside her, took every bit of pleasure she could offer and then found a way to give her even more.

"I'll bet eggs would taste good eaten off your belly, too," he said, his voice low and husky against the sensitive curve where her shoulder met her throat. "Those noodles were pretty tasty that way."

That's what a woman got for not having a supply of chocolate and whipped cream on hand, Alexia thought ruefully. Cold noodles in gooey cheese and butter slurped off her skin.

She wrinkled her nose, ready to remind him what a failure that had been, tastewise, when he kissed her.

Deep, intense. Mind-blowing.

Alexia melted.

Slowly, her lips still clinging to his, he pulled back and arched one brow at his plate.

She wasn't sure why she didn't want to. She had no idea where the strength to resist came from, but suddenly it seemed like the most important thing in the world. She needed a little distance, she realized. Some space to get a grip on this...what? It wasn't a relationship, was it? She didn't even know his last name. Had no idea what he did for a living. It wasn't as if the last two days had been silent. They'd shared plenty of words. It was just that most of them were in the form of directions, dirty talk or cries of ecstasy.

"I'd hate to ruin the taste of the eggs with the flavor of my body wash," she said, giving a little laugh as if it was a joke instead of a blatant excuse.

Blake didn't complain, though. Nor did he push the issue. He simply smiled, let her go and picked up his fork. He waited until she was seated before digging into the eggs on his plate.

The man was perfect. How was that possible?

It wasn't.

She settled in her chair, the brush of their knees sending sexual tingles up her thighs to tease her still-quivering flesh.

"Where are you from?" she asked after a few bites. She was suddenly aware that while she knew just how much pressure he liked when she stroked him, and how sucking on his tongue made him crazy, that was about the extent of her knowledge. "Are you a California boy?"

"No. I grew up in South Carolina, but now I'm more of a nomad."

She waited. But that was it. He didn't expand, he didn't explain. He just scooped up another forkful of eggs.

What the hell?

"A nomad, hmm? Does that mean you're just visiting, or will you be around awhile?"

He finished the last of his eggs, then gave her plate

a questioning look. Alexia obediently forked up some of her own while he munched on toast.

"I'm here for a while," he said. "I like the weather in Southern California."

"And we have great beaches," she said with a smile, remembering where they first met. And, she quivered a little, where they first made love.

He didn't smile back, though. His gaze darkened, then shifted. As if someone had slammed the book shut. The pain she'd sensed in the bar was there again, radiating from him like a silent sob of misery.

They'd spent two days sharing their bodies. Surely he'd share this with her, too.

She wanted to ask him what was hurting him so deeply, why he was hiding from it. Before she could find the words, he gave her a wicked look, then reached one finger into the jelly bowl and scooped out a dollop of glistening orange sweetness.

"Taste?" he asked, offering her his finger. "Your neighbor said it's plum. Made from her own trees."

Beneath the amusement in his eyes was a challenge. Purely sexual, totally tempting. She couldn't resist. Alexia leaned forward, sucking the tip of his finger into her mouth. Yum. The sticky sweetness had a tart edge. As she swirled her tongue around, licking all the way to the knuckle, his gaze deepened. Intensified.

"More?" he asked, his voice husky.

Power, unlike anything she'd ever felt before, filled Alexia. This man had had her six ways from Sunday. He'd climaxed more times than she was years old. And he'd done it on barely any sleep. Yet just the swipe of her tongue, and he was all hot and bothered.

Totally turned on.

She stood, arched both brows, then unbelted her robe. All it took was a shrug for it to drop to the floor.

"Gorgeous," Blake moaned in delight. He leaned forward to pull her onto his lap, but Alexia shook her head. Nope, it was her turn to call the shots.

"Strip," she ordered.

He grinned. Then, proving he was all for equality among the sexes when it came to loveplay, he stood, and in a few quick moves, had that incredible body bared for her pleasure.

Alexia dipped her fingers into the jelly jar, then smoothed them over his lower lip. With a delicate swipe of her tongue, she licked it clean.

"Yum," she told him.

He grinned, waiting to see what she'd taste next.

She swirled the sweet jelly around his nipples. Then she sucked them clean. They tightened gratifyingly, first one then the other, beneath her lips. She smoothed her other hand down his slender hips, over the rock-hard angles of his sexy butt.

She dipped her fingers in the jelly again, dropped to her knees and kissed her way down his belly. His body was a feast. Every inch delicious. And she wanted to taste him all.

"Nope," he said with a strained laugh, grabbing her sticky fingers just before they could spread the breakfast preserve over his erection. "That'd get in the way of what I have planned next."

"But I wanted to taste," she said with a naughty smile. Her hand still in his, she leaned down to blow a soft puff of air on the glistening tip of his dick.

It jumped.

She slid a glance up at Blake, noting the hazy, almost-stupefied-with-wanting look on his face. Still, though, he didn't release her hand.

So she tasted without jelly.

First with just her tongue, sipping gently at the tip of his dick. Then she slid it down the hard length, and back up. His fingers, wrapped around her wrist, trembled. She sucked the velvety rounded tip. Just the tip. He groaned out loud.

Before she could take his entire delicious length into her mouth, he used her wrist to pull her to her feet. Her breath shocked right out of her, Alexia gasped. Still holding her hand, he lifted the jelly-smeared finger to his mouth and licked it clean. Then he grabbed her by the waist, flipped her around and pressed her body between his and the table.

"You're the most delicious woman in the world," he murmured against the back of her neck, his lips moving along her shoulder in soft, wet kisses. Both hands reached around, cupping her breasts. Fingers tweaked, pulled, swirled the tips until they ached with pleasure. Her butt brushed his erection again and again as her hips undulated, desperate for release. Wanting more, and since his hands were busy, she pressed her own down between her thighs, preparing, readying herself for the delight she knew he'd give.

"Mine," he protested, one of his hands sliding down to cover hers, twining their fingers together so they worked the aching swollen nub in concert.

Alexia moaned, heat swirling, passion building tight in her belly. Before she could climb too high, too fast, Blake bent her low over the table.

Her face nestled in her arms, she let him position her, lifting her hips for his entry. Even with proof so many times over of how big, strong and fabulous he felt inside, she still gasped with shock when, his hands braced on her hips, he plunged deep.

Her fingers dug into the tabletop, the wood cool and unyielding under her. Her hips shifted. Back, forth and back again, meeting his thrusts.

One hand still guiding her hips, he slid the other between her thighs, flicking his finger over the quivering bud there.

She cried out with pleasure.

He thrust again. Flicked once more.

Two strokes, then three. Her body exploded. Stars danced a wild boogie behind her closed eyelids as she gasped, moaning his name over and over. The orgasm rocked her, her body pressing tighter to the table, to his hips, as if she could somehow wring even more pleasure from the climax.

Her moves were all the encouragement he needed. Blake's fingers dug into her hips, holding her still for his body. With a guttural moan, he plunged again, then once more. Then he groaned, loud and long. His thighs, so hard and strong, quivered against the back of hers.

Spent, totally empty, her body lay across the table as she tried to catch her breath. To find her thoughts. To remember her name.

"I have to go," Blake murmured, his lips brushing her shoulder, making her shudder as yet another tiny orgasm rocked her body.

"No," she protested. She wanted to lift her head, to roll over and grab on to him. But she didn't have the strength. There was nothing left, he'd drained her dry.

She heard him move away but still couldn't open her eyes.

"Look, I've got a thing tonight," he told her. His voice was distant, as if he was trying to put space between them. A hint of panic flamed in her stomach. Before it could grow, he continued, "But I should be done by eleven, midnight at the latest. I'll come back."

Alexia's lashes fluttered. She forced her head to turn so she could see him. She wanted to protest. To tell him to ask instead of inform.

She might even have plans.

Her brow furrowed.

Wait.

She did have plans.

"I'm busy tonight," she realized, not sure which she wanted more. To exert herself, proving that this was a two-way street and she'd be calling just as many shots as he would. Or to grab on to an excuse to ditch the admiral's retirement party and have another bout of mind-blowing sex.

"How busy?"

She sighed. She'd promised Michael she'd be there. And she'd promised herself that if she moved back, she'd make her best effort to get along with her parents.

"Very busy." Pulling a face at having to climb off the cloud of sexual nirvana, she rolled to her side. Blake's eyes heated to blue flames. "I've got a family thing going on."

She only hesitated a second before adding, "But I can be back by midnight."

He zipped his jeans, tucking his T-shirt in and giving her a long, contemplative look. As if he knew exactly what she was offering. Not just sex. Trust. A chance to see where this went. And, she admitted to herself with a sigh, rolling off the table, a boatload of expectations.

She could see the hesitation in his blue eyes. Knew he was weighing all that, probably against how fast he could hit the door. He stepped forward, sliding between her legs again and resting his hands on her bare waist.

Eyes open, staring into hers, he leaned down to meet her lips. Whisper soft, it was a promise, an acceptance. For the first time, his kiss didn't make her think, *Let's get naked.* It made her think, *Wow, there goes my heart.*

"Midnight, then," he said, kissing her one more time before striding to the door.

And just like that, she felt committed. She didn't know anything about him other than his name, that he was incredible in bed and that she'd trust him with her life.

Trust. That was the biggie.

Other than Michael, had she ever trusted another man in her life? Growing up with an emotionally—and often physically—absent father who ruled everything on a need-to-know basis, and a mother who didn't bother sharing important things like when or where they'd be moving next because she hadn't wanted to hear the whining, Alexia tended to demand a lot of information from people. Maybe it made her a little bit of a control freak, but she liked to know everything she could, before she made decisions.

And here she was, with a man who hadn't told her anything.

Alexia pressed her fingers to her lips, still sticky with plum jelly. The front door shut behind Blake.

"It's a date," she whispered to the empty room.

CHAPTER SIX

"CHEERS, BUDDY," Cade said, tilting his beer—in a glass, no tacky bottles at the admiral's retirement party—against Blake's. The sound was lost in the sea of well-modulated voices, yawn-worthy chamber music and the almost silent white noise of the air conditioner. "Gotta admit, the old guy has style."

Blake shrugged. He'd grown up poor enough to appreciate that using a glass instead of the bottle gave the guy doing dishes a chance to earn a living. But other than that, opulence confused more than impressed him. What was the point? Rich people were more worried about showing off their fancy than guys were showing off the size of their…muscles.

He didn't bother saying that to Cade, though. Compared to the Sullivans, Cade's family, Admiral Pierce might as well move into the trailer park Blake had grown up in.

"What do you think he's gonna do now that he's retired?" Cade asked idly, his mellow tone at odds with the sharp intensity of his gaze as he scanned the crowd. "Put on one of those flowered shirts and putter in the garden?"

"I hope someone takes pictures," Blake snorted. Then, after another drink, he shrugged. "He's mentioned doing consults in D.C., maybe put together some programs here on the base."

That was the great thing about Cade. No pissiness over Blake having an inside track with the admiral. Then again, Cade's uncle was a senator and his father owned half of Northern California. So he had plenty of inside tracks of his own.

"Why bother to retire, then?" Cade asked. "Retirement is supposed to be relaxing, isn't it? Like R&R every day?"

Blake grimaced. That was way too much relaxing for him. Like this party, that kind of deal just wasn't in his cards. He scanned the crowd again, looking for a waiter and another beer.

Unlike the poor civilian saps in tuxes, he and Cade, along with a bunch of bright shiny brass, got to wear their dress whites. It wasn't fatigues, but close enough to keep him comfortable.

"Sir," the waiter said with a little bow as he exchanged Blake's empty glass for a full one.

He shifted his shoulders against the constricting fabric. At least he used to be comfortable. For the first time since he'd put it on, it felt as if his uniform didn't fit right.

"What's up?" Cade asked after exchanging his own glass. "You've been antsy as hell all night."

"Just want to get out of here. This isn't my kind of thing."

"Dude, ya gotta party while the music's playing."

Cade's grin disappeared as the words cleared his mouth. That'd been Phil's favorite saying.

Blake stared into his own pilsner glass. They were trained for this. They went into every single mission knowing it wasn't just a possibility, but a probability, that sooner or later one of them wouldn't make it out. So what was with the emotional drama? When did it get easier?

"Landon, Sullivan, glad you could make it," the admiral said in a big, hearty social voice. As opposed to the big, gruff commanding voice he usually used to bark out orders. There actually wasn't a whole lot of difference in the two, except the slightly disturbing smile on his face.

"Congratulations on your retirement, sir," Cade said. "The base won't be the same without you."

You had to hand it to him, Cade rocked this social bullshit. And the admiral ate it up with a spoon.

"I did my best to leave a strong mark," he claimed before giving Blake an indulgent look that made the hairs on the back of his neck stand up. "And I like to think I'm leaving behind a legacy. That my influence will carry on, if you know what I mean."

"The mark of a great leader is the impact he leaves on his troops," Cade agreed.

Blake didn't have to look at him to know that beneath his social tone, his buddy was smirking.

"And speaking of legacies," the admiral said, pulling on that social smile again, "Landon, there's someone I'd like to introduce you to."

"Sir?" Shit. He didn't want to meet anyone.

"My daughter. A lovely young woman. Articulate, bright and gainfully employed. Top-security clearance, a solid portfolio, and being my daughter, she's well versed in what's required to support a military household."

Obviously Pierce didn't play matchmaker very often.

And Blake wished like hell he wasn't doing it now. He wasn't stupid. He knew what game the admiral was playing. The old guy liked Blake's story. SEAL, linguist, decorated soldier triumphing over a pathetic childhood. The son-in-law ad practically wrote itself.

Except Blake wasn't in the market.

"I'm sorry, sir," Blake said. "I'd be happy to make your daughter's acquaintance, but I won't be asking her out. I'm seeing someone."

It wasn't until he saw the shock on his superior's face that Blake realized this was the first time he'd said no. His shoulders twitched again. It wasn't as if he'd refused an order, he told himself. All he'd done was sidestep the questionable honor of being dangled in front of the admiral's daughter.

"Elliot, darling," Mrs. Pierce said, giving Blake an apologetic smile before dismissing him with a tilt of her head. "It's time for the toast."

"Excellent," Pierce said, arching his brow at Blake. "You'll wait, of course. I'd like to finish this discussion."

Blake almost saluted out of habit.

"I'm a soldier, not a lapdog," he muttered instead as soon as the old guy was out of earshot.

"What's the big deal? You meet his daughter, play nice, then skip out to hook up with that hot redhead again."

Blake frowned.

"What? You didn't think I could figure out why you've been mooning all night?" Cade laughed. "Dude, it's practically written on your face. I'm surprised you can drink that beer with the hook stuck so tight in your lip."

Like feeding jackals, denial was pointless. Besides, Blake shifted uncomfortably, he wasn't a hundred percent sure that he wasn't hooked good.

He was spared the need to think of a comeback thanks to a chiming crystal bell.

First time he'd ever been grateful for a speech.

The gratitude lasted about five minutes.

"I hate politics," Blake decided under his breath, not for the first time.

"You want to get anywhere, get anything done, you play the game." Cade shrugged as though it didn't matter. But his lips twisted, a bitter indication that he, too, thought the game sucked.

Blake ignored the droning accolades, letting his mind wander back to Alexia. As soon as this toast was over—regardless of who the admiral wanted him to meet—he was outta there. He wanted to see her. To talk to her. To taste and touch and have her.

No surprise, really, since he hadn't been able to get her out of his mind. Except the wanting to talk to part. That could probably be filed under shocking.

But as hot as things were between them, he knew she wasn't going to be satisfied with just sex much longer. She'd already been pushing, hinting. He remembered the aggravation in her eyes that morning. She wanted more, and if he wanted her, he was going to have to pony up.

He shifted, his uniform suddenly tightening like a straitjacket. Sharing his past wasn't an issue. Admitting his job? It was going to take a whole lot of charm to get her naked after he fessed up to being not only navy, but a SEAL, too.

He was pretty sure he had enough, though.

"Well, now..." Cade murmured, his grin wicked.

Blake followed his gaze.

He recognized the man first. Strawberry-blond hair fashionably tousled, alligator tuxedo lapels indicating not just custom, but way-out-there custom, and a ruby pinkie ring that glinted as he waved a friendly greeting to the crowd.

Michael?

What was he doing here? Was he a part of the entertainment? Blake wondered what he'd missed while he was obsessing over Alexia.

He watched the younger man reach out to assist someone onto the raised dais. His hand closed over slender fingers. It took an obvious tug to get the rest of the woman's body to move. Despite his confusion, Blake grinned. Somebody didn't like the spotlight.

Then, as people shifted, he saw who Michael was trying to drag onstage.

Her hair tumbled in loose curls over one bare shoulder, the red so deep it was almost black in places, so light it shone gold in others. Something black draped a tall, willowy body, the effect saved from elegance by the slender rose tattooed on her bare shoulder. The fabric was deceptively loose, but wrapped in a way that drew his eyes to the sweet curve of her breasts, the slender indention of her waist.

Breasts he'd tasted just hours before. A waist he'd gripped as he'd held her body over his, watching as she slid in a glorious rhythm, up and down his straining erection.

Alexia.

His sexy temptation.

His gaze shifted from her to the man of the hour,

suddenly seeing the resemblance in the shape of their faces, the arch of their brows.

The tiny hairs on the back of his neck that warned of trouble stood on end.

Alexia was the admiral's daughter?

Shit.

STANDING ON DISPLAY, Alexia kept her expression neutral and her shoulders erect. She hated these things. Her mother was as social as the admiral was bossy, which meant growing up there had been four over-the-top fancy functions a year.

Since Margaret Pierce came from money—lots and lots of money—that meant the parties were not only boring, but super-upscale boring. The only upside was that events on this scale meant that other than assuring themselves their offspring were in attendance and properly behaved, the admiral and Mrs. Pierce were too busy to do anything but ignore them all night.

When it came to her parents, Alexia usually believed that being ignored was best. But she'd forgotten how hellishly boring it was.

"Hide the ennui," Michael whispered. Thanks to her heels, he only had to lean sideways, so the exchange wasn't that noticeable. Good thing, since their mother was a stickler for social protocol.

"I'm swimming in ennui," she whispered back, her lips barely moving from their frozen smile.

Actually, she was swimming in anticipation. She glanced at the ornate grandfather clock on the landing and sighed. Only an hour till midnight. That meant a few boring speeches, a couple ostentatious odes to her father's brilliance, and whatever pompous response he ended the toast with, and she could leave.

Go back to her place and wait for Blake.

She'd been so amped up after he'd left, she'd finally dug into the packing boxes. Sure, she'd opened the first one in search of her favorite teddy, a confection of black lace and red satin. But within a few hours, she'd turned her barren bedroom into a comfortable oasis. One she'd be happy to spend another two days of sexual ecstasy in.

The image of Blake popped into her mind, his eyes intense, his incredible body poised over hers. So delicious.

She sighed, a soft fog of sexual warmth wrapping around her as it always did when she pictured the two of them together.

She couldn't wait to touch him again. To feel his body inside her. To taste the intense heat of his kisses. But first, before she let herself have any of that, the two of them would be sitting down for a little chat.

Because as wonderful as things were between them, she wasn't having sex with a stranger again. And, despite the fact that she now knew his body as well as she did her own, facts were facts. Blake was an *emotional* stranger to her.

"Why isn't Dr. Darling here to distract you?"

Guilt, sharp and cutting, sliced through Alexia's sexual fog. She had no reason to feel bad. There was no commitment between her and Edward, either concrete or implicit. It was stupid to feel guilty. Just because she'd spent the previous couple of nights rolling around naked in the sand, surf and sheets with the hottest, sexiest, most passionate man she'd ever met instead of calling the guy who wanted her to be his one and only?

She winced. Nope. No reason for guilt.

Michael's nudge reminded her that he was waiting for an answer. Since this probably wasn't the right moment to share her emotional confusion, she shrugged and went for humor instead.

"Are you kidding? Bring a date to a family affair?" she whispered back in mock horror. "That's never a good idea."

"It'd help you decide if you want to take the relationship plunge, though," Michael mused quietly. "What better way to see what a guy's made of than let him go up against the old man? If he caves, you know he's a wimp. If he cozies up, you know he's an ass."

Alexia shrugged. The only measure of her father she cared about was that any guy she was in a relationship with was nothing like the man who'd sired her. Other than that, she didn't care how he acted around the admiral.

She was just about to ask Michael to run interference once the toast ended—so she could slide out the door—when she caught the steely disapproval in her mother's stare. Alexia subtly nudged her brother, who straightened, too, both of them shifting their fake-smiling faces toward center ring as their father started speaking.

As the cadence shifted, winding down, she felt some of the tension seeping from her shoulders, out her fingers. They were in the end zone. She focused in on the words, listening to her father thank a laundry list of dignitaries, ranking officers and political cronies for their support of his career over the last four decades.

She leaned toward Michael.

"Think he'll include us?" she whispered.

"Nah," he whispered back. "The only time we come up in a speech is in terms of the challenges and struggles he's had to overcome."

"As soon as this is over, I'm outta here," she muttered.

"Not so fast. Remember, we're part of the receiving line. You have to stand and smile until everyone's done worshipping—I mean, congratulating Dad. Besides, you should stick around." Michael's smile was pure delight. "I'll bet your night improves."

"I'm sure it will."

Just as soon as she got out of here and called Blake. She surreptitiously glanced at the grandfather clock in the corner, noting it was already eleven-thirty.

Why couldn't her father have toasted goodbye to all his glory at a reasonable hour, instead of pushing it to the limits and forcing everyone to stay so late? She glanced around. Most of the guests were pretty darned old. They probably wanted warm milk and their beds instead of a boring speech and champagne.

Skimming the crowd, her gaze flew right past one particular face. Then, her brain screaming a warning, her eyes flew back so fast she probably lost a few lashes.

Blake?

Brow furrowed, she shook her head in denial.

What was he doing here?

Then her focus widened. Horror filled her with a cold, icy sort of misery.

No!

Her eyes bounced from his uniform to the medals

glinting off his chest, back to his face and then to the crowd of men he was standing with. SEALs.

Navy SEALs.

The man who'd driven her crazy, who had her thinking forever thoughts and craving a relationship, the one who made her want to play house—naked—was also the one thing, the only thing, on her forbidden-relationship list. Military. Elite military, and up until one speech ago, under her father's command.

How had she missed the signs?

Why hadn't he told her?

And when the hell would these speeches be over so she could run away?

BLAKE WATCHED the expressions chase across Alexia's face. Shock, then disbelief, quickly followed by fury. Then she shifted. Her body weight, the tilt of her head and her expression. It was as if she'd slammed the door shut.

Shit.

As much as he wanted to avoid any matchmaking from the admiral, he was equally determined to hold on to the sweet, pleasurable oblivion Alexia's body provided.

Hurry, hurry, hurry, he silently urged his commanding officer, knowing the longer Alexia had to stew, the harder it would be to charm her out of her snit.

Thankfully, the older man chose that moment to raise his glass in thanks. Blake absently followed along with the rest of the room, raising his, as well. But his eyes didn't leave Alexia.

A good thing, because as soon as the crowd shifted,

she lost herself in it. Clearly, growing up with military influence had taught her a thing or two.

Of course, Blake had some pretty solid training on his side. He noted the direction she was going, then skirted the outside of the crowd, cutting her off before she reached the door.

He placed his hand on her shoulder with just enough pressure to stop her escape. She hissed, a sound like cold water being thrown on a sizzling fire.

Blake dropped his hand.

"Surprise," he said quietly, suddenly very aware that they were surrounded by her family and his superiors. None of whom needed any details as to his and Alexia's relationship. "I didn't realize you were Admiral Pierce's daughter."

"And I didn't realize it mattered who my father was." Her tone was as cold as her eyes. A temperature he'd have sworn a woman as hot as she was could never drop to.

"It doesn't," he said, dancing out of that trap. Alert, knowing there were more to come, he weighed his words carefully. "I hadn't realized we had mutual interests."

She gave him a long, considering look that made him wish he was in combat gear.

"I hadn't, either. That's one of those things that usually comes up in conversation. Which is another thing we never had."

Blake shifted to block her exit again.

"Where are you going?" he asked.

"Away."

Blake had swum through the Arctic Ocean once and

swore it'd been warmer than her tone. Brows arched, he gestured to the open French doors.

"Why not go this way, then?" he suggested. "We can talk."

"No." Lips pressed so tight together they were white at the edges, she took a long, deep breath through her nose, then exhaled slowly. "No, thank you. I'd rather not go out on the patio. I'd rather not talk. I prefer to go home."

"I'll go with you."

"I prefer to go alone."

Before Blake could counter that, they were interrupted.

"Lieutenant," the admiral greeted with the biggest smile Blake had ever seen on his face. The empty champagne flute in his hand might factor in, but retirement probably didn't hurt.

"Sir." Blake shifted aside just a little so the older man could talk to his daughter. But instead of words, Pierce's smile dimmed and all he offered his daughter was a nod.

Then, proving that a dozen or so toasts hadn't affected his perception, his gaze shifted back and forth between them. "The two of you have met already?"

Blake waited for Alexia to answer.

"We said hello on the beach last week," she finally told her father.

"And?"

"And, nothing." Her words were as flat as her expression. Blake didn't get it. Alexia was unquestionably the brightest woman he'd ever met. Not just smart, although he was pretty sure she topped that chart, too. But bright in energy, in color. With her vivid red curls, her expressive face and her enthusiasm, she shone like neon.

Until now.

The color was still there. Her hair as red, her eyes as brown. Her smile, painted a vivid rusty rose, didn't alter. But she looked as if someone had flipped a switch and shut her down. Turned her off.

The last thing a woman like Alexia was meant to be was off.

Even pissed at him, she'd still shot off a few sparks. Like a woman with a fabulous temper who'd learned to control it. But now? Blake's gaze cut from her to the admiral, then back. What the hell was going on?

"I told you to plan on staying for at least an hour after the address to perform some specific social duties I required," the admiral informed his daughter, his gaze shifting from her face to her purse, clutched in white fingers, and then to the door.

"And I told you that I was here to celebrate your retirement, as mother requested. But that I'd have to leave as soon as the address was finished."

Blake was starting to get the impression that this wasn't a loving father-daughter relationship.

"I gave you an order, young lady. I expect it to be obeyed." The admiral gestured to Blake. "Luckily, the two of you have already broken the ice. Lieutenant Landon is one of my protégés. I'd like you to spend some time getting to know each other."

And there it was—Blake sighed—the last nail in his coffin.

He stepped forward, surreptitiously putting himself between father and daughter. Before he could defuse the situation, Alexia gave a chilly smile and shook her head.

"I'm sorry. We've spent enough time getting to know each other already and discovered we're completely incompatible. Now, if you'll excuse me…?"

Her icy smile skated over both of them before she turned heel and walked out.

Just walked right out the door.

It was a toss-up who was more shocked.

Blake, or her father.

Looked as if he didn't have quite as much charm as he'd thought.

"Excuse me," the admiral said stiffly before following her. Blake deemed it wise to stay where he was. Neither would welcome his presence at this point.

But he wasn't willing to let it go, let her go. Blake looked around.

There.

He made his way across the room to a small cluster of people.

"Excuse me," he interrupted, not caring about protocol or manners at this point. "Michael, I need to speak with you."

Alexia's brother's eyes widened as he realized who Blake was. He did a visual up and down, taking in the uniform, then offered a morose shake of his head. "Yep, we should talk."

He cheerfully excused himself from the couple, then gestured toward the same door Blake had tried to get Alexia through earlier. At least one of the Pierce siblings was willing to take a walk under the moonlight with him.

"I didn't know you were navy," Michael said as soon

as they cleared the French doors. With an elegant wave of his hand, he indicated they sit on the bench swing.

"Does it matter?" Blake asked, not wanting to sit since he saw this as more an interrogation than a friendly chat. Leaning comfortably against the wooden back, one foot cocked over his knee, Michael didn't seem to care.

"Not to me."

"But it matters to Alexia," Blake guessed. "Why didn't she say anything?"

"Well, it's not like you had an in-depth discussion there on the beach." Then he gave Blake a searching look, arched both brows and asked, "Unless you had a little tête-à-tête after the beach encounter?"

SEALs didn't break that easily. Apparently a denial or confirmation wasn't necessary. Michael gleefully dived right into conclusionville. "Ooh, this is juicy. Where did you hook up? And did you? Hook up, I mean? Obviously you did. No wonder she was all airy-fairy this evening. This is probably why she didn't want to bring Dr. Darling to the shindig."

"Who?"

"Some guy," Michael dismissed with another wave of his hand. "Doesn't matter. What matters are the details. When did you get together, where were you and what are your intentions? Those are the questions that need answering."

"What guy?" Blake persisted, shifting his body weight so he loomed rather than stood over the younger man. "What's his relationship with Alexia? Is she involved? Is he someone she cares about?"

"If she cared, he'd be here."

Blake rocked back on his heels.

He was here. But not with Alexia. There was a message in that somewhere.

"What's her issue with the military?"

"Well, you've met our father." For the first time, Michael's carefree facade cracked, showing a layer of bitter hurt. Blake had seen the same expression in Alexia's eyes in the bar, when she'd talked about military men. Seemed the admiral wasn't in the running for any father-of-the-year prizes.

"I'm sorry," Michael said, charm back in place as he got to his feet. "I really am. I think you'd be good for Alexia."

"So why are you sorry?"

"Because she won't talk to you again."

"You don't know that." Even though it was pretty much exactly what she'd said. But Blake didn't accept it. And what he didn't accept, he changed.

"Look, you're a great guy," Michael explained. "And Alexia deserves great, unquestionably. But she'll never date a soldier." He hesitated, as if he was worried about Blake's reaction. Then he laid a sympathetic hand on his shoulder. "I'm sorry."

Blake dropped to the bench swing as he watched the younger man walk away.

Up until three weeks ago, he'd loved his job. He'd trained for it, embraced it, lived for it. He'd never questioned being a SEAL. Never wanted anything else.

But in the space of the last couple of weeks, that same job he loved, he identified with, had taken two things that he hadn't wanted to give up.

His buddy.

And the most fascinating woman he'd ever met.

He couldn't do a damn thing about Phil. But he

could about Alexia. All he needed was a plan, a little strategy and the right hook. He'd get her back.

Damned if he wouldn't.

CHAPTER SEVEN

BLAKE GAVE ALEXIA an hour. Enough time to chill, but not enough to stew. He used the time wisely, stopping by Cade's to change into jeans. She hadn't been kidding when she said she wasn't a fan of a guy in uniform.

Truce wasn't going to be negotiated if he pissed her off from the get-go. Not that he expected an easy surrender on her part. She was too fiery for that. Too intense. Which was just one of the reasons he was crazy about her.

One of the reasons he refused to let her end this between them.

Parking his truck in front of her condo, he took a breath. Middle-of-the-night battles had a different feel than daytime skirmishes. An edge.

Prepared to win, he strode up to her door and knocked.

He figured she'd be mad at first, probably have that chill going still. He'd charm her a little, play the apology game, bring her around to admitting that he hadn't done anything wrong. Five, ten minutes tops and he'd be reveling in the pleasure of her again.

A few seconds later he knocked again.

He didn't have to look at his watch to know it was 1:00 a.m. Just like he didn't have to look at her brightly lit windows to know she was still up.

He waited a few more seconds, then pulled out his cell phone and dialed.

"You might as well answer," he told her machine when it picked up. "I'll stay here all night. Patience is a particular virtue of mine, remember? I can last all night, babe. You know that. Even when you're naked, gyrating over me and driving me crazy, I can hold out. Actually, I like waiting. It's like a personal test, to see how many times I can make you come before I can't control myself anymore."

Before he could detail all the things he'd liked that she did to push that control, the door swung open. Blake grinned.

Alexia's glare was lethal.

Her hair, sleek and sexy just hours ago, was brushed out in a wild frizz so it haloed her face like an angry red cloud.

Her face was scrubbed clean, the siren's glow that'd matched her evening dress completely eradicated. All that was left was a sprinkling of freckles across her nose and smudged remnants of mascara under her furious eyes.

His lips twitched. Was this girl-battle 101? Make the enemy think they don't want the goods so they walk away without bothering to engage?

Nope.

His gaze skimmed the huge sweatshirt, noting that Jon Bon Jovi was still sporting the big curls and guy-liner. The faded gray fabric enveloped her so well, her curves disappeared. Frayed cotton shorts drooped to her knees.

Her toenails were still a glittery, sexy red, though. Her legs smooth and silky looking.

Her translucent skin flushed with anger, she was just as sexy now as she'd been wrapped in that tiny bikini on the beach.

Not a chance he'd walk away.

He wanted those goods.

"We need to talk," he said. The sooner they did, the sooner he could strip ole Jon off her body and get down to worshipping those toes.

"Talk? You know the concept?" she asked, not shifting out of the doorway.

"I've been introduced to it a time or two," he said drily. Figuring she'd negotiate better if she thought she was calling the shots, he didn't push her to let him inside. Instead, he leaned against the door frame and gave her a charming smile.

She automatically stepped back, glowered, then stood her ground again. Damn, she was cute.

"I think the opportunity to talk has passed. I'm sure, as a military man, you're aware of how many battles have been lost not because of mistakes, but because of timing."

Blake wasn't sure if it was because he knew Pierce was her father, or if it was her tone of voice, so precise, cold and similar to the admiral's, but the resemblance between them was remarkable at that moment.

"I don't let other people's mistakes dictate my decisions," he told her. "And I've never lost a battle."

"Well, you won't be able to say that again, will you?" she taunted with a chilly smile.

Blake's smile wavered for a second. He'd figured she'd be angry, but this was a little over the top.

"Would you mind clarifying something for me?" he asked, running low on charm. Not waiting for her response, he continued, "I didn't do anything wrong. I didn't lie to you, I didn't cheat my way into your bed. I didn't even make any promises. I was respectful, honorable and up front."

He waited for her to acknowledge his largesse. Instead, she slammed her arms across her chest and glared.

Wow. Talk about standing guard over that mountain she'd constructed from a tiny pile of dirt.

"So, what's the deal?" he asked when he saw that's all he was going to get. "Why are you so angry?"

There.

The facts, simply laid out and incontrovertible.

He didn't expect an apology right away. He figured pride, the baffling twists of a woman's mind and maybe a little embarrassment at overreacting would have to be worked through first. He could wait.

His gaze skimmed her shapeless, colorless outfit again and his blood heated. He sure hoped she'd let him in so he could enjoy himself while he waited.

"Ah, those fine lines," she mused, relaxing enough to lean against the edge of the door she still gripped and crossing one ankle over the other. "The only problem with your argument is that you're ignoring intention. Communication isn't just the words we say, it's the message we intend to share."

"I don't want to sound crude, but what I intended to share was my body with yours. A good time, a lot of incredible sex and, as we spent more time together, maybe a chance to build more," he countered, reaching out to take her hand. He shoved his impatience back, telling himself this was part of what made her so appealing. Her fiery nature.

Then she moved her fingers away. His brow furrowed. But when she didn't close the door any farther he let himself start to relax. *Almost there.*

"Oh, yes, the wonders of sex. It was great, wasn't it?" she said, her smile wicked. He shifted, starting to feel a little nervous when it didn't reach her eyes. "And we both had the same intentions when it came to that. But one of us, unlike the other, hid pertinent facts in order to have all that great sex."

"I didn't hide a damn thing," he denied, starting to get irritated.

"No? You didn't hide your job, your lifestyle, your affiliation? Given that being a SEAL requires a level of dedication that's steeped in the blood, not sharing that was a deliberate choice on your part. Since I'd made my feelings about being involved with a military man clear, I can only assume that choice was made with the intention of hiding your career from me."

She sounded like a freaking lawyer. Or worse, he realized, gritting his teeth, a psychologist.

"You didn't share your last name," he countered.

"You're right." She inclined her head, the move sending her halo of frizzed-out curls wafting around her face. "And that makes me loose and easy. Which is still better than a liar in my book."

That was enough. Blake straightened, giving her a dark look. Name-calling? That's the best she could do?

"Look, you have some issues with your father. I get that. And I know he pissed you off with his little matchmaking game. But what does it matter? We're great together. You're not going to toss that away over him, are you? Because, what? You have some kind of

Pavlovian response, automatically rejecting whatever your father approves of?"

As the words cleared his lips, Blake cringed.

She froze. Everything except her eyes. Those were like fire. She gave him a long, slow once-over before meeting his gaze again. This time he almost stepped back. "Well, aren't you clever? Throwing out those psych terms like an expert. Clearly you've got it all figured out. So tell me, Blake… Do you know the meaning of closure? How about inductive reasoning? Or here's a simple one. Goodbye."

She didn't wait for his response before stepping back and slamming the door shut in his face.

Damn.

Furious with himself, Blake glared at the closed door.

He deserved to get shot down over that one.

Dammit, he'd just wanted a space from the memories, a chance to be a man instead of a soldier who'd just lost a brother-in-arms. What was it with women, always expecting a guy to spill his guts and blab like they did? He didn't want to talk about his job, or about Phil. He was escaping, not looking for a chance to wallow.

And if she'd wanted to know more about who he was, what he did for a living, then that was on her. She should have asked instead of pitching a fit after the fact.

He resisted the temptation to bang on the door again, shoving his fists in his pockets instead. Grinding his teeth, he stared unseeingly while his mind regrouped.

He wasn't finished.

He never gave up.

But, as much as it grated to admit, retreat was the only option right now.

Tomorrow, though?

Tomorrow, he'd win.

THE LAST THING Alexia wanted to do after a sleepless night spent crying over Blake was to face her father. She'd wanted to stay in bed with the covers pulled over her head and a bowl of hot fudge.

But she knew that walking out on his party was tantamount to a declaration of war. As with all conflicts the admiral oversaw, the battles would be played to win at all costs. But she'd spent her formative years learning strategy and figured she was as prepared as she could be.

She wouldn't win. Nope, she wasn't delusional. Going up against an admiral in the United States Navy, a SEAL trainer? She didn't stand a chance. This was all about mitigating damages.

The timing was crucial. A waiting period of just long enough for his temper to drop but not long enough for it to chill.

The combat zone had to be chosen with an eye toward tactics. Brunch at her mother's table didn't guarantee he wouldn't get ugly. But it did mean he'd have to stop to take sips of his coffee between insults.

Her weapons? Maturity and logic, and a gift for communication. As long as she kept her temper and presented her case in a diplomatic, intelligent way, the admiral would listen. He might not agree, but he'd listen.

So, there ya go, she told herself. *Ready to rock.*

Standing on her parents' porch, she pressed one hand to her churning stomach, said a little prayer and knocked.

She didn't recognize the housekeeper who answered, but followed her meekly down the hall. When they passed the French doors where she'd had her confrontation with Blake, she almost tripped over her own Jimmy Choos. Why'd he have to show up last night? Her eyes filled again, both fury and hurt making her want to hit something. It was like Cinderella at the ball, watching her prince turn into a rabid toad.

No. She clenched her fist around the strap of her purse and took a deep breath. This wasn't the time to think about Blake. All weaknesses, all worries, all distractions had to be ignored. Because eggs Benedict and mango aside, this was war.

"Mother," she greeted. Then, her fingers only trembling a little, she smiled at the admiral. "Father. Good morning."

"Alexia," her mother exclaimed. The older woman was perfectly made up. Her hair was more golden, like Michael's, than red like her daughter's, and fell in a smooth swing around a wrinkle-free face that didn't show a single sign of her late night. Ever the perfect hostess, she indicated to the housekeeper to bring in another plate even as she rose to give her daughter a kiss on the cheek. "What a lovely surprise."

"Lovely?" her father derided, snapping his newspaper shut and slapping it onto the table. He gave Alexia a dark look. "I had higher expectations of your moving back here, young lady."

For a second, just one sparkling bright second, Alexia's heart melted. He'd wanted her back? He'd anticipated her return?

"And this is how you behave now you're here? By insulting me and my guest?"

Silly heart, she chided, sliding into a chair and setting her purse at her feet to give herself time to blink away the unexpected tears.

"I'm sorry you saw it as an insult," she apologized when she looked up, her words sincere. "The last thing I wanted to do was hurt you."

She'd promised herself when she'd moved back to San Diego that she'd handle her relationship with her parents in a mature, dignified fashion. No hiding, no avoiding, no drama.

"I'm sure Alexia had a good reason for leaving," Margaret chimed in, irritation giving an extra snap to her words. "Let it be, Elliot. She's only been home a week, probably hasn't even unpacked yet. The last thing she needs right now is to worry about a relationship."

The tension ratcheting down a notch, Alexia gave her mother a grateful smile. It'd been rare growing up that their mother sided against their father. Allies must present a united front, after all.

"We'll have dinner next weekend," Margaret continued, gesturing to Alexia to have some fruit. "Just a quiet little get-together. You can invite the lieutenant then, Elliot."

Alexia's shoulders sagged. She fisted the crisp white fabric of her skirt between her fingers to keep from banging them on the table. She specialized in communication. Why could she never get through to her parents?

"I'm sorry, Mother," she tried again, calling on patience. "But I'm not interested in dating Lieutenant Landon. Not last night, not next week. Not ever."

"That's ridiculous," her father stated. "He's a fine

young man. A great career ahead of him. You're just being stubborn out of habit."

"No. I'm trying to be clear. I've just moved to town and, as Mother said, haven't even unpacked yet. I start a new job tomorrow, one that's going to take all my focus and concentration. I'm not interested in a relationship right now."

At least, not anymore. She pressed her lips together to keep them from trembling. Yesterday, she'd been wide-open to the idea.

"Speaking of that job," the admiral said, propping his elbows on the table and giving her a steely look. "I'd like for you to meet with the head of the Dillard Institute next week. They have an opening for an acoustical engineer. Now that you have top-level clearance, you'd qualify just fine."

"I have a job already. One I moved across the country for." Stress did a grinding little twist in her gut as Alexia realized that her walking out the night before was only the opening salvo to her father's list of issues. He had a whole arsenal of complaints to shoot her way.

Her father waved away her objection. "You'll need to change jobs. Did you see today's paper? There's a write-up about you and that sex-research grant in there. It's completely unacceptable."

Unacceptable. How often had she heard that over the years? Closing her eyes, Alexia tried to breathe past the knot in her chest. Why had she expected things to change?

"Are you paying attention, young lady?"

He never used her name. Maybe he didn't know it. All her life, she'd been young lady. And for this, she was making herself ill? Worrying herself into misery, all while apologizing for making an adult choice in a matter that was completely her decision?

Alexia opened her eyes, lifted her napkin from her lap and set it on the table next to her plate. She gave her mother, then her father, a distant smile and got to her feet.

"Where do you think you're going?" he snapped.

"I'd hoped that in moving back we could heal our relationship. If not come to love and enjoy one another, at least reach a respectful camaraderie," she informed them in the same smooth, distant cadence she'd used delivering her dissertation at the age of twenty-two. "Unfortunately, in the handful of hours we've spent in each other's company I've come to realize that would be impossible."

"You're being dramatic," Margaret said with a sigh, topping her orange juice off with more champagne.

"No, Mother, I'm being practical." Alexia bent down to pick up her purse, then faced her father. "You've made it clear that I'll never be good enough to meet your standards."

"You mean you won't try to meet them."

"Since that would require that I date men you choose, regardless of my feelings about them, and that I change my career to suit your preferences, then no. I won't."

"If you walk out that door, you're finished with this family." The admiral's voice was as emotionless as if he'd just recited the weather forecast. Of course, he probably figured the weather was more cooperative than his eldest child.

For the first time since she'd walked into her parents' house that morning, Alexia smiled. "That's the last thing you said to me when I graduated college and moved to New York."

She didn't wait for a response. There was no point.

THREE HOURS, FOUR IBUPROFEN and a cold compress later, Alexia lay on her couch practicing meditative breathing. The now-lukewarm cloth across her eyes dimmed the light while the soothing sounds of her relaxation tape played through her earbuds.

Suddenly, someone pressed a hand against her arm.

She screamed. Heart racing, she jackknifed. The damp terry cloth went flying one way, her iPod the other.

"Calm down," Michael said, both hands raised as if to prove he was unarmed. "It's just me."

"What're you doing here?" She eyed the cloth now hanging off the rosewood table, but didn't have the energy to move it. Instead, she dropped back to her pillow and tossed her forearm over her eyes.

"I heard you had brunch with the parents. So I brought ice cream."

Alexia shifted her arm just enough to peer out. Michael shook the white bag as proof.

"Your favorite. Double-chocolate caramel with almonds." He waited until she was upright before handing it to her. "The spoon's in the bag."

Chocolate might not fix everything, but it sure made suffering through it a lot easier, Alexia decided as she opened her treat.

"I can't believe I thought it would be different. How stupid is that?" She dug into the carton, pressing hard to fill her spoon.

"You aren't stupid. Most people have decent relationships with their parents. You probably just forgot that yours aren't human."

Alexia's lips twitched. Then she sighed, staring at the spoonful of chocolate for a few seconds before gulping it down. It was delicious, but didn't soothe the way it should.

"Besides, it's not the admiral and his missus that has you all tweaked out."

"Well, aren't you the king of perception," she muttered.

"Queen, actually." Michael grinned. "And to prove it, I'll continue my brilliant assessment."

Alexia curled her feet under her and gestured with the spoon for him to have a go at it.

"You're upset about the hottie from the beach, right?"

Alexia gave a jerk of her shoulder, pouting into the carton instead of meeting her brother's gaze.

"You had fun with him?"

"Do hours and hours of mind-blowing sex count as fun?"

"They do in my book."

"Then sure. We had fun. But that's all it was. Fun."

"And what's wrong with that?"

"Nothing." Getting up because the chocolate was starting to hurt her stomach, not because she wanted to avoid any aspect of this fabulous conversation, Alexia headed into the kitchen. "Water?"

"Sure. While you get it, you can tell me what you were hoping for from Blake."

Honesty.

Openness.

Forty or so more orgasms.

A chance to build a relationship.

"Nothing," she said, pulling two bottles from the fridge and letting the cool air chill the heat on her cheeks. She'd never been a good liar.

"Well, then you got exactly what you wanted," Michael decided when she handed him his water. "Too bad he didn't get what he wanted."

Sure he had. On the beach. In his truck. On her bed. In her shower. Hell, right there on her dining-room table. He wasn't a shy, retiring sort of guy. If he'd wanted anything more than that, he'd have said so.

A bitter weight settled in her stomach.

"How would you know what he wanted?"

"After you left last night he found me."

Alexia's feet dropped to the floor. Wide-eyed, she peered at her brother, trying to see what he wasn't saying.

"And?"

"And you're awfully interested for a woman who wants nothing from him."

"Why'd he find you?" she pressed, ignoring the dig.

"To ask what it'd take to get you to talk to him again." Michael crossed one slender ankle over his khaki-clad knee and sipped his water, then arched one elegant brow. "So? What'll it take?"

"For him to change careers. To get amnesia and forget he served with Father. To learn the importance of open, honest communication."

"He's not going to change careers. He's a SEAL, he's totally dedicated. Would you change careers for a relationship? I think not," Michael said reasonably. She peered at him, wondering if he'd been hiding in the kitchen during brunch.

"Then we have no chance of being together," Alexia stated, getting to her feet to pace. "Because me dating a solider, a SEAL, at that, well, it'd be like you dating a woman."

"Eww." Michael grimaced. "No need to be gross."

"But you get what I mean, right?" She stopped in front of her brother and dropped down to sit on the coffee table. "It's not like it's a bad thing for someone else. I'm not dissing the military itself, or the idea of someone else dating soldiers."

"It's just not your thing."

"Exactly," she said, grateful that he understood.

"Except Blake? He is your thing," Michael pointed out gently. "You had fun with him. You connected. Great sex? That's not just physical. Once or twice, sure. But days on end? That's a connection, Alexia. Sometimes a once-in-a-lifetime kind of connection. Are you willing to let your prejudices stand in the way of that?"

She sighed. Dropping her gaze to her hands, she watched her fingers twist together. Remembered how they'd looked against Blake's tanned skin, smoothing, touching. Caressing.

It'd been incredible.

Could she risk it? He was the kind of guy who'd demand everything. She'd already experienced that firsthand when it came to sex. Physically, there was no holding back with Blake. He gave one hundred percent and demanded just as much in return.

But she needed more than just physical.

Only a week ago, she'd wanted sex, had thought it was the most important aspect of a relationship. She'd wanted something that'd make her feel like a woman, sexual and strong and satisfied. And she'd got it.

But the bottom line was that he was a soldier. Not just military, in service to his country. But an elite fighting machine, specifically trained and totally focused on dangerous missions. Someone who'd always put country, squad and his career before anyone else in his life.

Men like that were exceptional. Special. And even though she hadn't realized it, that was part of what made Blake so incredible. So maybe she could live with that.

But another part of his job was keeping secrets. She'd never know what he did, where he went. She'd always come second, not just to the mission, but to the classified information that made up eighty percent of his life. By nature, military men kept part of themselves closed off. Private.

That, she couldn't accept.

"Give it a chance, Alexia," Michael said, almost pleading. "At least talk to him."

"Is he paying you?" she asked suspiciously, giving her brother a narrow look.

"I just..." He glanced at his hands, then shrugged and gave her a sad smile. "I just want to see you happy. If you're happy, you'll stick around."

Alexia reached over and squeezed his hand. "I'll stick around anyway, silly."

"No." Michael shook his head. "After all this, you're going to convince yourself that dating Dr. Darling is the right thing to do. Within a year you'll realize how much you hate it, working together will be a nightmare, and you'll quit and move away to escape the misery of it all."

She started to laugh, then realized he was right.

That's exactly what she'd do. Wrinkling her nose, Alexia asked, "When'd you get so smart?"

"I've always been smart. You just weren't listening."

"I missed you," Alexia said quietly, reaching out to take his hand. "I don't want to be that far away again. So how about this. You don't push me on dating Blake, and I'll promise not to date Edward. That way you won't drive me crazy, making me wish for what I can't have, and I won't ruin my career and run away."

"If that's the best I can get, I'll take it," her brother said resignedly. "But I still think you should give the Sexy SEAL a chance."

She'd already fallen half in love with him just based on their physical connection. If she gave him a chance—gave them a chance—the rest of the fall would be as easy as breathing.

And she couldn't—wouldn't—let herself fall in love with a man she couldn't communicate with. One who kept part of himself under lock and key.

"I can't," she decided quietly, wishing it didn't hurt so much. They'd known each other less than a week. She shouldn't feel as if someone was tearing part of her heart in two. "Because my prejudices would ruin the relationship in the end anyway."

CHAPTER EIGHT

Eight Months Later

"DUDE, YOU'VE TURNED into a total downer."

Cade's words echoed through the empty barracks in Qatar. The rest of the squad was off celebrating their return from Syria. Blake had turned down their invite to join in, wanting to sleep and decompress first.

"Sorry I'm not living up to your entertainment standards," Blake muttered, not bothering to open his eyes.

"You're mooning. Get over her already."

"I'm sleeping. As in resting up after a three-week recon."

Cade's sigh was a work of art. Loud, drawn out and filled with enough exasperation to fuel an obnoxious teenager for a week.

Blake almost smiled. But he still didn't open his eyes. He wanted to sleep. Sleep and work were great. In between the two? Not so great.

Not that he was mooning. That'd be stupid. And Blake didn't waste his time with stupid.

"You need to get over her."

"Over who?"

The silence was glorious.

If only it'd last.

"It's been months. You're so hung up that you barely

do anything anymore. Missions, the gym, the dojo, the range. That's your life. You're a cliché, man."

Sad, but true.

Michael had been right. After slamming the door in his face, Alexia hadn't talked to him again. Blake had called. He'd gone by her place. He'd done everything but tattle to her daddy.

Finally, he'd given up.

He wasn't going to waste his time on a woman who couldn't get past her father issues.

"I'm not a cliché. I'm not mooning and I haven't been a monk." There. He'd defended himself against all of Cade's accusations. Maybe now he could get some sleep.

"You're not putting anything into it, either. Sex with random strangers just to relieve the pressure isn't your thing."

"Don't you have a lovelorn column to write?" Blake snapped, sick of thinking about Alexia and totally pissed that Cade wouldn't let it go.

"'Dear Lovelorn LC, I've fallen for the girl I can't have and now can't get over her. How do I heal my broken heart?'"

It might have been funny if it wasn't way too close to the truth.

"Sullivan, you're a pain in my ass."

"Landon!"

Thank God. An interruption Cade couldn't ignore.

"Sir?" Blake sprang to his feet, coming to attention despite the fact that he was off duty, in his boxers and, *seriously,* trying to sleep.

"New orders. Report to the captain."

EYES FOCUSED ON the silver eagle gracing the plaque of the United States Navy, Blake stood at attention. The brass behind the desk ignored his presence, multitasking paperwork and a phone call instead.

Shoulders firm, chin high, senses alert, Blake knew his face didn't betray any irritation at waiting, even though it'd been ten minutes already. Nor did any of the questions he had on his mind show in his expression.

He wasn't wondering why he had been pulled from his assignment and ordered back to the Coronado Naval Base without the rest of his team.

Nor was he curious about why this meeting was deemed classified.

Both of those were pretty much Standard Operating Procedure.

The question burning in his gut was why the hell he was reporting directly to Rear Admiral Lane.

Plenty of orders had come down from Lane, but they went through the chain of command. Blake had never had a face-to-face with the rear admiral. He hadn't even seen the guy in person since Admiral Pierce's retirement party last September.

Anger fisted tight in his gut, the same as it always did at the memory of that night.

As he had so many times in the past, he reminded himself that it was stupid to get worked up over a woman he'd barely known. The only reason Alexia was still intriguing was because he hadn't got to spend enough time with her for the shine to wear off. Great sex, a body that haunted his dreams and a personality that had almost convinced him there was such a thing as relationships outside of bed... Nothing to obsess over.

He'd slept with plenty of women in the past few months, enough to wipe away the memory of that wild encounter. He wasn't a sentimental guy, nor was he the kind who fanatically crushed on some long-forgotten—or supposed-to-be-forgotten—chick.

Nope. No reason to be angry.

No point in remembering the exact texture of her lips, the scent of her hair in the moonlight or the feel of her soft curves pressed into his chest. It was ridiculous to wish he could see her, just one more time, poised naked above him, waiting to ride them both to the heights and depths of passion. The last thing he needed in his life was the distraction of wondering how she was liking her new job, whether she'd adjusted to life in San Diego or if she still missed New York. If she'd unpacked everything and if she'd got to the beach yet this year.

With the same discipline he used to push his body to its limits, to train with the elite and to succeed in missions that most would deem impossible, Blake shoved the memory—and all its accompanying emotional tension—out of his mind.

Better to focus on wondering why the hell he was here.

More for distraction than because he figured he'd find an answer, he started running through a mental list of all the known conflicts that might require a one-man mission.

He hadn't come up with a single idea by the time the rear admiral wound up his phone call.

"Landon," Lane acknowledged when he hung up the receiver.

Already at attention, Blake shifted all of his focus—physical and mental—to his commanding officer.

"Sir."

"You were recently in Syria."

Since it was a statement, not a question, Blake didn't respond. Still staring at the eagle, he was aware his mind raced. The last mission had been a success. The team had even received a thumbs-up from the commander in chief on a job well done. Where was this going?

"In the last year, you've spent six months deployed in the Middle East, completed seventy-two missions and earned yourself three commendations."

That sounded about right. The rear admiral wasn't looking for confirmation, though.

"You have a reputation as a strong team player. A man who understands orders but can think on his feet."

What SEAL didn't?

"You've proven that you're a stickler for the rules of engagement, and will follow them to the letter."

It was all Blake could do not to roll his eyes.

Any guy on the team could be standing here. None of this commentary was unique to Blake's career. So where was the old guy going with it? He wasn't evaluating Blake's service history to fill conversation gaps. It was some kind of test.

One, Blake figured, that he'd already won—or lost, depending on the perspective—given that he was standing here.

But what was at stake?

"While your service record shows an affinity for teamwork and leadership, your C-Sort indicates a leaning toward autonomy and self-reliance. That suggests that you work well alone, possibly even better than you do on a team."

His C-Sort? The admiral had dug all the way back

to Blake's initial psych screening for this assignment. What the hell was going on?

For the first time since he'd walked in, Blake stared at the rear admiral. Frowning, he processed the furrow in the older man's brow, the cold sheen in his narrowed eyes.

Whatever was going down, it was big.

"Am I being removed from my team?"

"Temporarily reassigned."

With a quick jerk of his chin, Blake acknowledged the new assignment and waited for further orders. And, hopefully, clarification.

The rear admiral looked out the window for a few seconds, as if sorting through which information he wanted to share. Then, his lips compressed almost white, he met Blake's gaze again. He straightened, hands clasped behind his back, took a deep breath then spoke.

"There's been a kidnapping. A civilian with military ties and potentially dangerous information was forcibly removed from her home two days ago. Operatives have discerned the group behind the act and pinpointed her location."

The words *her* and *military ties* added a layer of urgency to an already volatile mission.

"The cell is based inside the continental United States," the rear admiral informed him. "The leader of this branch of terrorists, as well as a number of those serving him, is a U.S. citizen."

Touchy. And way outside the SEALs' usual M.O.

"In two days' time, a team will neutralize this cell. Every effort will be made to keep the targets alive."

Blake gave a mental grimace. Targets had an unfortunate way of becoming collateral damage. Hostages, even more so.

"Your orders are to extract the hostage. You will go in alone, answering only to me. You will have twenty minutes before the team deploys. You will inform nobody of this assignment, nor will you coordinate with the team itself."

His mind took off in multiple directions. One part wondering why the hell his role in the mission was on blackout. Another part assessing what he'd need to do to pull it off without risking the team's mission or the safety of the hostage. Yet another part was already shifting into mission mode, emotionally distancing himself at the same time he set in place the expectations for victory.

"You were specifically requested for this assignment, Landon."

Blake frowned.

As a SEAL, his training was intense and his skill set diverse. But so was the rest of his team's. He was the Assault Force commander, the radioman and a linguist. And he was damn good at what he did. But, again, so were a lot of the team. So why him, specifically? Blake waited. If Lane wanted him to know who'd put in that request, he'd say so.

The rear admiral shifted. It wasn't the uniform, the rank or the shock of white hair against a rock-hard face that made the man intimidating. It was the cold look of determination that said this was a guy who'd do whatever it took to get the job done, not because he felt the consequences were worthwhile, but because he didn't even see consequences. Only the goal.

After giving Blake another assessing look, he

pressed the intercom button on his desk. He didn't say anything though. Just waited.

Blake waited, too. But for less time than it took to exhale. The private door to the right of the rear admiral opened.

His mentor, his recruiter, the man who'd shaped the direction of Blake's career and had fathered the sexiest woman alive, stepped through the door. Pierce didn't say a word. He just stood at ease, his face unreadable as he stared at Blake.

The rear admiral lifted a file from his desk, tapped it a couple of times against his thigh while giving Blake another of those assessing looks. Finally, with a lengthy stare at the admiral, he handed over the file.

"Your assignment." Unspoken was the order that it be read and memorized here in this room. Blake had access to the information, but the contents would stay under lock and key.

Used to that, Blake glanced at the admiral again, but got nothing. Then he unwrapped the cord holding the folder closed and pulled out the stack of papers. On top was an eight-by-ten color photo. His heart stopped. His breath jammed in his throat. A feeling he barely recognized as fear clenched his belly.

His gaze flew to the admiral's.

"Sir?"

Pierce's jaw tightened. His eyes dropped for one second to his hands, then met Blake's again.

"I'm calling in a favor on this. A number of them, actually. I'm sure you understand why."

Shocked, Blake looked at the file again but didn't respond.

Pierce came around the desk in swift, determined

strides. He didn't stop until his face was inches from Blake's.

Through gritted teeth, he commanded, "As of this moment, and until the mission is complete, you report directly to me and Rear Admiral Lane. You will rescue her. You will keep her safe."

Cold blue eyes bore into Blake as if imprinting the orders on his brain.

"You bring my daughter back. Safe and sound, Lieutenant."

The *or else* didn't need to be said. The message was implicit in the admiral's furiously set jaw, and in the vicious bite of his words.

"You will rescue her before the team storms the compound. You will get her out, safe and whole. And you will keep her hidden and safe until you get my order to bring her back home."

Blake didn't have to ask if this mission was sanctioned. He knew the rear admiral was dancing on a fine line, doing this favor for his old friend. But he hadn't crossed it. Even if he had…

Blake's gaze dropped to the photo again. Alexia's face stared back at him. An official government ID shot, her brilliant hair was pulled back, but wayward curls escaped to dance happily around her face. The photo captured the brilliant brown of her eyes, the same brown that haunted his dreams. Her smile, with that sexy overbite, was just this side of wicked. He remembered how soft those lips had been under his. How sweet and sexy she'd tasted.

He tried to bank the fury savaging its way through his system. Emotions had no place on a mission. Not a successful one. And this one, he promised himself, would be a success.

He met the admiral's eyes, his own hard with determination.

"I'll bring her back, sir. Safe, sound and secure."

IF SHE COULD JUST KEEP breathing, Alexia promised herself, she'd survive with her life, her sanity and maybe—by some miracle—her faith in humanity.

Eyes closed, carefully inhaling through her teeth to try to block the rancid smell in the room, she focused on calming her mind.

In.

Out.

Just keep breathing in and out.

Don't think about anything but breathing.

"You're going to hyperventilate if you keep sucking in air like that."

Her next breath slid through her teeth with a hiss as she slitted her eyes open to glare at the man across the dining table from her.

The source of the rancid smell, his scent perfectly fit his personality. She'd memorized his features as a part of her promise to herself that she'd not only get out of this nightmare, but that as soon as she did, she'd have as much ammunition as possible to fry his ass.

Short, probably about five-seven, he had that small-man syndrome, flexing his power left and right. Dark hair, brown eyes, a nondescript face marred by a small scar on his chin, he had the beady-eyed look of a rat. Which made sense, since he had the personality of a rabid rodent.

A rabid rodent with a large contingent of creeps on

his payroll. The creeps who'd grabbed her on the sidewalk in front of her condo. The creeps who'd put a hood over her head, hauled her to the snowy regions of hell, aka the wilds somewhere in Alaska. The creeps who'd taken turns guarding her when she was locked in her room or the makeshift lab they'd set up. Or, she slanted a look sideways at the big bruiser leaning against the wall of the large dining room, wherever she happened to be. Then there were serving creeps, administrative creeps and, she'd discovered when she'd stood on the back of the chair in her tiny room to peer out the tiny barred window, a tidy number of creeps guarding the perimeter of the icy compound.

"You might as well say something," the rat instructed, his bored tone at odds with the irritated tapping of his glossy fingernail on the arm of his chair. "You're not going back to your cozy room until you detail the progress you made in the lab today."

A seven-by-seven space with no heat, a cot-sans-sheets, a blanket and a spindle-backed chair and rickety floor lamp didn't quite say cozy to her. But to a rat, maybe that was heaven.

Alexia deliberately took a deep, loud breath in, then exhaled. But she didn't speak.

He tapped louder.

She almost smiled. These tiny rebellions were pointless, but they were all she had. It'd been four days. Four long, nerve-shattering days since she'd been grabbed. Someone had to notice she was gone by now. Michael would have alerted their father. He might not be much in the way of a great parent, but when it came to protecting the interests of the United States and its citizens, he was hell on wheels. Which meant he'd get her out of here soon. At least that's what she'd been promising herself.

For four days.

The first day, exhausted from terror and travel, she'd begged to know why they'd abducted her, pleaded to be released. The rat had said he'd fill her in on what she'd need to do to stay alive in the morning. After she had a nice little rest and time to think about all the possibilities, he'd gloated. Then he'd locked her in that dark, dank *cozy* room.

The second day, fury overshadowing her bone-numbing fear, she'd tried threats as soon as he unlocked her door. The rat had laughed in her face before instructing her to follow him to the dining room. Couldn't have her wasting away from starvation until she was done with her new job.

Since the Science Institute had refused his many legitimate requests, he'd decided it was time to get what he wanted the illegitimate way. Through force and kidnapping. Since she was the public face of the institute's subliminal project, she was clearly—at least in his mind—the expert. It would be her duty, he'd explained over smoked fish, runny eggs and undercooked bacon, to develop a new subliminal program. One that would take the technology she'd been developing for sexual healing and use it to stimulate and heighten anger.

She'd tried to reason with him. The science of true subliminally enhanced emotional response was new, she'd explained. Unlike the cassette tapes of years gone by with their spoken message whispered through soothing music, actually effecting a specific, targeted emotional change via brain waves. Her psychological focus was human sexuality, not anger. She'd never studied how sound related to human perception of negative emotions. She wasn't a neurologist, she didn't know where anger was triggered in the brain, so she couldn't create a program that would target it.

He'd pointed a fork dripping with egg and bacon grease her way and suggested she get her ass to learning before he lost patience. Then he'd had her escorted to what he called her new lab. A room barely bigger than the one she'd slept in, it was fitted with a desk, a workbench and two chairs. A used and slightly beat-up-looking stack of audio and digital equipment littered the bench, including a processor, data streamer and a closed-loop stimulator. Next to that was an array of psych books and a digital tablet.

After ordering her to work, he'd left her there until this morning. With bargain-basement equipment that did her no good, a pile of books that meant nothing, no research access and a ton of time for her brain to scramble between terrified images of what would come next, to blinding hope that someone would get her the hell out of there before she had to face the rat again.

But here she was, pretty much running out of hope.

So she was tuning him out. The games, the threats, the fear. Four years of yoga breathing and tapping into her long-abandoned meditation practice were all she had left.

With that in mind, and yes, because she'd seen the irritation on his face, she closed her eyes again and inhaled deeply through her teeth.

"You're doing it wrong," the whiny voice snapped. "You're supposed to inhale through your nose. It's a filter. Are you sure you're a scientist? You don't seem to know very much."

Alexia's eyes popped open, followed quickly by her mouth. Luckily, she saw the gleam in his beady eyes before she spit a word of defense.

She clamped her lips shut.

"I'm not surprised, actually," he mused, contemplating the slab of bloody red steak on his fork. "Disappointed, but after your lack of progress these few days, not surprised at all."

Shifting that same contemplative stare to her face, he wrapped his fat lips around that huge chunk of meat and chewed. A trail of blood dripped down the side of his mouth, over his receding chin, then plopped on the front of his white shirt. He didn't seem to notice.

He was waiting for her to rise to the bait.

Alexia refused.

His eyes gleamed, as if the more defiance she showed, the happier he was.

"I'd have thought a woman like yourself, with all those fancy degrees and who's made a show of thumbing her nose at her family, would be a little smarter."

Alexia's blood froze. She'd figured this was all about her research. But if he knew who her family was, that changed things. Was this really about creating an anger switch? Or did it have something to do with her father? If the latter, why the elaborate charade?

"Please," she said, trying to sound reasonable and calm instead of freaked-out and frenzied. "Just let me go. I can't do what you're asking. You're smart enough to have researched the technology yourself. You know the equipment you have here isn't adequate. The research isn't cohesive enough to work with."

Yes, she was playing fast and loose with the terms *smart* and *research* there. But she figured saving her life was a good enough excuse to employ a few lies and fake flattery.

"You're on the verge of a breakthrough. You just did an interview on TV last month. It's in the papers, other scientists are commenting on it in their blogs," he said, shaking his finger at her as if she had done something naughty.

Blogs? Seriously? Alexia's nerves stretched tight, ravaged from alternately fearing for her life and peering into corners looking for the hidden cameras that would prove this was all some elaborate, sick hoax.

"So there's no reason you can't take the same research and give it a little twist. Passion is just as easily channeled into anger as it is into something as trivial as sex."

"I told you, it's not a simple matter of flipping a switch. My research has been focused on the physical body and healing. Not on the emotions. I don't know how to tap into anger, fury or any of the other destructive emotions you want."

His contemplative stare didn't change. He didn't even blink. Maybe he was more snake than rat.

"Perhaps you just need a little motivation," he decided. That damn finger still tapping, he tilted his head to one side as he gave her body a thorough inspection. Her skin crawled as if someone had just dipped her in a vat of lice.

"You're a pretty woman. Robert—" he indicated the henchman who most often guarded Alexia "—has expressed an interest in your charms. Perhaps I should reward his exemplary service, hmm?"

Her eyes blurry with fear, Alexia's gaze slid to the henchman, whose own beady eyes were gleaming with lust. Bile rose in her throat, but she was too paralyzed with terror to even throw up.

"Of course, Robert did go a little far with his last reward," the rat continued in that same contemplative tone. "She was useless to us when he was through. It's hard to see much through the snowstorm, but if you look out your window, you can see her grave just on the other side of the electric fence."

Black dots danced in front of Alexia's eyes, her breathing so shallow she didn't think any oxygen was reaching her brain.

"I'm more inclined to wait on the reward," he said slowly, pausing to sip his wine, giving her time to take a small step back from the panicked cliff she'd been about to dive over. "Myself, I find rape a poor persuasion. If the mind is broken, the body isn't good for much except more of the same. And I need your mind in good working order."

Alexia wasn't sure if her mind would ever work again, even as it shied away from the hideous images she couldn't stop from running through it.

"So many possibilities to consider," he mused, now tapping his lower lip as if that would help him decide. "I'll have to sleep on it and let you know in the morning."

His smile slid into a smirk. "In the meantime, I suggest you trot on over to the lab and see what you can do now that you're a little more motivated."

"You can't do this," she breathed, half denial, half prayer.

"I can do anything I want," he said with a dismissive wave of his hand. "Go. Robert will see you to the lab."

Alexia got to her feet, subtly resting her fingertips on the edge of the table until her knees stopped shaking enough to support her.

"Go on," the rat ordered, flicking his fingers toward the door. "Get to work."

Yeah, she decided, trying to find the fury through the choking waves of fear threatening to overwhelm her.

He was definitely a snake.

CHAPTER NINE

FOURTEEN HOURS LATER, Alexia finally understood what it was to have fear leach every ounce of energy from a body.

She was completely numb.

She cradled her head in her arms and tried to stop her teeth from chattering.

From her bare toes—made colder every time she glanced at the window to see the white blizzard of snow swirling outside—to the top of her aching head, she was ice.

Desperate for a focal point other than the hideous visions her captor had stuck in her head, she had resorted to digging into the books. Somewhere around hour three, she had filled a notebook. Not anything that'd produce the results he wanted. But maybe enough to make it look as if she could, which might buy her some time.

The words were a blur on the page now.

It took Alexia a minute to realize that was because she was crying, her tears making the ink run.

A sound, barely a whisper of the wind, caught her attention. Her body braced. Tension, so tight even her hair hurt, gripped her. Barely daring to breathe, she shifted her head just a bit in her cradling arms so she could peek over her shoulder.

Crap.

She blinked, trying to focus on the figure standing inside a window that should be too tiny for a body to fit through. The freezing air wrapped around her like a shroud, making her blink again.

Her shivers turned to body-racking shakes. Alexia still didn't bother raising her head.

"I sure wish hallucinations came with temperature control," she muttered to her biceps.

The figure moved. She blinked a couple of times, waiting for it to fade. But it came closer.

And closer.

The closer it came, the more sure she was that this was pure fantasy, woven by a generous mind eager to give her a sweet escape.

"Let's go," the fantasy ordered. She wasn't surprised it sounded like Blake. All her fantasies revolved around the sexy SEAL. Most were naked, though, and the only shivers involved were sexually inspired.

"Sure, I'll go with you," she bartered in a teasing tone. Might as well humor her mind, since it'd gone to all this trouble of creating her dream man. "But if I do, you have to reward me with kisses and sexual delights. I've done the calculations. By showing up at the party and outing yourself as forbidden fruit," she informed the hallucination, "you deprived me of at least twenty-seven orgasms. I figured that's how many I'd have gotten before the heat ran its course."

The figure froze for a second, then he shook his head as if clearing his ears of static.

He looked like a walking arsenal, with an automatic weapon slung across his shoulder, pistols at both hips and a slew of scary-looking devices on his utility belt.

He wore a white snow-camo jacket and hood with a cloth mask covering the lower half of his face. All she could see were his eyes. They were the same vivid blue she remembered, then they grew distant again. Assessing, constantly shifting around the room, and almost as cold as the snow outside.

"Twenty-seven, hmm?" He stepped over to the door, his moves slick and silent. He pressed an ear against the wall, checked some gadget in his hand, then gave her a commanding wave of his hand as if ordering her to stand.

"Tell you what, let's get the hell out of here, and then we can talk about payback on those orgasms."

"Payback is double," she decided then and there. Why not. It was her fantasy after all.

For a brief second, she saw amusement flash in those bright eyes. For that instant, she felt the same connection that'd zinged between her and the real Blake Landon almost a year ago. Her heart sang with joy, so sure it'd found its perfect match.

Silly heart.

Then he shifted, shrugging a pack off his back. He dug into it, pulling out things even more tempting than fifty-four screaming orgasms.

Warm clothes. Thick socks, heavy boots and a coat.

She moaned. A heavy coat, with a furry hood.

This fantasy just kept getting better and better.

A cold wind whipped through the room. Ice showered her back and freezing snowflakes flecked her hair and face.

Slowly, terrified if she moved too fast he'd disappear, Alexia raised her head off her arms.

He was still there.

She blinked.

He held out the socks and boots.

Wetting her lips, she hesitated. Then, having to know one way or the other, she reached out. The wool socks were like fire, hot and welcoming.

The boots waggled. Her gaze flew from the sturdy cold-weather footwear to the man's face. He was real? He was here to rescue her?

Alexia's mind couldn't seem to take it in.

Thankfully, though, her body was all over the idea, grabbing the socks and yanking them over her frozen toes.

"You're real?" she whispered, reaching out for the boots.

"As real as you are, sweetheart. Let's get our asses in gear. We have five minutes before this place is blown to hell."

She should be scared, shouldn't she?

Or relieved?

Excited or ecstatic or grateful.

Maybe the weather had frozen her emotions, too, because she couldn't feel a thing.

Except the cold.

Like moving through a dream, Alexia snuggled herself into the warmth of the white camouflage winter gear. Her brain was foggy as she tried to accept that Blake was real. The possibility that he was a figment of her desperate imagination didn't stop her from following him to the window, though.

Her movements were stiff as she took his hand to help her climb onto the chair, wishing she could feel him through their thick gloves, her body feeling as if she'd just recovered from a vile flu.

He was real.

He was here.

She was rescued.

"Is there a team outside?" she asked. As much as she wanted out of this room, she knew there was an arsenal pointed at the window, armed guards who'd be thrilled to use her for target practice and a seriously strong chance that she'd break a leg crawling out a second-story window.

"We're on our own," he said quietly, stepping up to the window, too, and using his infrared binoculars to check the landscape. "There's a rope hanging just outside the ledge. Do you see it?"

"On our own?"

How was that possible? SEALs operated in teams.

Suddenly her brain sparked to life. Like a limb waking, the tingles were painful as she tried to figure out what was going on.

"Where's the rest of the team? Your backup?" It was unfortunate that her words came out shrill with an overtone of hysteria. But, well, she was pretty close to hysterical, so it was only to be expected.

"We're the team, you and I. We're not going to need backup because nobody's going to be paying us any attention in—" he glanced at his watch again "—four minutes."

He wasn't hysterical. She frowned, peering at his face to try to see if his mellow certainty was an act or if he was really okay with being a one-man rescue show.

The more she looked, the calmer she became. As if she was absorbing his confidence and strength. Granted, he was almost completely shrouded in warm winter gear. But his voice, his stance, his entire persona were one hundred percent assured. He was trained for this, she told herself. He'd done hundreds, maybe thousands, of missions in much riskier situations. He'd served during wartime, for crying out loud.

But that was him.

She was pretty much a wimp.

"We're really on our own?" she whispered. Then, with a shaky breath, she glanced at the rickety desk and sad stool. Maybe she should stay here.

"Do you trust me?"

Her gaze flew to his face. Covered in goggles, surrounded by a cinched hood, she could barely make out his features.

"Do you trust me?" he repeated.

Her heart sighed, even as terror clutched her guts. They'd have to sneak through a terrorist encampment filled with gleeful murderers to hide in a vicious snowstorm. Just the two of them, with no backup. No access to help. Nobody to rescue them if something went wrong.

Of course, if they stayed here, they'd be blown to bits in four minutes.

Alexia wet her parched lips, then nodded.

"I trust you."

Blake moved closer. He took her right hand, so warm now inside its heated glove, and tucked it up inside the wristband of her coat. Then he did the same with the left.

Alexia's body came awake much faster than her mind had. Warmth, not felt since the last time he touched her, slid through her body. Like liquid pleasure, it permeated, slowly trickling all the way to her toes.

He tugged on the zipper of her coat, snugging it up to just below her throat, then with hands so gentle she almost wept, he smoothed her hair away from her face and lifted the hood of the coat. The fabric was so thick, so warm. When he pulled the strings closed to cinch it tight around her face, she felt as if she was in a sound tunnel, the beat of her heart amplified in her ears.

He let go for just a second to reach into the pack and pull out a pair of goggle-like glasses, sliding them onto her nose. Then he tugged the zipper higher, snapping the front of the jacket tight so not a whisper of cold air could touch anything but the little bits of her face still exposed.

Alexia wasn't sure she'd ever felt so protected. So cared for.

"Do whatever I tell you," he said softly, his gaze intense as he stared into her eyes. "Stay low, follow in my exact steps. I'll get you home safe and sound. I promise."

Unable to believe otherwise when he was looking at her like this, she nodded.

"I need you to really trust me, Alexia. Not because I'm the lesser of two evils, but because you have complete faith that I'll keep you safe. That I know exactly what I'm doing, that I'm damn good at it and that you know without a doubt that I'm going to get you out of here."

The huge lump in her throat made it hard to swallow, so Alexia just nodded instead of speaking.

"You're sure?"

She took a deep breath, then swallowed again. "I trust you, completely," she promised breathlessly.

His smile was like the rising sun. Warm, vivid and

beautiful. She melted. Then, his hands still on the zipper of her jacket, he tugged her closer. Bent his head and kissed her.

Oh, baby.

His lips were as soft, as delicious, as magical as she'd remembered. The kiss was short, way too short, but so sweet she would have cried if she wasn't afraid the tears would freeze on her face.

He slowly pulled back, his eyes still locked on hers. Then he flicked a button in the side of the goggles, activating a buzzing in her ears. Communication device, she realized.

"What's that for?" she whispered, her breath an icy mist between them. "Luck?"

"I don't need luck, sweetheart. I'm the best. That's why I was handpicked to rescue you. That—" he kissed her again, just a quick brush of his chilly lips against hers "—that was because I've missed you."

Nothing like fogging a woman's brain and sending her heart into a nosedive of delight to get her to climb out a tiny window into an enemy-filled snow-hell.

She didn't know if she should admit she'd missed him or not. If she did, it'd be like a deathbed confession, said because she knew she'd never have another chance. Call her superstitious, but she'd rather wait to make any emotional declarations until they were safe.

"Lucky me," she said instead, putting all the things she couldn't say into her smile and hoping he understood. "I'm glad I rate the best."

BLAKE WISHED SHE hadn't smiled.

It touched something inside him, ratcheted the stakes so much higher.

He was here to do a job, and he couldn't do that job if he let emotions in. Any kind of emotions. The key to a successful mission was a clear mind, the ability to think three steps ahead and a solid handle on the outcome, while keeping a fluid sense of the steps in between.

He'd learned early in his career that the only way to succeed was to shut out fear. Worrying, in any form, was the equivalent of strapping a bull's-eye on his back.

He shouldn't have kissed her.

He was on a mission.

She was his mission.

Kissing the rescue target was totally against protocol.

He hadn't been able to resist.

Blake hefted his pack onto his shoulders again, then checked the time.

Two minutes.

"Let's go."

He made sure she was situated on the chair, then grabbed the windowsill and pulled himself up. He glanced at her again.

"Promise. You do exactly what I say."

"Promise."

"Even if I say run, without me, you'll do it. The coordinates, a compass and a GPS are in your jacket. Don't take it off."

Her eyes were huge behind the protective lenses. Her nod was a jerk of her chin. But her lips were pressed in a determined line, and if her hands were shaking inside her gloves, the tremor was mild.

She'd hold up.

Blake glanced at the compound again, then reached

down to pull the cloth, embedded with a tiny communication wire, across her lower face. Then he did the same to his own.

"Ready?" he whispered.

She gave a tiny start, indicating that she'd heard him through her headphones, and nodded again.

"Then let's rock."

He flipped the switch on his lenses, triggering the heat sensors. Two guards on the east side, one on the west. He glanced at his watch.

One minute.

One hand holding his weapon, Blake shimmied through the window, gripping the stones surrounding it and pulling himself free. He reached in to aid Alexia, but she'd already grabbed ahold of the sill and had herself halfway out. He took her hand, pulling her up so her toes were balanced on the sill and the rest of her against the stone wall, then bent low to snag the rope.

"Wait until I'm down, then follow," he said quietly.

Her gaze ricocheted around the compound as if she was watching for the devil to come riding in. But she nodded. Using the rope, his back to the wall so he could watch for threats, he quickly lowered himself to the ground. He sank into the snow to midcalf.

It only took him a second to reach into the small white pack he'd stashed at the base of the wall and pull out the snowshoes. Fully alert, his finger still on the trigger of his revolver, he swiftly stepped into them.

"Go," he told Alexia.

She flew down the wall. He winced twice as her body bounced off the stones, but she didn't slow. Clearly she wanted the hell out of here.

He liked giving a lady what she wanted.

"Put these on," he told her as soon as she'd released the rope. She squinted at the snowshoes, then nodded. He made sure she knew what she was doing as she put the first one on. He glanced at his watch as she finished the second.

One minute past. The explosion should have already happened, providing cover for their escape. He scanned the guards again. Still in place.

Recalling one of Phil's favorite sayings, *no worries, no bull's-eyes,* he reached into his boot and pulled out his backup Glock.

"Ready?" he asked Alexia, giving her a once-over.

"Ready."

He handed her the gun.

Her gasp echoed in his ears. But she took it. With a sureness that'd do the admiral proud, she checked the clip, the safety. Her breath just as loud in his speaker again, she nodded.

What a woman.

Grinning behind his mask, Blake tilted his head to the north. Time to go.

As soon as he stepped a foot from the building, he was buffeted by driving snow.

"Hold on to my belt," he instructed.

A second later he felt the pressure of her fingers. Good. Now he could focus ahead without needing to check her progress.

Without the wind and snow, they could have made the hundred and fifty yards to the fence line in less than half a minute. But running at a crouch through a foot of snow took twice that.

When they reached the bare expanse of wire fence, he stooped. Alexia did the same. Watching constantly, he pulled out what looked like a pair of tiny rubber pincers. He'd come in overhead, rappelling from the trees to the top of the building. To leave, they needed to cut the barbed wire.

He hesitated. As soon as he clamped the wires, an alarm would sound. If the compound had already been hit, the chaos would have covered their escape.

This, or the gates, were the only way out. Orders were to stay covert and not to engage the enemy.

So they'd stick with the plan. And run a little faster.

He took a deep breath.

Then, knowing what was likely to come, he looked at Alexia. Her brown eyes were huge, her lips white. Still, she gave him a reassuring smile.

"So far so good," she whispered.

He nodded.

"As soon as I cut this, we're tagged. There's a vehicle waiting a mile to the east. In it is a radio in case you have to communicate with anyone." He hesitated, then decided she was strong enough—had to be strong enough—to face reality. "If we're engaged, you keep running. Don't wait for me. Don't look back or try to help. Head for the vehicle, get the hell out of here."

"But—"

"Get the hell out," he repeated firmly.

Her chin trembled. He watched, fascinated, as she breathed in, seeming to suck strength from the air. She squared her jaw, resolve steely in her eyes. And she nodded.

"Attagirl," he whispered.

Then he clamped the wires.

The world exploded. Fire filled the air. Rocks flew.

The ground shook. Alexia ducked low, covering the back of her head with her hands.

"And there's the cavalry," he said with a grin, cutting the wires. "Go."

She gave a wide-eyed look at the now-flaming building, bodies scurrying like rats to and from the inferno. Then she crouched down low, sliding through the wires he'd cut.

"Hold my belt and keep up," he told her as soon as they were clear. "Most of the enemy will be focused on the invasion. But if they're smart, they'll have people securing the perimeter."

"They didn't impress me as being too smart," she said, showing a little of that sass he remembered so fondly. "But they did have the devil's own luck on their side. So run as fast as you want. I'll keep up."

The rapid-fire pinging of automatic weapons got louder. The team had engaged, he noted. And since they had no idea he or Alexia were here, they'd be taken as the enemy if spotted.

"Let's go."

Taking her at her word, he set off at a low, crouching sprint. Moving through the snow, both the thick ground cover and the flurries buffeting them backward, was hardly fast. But—he checked his GPS to make sure they were on track—they were making progress.

"Hold," he ordered. He stopped, still hunkered down, and scanned the area for signs of body heat. Nothing.

"Okay, let's go."

"Go? Where? How?"

"Vehicle," he said, gesturing to what looked like one of the many snowdrifts in the blurry white landscape.

When she shook her head in confusion, he pushed through the snow—hip-deep here—and unerringly found the loose end of the white tarp. With a tug, he uncovered the snowmobile he'd stashed.

"This is a vehicle?" She gaped. "Are you sure?"

He grinned, swinging one leg over the seat. "Climb on."

Giving him, then the snowmobile, a doubtful look, she shook her head before climbing on behind him. There wasn't much sexy about the half foot of fabric between their bodies, but Blake's blood still hummed when her thighs clamped tight against his hips. Her arms wrapped around his waist, holding tight to his jacket. As soon as she felt settled, he pressed the ignition and, with one last glance at the flaming sky to the west of the trees, took off.

They flew across the snow, flurries pounding against them as if protesting their escape. He watched his GPS, double-checking the few landmarks along the way to make sure they were on track.

Twenty minutes later, after taking a couple side trips and doubling back to make sure they weren't followed, they reached the side of a mountain. He cut the snowmobile's engine and, muscles trembling from the exertion of holding the vehicle steady in the intense winds, looked around. The helicopter would pick them up on top. At the base, camouflaged by icy brush and snow, was a domed tent. He didn't see any new tracks in or out, but wasn't taking any chances.

"I'm going to make sure it's secure. You move forward and take the controls."

He dismounted, waiting for her to grip the handlebars. As soon as she did, he pulled out his infrared binoculars again and checked the perimeter. Five minutes later, but never losing her from sight, he returned to the snowmobile. Alexia hadn't moved. He could tell because she had at least three inches of snow on her now.

"All clear," he told her.

Her eyes were huge behind the plastic lenses, swimming with exhaustion, fear and relief. She didn't move, though.

"Ready to get out of the snow?"

Her nod was more along the lines of a shiver.

Knowing he needed to get her to warmth quickly, Blake opted for the fastest route. He reached out and lifted her into his arms. She didn't make a sound. She did, however, wrap her hands around him and hold tight.

He liked how it felt, even through the miles of insulated fabric between them.

When he reached the tent, he shifted her, but didn't let go. He tugged open the Velcro closure, then unzipped the canvas. It wasn't until they were inside, lamp on and flap secured again, that he put her gently on her feet.

He waited until she'd stopped swaying, then unhooked the scarf from his hood and grinned.

"Welcome to your temporary home sweet home."

CHAPTER TEN

ALEXIA'S HEAD WAS SPINNING. She wasn't so sure her body wasn't, too.

The last five days had been surreal. Like something out of a horrible nightmare that not even her own subconscious would torture her with. And now it was over?

Or, she blinked and looked around the tent, almost over?

The tent was awfully well equipped for a temporary stop. Two cots, a cookstove, an array of equipment that looked as if it could control rocket ships. A small arsenal in one corner and a table and chairs in the other. And Blake in the center. Boxes were piled at the back wall and, she squinted, there was a stack of books on one of the cots.

As always, her gaze landed on Blake.

Nerves that'd gone numb on the bone-bruising flight over the snow started coming to life again with big, snapping bites.

He wasn't paying any attention, though. He'd pushed back his hood and now set his goggles aside so he could pull on a radio headset.

She watched carefully, noting what buttons he pushed, which switches he flipped.

"Base, this is Boy Scout. Hostage secured. Will await your go. Boy Scout out."

"That's it?" she asked, frowning as he turned everything off with a push of his finger. She wanted to grab the radio and yell into it. To insist someone hurry the hell up and come to get them. She wanted to go home, dammit.

"That's it," he said.

No, she wanted to moan. She wanted a shower and warm clothes. A bowlful of hot fudge. Her own bed, popcorn, to hug her brother.

"Where are we?" she whispered, more than ready to hear him say the icy bowels of hell.

"Alaska. North Slope," he told her as he moved around the perimeter of the tent, turning on small heaters so the space was soon a warm cocoon. Then he flipped on a series of tiny monitors. At first they all looked white, as though they weren't tuned in. Alexia stepped closer, her eyes narrowed as she realized the white was snow. Then she saw the angled rock he'd parked the snowmobile behind.

Security cameras.

Did he really think someone might follow them? That, and a million more questions chased through her mind. But the first ones to tumble out were, "How long are we waiting here? Is someone picking us up? Who sent you to get me?"

"We're here until we're told otherwise," was the only answer he gave.

"Is that going to be hours? A day? Two? What's that mean?" Alexia realized her voice had hit a pitch high enough to trigger an avalanche, but she couldn't help herself. Feeling trapped, barely able to breathe, she yanked the kerchief from her face and ripped at the strings tying her hood closed. Her fingers, clumsy and fat in the thick gloves, couldn't undo it.

Her breath was coming in gasps now. Black spots sped across her vision, racing one another from side to side. Before she could give in to the scream building in her throat, Blake was there.

His knuckles were warm as they brushed her frozen face, fingers making swift work of the ties, before he gently pushed the hood back and pulled the goggles off.

"Breathe," he instructed quietly. "Pull the air into your belly. Attagirl. Hold it, then let it out."

Her eyes locked on his, she followed his breath, listened to his instructions, and slowly, painfully reeled in the fragile threads of her control.

"Sorry," she murmured as she started to feel like herself again. The heat warming her cheeks should have been welcome in this bitter cold, but shame was never comfortable.

"Nothing to be sorry about," he told her as he continued to gently release her from the coat's bindings, then slipped the gloves off her hands. If he tried to take her boots and socks, she just might have to smack him. It'd be a long time before she wanted to be barefoot again, she realized. "You're exhausted, stressed and probably starving. The natural expectation after being rescued is to go home."

"Can you tell me why I can't?" she asked in a low whisper, not taking her eyes off his. She waited for him to prevaricate or outright refuse. That's what her father would do. All information—right down to which state they'd be attending school in the following month—had always been imparted on a need-to-know basis.

"This is a two-stage mission," he explained. "Rescuing you is stage one. Neutralizing the enemy is stage two. If we're pulled out, it could compromise the team's efforts. Added to that, it's nighttime. It's safer to wait until light to head out again."

Alexia's jaw dropped.

"What?" he asked, pausing in the act of taking off his own jacket and hanging it with hers on a hook.

"You, well… You answered my question." She realized how stupid it sounded when she said the words. But she'd never gotten answers as a kid. Had been told time and again that good little soldiers followed orders without question—that questioning was a sign of disrespect, of showing doubt toward one's superior.

"You didn't ask for classified information," Blake said, dismissing what she thought of as a miracle with a laugh. "I'll answer whatever I can. You have the right to know what's going on."

It was as if he'd twisted a spigot. Before she realized it was happening, Alexia's cheeks were wet with tears. Her breath came in hiccupping gasps as she fell apart.

He looked at her as if she'd just turned into an alien giraffe with four heads and an Uzi pointed at his man parts. Horrified, shocked and desperate to make it stop.

"I'm sorry," she wailed, trying to control her sobs.

"What…" He shook his head, clearly realizing that this wasn't the time for a reasonable discussion. Then he crossed the tent and pulled her into his arms.

She didn't care that she'd spent months being angry with him, or that she'd imagined countless scenarios in which he saw her again and, miserable and unable to get his party on *sexually* without her, he'd begged her to let him into her life again.

In her imagination, she'd always turned him away.

In real life, she grabbed on as if he was the only oxygen in the room. As soon as she did, her tears slowed. Her heart stopped aching. She felt like a scared little girl and he was her security blanket. Now she wanted to wrap him all around her.

"I don't know what's wrong," she said, her words as shaky as her breath. "I'm safe, right? I'm away from that lunatic and his insane demands. He can't hurt me. His henchman can't touch me, right?"

Blake's arms stiffened around her, his fingers digging into her spine as he pulled her closer, tighter. As if he could wrap himself around her as a shield, keeping her safe. Protected.

"You're safe with me," he vowed.

She never wanted to be anywhere else.

Realizing she'd plummeted into dangerous thinking, Alexia drew in a little more of his calm, got her thoughts and her breathing under control, then slowly pulled back.

"Thank you," she said, wrinkling her nose in embarrassment. "I'm sorry to cry all over you. I guess SEALs really are trained to handle any emergency."

His eyes narrowed, as if he knew she'd tossed his job out to put a wedge between them. He didn't call her on it, though. Maybe he liked the wedge? Alexia frowned, then rubbed her damp cheeks dry.

"I don't suppose you have a hairbrush, or something I can use to wash my face," she asked. "Or, you know, a hairdresser and manicurist stashed in one of those packs."

"There," he said, pointing to the bunk on the left. On it were two packs, one smaller, one larger. "Clothes, toiletries, whatnot. Over there is a makeshift bathroom. No bathing facilities, but you can change."

Alexia followed his gestures, then looked back at him and wet her lips. Get naked, with just a flimsy piece of fabric separating them? Her body trembled at the idea, wanting desperately to beg him to get naked with her. But that wasn't going to happen, she warned her body. He was off-limits. Totally wrong for her, and she wasn't stupid enough to make the same mistake twice.

"Thank you," she murmured, lifting the pack and digging in to find not only a hairbrush and toothbrush, but ponytail holders, thick wool leggings, thermal underwear and a sweater. She wanted to ask who his personal shopper was, but figured the less said to bring attention to the fact that she was about to get naked, the better.

"I'll get dinner ready while you change," he told her.

Alexia narrowed her eyes. He didn't sound as if he cared that she was going to strip down. Not excited, not intrigued. Nothing.

Fine. It wasn't as though she wanted him to want to see her naked. She'd ended that part between them and for a damn good reason.

When Alexia realized that it was taking all her control not to add *so there* and stick out her tongue, she sighed. Clearly, the ordeal was messing with her way too much.

It might have been residual irritation, or probably nerves that she'd give in to her body's urgings and call out for him, but Alexia changed in record time. She didn't want to touch the nasty, five-days-worn clothes once she'd stripped them off, but it wasn't as if the tent came with maid service. So she bundled them up and, noticing a couple of small plastic bags tied to a rope, stuffed them into one. There. Trash.

She used the canteen water to brush her teeth and wash her face, then spent a luxuriously long time running the brush through her tangled mass of hair.

Once it was pulled into a tidy French braid and she felt clean and warm and real again, she pulled back the curtain and rejoined Blake.

Why, oh why did she have to have values? He looked so deliciously sexy standing there in winter camo fatigues tucked into his boots and a long-sleeved white T-shirt. She tried reminding herself that the silver chain she could see along the back of his neck belonged to his dog tags. Making him a soldier boy. *Off-limits, Alexia,* she wanted to yell. But her body didn't care. All it could see was how great he looked.

"Hungry?" he said, giving her a friendly-yet-distant look over his shoulder.

Clearly, he had no problem forgetting about the two days of constant, mind-blowing sex they'd shared. She sniffed. Either that or they hadn't blown his mind enough for him to see her as anything but a mission objective.

And that kiss. She forced herself not to sigh and melt at the memory, since she now knew it was probably just his way of reassuring her. Keeping her from getting hysterical. Or, who knew, maybe luck, as she'd first said.

Before she could pout too much, her stomach—the only part of her body not craving Blake's touch—growled.

"Hungry it is," he said, grinning and setting two plates, steam rising temptingly, on the table.

Alexia placed the pack on her designated cot and joined him.

"Field rations?" she guessed with a grimace. "My father used to insist we have them for dinner once a month. It was supposed to make us appreciate what soldiers had to deal with while protecting our way of life."

"Did it?"

"No," she remembered, wrinkling her nose. "But it did solidify my determination not to serve in the military."

Blake's grin warmed her more than all the space heaters combined. That feeling—and starvation—got her through the first few bites. Then the flavor hit her taste buds.

She poked into the open food box he'd set between them until she found salt. It took two packets before she could get through the other half of her meal. She glanced at Blake, who was spooning up his as if it was covered in chocolate.

"You don't actually like this—" she was hesitant to call it food "—stuff, do you?"

He shrugged, still scooping up the tan goo. "It's not that bad. Growing up, I was mostly hungry, so I tend to focus more on filling my belly than the taste threshold."

She wanted to ask why he'd been hungry. What his upbringing had been like. Was that a part of why he'd joined the military? For three square meals—or the equivalent? She wrinkled her nose at the mushy stuff on her plate. Did he have siblings? A family? Were they still hungry or had they found their way?

A million questions raced through her mind, but

she couldn't ask any of them. She felt it was private, that she had no right to poke or prod. She'd been fine with the right to lick her way down his body and to do a naked dance on his face, but ask personal questions? Totally taboo.

Which was ridiculous. So was the fact that while she'd claimed to want communication with him in the past, she'd never wondered any of those things. She'd only focused on the parts of his life that she thought impacted her. And then, when she'd found out just how strong that impact was, she'd slammed the door shut.

She poked her spoon into the stew again, trying to control the urge to cry. Again. God, she was a mess.

"If you eat all your dinner, I have chocolate for dessert," Blake said in a singsong voice.

Her eyes flew to his face.

"Chocolate?"

"Yep. Chocolate bars, chocolate powder, chocolate syrup."

"Noooo," she breathed in a reverent moan.

"Yep."

She looked around the tent, wondering where he'd hidden it. She hadn't seen any in the box of gross dinner choices. Then, because chocolate made everything more appetizing, she dived into the stew, eating it fast enough that she didn't have to taste it.

"There," she said three minutes later, holding out her cleaned plate. "Chocolate time."

"You're done already?" Surprise clear in his blue eyes, Blake laughed. But he took her plate, put it in a bag, then pulled a small knapsack from beneath one of the bunks.

"It's all yours."

Her fingers trembled, not a new thing for her this week. But this time it was excitement shivering through them as she undid the buckles.

"Yum," she moaned again when she saw the stash inside. At least two-dozen chocolate bars, three cans of familiar brown syrup and a large pouch with two sections, one with brown powder and the other with white. Chocolate milk to go, just add water?

Her fingers had already wrapped around a candy bar when she realized this was a lot of soothing sweetness. Enough to last awhile. A long while.

She bit her lip.

"Should I be rationing it?" she asked Blake quietly.

He paused in the act of emptying another pouch onto his plate and met her eyes. His gaze shifted to the radio, then scanned the monitors before meeting hers again.

"Just enough so that you don't make yourself sick," he said.

Alexia still hesitated.

"We're waiting until we get word that the compound is secured and the team has neutralized everyone inside," he told her, his voice so quiet and matter-of-fact that it took her a second to realize he was filling her in on the mission objective. "As soon as they give the all clear, someone will contact us with pickup coordinates. How long that takes simply depends on the level of resistance the team meets back there."

"The guy was crazy," she said, carefully pulling a single candy bar from the knapsack, then deliberately closing the flap. "He talked about starting a war, about the loyalty of his troops. There were too many there for me to count."

"Numbers don't matter. Strategy is what counts. And SEALs rock the strategy."

"I've heard that rumor," she said with a smile. "Is this your usual job? Hostage hand-holding?"

His lips twitched. He crossed the tent and stopped in front of her.

"What are you doing?"

Alexia held her breath as excitement swirled in her belly. Personal prejudices being what they were, she'd never been turned on by a guy in uniform, or in camo or even wearing dog tags and low-riding jeans. Soldiers were totally not her thing.

Except Blake.

She was horribly afraid that if she wasn't careful, he'd become her *every*thing.

He reached out and took her hand in his. His fingers entwined with hers, then he gave them a gentle shake.

"Holding hands."

BLAKE LOVED THE WAY she laughed. The sound of it, rich and husky. The way it made her dark eyes dance with delight. The look of her face, all lit up and happy.

He loved the feel of her fingers, slender and warm in his. Relief so intense it made him want to drop to his knees poured through him. She was here. He'd got her out alive, safe and sound.

He couldn't claim he'd never been worried on a mission. Since Phil's death, worry was a second skin, always looming, never comfortable. But scared? He'd never understood real fear until he'd opened that file and realized Alexia was his target. He'd used the fear, iced it down and applied it to fuel his moves, to make sure he was hypervigilant. To get Alexia to safety.

They weren't quite there yet. But at the sight of her smile, watching her come back to life as the terror started to fade, he was filled with so many emotions he'd never felt before. It made him wish for things he'd never thought of. Made him care, way too much. Cade had accused him of mooning over Alexia. Blake realized now he'd just been waiting.

And if he'd had the words, if he had a clue what to say, he'd have made some big emotional declaration.

His gut clenched, the hair on the back of his neck standing on end.

He owed his life to those warning signals, so he automatically stopped, mentally gauging the danger.

Alexia, he realized.

She wasn't a threat to his physical safety.

She was a threat to his way of life.

If he let these emotions grow, he'd give in to anything she asked. Like leaving the military. Giving up his career. Growing out his hair. Hell, he was pretty sure he'd even get one of those dogs women carried in their purses if she asked.

Slowly, trying not to make a show of it and get her upset again, he released her hand.

He'd rather have the fear back.

Or at least that nice safe distance time and her anger had provided. Because now that she was here, right here in front of him again? With all these crazy thoughts and emotions going on? She was a bigger danger than the wannabe terrorist and his cadre of idiots back there.

"I guess hand-holding really is a part of your job description," she said, her laugh a little stiff. He wondered if she'd been hit with emotional overload, too. He doubted it. She'd already faced the threat of her life's destruction. Flicking him off again probably didn't even register.

Good. He just had to keep it that way. Make sure his position as a SEAL, his connection with her father, stayed clear in her mind.

That'd keep her hands off him.

And hopefully he had enough training and self-discipline to keep his own off her.

Before he could dismiss the hand-holding as a nothing gesture, or figure out a way to bring her dad into the conversation, the radio light flashed, a low buzz indicating a message was coming in.

Saved by an unexpected communiqué. Not wanting to alarm Alexia, he kept his smile in place.

"Well, hand-holding and answering the phone. Or radio, in this case," he said, walking over to see what was there.

His expression didn't change as he read the intel.

The compound belonged to one Hector Lukoski. The son of a known terrorist with Syrian ties, Lukoski was trying to make a name for himself apart from his father. Well trained in defensive measures, he had an underground hideout. The team had confirmed that there was only one way in or out, and had it covered. But short of blowing his lair up around him, they were forced to lay siege and wait. No action would be taken until new orders were issued, at least twelve hours from now.

He tapped a few keys to signal that the message was received.

Alexia wasn't going to like the news.

Nor, he remembered, was he supposed to tell her.

The message was in code, so she wouldn't have to

know. Wouldn't have to worry. His brain raced, pulling together a plan. He'd make her some hot chocolate, dim the lights and talk her into going to sleep.

It wasn't a very elaborate plan, but sometimes simple was best.

"What's going on?" she asked.

"Just a weather report," he said, tapping the screen. "It looks like it's going to snow."

"Ha-ha." Giving him a narrow look, she got stiffly to her feet and, after taking a second to bend in half and touch her toes, she crossed to the bank of radios and monitors and peered at the message.

"A weather report? Seriously?"

"SOP is to check in every two hours. A weather report is a simple message to use. If it was somehow intercepted, it says nothing. And it's always good to know the weather."

He couldn't tell if she was buying it or not. That was the trouble with Alexia. Half the time, she was an open book, easy to read and ready to share. The other half made him feel like an untrained schoolboy trying to talk to his first girl. Clueless and inept.

"Well, at least the navy has a handle on the weather," she finally said.

His shoulders relaxed and he let out the breath he hadn't realized he was holding. He didn't want her worrying. Which would be fine if it was because her worrying would make the mission more difficult. But he knew that wasn't why. It was because he hated the idea of her suffering in any way.

Cade was right. He had a problem.

"Ready for some hot chocolate?" he asked, doing

what he always did when faced with a problem. Taking it down one step at a time.

"Sure." She glanced at the now-blank screen again, then followed him over to take her seat at the table. "Can I help? It seems like you're always cooking for me."

That's because with the exception of the field rations they'd just had, he'd ended up eating a bit of every meal off her naked body.

Don't go there, he warned himself. His imagination didn't listen, though. As he heated the water to mix with powdered milk, his brain threw out a dozen or so images of the way Alexia had looked covered in plum jelly. Or in cream sauce. Or in soapy bubbles that slid, slow and thick, down her bare breast. The tip beaded in pouting delight, just waiting for his tongue.

"Shit," he muttered, shaking the splash of hot water off his hand. *Focus, dammit.* He removed the pot of boiling water from the burner, dumped the white powder in and stirred.

"You're making a mess," Alexia said, tilted almost sideways in her chair so she could see what he was doing. "Are you sure I can't help?"

Blake looked down at the table. The burner was sizzling with specks of watery milk. Powder pooled around the pot like mounds of snow. He'd stirred so hard that the back of his hand looked as if he had white freckles.

"Here," he said, pushing the pot, spoon and chocolate powder toward her. "Have at it."

Needing to move, wishing for action—any action that didn't involve Alexia's naked body—he strode over to the monitors to check the display, then to the tent flap, pulling down the pseudocurtain and looking out.

It was still white.

Go figure.

"Did you want some?"

Some of her? Oh, yeah.

"No. Thanks," he added, trying to soften the bark. He glanced back to see she'd poured half the mixture into a tin cup. She held up the pot, looking at him questioningly.

He really needed to get a grip. This was just an adrenaline-induced loss of control, combined with seeing someone he'd been obsessing over. No big deal.

Time for phase two of his plan. Get her the hell to sleep.

He crossed the tent, reaching for the pot. Their fingers brushed. He wanted more. He was desperate to touch her again. Even if it was only her fingertips or her hair. He still had dreams about that hair. She'd brushed it back into some twisting rope, the red glowing in the soft lamplight. He remembered the feel of her hair in his hands, trailing down his body. The silky feel, the sweet scent.

In an instant, he went from soldier to man.

Horny, turned on and ready to rock, man.

"How is it?" he asked, his voice a little hoarse.

"Surprisingly good." She sipped again, then arched one brow. "Are you sure you won't have some?"

"I'm still full from dinner," he said. And desperate for more space than the small tent allowed. "But you must be exhausted. Why don't you finish your drink, then try to get some rest."

"I was hoping we could chat." Her smile was sweetly

mischievous, making Blake want to howl and beat on something. She was supposed to be overwrought. Not cute, dammit. He'd never had to fight off all these sexual and emotional needs while he was on duty before. And couldn't say he was liking the new experience much.

"Chat? About what?" he asked.

"I thought we'd talk about why you were assigned this mission. If hand-holding isn't your usual thing, then what is?"

"I'm the radioman. Communications, languages, they're my usual things."

"That's kind of funny," she said in a tone that didn't sound as if she was enjoying the humor. She stared into her cup for a second, then met his eyes. "We're both communications specialists."

She stopped there, as if she were standing against the door between now and then and wasn't sure she wanted to open it.

"And you think we didn't communicate," he said, figuring they had to step through the door sooner or later.

"You think we did?" she asked.

Her tone wasn't challenging. It was simply curious. He wondered if she'd burned through her supply of negative emotions. He'd seen it before. It was like watching someone hit rock bottom, so they operated in an emotional vacuum. It wouldn't last. But as chickenshit as it was, he sure hoped they were picked up before she tapped into a new supply.

He hesitated before responding, though. There was a good chance she still had plenty of mad tucked away in there. And despite his wanting distance between them, this was a damn small tent to be sharing with a pissed-off woman. Still, he could only answer honestly.

"I thought we communicated just fine. We were focused on one thing, and we got our wants and needs across to each other pretty damn well."

Something flared in her dark eyes. Interest. Heat. A dangerous curiosity. Blake braced himself. But as quick as it'd flamed, she banked it. With short, deliberate moves, she set the cup on the table and got to her feet.

"It just hit me how exhausted I am. I'm going to go ahead and sleep."

He didn't let the relief pour in until she'd climbed onto the cot, still fully clothed, and covered herself with the thermal blanket. To help her along, he dimmed all the lights.

"Good night," he said quietly.

She didn't answer for a second. Then, her voice a sigh, she said, "'Night. And thank you."

CHAPTER ELEVEN

BLAKE LISTENED TO Alexia's breathing. As if he could coax her into relaxing, he breathed along with her, slowing, soothing. After a few minutes, he knew she was asleep.

That's when he let himself relax.

He should sleep. The perimeter alarms were on. If anything heavier than snow crossed them, he'd know. Still, he hesitated. He didn't trust Alexia's safety to machines.

For just a second, he let his frustration at being on this side, tucked away from the action, pound through him. He wasn't made for sitting it out. Not even with a beautiful woman.

His watch set to ping him in thirty minutes, he forced himself to sink into the cot. Eyes closed, he tried to put everything—especially the woman sleeping three feet away—out of his mind. If he wanted to keep her safe, he had to be in top form. To be in top form, he needed sleep. He wouldn't sleep if he was imagining her naked except for those leather combat boots.

It was the boots that did it. He focused all his attention on those, and slowly felt himself sinking into a doze. He was a breath away from sleep when he heard something.

He jackknifed up and flew from his cot. He pulled a sobbing Alexia into his arms.

"Baby, it's okay," he soothed, brushing the damp tendrils of hair off her face. By the lights of the monitors, he could see the terror in her eyes. "There's nothing to worry about anymore. I'm here. I've got you."

"Hold me," she begged, wrapping her arms so tightly around his waist, his breath shortened. "Don't let me go. Don't let anything happen."

"I'm holding you." To back up his claim, he ran his hands up and down the back of her thick sweater.

"Hold me tighter. I've never been so scared, Blake. I close my eyes and I can see him again. See the glee in his nasty rat face as he threatened me. He promised to let his men do horrible things to me."

Fury pounded through him, racing past frustration and damn near knocking out his control.

"You're safe," he told her again, brushing a kiss against the silkiness of her hair.

He didn't know if it was because she needed the assurance of seeing his expression, or if it was a reaction to that kiss. But Alexia peeled her cheek off his chest and leaned back. Just far enough that they could look into each other's eyes. Feel each other's breath on their faces. Blake knew he should get up. He was on duty. He was sworn to protect her. Hell, her father had handpicked him to keep her safe.

Every reason—and there were a lot—that he should get the hell up and away from her crossed his mind.

He looked into her eyes, the dark heat there calling to him, touching something in his heart that he couldn't resist.

"Just letting you know ahead of time, this is a huge mistake and I'm sorry," he said.

Her brow furrowed, but before she could ask what he meant, he kissed her.

IT WAS LIKE WAKING from a nightmare and finding herself safe, cocooned in pleasure. Like coming home. As Blake's lips sank into hers, Alexia felt right for the first time in months. His mouth was so soft, so sweet. His body so warm and hard as his arms enfolded her and held her close.

She wanted more. Needed him with a desperate, clawing need. With him, she was safe. With him, she was whole.

Her mouth moved under his, their lips sliding together then slipping apart. At his touch, the tension and terror that had gripped her fell away. At his kiss, the horrified images of the last four days dissipated, like smoke.

He was heaven, pure and simple. It was as if nothing could scare her, nothing could hurt her as long as he was close.

Slowly, he released her lips and pulled away. Her fingers clutched his shoulders, trying to keep him from moving, from leaving.

"You were crying," he said, his fingers gently wiping dampness she hadn't even realized was streaked over her cheeks before sliding along her hair to cup the back of her head.

Well, that was hot. Nothing sexier than sobbing in your sleep. Alexia frowned, her shoulders drooping, right along with her sexual bubble.

"That's why you kissed me? Because I was crying?"

He hesitated. She could tell he was debating. The easy way, or the truth. She should make it simpler for him. After all, the man had rescued her from a stinking lunatic. But she wanted more, she wanted…well, hard. Him hard. Better yet, him hard inside her.

"I kissed you because I couldn't resist," he said, his fingers now sliding into the braid at the back of her head, loosening her hair, massaging her scalp in a way that made her want to purr. "I shouldn't have, though."

The tension that had been building again started to fade. Joy bubbled up, filling her smile with a little extra sparkle. Excitement started growing again as the hope of sex, and yes, those incredible fingers, worked their magic.

"Why not?" she whispered, her hands roaming his back, delighting in the play of strong muscles beneath his shirt. Her reasons why not were a mile long.

Better to focus on his reasons instead. That way she could brush them aside and get on to the good stuff.

"Because you're you and I'm me."

"Ah." Alexia couldn't help it. She laughed. "That's succinct."

His lips twitched, but he didn't smile. He gave her a serious, peering-all-the-way-into-her-soul kind of look instead.

"You're the admiral's daughter. I'm a SEAL. You're looking for a transparent, open relationship. I live in the shadows. You're the victim under my protection. I'm charged with the mission of getting you home safe."

As if his words had flipped open the tent flap, the chill of reality crept over her. Alexia's fingers stopped caressing his back, then slowly fell away.

Looked as if their lists were pretty similar after all.

"Well, those are some solid reasons," she acknowledged quietly. How could she argue with her own justifications? If they both had them, they were even more rational than just her making them up in her own head, right?

Alexia sighed, wishing she could go back to believing that she was overreacting.

On his face she saw the same frustration, the same reluctance that she felt. He eased away.

She shivered, her body instantly missing his warmth. She wanted to pull the blankets around her, but doing so would mean he had to move. And sex or no sex, she wanted—needed—him close for as long as she could keep him.

"Yeah. Good solid reasons why we should keep things smart," he said, sitting upright. He shoved one hand through his hair, making it stand up in short spikes, and gave Alexia a stiff smile. The only reason she was able to smile back was because she could see that stiffness echoed in his tented fatigues.

Her breath caught in her chest, adding to the surreal buzzing she heard in her head. It was like standing, starving, outside a bakery, staring at a window display of her very favorite, most decadently delicious pastries. Or in this case, cannoli. Her eyes traced the ridge of his pants and she corrected that to jumbo cannoli.

"Smart is good," she agreed absently.

"Smart is necessary," he told her, his words a little more clipped than usual. He was only saying them because it was *the right thing to do,* she realized.

"We're two intelligent, mature adults who know how to control our urges." Her fingers traced a design on his thigh, reveling in the corded muscles she could feel, even through the heavy cotton of his pants. Slowly, as if she was sneaking up on it, her fingers trailed closer and closer to the ridge of his impressive erection.

His gaze narrowed, eyes calculating. As if he was figuring out just how to turn this to their advantage. Their *naked* advantage.

"Just because there's this thing with us," he said, waving his fingers back and forth between them as if there were an electric field there, "that doesn't mean we have to give in to it."

"Of course not," she agreed with a strained laugh, her nipples aching and heavy as every breath brushed them against the thermal fabric of her shirt. "We're not animals, after all."

"Nope. Not animals," he agreed, his eyes locking on her sweater-covered breasts, heating. Making her nipples tighten even more. "We know better than to get into something that we've both clearly accepted is bad for us."

"So bad," she breathed, her eyes lifting from his crotch to meet his slumberous gaze. "So, so bad."

"So we're having wild, uncontrolled animal sex, right?" he asked, his hand reaching out to hover over—but not quite touch, dammit—her aching nipple.

"Oh, yeah. Hurry and get your pants off," she ordered, saving time by yanking two sweaters at once over her head. When her face cleared the fabric, she saw that Blake had pulled off his long-sleeved T-shirt and was unlacing his boots. What was with military footwear? she wondered, wanting to cuss at how long it took. Clearly, whoever designed it didn't have fast sex in mind.

For the first time since they'd met, Blake showed a

lack of grace as he hopped on one foot, trying to untangle the mile-long laces on his snow boots.

Wanting to hurry him along, Alexia took a deep breath and yanked her thermal undershirt over her head. Braless, since she'd thrown out everything she'd been wearing in that hellhole, her torso was instantly covered in goose bumps.

Until Blake's gaze, hot and intense, warmed her like a caress.

"Damn, you're gorgeous," he breathed.

Then he lost his balance and toppled onto the other cot.

The crash was deafening.

She paused, her pants unzipped and her hands on her hips to shove them down, and met his eyes.

Desperation turned to laughter. Her gaze still locked on his, Alexia clapped her hand to her mouth to try to contain the chortles. But when he grinned, she couldn't hold back.

Giggling, she pulled the blanket over her nudity and shifted into a sitting position to peer at Blake. Already on his feet—gotta love that physical conditioning—he was pulling the cot back into an upright position.

"Are you okay?" she asked as soon as she got control of herself.

"Yeah, but the cot's a little worse for wear." He kicked at one of the legs with his stocking-clad foot to indicate the bent metal.

"Oops." Alexia wrinkled her nose at the damage.

"Can't say I don't know how to show you romance," he told her, still smiling.

"Well, one of us was definitely swept off their feet." Then she hesitated. Without the haze of his sweet rescue of her from her nightmare, or the reckless desperation that had pushed them toward fast-and-furious sex, they were left with… What?

A choice.

Alexia's gaze fell to the plain black wool blanket she'd wrapped herself in, her fingers twisting then untwisting the hem.

She felt, rather than saw, Blake drop to his haunches next to her cot. Slowly, after taking a fortifying breath, she lifted her gaze to his.

He was so damn gorgeous. Blue eyes so warm, so inviting, and a mouth that was sexy whether he was smiling or frowning. Sexiest on hers, though. She could see the patience in his gaze. The comfortable acceptance that this was her choice.

It'd been so hard to get over him last time. She'd shoved her feelings about him, her wishes and regrets and longings, all into a box in the back corner of her mind. Then she'd pretended it didn't exist. All but the anger. That, she'd held on to. Used as a weapon to beat down any thoughts she had of maybe peeking into that box.

This time, though, she wouldn't have that anger. This time, she couldn't blame him for anything that wasn't his fault, as she had before.

This time, she was accepting him exactly as he was, completely aware of his loyalties. If they had sex, *this time* she was one hundred percent responsible for her choice. For her feelings. For whatever happened next.

Alexia's fingers shook a little as she stared into his eyes. There, she saw acceptance, appreciation and a heat that went deeper than passion. A heat she couldn't resist. Terrified, but unable to do otherwise, she dropped the blanket and opened her arms.

Blake gave an appreciative moan, traced his finger around one areola, then the other. Looking as if he was about to partake in the Fountain of Youth, he leaned forward to sip delicately.

Alexia's own moan was high and breathless.

Then he moved. Rising to his feet, he stood like a warrior god of old, his broad shoulders tapering in a golden line down to his slender waist. His cock jutted proudly over thick, muscled thighs. Unable to resist, Alexia lifted herself to one elbow and leaned forward to blow lightly on the straining tip of his erection.

It jumped, as if coming to attention.

She slanted him a wicked look, then leaned closer to run her tongue around the velvety head. His fists clenched at his hips, but he didn't move. Didn't try to take control.

"Yum," she murmured before taking him into her mouth, sliding her lips on and down the hard length of him. His fingers splayed, as if he was going to grab her, then he fisted them again. As a reward, she sucked, hard, just the tip, and made him groan out loud.

"My turn," he insisted, lowering himself to the cot and sliding over her body. "Otherwise you might not get yours."

"Oh, I'll get mine," she guaranteed, her bare feet skimming up the back of his hard thighs before she dug her heels into his butt and pressed her aching core to his erection. "You're going to give it to me."

"Yeah. I'm going to give it to you all right." His teasing smile was the last thing she saw before his mouth covered hers. All it took was the touch of his tongue against hers and Alexia went crazy. She needed him. All of him.

"Now," she demanded.

"I'm not done," he said with a strained laugh as his fingers slipped between their bodies and down her belly to cup her curls.

As soon as he touched her swollen clitoris, she shattered. Stars burst, heat exploded. Her entire body convulsed, trembling with the power of her orgasm.

He moved like lightning, thrusting into her with a low, animalistic growl that turned her on even more. He took her hands in his, dragging both their arms over her head. Their eyes locked as his body rose over hers. Excitement swirled, deep and low in Alexia's belly. Every nerve ending was electrified, raw with pleasure. Blake arched his back, then slid into her again in one deliciously slow thrust.

Her body contracted around him, reveling in the feel of his hard length as it moved in, out, in. Slow. So slow she could count her heartbeats between thrusts. So slow she wanted to cry from the pleasure of it.

He pulled her hands higher. Alexia gasped, arching her back against the pressure. She shifted onto her heels. The angle change meant the length of his cock now slid against her G-spot, that electrified, pleasure-charged sensor sending tight, tingling spirals of pleasure up, higher and higher in her belly. Blake bent his head, taking the beaded, aching tip of her breast into his mouth. The spirals climbed higher, grasped tighter.

Her breath came in pants now. Passion swirled, gripping her. Her body tensed as he teased her nipple deep into his mouth, then sucked. When the edge of his teeth scraped along the sensitive flesh, she exploded.

She wanted to close her eyes. To escape into the decadent ecstasy as it washed over her, pulling her deeper and deeper into delight.

But Blake wouldn't release her gaze. Like a magnet, he held tight, forcing her to let him watch her orgasm, to see all the way into her soul as she let go.

As she exploded. Her body, her emotions, the very core of her being all laid bare to him as passion took over. She whimpered at the power, unable to do anything but feel. And it felt incredible.

Slowly, drifting like a downy feather, she floated back to earth. Her heartbeat was still so loud in her head she couldn't hear a thing. But awareness was returning to her body. A body that was still shivering with the aftershocks of pleasure, like mini-orgasms rippling through her.

And no wonder.

Blake was still inside her. Still moving, slow and steady. Building, tantalizing. Teasing her with his control.

Time to shift the balance of power, she decided.

She reached up, threading her fingers through his short hair, and pulled his mouth to hers. Her kiss was sweet at first. A gentle thank-you for the delectable orgasm.

Then, as he sank into it, she took it deeper. Her tongue stabbed, her teeth nipped. He stiffened, the smooth rhythm of his thrusts shifting. Jerking.

Alexia let go of his hair, pushing against his shoulders. Then, in a move that made her grateful for her thrice-weekly pilates class, she gave a big push, and switched positions so she was on top.

"Yum," she whispered.

A wicked smile played about his kiss-swollen lips and he gave an appreciative nod. "Yum, indeed."

He angled his body so he was half raised, his head leaning against the wall of the tent, his hands cupping both her breasts. Holding them in position for his mouth.

Alexia wrapped her legs around the back of his hips, her heels digging into his butt.

Then she set the pace.

Fast. Intense. His face tightened as he drove into her.

"Now," he demanded in a low, guttural tone. His face drawn taut, his muscles tense, he stared into her eyes.

She'd never felt such intimacy, such a touching of souls, as she did in that second. Blake, the connection between them, had become her entire world. Her entire focus.

He thrust harder. His eyes narrowed. He sucked air through his teeth. Feeling more powerful than ever before in her life, Alexia shifted higher, swirling her hips to meet his. Then she clenched her core muscles, grabbing his cock, holding tight.

He exploded.

Hers, she thought as his breath caught.

He was all hers. And she didn't want to let him go.

Ever.

BLAKE WAS ENGULFED by the intensity of the passion pounding through his veins. The orgasm grabbed ahold, ambushing him with its power. As he poured himself into Alexia's warmth, his body shuddered, his arms shaking as his muscles tensed to the point of shattering.

His orgasm triggered hers. Still spinning out of control, he watched through narrow, passion-blurred eyes as she went over. Her body tensed, arching her back. Her breasts, lush and gorgeous, bobbed in time with her frenzied gyrations. She tilted her head back, her moans filling the tent. Filling him with power, his ego swelling so he felt like a he-man. All-powerful, totally awesome.

"Wow," she breathed a few seconds later, staring down at him. Damp tendrils of hair stuck to her face, her skin glistening in the dim light. Slowly, as if all her bones had melted, she sank onto his chest.

"Definitely wow," he agreed, lifting her chin for a kiss. He wanted to say more. To find words to express how incredible he felt with her, how great that had been. But he couldn't. Besides, she looked exhausted.

Telling himself it was the gentlemanly thing to do and not chickenshit, he kissed her again, then rolled so they were on their sides.

She curled into his body as if they were one. Blake closed his eyes against the emotions buffeting him. Passion, still flaming hot, led the pack. But right behind it was a tenderness, a gentle sort of sweetness he'd never felt before. It scared the hell out of him, so he focused on the passion instead.

He wrapped his arms tight around her, giving himself a brief moment of sweet surrender before he hitched her higher, his lips latching on to her breast.

"What are you doing?" she gasped, sounding half asleep.

"I'm not finished."

"Oh, yes, you are," she said with a gasping sort of

laugh, her fingers digging into his shoulders. "I felt you finish, bud. Don't try to claim otherwise."

Kissing her, a soft, gentle brush of his lips over the swell of her breast, he gave her a wicked look. "I would never claim that was anything but fabulous. But I'm not finished."

"You've got to be kidding."

Then his fingers found her. Still wet and swollen, he flicked his thumb over her quivering clitoris. She gasped, her head falling back against the pillow and her nails leaving tiny crescents in his skin.

"You're not kidding," she breathed. "How..."

Her words trailed off when he slid lower, kissing his way down the center of her body. When he reached the flaming curls at her apex, she moaned, shaking her head as if she couldn't believe he was there. But her thighs fell to the side, making room for his shoulders.

This time, when he emptied himself in her, he knew he was done. There. He'd given her all he had.

Every drop.

Every bit of pleasure.

Every ounce of himself.

He collapsed, pulling her tighter into his arms and rolling so he wouldn't crush her. It was all he could do not to groan out loud as he realized what he'd done.

He'd gone and fallen in love.

He was so screwed.

CHAPTER TWELVE

BLAKE CURLED HIS BODY behind Alexia's, his arms wrapped around her waist and fingers twined with hers. It was the closest he could get without being inside her. But give him another five, maybe ten minutes, and he'd be up for that again, too.

She was quiet in his arms. Too quiet. He could tell she wasn't floating on a cloud in sexual nirvana. Not with all the tension he could feel radiating off her.

Give him another five, maybe ten minutes, and he'd get rid of that, too.

"You never asked me what happened at the compound," she finally said, her words painfully low. "Is that a part of your orders? You're on pickup-and-delivery service, but not allowed to know what's in the package?"

Protocol clearly stated that he was exactly what she'd said—pickup and delivery. His orders had been clear. Don't grill her. Debriefing would be done by higher-ups. Besides, Blake winced, trauma, PTSD—she was going to be carting around plenty. But he wasn't equipped to deal with it. Hell, with her psych degree, she was better prepared than he was.

Distract and delay, he decided. Until she could talk to someone who knew how to guide her back to feeling safe.

"I'm pretty sure I just explored the package pretty thoroughly," Blake said, laughing a little before he leaned down to gently bite the back of her shoulder. Ah, the perfect distraction. Alexia gave a delighted shudder, pressing her hips back against him. He felt life stirring again, and was tempted. Oh, so tempted to let their bodies take over again.

But even though they didn't have a future, even though his reasons for them not being together were all still strong and solid, he couldn't do it. He couldn't go the same route he had before. He'd seen the questions in her eyes last fall, had known she wanted to talk, to connect in more than just a physical way. He could use the typical guy excuse that talking about emotions was stupid, a total girlie thing. But he knew that wasn't what she was looking for. She just wanted to know more about the guy she was sleeping with than his favorite position and what moves sent him over the edge.

Blake had hurt Alexia once because he'd taken the easy route. He wasn't going to do it again if he could help it.

"SOP in a rescue is to get in, get the victim and get out. We're not supposed to ask questions unless it pertains to completing the mission," he explained.

"Is that what I am? A *standard operating procedure?*" She didn't sound angry. Nor did her body stiffen or shift away. She simply looked at him with patient curiosity. As if she could wait, that she totally trusted he'd get to the right answer eventually.

Blake frowned. Why didn't she ever react the way he expected? They had sex, and instead of falling into a satisfied stupor, she started thinking about her captivity. He inadvertently labeled her and she laughed it off. Would he ever understand how her mind worked? What her emotional triggers were?

"There's nothing standard about you," he said honestly. "The truth is, I don't do this kind of thing well."

She twisted in his arms so they were face-to-face. Her hair, free of the braid again, haloed around them like red flames. Her slender shoulders and silky skin made for a gorgeous distraction. Blake wanted to pull her tight against him, to tuck her head into his chest and distract her with sex. But the way she was staring at him made it clear she wasn't going to go for it.

"What kind of thing?"

"The emotional aftermath," he said with an uncomfortable shrug. "Dealing with the trauma. You went through hell. You deserve to talk to someone who understands how to guide you through the healing process. I'd say the wrong thing, or pat your head because I don't know how to react, or cuss and punch something. And you don't need anyone making it worse for you."

Her eyes turned to liquid, her smile trembling a little at the corners.

"You are so sweet," she said quietly, brushing her fingertips over his lips in a whisper-soft touch almost as intimate as a kiss.

"No. I just don't want to talk the emotional stuff," he dismissed gruffly. But inside, he felt like a little boy doing backflips. All excited because she thought he was sweet.

"But you would, wouldn't you? If I had to talk it through, if I couldn't wait for a professional who knew how to counsel me, you'd let me work it through with you?"

Blake would rather take a bullet. But, keeping his cringe inside, he nodded.

Her smile was bright enough to light the entire tent. With a husky laugh, she hugged him tight. Her bare breasts pressed temptingly against his chest while her legs twined with his.

"Sweet," she told him. "You are so seriously sweet. Sweet enough that I won't put you through that."

"Thank you," Blake breathed. Then, because words weren't enough, he leaned down to kiss her. Their lips melted together, heating him through and through.

Maybe their five-minute wait was up…

Before he could find out, she leaned back to break the kiss and smiled again.

"So all that hand-holding you do is restricted to the rescue," she teased. "Not the recovery?"

"We should all do what we do best. And leave the things we do worst for someone else."

"And what do you do best?"

"Whatever I set my mind to," he told her. It wasn't bragging. He was damn good at what he did.

"Do you ever worry?" she asked, her fingers tracing a pattern on his chest, but her eyes locked on his. "Does it ever just seem like it's too much? The constant living on edge, the missions and danger and never knowing what's next?"

"It's my life. Danger, the unexpected. They're second nature. Like breathing." Unable to resist those lips, already swollen from his kisses, Blake leaned down to kiss her again.

When he leaned back, she gave him a look that said no distractions allowed. Blake was tempted to see how long it would take to make that look change into passionate surrender.

But finally, with those patient eyes locked on his, he sighed and admitted, "Yeah, sometimes. I didn't used to worry. I'm serious when I say it's a job. I'm highly trained, and damn good at what I do. So doing it isn't a worry."

"But?"

How did she know there was a but? He replayed his words, his tone. There hadn't been a but in there, dammit.

"You know, you wasted that psych degree of yours," he teased, trying to laugh it off.

Despite her smile, she suddenly looked sad. Stressed. He could feel the tension tightening in her lower back.

"What?" he asked. "Why does that bother you?"

"That's what my father said the last time he spoke to me. He wanted me planted somewhere safe and sound, billing fifty-minute hours and poking into people's heads."

Weird. Blake hadn't taken the admiral to be a touchy-feely, get-in-touch-with-yourself kind of guy.

"I guess parents have their own vision for our lives, and it doesn't always mesh with our own."

"Or we have a vision for our own life that doesn't fit theirs," she said, her words only a little bitter.

Same thing, he started to say. Then he realized it wasn't.

"Did yours?" she asked, her fingers tracing a design on his chest. Sliding lower, tighter.

"Did mine what?" he responded absently, all his attention focused on where she'd touch next.

"Did your parents' vision suit you? Or did your vision suit them?"

Her fingers forgotten, Blake snorted. "I didn't rate high enough to merit visions. My old man walked out when I was three, and my mother's view was usually blurred by vodka. She didn't care what I did. Or what I didn't do."

Alexia's fingers shifted upward, teasing the hair on his chest, then rubbing in sweet, soothing circles. "She must be proud now, though, right? You've been decorated so many times. Won so many honors."

Blake arched a brow. How did she know what he'd done?

She looked stubborn for a second, then sniffed. "So I checked your records. So what?"

He couldn't help it. He laughed, then kissed the tip of her nose. She was so freaking cute. Her sexiness was blatant, always right there like a punch in the face. Her brains were subtle, a backdrop to the sexy. Again, always there, but not something she shoved down your throat. But the cuteness? The vulnerable sweetness? That's what got to him. She hid it a lot of the time, so when it peeked out, it was extra special.

"So I'm glad you were curious enough to want to check me out," he said softly. Then he grimaced. He didn't want to talk about his past. It wasn't something he was ashamed of, but it wasn't his world anymore. Still, honesty deserved honesty, so he told her, "My mother doesn't care about any of that. I'm not even sure she knows I made the SEAL team. When I refused to send home my paycheck, she wrote me off. Said we were through. It's been six years and I can't say I miss her."

Horror, anger and a sort of recognition all mixed together in Alexia's expression. She kissed his chin, as if kissing away any hurt he might still feel.

"Even when we don't care, it still hurts when they close that door, doesn't it?" she said quietly.

Blake frowned.

"What doors are closed to you?" he asked, even though he was pretty sure he knew. He hated that the admiral, a man he honestly looked up to and thought a great deal of, could be so flawed as a father.

"My father disowned me last fall. Again."

Last fall?

Shit.

"Because of me?"

Her smile was pure appreciation.

"No, although my unacceptable behavior toward you did trigger the discussion."

"By discussion you mean fight?"

Alexia gave him a sardonic look. "I thought you knew my father. One doesn't fight with the admiral. One listens. One obeys. Or one is disowned."

"I was the trigger. What was the bullet?"

"He doesn't find my career acceptable. It's embarrassing to him and my mother that I focus on sexual behavior. They'd rather I use my psych degree working for the government. Or barring that, they want me to go into private practice in a tidy little office somewhere and talk sexual behavior behind closed doors, where it belongs."

"But you said what you're doing will help a lot of people."

"It will. In the last year, it has, actually. We just received a huge grant to further the work, which is probably what brought the wrong kind of attention." She was quiet for a second, then shifted one shoulder as if it didn't matter. "Fitting, my father would say. To my parents, subliminal programming to heal sexual aberrations is nothing more than *self-indulgence for the weak.*"

"That's bullshit." It pissed him off that she would blame herself, even in a roundabout way, for the kidnapping, or for her parents' narrow views. "You make a difference. And you love what you do. Don't let bullies push you into sidestepping that passion. Even if one of them is a terrorist and the other your father."

Alexia's tension faded, her body relaxing into his again as she laughed.

"I guess that's what you do, isn't it? Stop tyrants from getting away with bullying."

"That's one of our specialties," he confirmed. Blake was always proud to be a SEAL, to serve his country. But seeing the admiration in Alexia's eyes added a nice layer of muscle to that pride.

"So why did things change?" Her tone was pure compassion, so understanding and sweet that he wanted to lay his head on her shoulder and let every pain he'd ever had drain away. "You said you don't worry about doing your job. But you worry about something else now, don't you?"

Blake went as still as if she'd pulled the pin from a grenade and tossed it to him. One wrong move and there would be emotional spattering, all over the place.

"Maybe you can sideline with that psych degree," he joked stiffly, wondering how the hell she'd circled back. Hadn't baring her own woes been a distraction?

You'd think the sad, pathetic story of his childhood was enough to listen to. She still wanted more?

"You don't have to tell me," she said, sounding compassionate and soothing. He could feel the hurt in the set of her shoulders, though. See it in the stiffness of her smile. "I just, well, you were hurting before. Last fall. It made me sad to see the unhappiness in your eyes."

Blake clenched his jaw. She'd known then that he was hurting? Was he that transparent? For just a second, he frowned. That wasn't why she'd slept with him, was it? Pity sex? As quick as the thought came in, it faded. There had been nothing pitiful between them, and he'd be a fool to start thinking that way.

"That was a rough time," he said, figuring he could let it go at that. Then, hoping she'd accept it as enough of an excuse, he added, "I'd served on three back-to-back missions and was hitting burnout."

"That's got to be hard. Like an adrenaline rush that doesn't stop. I'd think you'd face quite a lot of exhaustion." She sounded so understanding that Blake had to close his eyes against the emotions her compassion unleashed. He wanted to kick himself. He'd had access to this much caring, this much sympathy eight months ago. And instead of opening to her, he'd locked everything up tight, deep inside where it could fester and ferment and grow. Damn, he was smart.

"You don't really notice the exhaustion," he heard himself saying. "At first, the back-to-back element gives you an edge. You're always on, always primed. That makes for a pretty effective weapon."

"But after a while, a bow drawn taut loses its intensity, doesn't it?"

He nodded. "Yeah. That's when things happen."

"What happened?" she whispered, her words a breath of comfort over him. No demand, no surprise, it was as if she'd known there was something aching there and she wasn't going to pry it loose, but simply wait until it surfaced so she could scoop it away.

"We lost a guy."

He watched her face as he said it. Waited for the judgment. The shock or horror. But her expression didn't change. Her dark eyes might have melted a little more, but that was all. Instead, she shifted, leaning closer to brush a soft kiss over his lips.

Comfort.

Healing.

Acceptance.

For the first time since he'd watched the life drain out of his buddy, Blake felt those things. All because of a tiny little kiss.

No, he realized.

Because of Alexia.

He waited. Now that the door was open, she'd ask questions. She was intuitive enough to sense his loss was more than just a team member—although that'd be devastating enough. She'd make him talk about Phil. About what he'd meant, how hard it was to adjust to life without him.

Blake's stomach, cast iron in battle, shuddered.

"That has to haunt you," she said quietly. "And make you second-guess your decisions, be extra cautious when it's costing you to slow down and be careful."

Blake drew back to stare at her. That wasn't prodding and poking. That wasn't pushing him into facing things. Where was the emotional aggression? She was trying to kill him, wasn't she? Or worse, make him fall in love with her.

"You need to remember that life's short," she said, her palm skimming his cheek. "We don't get to pick the how or the where. All we get to do is live the days we're given to the fullest."

Blake had fallen off a cliff once. You'd think it would be a wild and fast plummet to the ground, filled with fear of the pain that was surely waiting on impact. And it had been. But it had also been surreal, a time to assess every decision, every mistake and totally analyze the misstep that had brought him into the free fall. It was oddly comforting to know that dive to the death provided plenty of time for regret.

That's how he felt right now. He was falling. He could feel it and knew there was no reversing the direction, no halting the fast plunge. That the landing was going to hurt was unquestionable. That he'd regret not watching his step was guaranteed.

Yet, for all that, if someone tossed him a rope to haul him back to safety, he'd have refused. Because some things just had to happen.

Like falling in love with Alexia.

BLAKE WAS LOOKING at her as if he could see all the way into her soul. As if he knew what was in her heart and was waiting for a confession. Alexia swallowed, wondering what had just happened. And how she was going to deal with it. Because whatever it was, it felt huge.

And she didn't mean the erection rubbing against her thigh.

She figured she had three options.

Reach down and slide her fingers over that erection, so they both changed focus to something a lot more pleasurable.

Voice any of the dozens of questions clamoring in her mind, like, who had died? How close had Blake been to him? How was he dealing with the loss after all these months? And oh so many more nosy, prying queries.

Or she could face her own fears and ask him what he was feeling. Ask him what it was like to face the death of someone he cared about, and how he could keep on when he could be next.

She could ask him if she was just an escape, a way to get his mind off those worries. A warm pair of arms and an easy distraction. Or if she was more. If they could be more, together.

That last one was a little terrifying.

Could she deal with whatever he was feeling? Was she ready to hear it? If she asked Blake to open that door, she'd have no choice but to face whatever emotions were on the other side. And then, in the name of fairness, she'd have to give him access to her emotional closet, too. That secret place where she stashed all the feelings she was too afraid to deal with.

She wanted to go with the first option. But she knew she'd hate herself if she didn't at least try to open the emotional door.

"Since life is so short," she said, picking up from the last comment she'd made, "don't you think it's important to be honest about what you want?"

"I honestly want you," he said, his words teasing, but the look in his eyes deep and intense.

And there she was, back to choosing between the easy route—sex—or the harder one of emotional honesty. Before Blake, Alexia would have sworn that she'd always pick emotional honesty. But it was easy to think that when there was very little at stake.

She took a deep breath, then asked, "And what else, besides me, do you want?"

She figured he'd sidestep. Dance away or turn the query back to something sexy. A part of her hoped he would. Then she'd know she'd tried, given it her best, but that it was all his fault they couldn't dive into the messy, core-wrenching pain of honest feelings.

"I want to make a difference. I want to know I've done my best." He looked past her for a second, as if he was scanning his want list. Then he met her eyes again, and made Alexia's heart stutter. "I want a full life. One that's more than just the military. I want a home. Someplace, someone that accepts me for who I am. For what I am."

Stuttering just a second ago, now her heart tripped, not sure if it should run toward him or skitter away in fear. He wanted everything. And she knew he'd give everything in return.

Frozen, more afraid in that second than she'd been when the rat terrorist had offered her up to his henchman, Alexia tried to figure out what to say.

Suddenly a loud buzz rang out. Lights flashed.

Blake's expression shifted from sexy man to soldier in the blink of an eye as he looked past her shoulder toward the equipment bank.

Fear, already hunkered down in her belly, exploded. "Is that them? Did they find us?"

"No," he assured her, sliding from her arms and the cot. He moved toward the equipment, grabbing his pants as he went. "It's just a message. We check in every couple of hours, remember. Nothing to worry about."

Bless the navy, she thought as the tension poured out of her, leaving her limp and exhausted. Maybe after some sleep in her own bed, some time to sort through her own thoughts, she'd be ready to talk emotions with him. Ready to share what she felt—hell, maybe she'd know what she felt.

But right now, this second? She was just grateful for the interruption.

She watched him answer the radio call, too relieved at the emotional escape that she wasn't even curious about the message.

Then she shivered. Without his body there keeping her warm, she was chillingly aware that she was naked. She tugged the blanket closer, but it didn't help. As she watched him pull his shirt over his head and tuck it into his fatigues, she reluctantly reached for her own clothes.

Interruption or not, they were going to have to finish that conversation. It would have been so much easier naked.

She'd got as far as tugging the second pair of socks over her feet when he returned to her side.

"Time to go," he told her.

"What?" Shocked, she stared at him, trying to read more in his face. More what, she didn't know. All of a sudden, fear gripped her belly. This tent wasn't home. It wasn't even civilization. They were in the godforsaken middle of frozen hell. But this tent had become a haven. Safe and secure.

Now they had to leave?

He sat opposite her, tugging on his boots.

"They took Lukoski at 0400. The area is secure." He looked up from tying his laces to give her a quick smile. "You get to go home."

"Home." The image of her condo, with its bright colors and big soft bed, filled her head. Even better, the beach only five minutes away. Hot sand, warm water. She was going to spend her first two days home curled up under her blankets, sleeping like a baby. And the next handful on the beach soaking up as much sunshine as her body would hold.

"Can't go until you put your boots on, though," he prompted, handing them to her as if to hurry her along. She tugged, tied and stood in under a minute.

Not bad time for having spent part of it peering at her lover, trying to figure out why he felt so far away all of a sudden.

"Ready," she said as her head popped through the top of her sweater.

Busy with their outer gear, Blake didn't say anything.

"What about all this?" She gestured to the tent, the equipment. "Do we pack it up?"

He shook his head.

"A team will come in later, after we get you out of here."

"We should do the dishes." She looked at the cots, one pristine with blankets still tight enough to bounce a quarter on, the other mussed and tumbled, with two imprints clear on the pillow. "Or at least make the bed."

Blake followed her gaze with unreadable eyes. Why was he so distant now? Was he ashamed of what they'd done? Was he so tied to rules and regulations that he regretted their lovemaking? Or just that he'd opened up to her? Hadn't he meant what he said about wanting a full life? Or had he meant it, but realized that it simply didn't apply to her.

He handed her the heavy coat she'd worn on the trip in, then shrugged into his own. Before she could finish zipping hers closed, he tossed the can of chocolate into the trash bag, shook out the blankets and gave the pillow a good, solid punch.

Alexia winced. Her heart wept as she forced herself to finish securing the coat.

Good thing she hadn't bared her heart. It looked as though he was finished here.

CHAPTER THIRTEEN

BLAKE WANTED TO punch something harder than a lousy pillow. A brick wall. A steel door. An angry lion. Anything.

Why then? Why did the call have to come then? Why not in an hour. Or two, even. That would have given him time to deal with the emotional mess he'd fallen into. To finish the discussion and bring, what had she called it before? Closure?

Yeah. *Closure.*

Because facts were facts. Feelings, no matter how intense and inviting, wouldn't change them. He wouldn't—couldn't—ask her to be a part of the life he'd chosen. No matter how much he loved her.

"Are you ready? The rescue team is meeting us at the top of the mountain in fifteen minutes."

"We have to climb a mountain?"

He wanted to laugh. He wished he could find a little humor in this ending. Some way to leave them both with smiles. But he couldn't.

"The rescue vehicle can't make it down to this elevation," he explained, his voice a little stiff. "It's not a big climb and there's a pulley system in place. It'll be like taking an escalator to the second floor of the mall."

"Just like the mall," she muttered, looking as irritated as he felt all of a sudden. "Except for the freezing temperatures, wind trying to knock us over and blinding snow. Maybe we could get a cinnamon bun when we get to the top."

Blake felt rotten. He knew she was reacting to his tone, to his attitude. Just because he knew they had no future didn't mean he wanted to make her angry. Or worse, upset.

There you go, Landon, he mocked. *Rescue a gal from a raving lunatic, have sex with her all night even though you know better, then make her feel lousy about it. The Stud of the Year trophy should arrive any day.*

"Cinnamon buns, hmm?" he said, trying for a light tone. He took a deep breath, then crossed over to finish securing her winter gear. "I'll see what I can do."

He made quick work of her gear. Within seconds, she was ready to brave the elements. Swathed like a mummy, her face concealed and her vivid hair under wraps, she was all eyes. That should mean she was less expressive. But those eyes spoke volumes. Worry, sadness, a regretful goodbye. They were all there, screaming at him loud and clear. So were the embers of passion, so easily ignited between them. All it'd take was a look in return. A word, not even a promise.

And he could keep this going.

She'd regret it, eventually.

She'd hate his job, his connection to a man she felt so negatively toward.

He'd hate hurting her, resent the silent—or eventually not-so-silent—pressure to change.

But between now and that happening, they could have a whole lot of time exploring that passion. Having incredible sex. Enjoying the hell out of each other.

That was living in the moment, wasn't it?

Even though you knew the moment was going to hurt like hell eventually.

"Let's rock and roll."

With that, and a quick smile, he pulled his own face gear into place and gestured her out the tent flap.

They didn't say another word, even when he hooked her safety line and showed her how to climb. It took them a solid ten minutes to traverse the ledge. When he'd arrived, after setting up the tent, he'd put the pulleys into place and carved hand- and footholds into the icy snow. They'd filled in a bit in the thirty or so hours since, making for a few dicey moments. But mostly it was a simple, easy extraction.

As before, Alexia kept up. He wanted to tell her she had military in her blood. She was as good, as solid, as many of the people he'd served with. But he didn't think she'd see that as a compliment.

At the top, he dug his fingers into the deep snow and heaved himself over the edge. Then he reached down for Alexia. Without hesitation, despite there being a thirty-foot drop behind her, she let go of the mountain and put her hand in his. He pulled her up, first over the edge, then to her feet.

They both looked around.

The sound came first. Like a purr beneath the roar of the wind, it slowly grew. Lights, blurred and hazy, bobbed toward them.

"Your chariot," he said, recognizing the light pattern, but still gesturing her behind a rock and pulling his gun. SOP until he saw the driver and knew it was safe.

"Boy Scout, this is Magic Carpet. Do you read?"

"This is Boy Scout, I read. You're in our sights."

"The package is ready to go?"

"Affirmative." The package was staring at him through huge brown eyes as she listened to the communication through her own headset.

"Handoff is imminent. CHAOS will take delivery in person. Magic Carpet out."

Shit.

The admiral was in the Snow Trac?

He should warn Alexia. He might have wiggled out of personal responsibility for not telling her his connection to her father in the past, given the situation. But this time? He knew who her father was, where he was and, Blake eyed the lumbering vehicle still a mile away, just exactly when he'd arrive.

Telling her was against regulations.

Not telling her was the end of their chances together.

He pictured Phil's mom's face at the funeral. Someday, it could be him in the flag-covered box. Could he ask Alexia to accept that? To take the chance that someday she'd be sitting there, accepting a folded flag and military condolences?

Because he loved her enough to want forever, he realized with a painful grinding in his heart. And forever was something he couldn't promise.

Better to promise nothing, to ask nothing. And to make nothing available. She wouldn't get hurt that way.

And his hurt? The excruciating, gut-wrenching misery in his heart? Hey, he was a specially trained soldier, equipped to push through any pain and survive.

"Thank you," she said, her voice soft as a whisper through his headset.

Afraid of what else she'd say, Blake quickly shook his head, then pointed at the Snow Trac vehicle rumbling across the white expanse. Privacy time was over. Communications were open now. Wide-open.

Blake clenched his jaw.

Time to say goodbye.

ALEXIA WATCHED THE huge monstrosity trudge toward them, looking like a giant metal turtle crossing the snow. It was her way home. Escape from the bizarre hell her life had turned into this last week.

So why did she have a desperate urge to shimmy back down the side of the mountain and hide in the tent?

Or better yet, burrow into Blake's arms and beg him not to let her go.

He hadn't let her thank him. Because they'd be overheard, or because he wasn't comfortable with the praise, she didn't know. But he'd saved her. Saved her life. Saved her virtue. And quite likely saved her sanity.

He was a hero. She watched him as he stood between her and the oncoming rescue vehicle, rifle at the ready. Even though he'd talked to them himself, he wouldn't take a chance with her safety until he was sure it was U.S. military in that snow-tank thing.

Everything he'd done suddenly crashed over her. All because he was a soldier. A SEAL. A hero. How could she take issue with that when it was because of all those things that she was alive? How could she ever wish him to do anything else when he was so fabulously talented at being a SEAL? As long as there were freaks and lunatics and evil in the world, men like Blake stood against them. Kept the rest of the world safe, just as he was keeping her safe now.

She wanted to thank him again. To tell him how

much he meant to her, how much she appreciated what he did. And how wrong she'd been to reject him based on his job.

She wanted a chance.

A chance for them.

But now it was too late.

As if mocking the timing of her realization, the Snow Trac grumbled to a loud, whining stop twenty feet away. The lights flashed. Code, she realized as Blake lowered his weapon.

"Your chariot," he told her, gesturing to the vehicle.

Everything she wanted to say was bottled up inside her like a shook-up soda. All intense and mixed up and ready to burst. She wanted to tell him so many things.

But she'd had her chance.

As she'd done so many times in the last day, she hooked her fingers in his belt and put her feet into the indentions he made in the snow.

They reached the vehicle and he gestured her to come around. Two soldiers stood on either side of the open door, both with rifles at the ready. Covering them, she realized with a nervous shiver.

"Be safe," Blake said as she moved toward the steps.

"What?" She turned back, shaking her head.

"Aren't you coming?" He had to be. She had so many things to say to him. So much to try to work out. "You're not staying here, are you?"

"I'm meeting my team back at the compound for cleanup," he said, sounding as official as if he'd been delivering a report to a superior. Or talking to a stranger.

Despite their audience, not caring how it was perceived, Alexia reached out one gloved hand. Before she could figure out what to say, how to say it, a familiar voice harrumphed.

"Well done, Landon. Now, move on to phase cleanup."

Ice formed along Alexia's spine. She felt like one wrong move and she'd crack into tiny pieces.

Suddenly as cold as she'd been in that tiny cell, she turned to face the man in the doorway of the Snow Trac. Like her and Blake and the rest of the soldiers, he was dressed in white camouflage, a helmet, mask and goggles obscuring his features. No matter, she'd know him anywhere.

"Father," she greeted quietly. "I didn't realize you were here."

"Let's go." That's all he said. No greeting. No explanation. Just an order.

Heart heavy, Alexia looked back at Blake. His lack of reaction told her that he wasn't surprised to see the admiral. He'd known he'd be there. And he hadn't warned her.

If he'd held up a sign that said Not Interested, the message couldn't have been clearer.

Shaking, her knees so wobbly that only pride allowed her to manage the steps into the vehicle, Alexia suddenly wanted to be gone. And she never, ever wanted to see snow again.

"Lieutenant," she said, looking over her shoulder to give Blake a nod to acknowledge all he'd done. Including breaking her heart. "Thank you."

"YOU SURE YOU DON'T WANT some chocolate cake? Or maybe ice cream? I can run out and get fresh strawberries to go with it."

It took all her strength for Alexia to pull her gaze from the view of her parents' garden. The entire time she'd been doing her *hostage routine,* as her brother had termed it once he'd stopped crying, she'd fantasized about her own bed. Yet three days after she'd climbed into that Snow Trac and rolled out of hell, she still hadn't made it there.

At first, it was easier to stay here. Her father's connections and pull had meant the debriefing team and the navy psychologist made house calls. The admiral's gruff attitude had meant that Edward, filled with guilt that she'd been kidnapped for research he'd instigated, kept his exhausting visits to a minimum. And her mother's newly found nurturing streak—and her chef—had meant that Alexia was pampered beyond belief. Margaret had even called in her beauty team and a masseuse that morning to give her daughter some much-needed pampering.

"I'm okay," she told her worried-looking mother. She'd never realized Margaret had the hovering gene, but for the last couple of days it'd been out in megaforce. "I'm still full from lunch."

"Lunch was four hours ago. You're not eating enough."

"I was only gone five days, Mother. Not nearly enough time to lose weight and need constant feeding," Alexia said with a teasing look. She patted the belly of her jeans to show it still wasn't flat.

Her smile faded as her mother's face crumpled. And not, Alexia knew, because she was horrified at her daughter's curves.

"Don't," she begged, sliding from the bench seat and wrapping her arms around her mother. "Please.

You keep crying and I'm going to need a transfusion. You know I'm a sympathy weeper."

"I was scared," Margaret admitted. "I've never been scared like that before." Her fingers clutched her daughter for just a second before she sniffed, stepped back and carefully dabbed the dampness from under her eyes.

Alexia dropped back to the window seat and stared in shock.

"You were scared?" But she'd seemed so calm when she'd welcomed Alexia home. Margaret had gotten a little weird, with the hovering and all. But Alexia hadn't realized that was fear.

"What do you think?" Margaret snapped. "My daughter, kidnapped by a lunatic. Hauled off to some icy hellhole. We didn't know who, or why. And when we did, it was even worse."

She paused to take a deep breath, then continued. "I was terrified. Your father was, too, although he tried not to show it. He called in every marker he had, Alexia. He handpicked the SEAL team, he demanded the best to rescue you. Even then, we had no idea…"

Her words trailed off, and she sniffed, but held her hand out to say she was getting control of herself. So Alexia stayed seated. Truthfully, she was too surprised at the idea of her father worrying to have the strength to stand.

"Michael and I waited here, of course. But your father refused to. He insisted on going to Alaska to get you. He even yelled at Daniel Lane."

"He yelled at the rear admiral?"

Reeling a little and not sure how to deal with it,

Alexia absently patted the cushion next to her. To her surprise, her mother took the invitation and sat.

"As I said," Margaret told her with a quick, uncomfortable pat to the knee, "I've never been so scared."

"You must have been, though. I mean, Father served his entire career in the military. He fought in two wars. How was that not scary?"

Heck, just thinking of Blake doing cleanup at that nasty compound gave her chest palpitations.

"Because that was his job," Margaret said with a flick of her bejeweled wrist, as if dismissing the question as ridiculous. Alexia waited to feel slighted, stupid, as she would have so often in the past when her curiosity was rebuffed. But her mother didn't seem to be closing the dialogue. Just responding.

"It's that easy? Because it's his job, you weren't afraid?"

"Darling, he was trained to fight. Trained in strategy. He knew how to use weapons and all of that big scary equipment and had an entire platoon of men just as well trained, just as dedicated, fighting at his side. As I said, it was his job. And he was very, very good at it."

"But his job put him in constant danger. He had people shooting at him, trying to blow him up. Didn't that worry you?"

"Did you watch the news yesterday?" Margaret asked.

Shaking her head no, Alexia frowned. What did that have to do with anything?

"I don't recall what city it was—I just caught the tail end of the newscast. But it was rush-hour traffic and someone became angry. He stopped his car in the middle of gridlocked traffic, pulled out a weapon and started shooting. He killed three people before he was stopped."

Alexia's breath caught at the horror. "Those poor people," she breathed.

"Exactly. They were only trying to get home, living their safe day-to-day lives. And someone tried to kill them." A combination of anger, disgust and pity creased Margaret's face. "At least a solider is trained and prepared. Nobody knows when their time is going to come, darling. It could be on a mission, or at the grocery store. So sitting around wringing one's hands and worrying is a waste of time and energy, don't you think?"

She nodded, and the little ball of terror that'd knotted in her belly when she realized she was in love with Blake started to unravel. But right next to it was a bigger fear, one that was still tied tight.

Taking a deep breath, she asked, "But what about the rest? The fact that most of his life is dedicated to the service. That he keeps tons of secrets from you. How does that not bother you?"

Her mother looked stunned for a second, as if she'd never considered those questions. Then she shrugged.

"Well, that too is a part of his job, isn't it? I knew it when I married him, so why would it bother me? As for the secrets..." She glanced at the door, then laughed and lifted both hands as if to say *well?* "Darling, I have plenty of secrets of my own. Secrets that your father will never find out about."

Alexia's eyes rounded with shock.

"Noooo?" she breathed.

"Mine might not be along the lines of military intelligence, but they're juicy enough. Like the true color of my hair, for instance. Or my real weight and collection of Spanx. Your father thinks I eat half a grapefruit every morning, but has no idea I have a bowl of Cocoa Puffs after he leaves for the day." Margaret tapped one manicured finger on her lips as she considered what else she might be hiding from her husband. "There are the two credit cards he doesn't know I have. For my girlie purchases, of course. He has no idea that I love trash-talk television in the daytime, or that when he's out of town I eat chocolate in bed."

"And you keep all this from him?" Alexia felt stunned, not so much that her mother kept secrets, but that she had such fun ones to hide.

"Of course. It's all a part of my job of being happy while presenting the ladylike image that's so important to supporting your father's career. And don't you forget, this information is classified, young lady, and disseminated only on a need-to-know basis."

Alexia laughed until tears trickled down her cheeks. Her mother, watching with a bright smile, reached over to tuck a curl behind her ear, letting her fingers smooth her daughter's cheek as she did.

Smiling, Alexia was pretty sure this was the closest, the happiest, she'd ever been with her mother.

"Why didn't you ever share any of this with me before?" she asked.

"You never wanted to hear it before, darling. You were too busy rebelling and finding your own way." Margaret patted her daughter's knee, then rose. "And you do have a habit of holding on to anger, Alexia. Long after a battle has ended, you're still there in the trenches, ready to aim and fire again. Which makes communication rather difficult."

Well, there you go. Alexia's shoulders sank under the weight of that truth. Her parents weren't perfect. Nor was she so overwhelmed by the emotions of her ordeal into thinking they were even great. They were self-absorbed, stubborn, close-minded and ambitious.

But, she realized, so was she.

"Mother, is it okay if I stay here again tonight?"

"I'd love it if you did," Margaret said. Then her smile dimmed a little. "But we do have company coming for dinner. You're free to join us, or if you're still feeling melancholy, you can take your meal in your room."

"I'll join you," Alexia decided, surprising them both. Hey, maybe a meal where she wasn't *holding on to anger* would be interesting.

"I'll let the cook know," Margaret said, her eyes bright again.

She left with a quick wave of her fingers. Alexia heard her in the hallway, then her father's deeper tones. He was home from the base. Other than his insistence on being there for the debriefing—which she'd thought was to make sure she didn't embarrass him but now wondered if it was for support—she hadn't seen him since their return from the North Slope. And even that she didn't remember much of. After ten silent, miserable minutes in the Snow Trac trying not to cry, she'd fallen asleep only to wake on an aircraft carrier just before it set down in Coronado.

Should she go talk with him?

Try to discover if there might be a bridge between them like the one she'd found with her mother?

Ask if he had news of Blake and whether or not the team was back yet?

Double-check to see if she'd drooled all over the cot in his aircraft carrier?

She should.

If she wanted an open dialogue and communication between them, it was up to her to take the first step.

And maybe her mother had a point. Maybe she did hold on to anger, creating walls where there didn't need to be any.

Then again, what if all he wanted to do was lecture her? Or chide her on her career choices? Or any number of other negative things.

Things had always been cut-and-dried between them—her father was the jerk, she was the poor, misunderstood and unappreciated daughter. He was rigid, she was strong. He was wrong, she was right. Simple as that.

Now she didn't know. Wasn't sure.

"Who's in the mood for cinnamon buns?"

Saved from talking herself into approaching her father, Alexia gratefully looked up to see her brother standing in the doorway, a white, aromatic bag in hand.

"Michael," she greeted, rising to give him a tight hug. "Are you here again? I thought you had a show today."

"Show, shmow. I took a little personal time. It's not every year that my sister scares the crap out of me, after all."

"That seems to be today's theme," Alexia said, taking the bag even though she wasn't hungry. At this rate, she'd be ten pounds overweight before she ever made it home.

"Are you okay?" Michael asked, pulling a chair over and straddling it. "What scared you? Flashbacks? Nightmares? Split ends?"

Alexia's lips quirked. She pulled a piece off the bun, but didn't eat it. "Mother said she was scared. When I was gone, she said you all were. I mean, I knew *you* would be. But I didn't even consider that they would."

"She was pretty freaked," Michael said. "And yeah, I'd have to say Father was, too. He cussed up a storm, threw a few things and ordered me to stay here and take care of Mom while he dealt with this mess."

Alexia's lips twitched. "This mess?"

"Yeah. But he didn't mean you for once," Michael teased with a wink. "He was talking about the Science Institute. Dr. Darling was being a total ass about the rescue, wanting to do some CYA before bringing in the authorities. He didn't want the news leaking before he'd talked to the investors."

CYA. Covering his ass, indeed.

"That Edward sure is a peach," she said sardonically. She wasn't surprised, though. He'd been in contact with the terrorist for almost a year and hadn't caught on that the guy was a murdering lunatic. If that got out, he wasn't going to look so good. And bad press could slam the door shut on the flow of money to the institute. But still, the man had claimed they were perfect for each other. Maybe he'd have been in a bigger rush to rescue her if she'd slept with him.

As if reading her mind, Michael nudged her shoulder with his. "Good thing you didn't date the guy, hmm? I mean, what a wank."

She made a sound of agreement, staring out the window again. She'd thought Edward's only drawback was that he didn't turn her on. But it looked as if all the communication skills in the world didn't make a guy a hero.

"Are you staying for dinner?" she asked.

"Are you?"

"Sure. Mother said there would be guests. But you can sit next to me and keep me entertained."

And distracted. Because all this self-reflection was really messing with her resolve to accept that things were over with Blake.

Of course, resolve or not, it didn't really matter. He was the one who wanted nothing to do with her.

CHAPTER FOURTEEN

BLAKE STOOD AT ATTENTION, waiting for the admiral's signal.

"At ease," Pierce said as he moved behind the imposing desk in his home office and sat like a king on his leather throne. "You're a guest, Landon, relax and have a seat."

Right.

Blake sat, but he didn't relax. The venue was a little more informal than headquarters, where he'd had his first debriefing. And he might be the admiral's dinner guest, but that didn't change the fact that this was a formal interview.

"You've already received official acknowledgment of a job well done," the admiral said, his fingers steepled in front of his chest as he regarded Blake. The look on his face might have been friendly, but it was hard to tell. Granite didn't bend well. "I'd like to offer my private, personal appreciation, as well. You got my daughter out, kept her safe and delivered her without harm. Her mother and I are grateful."

Blake stared. For real? He hadn't taken the admiral as a gratitude kind of guy.

"Thank you, sir," he said. Then, knowing he shouldn't, he still asked, "How is Alexia doing? Has she recovered from her ordeal?"

Meaning the "kidnapping and grueling weather" ordeal. Not the "sex on a cot and subsequent pseudo rejection from him" ordeal. Blake ground his teeth, still not sure if he'd done the right thing. Or more to the point, still not sure he was glad he'd done the right thing.

He missed her. He'd spent eight months missing her, but telling himself she hated him had made it easier to resist the urge to reconnect. Now that he knew she didn't hate him…? The urge was like a noxious rash, growing and spreading at lightning speed, making him crazy.

"According to the psychologist, she's processed the trauma in a healthy way and isn't likely to have long-term issues as a result." Before Blake could process how stupid that sounded, the admiral continued, "According to her mother, she's fragile and underfed, but just needs some time and TLC. And if you listen to her brother, who knows her best, she's stewing over something and needs to go shoe shopping."

"Shoe shopping?" Blake deadpanned.

"Apparently it's a cure-all," the older man said, looking both baffled and embarrassed. Then he pulled his official face back on. "The bottom line is she's fine. A great deal of the credit for that goes to you."

"I'd say the credit for that goes directly to Alexia," Blake shot back without thinking.

And immediately regretted it. The admiral got a wily, weighing sort of look in his eyes. Then he nodded as if Blake had just made some grand confession.

"I'm going to step outside of protocol for a moment," Pierce said, folding his hands on his desk. He leaned forward, his face creasing in a granitelike smile. "I'd like to talk to you, not as your commanding officer, but man-to-man."

Blake's brows arched. Technically, since he was retired, the admiral wasn't still his commanding officer. *Technically.* Still, it was the man-to-man part that was worrying.

"You and my daughter have..."

Oh, shit. Have what? Had inappropriate relations? Had a hundred or so mutual orgasms? Had enough emotional intensity between them to fuel a soap opera?

"You have a lot in common. You're both young and single."

Blake waited. Was that all Pierce had? Or did he simply not know enough about his daughter to make a list. Blake could. They liked the same music and laughed at the same jokes. They both liked the beach and hated being cold. They were communications specialists who specialized in avoiding communication. They had a sexual chemistry that could blow up both their worlds, and a mutual love for chocolate.

"You're both intense, focused individuals with strong ethics and career goals," the admiral finally said, a hint of triumph in his tone. Yep, the old guy really knew what young single people were looking for in each other.

"Sir, are you trying to set me up with Alexia?"

After she'd reacted so well to it the last time?

"*Set up* is such a juvenile term. Let's just say I'd be amenable to the idea of you and my daughter building a relationship together."

In all his consideration of whether a relationship with Alexia was a good idea or not, in all his continual recounting of the pros and cons, he'd never, once, factored her father's approval into the mix.

Now that it was front and center, he still didn't care. If he and Alexia were going to try to work things out, it'd be between the two of them. It didn't matter to him whether the admiral was cheering them on, or doing his damnedest to roadblock them.

But they weren't going to try, because there was no point. A relationship between them would eventually hurt Alexia. Blake figured it was better to hurt her a little now, instead of a whole lot later.

"I'm sorry, sir. But I'm not in the market for a relationship. Besides," Blake couldn't resist adding, "I have a dangerous career. The chances of my being hurt, or killed, aren't insignificant. That's a lot to ask someone to live with."

That the admiral waved his concern away didn't surprise Blake. But his next words did. "She grew up with the realities of a soldier's life. She knows danger is relative. There are plenty of other dangerous careers. Police work, firefighting. Hell, my daughter just proved it's not even safe to work in a science laboratory. She's not going to worry about how safe your job is."

He wanted to believe that. He wished like crazy that he wouldn't be condemning her to a life of misery if he pursued this heat between them. But the image of Phil's mother's face wouldn't fade from his mind.

"I'd worry, sir. You know as well as I do that our work requires total focus. How can you give it that focus if a part of you…" Blake winced, realizing he was treading dangerously close to sappy greeting-card territory here. But he still wanted the answer. "How do you do your job right if your thoughts are back home, worrying about the people who are worrying about you?"

"You do it because they expect you to. Because they believe you're damn good and trust your training is the best." The admiral shrugged, then poked a beefy finger at the framed photo of his wife sitting on the corner of his desk. "You make sure they understand your reasons for being a soldier, that they are strong enough to support you. And you let them blubber when they have to. Give them some pats on the back, a little reassurance and make sure they know how you feel. Then, if something does happen, they're ready. They know why you did what you did and they know your feelings for them. With that, once the shock is over, they can accept it."

Well. Nonplussed, Blake stared. Talk about sappy greeting-card fodder.

But sappy or not, maybe the admiral was right. Blake had taken the loss of Phil hard, but he'd never questioned continuing to be a SEAL. He'd never questioned Phil's dedication to his job. Nor, he recalled, had Phil's mom.

"The only concern your career would have to my daughter is the secrecy. She's a stickler for talking. Communicating and all that rot." The admiral shook his head as if the idea of a couple communicating with each other was bizarre.

It was as if someone had just flicked on a bright light straight into his brain, and Blake blinked with surprise. Not only at the totally accurate insight, but that Pierce actually knew his daughter well enough to make it.

Still… He couldn't—wouldn't—change who he was. So secrecy was just as valid a reason as danger to avoid getting hurt… No, he corrected, to avoid hurting Alexia.

"I appreciate you considering me suitable for your daughter," Blake said, doing a careful verbal tap dance. "But, again, my career is my priority right now. I don't feel there's room for a relationship. Sir."

He tacked that last word on because the old guy's face looked as if it was going to crack.

Instead, it was the man's fist against his desk that snapped.

"She needs someone strong. Someone who will guide her, keep her out of trouble."

"She's strong enough to guide herself," Blake pointed out, starting to get a little irked. "And the only trouble she's been in was through no fault of her own. I hardly think that calls for parental interference."

Blake tossed the words out like a grenade. With a lot of caution, full awareness that they were going to cause an explosion and a mental warning to be ready to duck and cover.

"You don't think being held in a terrorist cell, by a man convicted of five murders to date, is call for parental concern?" The admiral's expression was neutral, but his tone could cut ice. Both fists on his desk, he leaned forward with a lethal glare. "She won't listen to her mother or I, so she needs someone there. Someone who will protect her. Who will caution her and guide her into making more intelligent choices. To quit this ridiculous job and do something else. Private practice, counseling. If she'd done that before, perhaps she wouldn't be fragile, underfed and needing to buy shoes right now."

Blake wasn't sure how anyone could question

Alexia's intelligence. But he figured he'd give Pierce the benefit of the doubt and call this fatherly concern. Or something.

"She doesn't want to do counseling," Blake said with a frown. "She wants to do research, to help people on a larger scale."

"She has two degrees. There's absolutely no reason for her to be involved in such a crackpot field except as an embarrassment to her family."

"She's researching subliminal sexual healing because she believes in it," Blake said slowly. A man of few illusions, he was still surprised that the admiral would go so far as trying to set his daughter up in a relationship in order to control her career choices.

"She could believe in something else just as easily," the older man said.

"She believes she's making a difference in the world."

"She's going on television and talking to reporters about sex."

"She's trying to help people who've been abused and have no other options. That means keeping the topic, and the funding, fresh and relevant. Yes, she's talking sex. But she does it with charm, humor and compassion."

If Blake tried, he was pretty sure he could hear the admiral's teeth grinding together.

"I could find a way to make this an order, Landon."

"Your daughter isn't under your command. Sir." Bitterness coating his mouth, Blake bit off the title. For the first time since he'd joined the service at eighteen, he actually wished he could spit on it.

"But *you* are. And you have influence with her."

Since the admiral still served on base as a civilian adviser, Blake had to give him that point.

"I don't have, nor would I use, influence to coerce someone into leaving a job they love. I would resent someone doing that to me, and would expect the same resentment in return."

Clearly, that wasn't what Pierce wanted to hear. His face closed tight, the admiral steepled his fingers, then launched his pièce de résistance. "I've still got pull on the base. You'd be smart to follow my orders."

The threat hung between them.

And it was a doozy. With the right word in the wrong ear, Blake could be off the SEAL team. He could be dumped in a training camp somewhere, teaching BUDS to swim. He could be doing push-ups in Guam.

The admiral had that kind of power.

Blake didn't give a damn.

Ready to refuse, he took a deep breath and rose to his feet. Before he could say a word, there was a soft tap at the door.

He and the admiral both turned.

It was Alexia. Blake almost dropped back to his seat. Damn, she was gorgeous.

"Gentlemen," she greeted softly. The look she gave Blake was guarded. Impossible to read.

"Yes?" her father barked.

"Mother asked me to let you know dinner is ready," Alexia said quietly, addressing her words to her father but not taking her gaze off Blake.

"Very well." The admiral's chair squeaked as he rose. "We'll continue this discussion after the meal, Landon."

"I think we've finished it already, sir."

He should care that he'd just put his career on the line. It should matter that he was risking everything, his job, his identity, his world, in refusing the admiral's request that he manipulate Alexia.

But all Blake could see, focus on, was her. Standing in the doorway, she looked like sunset.

Her curls tumbled, soft and flowing, over bare shoulders. Unlike the last time they'd been together, when the only color on her face was the bruises under her eyes and her cold-chapped cheeks, she was fully made-up. Like a siren, her eyes were deep and mysterious, her lips red and luscious. She wore a sundress of bleeding turquoise and purple, the silky fabric hugging her curves, then flaring from the hips to swing, full and frothy, to her knees. It was an old-fashioned look, like something a fifties pinup would wear. It suited her perfectly.

She was gorgeous.

He wanted to reach out and touch her. To see if she felt as good as she looked.

"Ahem."

Blake's gaze shot to the admiral. The older man stood in the doorway glowering. Not nearly as encouraging a look as the old man had offered when he'd been hoping to hook his daughter up with Blake. Then again, he'd clearly thought Blake a lot more malleable then.

"If you don't mind, Father," Alexia said, finally pulling her gaze from Blake's to give the admiral a small smile, "I'd appreciate a few moments alone. I wasn't able to thank Lieutenant Landon adequately before. I'd like to now."

"Dinner is waiting."

Blake wondered if his invitation to dine was still

good. The other man didn't say otherwise, though, so he figured it was.

"It'll just be a few moments," Alexia said. Then, in a move that shocked all three of them, she laid her hand on her father's arm. "Please."

For a second, the admiral looked as if she'd pulled a gun on him. Then he gave a gruff nod, awkwardly patted her hand and turned to go. He even pulled the door shut behind him.

"Holy shit," Blake said, almost whispering. "How'd you do that?"

"I'm really not sure," she told him with a little laugh, giving the closed door a wide-eyed look. "But enjoy it while you can, since he'll probably be back soon."

Blake's grin only lasted a second, then faded as he stared at her. Damn, she looked good. Now that they were alone, he wanted to grab her and hold tight. To haul her off to the nearest private space that didn't have her father's stamp on it, and have his wild way with her.

He wanted to get the hell out before he gave in to any of those things and hurt them both.

"We should join them," Blake said, gesturing to the door and wherever beyond it the dining room was.

"In just a second." Looking at her feet, shod in impressively high fuchsia pumps, Alexia chewed on her lip, then gave a sigh and met his eyes. "I really do want to thank you. I also wanted to apologize. And, as soon as I confess, I'll have to do both of those again, but I should get the first one out of the way, well, first," she babbled.

Blake stared at her, trying to unravel her words.

Despite the gravity of her tone, her eyes danced as she watched him try to work it out.

"What do you want to thank me for?" he asked, starting at the top.

"For rescuing me." She held up one hand as if to halt his objection. "Yes, I know I thanked you already and you will claim it was just your job. But this is for more than rescuing me."

"You want to thank me for holding your hand?" he asked, trying to make a joke out of what was surely going to be an emotional mess.

"Well, you are pretty amazing at the hand-holding," she teased. Her voice was low and sexy, bringing back all kinds of memories of her naked body, his exploding climax, the sounds she made as she took her pleasure.

God, he wanted her. And not just sex with her. He wanted that about as much as he wanted his next breath, but thinking about it in the admiral's office gave him visions of the brig.

"But I wanted to thank you for a little more than that," she said, pulling him off the ride to fantasyland. "I was scared. Even after you got me out of that nightmare, I was scared. You kept me from falling apart. You made me feel safe."

"That's my job," he dismissed, trying to shrug the discomfort off his shoulders.

"Yes, that's the point. It is your job. Your job, what you do, makes people feel safe." She stepped forward, close enough that the familiar, heady scent of her shampoo enveloped him in a subtle cloud. "I threw your career in your face last year. I used it and, well, your connection to my father as an excuse to slam the door shut between us."

Since Blake had done exactly that himself, he'd have to be a pretty big ass to hold a grudge. Or even to pretend to, for the sake of keeping a wedge between them. "You have every reason to see my career as an issue," he told her. "It is one. I'm not a good relationship bet. I'm not going to be around a lot of weekends to go out. I'm not a 'home at five for dinner' kind of guy. I live on the edge and that takes a toll."

He shoved his hands into the front pockets of his slacks and resisted the urge to kick the thick leg of the admiral's desk. That was all true. That, and so much more. But he wanted, insanely and with all his heart, to ask her to take a chance anyway. To let him love her, despite those challenges.

But he couldn't. He loved her too much to ask that of her.

"My career is who I am," he said with a resigned shrug. "Relationship success with guys like me is pretty hard to come by. So rejecting me last year? That was a smart move."

"You think I was right to reject you?"

His wince was minuscule, more an ego reflex than regret.

"I think we have too many things stacked against us. My career, your upbringing. Your father, my…" His voice trailed off. Even in the name of full honesty, he couldn't bring himself to admit that he was still grieving. Instead, he shrugged as though his heart wasn't weeping like a sad, little baby. "Like you said last year, the issues between us are too big."

ALEXIA FOLDED HER FINGERS together, then flexed them apart before twining them together again. He listed all the same reasons they shouldn't be together that she'd already told herself.

She should be grateful. And to show that gratitude, she should finish her thank-yous and let the man have his dinner.

"You're right," she told him. "Your career is a big part of who you are. Just as mine is a big part of who I am."

She saw it, the flicker of anger in his eyes. It was that fury on her behalf that did it. That tipped the scales over from smart to heart.

"Which brings me to the confession, apology and second thank-you," she said, surreptitiously stepping closer. Close enough to breathe in his scent. To feel his warmth. To see deep into his eyes and revel in the heat there.

"You might want to make it fast. I doubt your father's going to wait long before reminding us we're missing the meal," he said, looking toward the door then back, shifting from one foot to the other. Was he nervous? How sweet was that, Alexia thought, almost smiling.

"Actually, my mother knows I wanted to speak with you. She'll keep Father from interrupting." Yet another shock to add to the many of the day. All it'd taken was a request and the word *please* and her mother had been happy to run interference.

"Okay. Confession?" he prompted, shifting away a few inches.

This time she did smile. She liked that she made the big bad SEAL worry. It gave her hope for the rest of this discussion.

"I listened at the door," she told him softly. Then, using his shock, she stepped right into his space and looked up at him with wide-eyed innocence. "I heard my name and couldn't help myself."

"Your father doesn't like your job," was all he said. He didn't rat out the admiral's threats. He didn't claim heroship for standing up for her. This was it, she realized. Her chance to use that angry-grudge habit her mother had commented on and turn it into Blake keeping secrets from her.

Except she knew better.

"My father is commanding, overbearing and arrogant," she said with a shrug. "But he's also right."

"That you should leave your job?" That shocked him and caused just a little anger, if his frown was anything to go by. "Why? Because he's got a puritanical streak? Or because some asshole terrorized you and tried to use you to create a weapon?"

"Why does it sound like you'd be equally angry if I answered yes to either of those?" she mused.

"I think its bullshit that you let anyone bully you. For any reason."

Alexia nodded. "I agree. Nobody has the right, even in the name of love, to try to control someone else's life."

Blake frowned. "Even if you think you're doing it to keep them safe? Or because you believe a relationship can't exist on half-truths?"

"You know, there are elements of my job that are classified. That I'm not supposed to discuss," she told him, twining her fingers with his. He didn't pull away, but she could feel the tension in him, as if he wanted to run. Or grab her. She figured if she held on long enough to stop him from doing the former, he'd go for the latter. "Would you have an issue with that? I mean, my job revolves around sexuality. I'm constantly dealing with people's sexual fantasies, figuring out what turns them on. I'm a scientist. We do a lot in the name of experimentation."

She left it there, with all that innuendo hanging out exposed and ugly.

He frowned, as if he'd never thought of her job in those terms before. Then he gave her a *nice-try* look.

"So you'd be okay with a relationship filled with secrets? One that didn't have total openness and honesty?" he asked, his tone calling bullshit on that.

"No."

He nodded, as if he knew he was right.

"I need total openness and honesty in a relationship," she said slowly. "Or I should say emotional openness and honesty."

"I can't stop what I do, Alexia." He lifted both her hands to his lips and brushed her knuckles with soft kisses. Then, sounding as if he was ripping the words from his gut, he added, "Not even for you. And what I do is dangerous. I lost one of my best friends last year. He caught a piece of shrapnel right in front of me. I know how it feels to have to go on after that. I've seen how hard it is on the people left behind. I've lived it. I can't ask someone to do that for me."

"You see," she said, inching just a little closer so the wide hem of her dress brushed his legs. "That's emotionally open and honest. That's what's important. Not the details of a mission or the location of your next raid."

Frowning, he shook his head.

"I don't think you heard me."

"I did," she promised. "I heard every word. But I responded to what really mattered. I'm okay with the danger. That's what my father was right about. I grew up surrounded by hundreds, thousands of men who lived with that danger. And most of those men are still around. You are specially trained to deal with that part of your job. That doesn't mean training eliminates the danger, or that horrible things won't still happen. But they happen anyway."

"Like your kidnapping," he said quietly.

"Exactly." *Thank you, Father,* she mentally sang, grateful that the admiral had laid the groundwork for that argument. "But the secrets, the danger? If we can communicate, if we're emotionally honest, then we can work through any issues those things create."

He didn't look as distant and closed now, but his blue eyes were still cautious. Watchful. As though he knew there was a flaw in her argument, but he just hadn't found it yet.

Because he was so worried about a trap, Alexia stepped away. Put some distance between them. Just because she'd reached a place where she felt good about pursuing this relationship, where she'd justified it all in her mind, that didn't mean he had. Or that he would.

Fear clutched at her belly. Her breath tight, she tried to remind herself that she'd faced death, dammit. This chasing down the man she loved? Piece of cake.

She pressed her hand against her churning stomach. Okay, so maybe more like an entire decadently rich, double-fudge-chocolate cake eaten in its entirety in a single sitting. In other words, she felt like puking. But it'd be worth it, she promised herself.

"I have a relationship with your father," Blake said as if he were laying another card on the table, slowly showing his hand one point at a time. "He's no longer active on base, but he was my mentor for years. He'll continue to have input into my career."

Then he grimaced and added, "Unless he follows through on those threats, of course. Then I'll probably be stationed on Guam."

"Ironically, I'm starting to think I might have a relationship with my father, too," she said, still not sure how she felt about that. "I doubt it'll ever be a close one, or even cordial. But I'm beginning to believe that maybe it doesn't have to be antagonistic and angry any longer."

"Wow," he breathed.

"I know," she said with a laugh. "Look at me, all grown up."

His gaze skimmed her body, as if reminding them both of just how grown up she was. Her blood heated, her breath slowed. She wanted him like crazy, and dammit, they had to get through this issue and then dinner with her parents before she could have him. So they'd better hurry up or she wouldn't be able to resist giving him a toe massage during the dessert course.

"If your job wasn't an issue, if the danger and secrets didn't exist, would you want to be in a relationship with me?" she asked, putting it all on the table. The questions, the opening, her heart. All there for him to take or leave.

"They are an issue."

"If they weren't," she insisted, giving him a *quit-being-stubborn* look.

"If they weren't an issue," he said slowly, so slowly she wanted to scream at him to quit tormenting her, "I'd be begging you to go out with me. I'd be doing my damnedest to sweep you off your feet. I'd have you in bed so fast, the sheets would catch fire."

Relief, pleasure and excitement poured through Alexia, making her want to grab him close for a hug, then dance around the room laughing.

"Then why are you making them an issue? I've made my peace with them, so now it's up to you. It's not because of me that these things stand between us." There it was, the truth gauntlet. Tossed between them in challenge. Now it was all up to him.

"I watched what it did to Phil's family, saying good-bye to him," he said quietly, his eyes boring into hers with an intensity that made her want to cry. "I saw the devastation. How could you ask me to do that to you?"

"There are no guarantees, Blake. All you can do is make every day we have together one that I could treasure, in case something did happen. Isn't that all anyone can do?"

He frowned, looking as if he was turning her words over and over in his mind. Trying to find the flaw, to figure out how to dismiss them.

Alexia wanted to tell him to get over it already. To agree they had a chance. She wanted to run from the room and hide, so she didn't have to face rejection. And mostly, she wanted to grab back the last eight months, to go back to the time that he'd believed they had a chance. Before her fears had fueled his, before she'd given him enough reason to believe that she wasn't strong enough to handle a future with him.

But she couldn't. Instead, she had to accept that she'd given it her best. With all his issues on the table, she'd answered each the best she could.

Well, she did have one argument left. But it made

her feel naked. Terrified. And, again, a little like throwing up.

Faced with probable rejection, she couldn't do it. She couldn't tell him she loved him, only to be turned away.

"Here's the thing. I can't date you," he finally said, his words low, quiet. As if the words were torn from him.

It took all her willpower to keep her smile in place and not look as if she'd just been kicked in the gut. But Alexia did it. Hey, something to be proud of.

"Well, then..." She took a breath, still smiling, dammit, and looked around. "I guess we should go in and join the dinner party. I'm sure our presence will help my father's digestion."

And the sooner she took him into the dining room, the sooner she could get a sudden migraine and have to go lie down. Looking forward to that, Alexia turned toward the door.

She didn't make a single step before Blake grabbed her hands and drew her back.

Gasping, she started to pull away. Then realized she was exactly where she wanted to be and stopped, sliding closer to him with a challenging look instead.

"Yes?" she asked in a long, slow drawl.

"Here's the thing," he said, sliding his fingers into hers and pulling her close so both hands were captured in his behind the small of her back. "I can't date you, because that's not enough."

"You want sex, too?" she teased, shifting just a little closer so her hips brushed his.

"Hell, yeah," he responded, grinning. Then he shook his head and gave her a chiding look. "But that's not where I was going."

"I thought that's always where you wanted to go."

She was having trouble containing the giddiness she felt. Crazy, since she wasn't even sure what she was giddy about. But she needed the answer to what was standing between them as much as he needed to say it, so she bit her lip and said, "Sorry. Why can't you date me?"

"We've got stuff between us, things that can be problems. I know your father will interfere. I know my career, your temper, they'll be challenging. But the things that matter, they're stronger."

"My temper?" she asked, giving him a wide-eyed look. Then her brow twitched. Hadn't her mother mentioned that very issue earlier? Clearly she had some self-reflection to do. Especially if it might fix the problem between her and Blake. "What are the things that do matter to you, then?"

He gave her a look so intense, her stomach plummeted to her toes and hid.

"I want a future. A commitment. A chance to see if this thing between us—the explosive heat and sweet humor and weird wavelength connection—to see if those are real. If they last."

A future? This time when Alexia bit her lip, it was to keep herself from crying with joy.

"They've lasted over eight months," she said, smiling so big her face actually hurt.

"I want to see if they last day in and day out. If we can both do our jobs, live together and still do that emotional honesty thing that's so important to you."

"Do you think we can?" she asked, willing to put one thousand percent in but needing to know he was just as committed.

"I think I love you enough to make sure we do," he said quietly. So quietly that it took a second for his words to sink in. Alexia's eyes rounded. Her heart jumped. The only reason she didn't throw her arms around his neck and squeal was that he had her hands still clasped behind her back.

"You love me?" she repeated quietly. "Me, with the temper and the sex job and the nightmare of a father? Me who insists on talking through all these emotional things and will always be asking you how you feel?"

"You, who are sweet and sexy, smart and funny. You who keep me from hiding inside myself," he said quietly, resting his forehead on hers. "You who make me feel like a hero, and keep me on my toes."

"Yep," she decided with a giggle as she pressed tiny kisses over his face. "That's me. The same me that loves you right back."

Blake's eyes closed, as if in thanks. Then he took her mouth in a kiss filled with as much passion as it was promises. With as much hope as there was heat.

"What d'ya say we skip dinner?" he said against her lips.

"Sneak around the back?" she suggested, tilting her head toward the glass door leading to the side yard. "My father will have a fit."

"I live for danger, remember." Grinning, he slid his arms under her and swept her off her feet.

Still holding her close, he nudged open the French doors and carried her through.

Alexia held on tight, her head snuggled against his chest.

"My hero," she whispered.

* * * * *

Regan Macintosh doesn't trust Jamie Quinn's roguish charm, but her resolve to keep the sexy stranger away is starting to wane...and if she's not careful, their hungry passion could make them both lose control.

Read on for a sneak preview of
THE MIGHTY QUINNS: JAMIE,
the latest book in Kate Hoffmann's beloved series
THE MIGHTY QUINNS.

Regan walked out into the chilly night air. A shiver skittered down her spine, but she wasn't sure it was because of the cold or due to being in such close proximity to Jamie. Her footsteps echoed softly on the wood deck, and when she reached the railing, Regan spread her hands out on the rough wood and sighed.

She heard the door open behind her and she held her breath, counting his steps as he approached. She shivered again, but this time her teeth chattered.

A moment later she felt the warmth of his jacket surrounding her. He'd pulled his jacket open and he stood behind her, his arms wrapped around her chest, her back pressed against his warm body.

"Better?"

It was better. But it was also more frightening. And more exhilarating. And more confusing. And yet it seemed perfectly natural. "I should probably get to bed," Regan said. "I can't afford to fall asleep at work tomorrow."

HBEXP0117

He slowly turned her around in his arms until she faced him. His lips were dangerously close to hers, so close she could feel the warmth of his breath on her cheek.

"I know you still don't trust me, but you're attracted to me. I'm attracted to you, too. I want to kiss you," he whispered. "Why don't we just see where this goes?"

"I think that might be a mistake," she replied.

"Then I guess we'll leave it for another time," he said. "Good night, Regan." With that he turned and walked off the deck.

Her heart slammed in her chest and she realized how close she'd come to surrender. He was right; she was attracted to him. She had wanted to kiss him. She'd been thinking about it all night. But in the end common sense won out.

Regan slowly smiled. She was strong enough. She *could* control her emotions when he touched her. Though he still was dangerous, he was just an ordinary guy. And if she could call the shots, maybe she could let something happen between them.

Maybe he'd ask to kiss her again tomorrow. Maybe then she'd say yes.

HBEXP0117